BLOOD OATH, BLOOD RIVER

Downwind:
the areas that
received fallout
from nuclear testing

MICHAEL RICHAN

BLOOD OATH, BLOOD RIVER

A *DOWNWINDERS* NOVEL

DANTULL

By the author

THE RIVER SERIES

The Bank of the River

A Haunting in Oregon

Ghosts of Our Fathers

Eximere

The Suicide Forest

Devil's Throat

THE DOWNWINDERS SERIES

Blood Oath, Blood River

BLOOD OATH, BLOOD RIVER

ISBN-10: 1-50022-637-8 / ISBN-13: 978-1-50022-637-4

Published by Dantull (148514177)

First printing: June 2014

www.michaelrichan.com

PREFACE

Blood Oath, Blood River is a work of fiction, set in a real place and culture. Local Mormon vernacular is used in the story to keep the characters authentic. People not familiar with the local and cultural terms might find some of them unusual and confusing. While the novel itself defines most of the important and relevant terms within the context of the story, a glossary is offered at the back of the book for those who would like to have the terms better defined. The type of definitions offered in the glossary (along with references to outside sources and more information) would have been too disruptive to include in the narrative.

1

Deem pressed herself tightly to the cold stone wall. She looked up – she couldn't see the top of the winze, which was good – it meant the ghosts up there couldn't see her, looking down. She could hear the moaning of more ghosts down the adit to her left from where she'd just come. They'd be on her soon. She only had moments.

Trapped! she thought. *How'd I let myself get into this?*

"Whatever you do, don't get cornered in here," she remembered her father saying when they'd enter a cave or an abandoned mine together. He'd been gone for a couple of years now, but the things he used to say were still vivid in her mind. *He'd be pissed at me right now,* Deem thought, *letting myself get caught like this.*

She thought she was being nice. It was Erin's birthday next week, and she thought she'd get her good friend a rare and exotic birthday present – iridium. And not just any iridium, but the stuff from the Tillburton mine near the Utah-Arizona border. The Tillburton had seen some of the most intense radiation fallout from the nuclear testing years ago, and everything in it was fucked up, including the iridium. It was also one of the most haunted abandoned mines in the area.

Erin's worth it, Deem thought as she started into the mine a half-hour ago. *Won't she be surprised?* Iridium was rare, and this fucked up iridium was a dream: special attributes that exhibited themselves only in the River. The perfect birthday present for someone who's gifted, like Erin.

Yeah, right, Deem thought now, as she pressed herself against the rock. Getting in had been a breeze, and thanks to a device she'd borrowed from Winn, she was able to locate and remove a small piece of iridium easily enough – but getting out was now a nightmare. She carefully removed her canteen and took three large gulps. The concoction stung as it passed the delicate linings of her throat and made its way to her stomach, where it would radiate out and hopefully provide some additional protection for the next few minutes.

The moaning was close now, and she knew the ghosts would be upon her within seconds. She reached up, turned off her headlight, and tried to take shallow breaths.

Total darkness surrounded her. Her ears pricked up, attempting to compensate for her lack of sight. She badly wanted to drop into the River, that flowing, invisible stream of knowledge that most people couldn't see, but "gifted" people like herself could enter. She knew if she did it would only give her away. Downwind, in the wake of the nuclear testing, the radiation from the fallout changed the things in the River, the same way it changed people. The humans developed cancers and mutations, but the ghosts mutated in bizarre, stranger ways. She couldn't take the risk that these ghosts might be the kind that get angry if they see someone in the River, or worse, could become corporeal and attack. Not all ghosts downwind could do it, but if these could, she'd be fucked. You had to assume the worst. Best to try and hide.

The moaning increased, and Deem knew they entered the part of the tunnel she was in. Several voices arrived and slowly moved past her, their moaning sending a chill down her spine as they drifted next to her.

"Darla?" one said, calling into the dark.

"You're a dark horse," another said, passing by her face.

The room slowly filled with voices and moans. She tried to ignore them. The voices were easier to ignore; the moans were not.

"Mouth to ear!" one kept saying.

She felt their coldness brush her face as they passed by. She wanted to whimper, but she knew better. The voices swirled around her, different timbres and tones, an old woman, a young man, everything in between.

"Darla, is that you?"

"I'll rip you open!"

"Hand to back...mouth to ear..."

The room reached a peak of noise, and Deem was unable to make sense of anything. She pressed her eyes closed and wished she could close her ears too.

After several painful minutes the sounds began to diminish. Some were going up the winze, some were returning back down the adit.

After all the sounds had left, Deem let herself exhale and step away from the rock wall. She could still hear the moaning above her in the passageway the winze led to – but it was diminishing. She turned on her headlamp.

The adit she was in was empty and silent. She looked up the winze. Silence up there, too.

Time to move, she thought.

She grabbed the wooden ladder and began climbing up the winze. It was a twenty foot climb, and she emerged onto the rock floor of another adit running in two directions.

Let's hope they went deeper into the mine and not the way I need to go! she thought as she took the route that led to the exit.

She had been trapped by ghosts in mines before. Her father showed her how to hide from them, but he was insistent she not put herself in harm's way by making sure they were distracted or not active when she went into a mine. Deem thought she had followed his advice, and she grabbed the pulsebox from the floor of the passage as she passed it, heading out. *All the good this thing did me,* she thought.

The pulsebox was something she and her father developed. It sent out a signal that could be used to either attract or repel ghosts in a mine. This time she placed it near the top of the winze before she descended, hoping it would keep the ghosts away from this junction, an area she knew she had to return through in order to get out of the mine. *They must have mutated again,* she thought. She would have to fine-tune the box to work against their new state.

Mutations were a constant problem in the River. The congenital malformations humans suffered from the fallout of the testing seemed to diminish after several generations, but in the River, they were still happening, as though the half-life of the radiation didn't matter. It was one of the reasons she never felt the need to carry one of Winn's EM guns, although he was constantly offering one to her. She felt carrying one was a waste of time, since there was a good chance the ghost you attempted to use it on might have mutated to the point where the gun wouldn't work on them. Winn was forever adjusting the guns, trying to make them effective on the widest range of ghosts they were likely to encounter. *But what good are they if they'll fail ten percent of the time?* Deem thought. *Not good enough odds for me to carry one.*

She tossed the pulsebox into her backpack and picked up her pace, turning at the next junction to take an adit running to the right. It soon joined up with a major passageway. *Three hundred feet and I'm outta here,* Deem thought. *Erin better like this present. If she doesn't, I'm going to be pissed.*

Erin was a good friend of hers, maybe her best friend. They'd grown up together in Mesquite. When she was fourteen Deem learned that Erin was gifted too. The two had been inseparable until Erin's mother, Jenny, took a new job in Kingman, moving her three hours away. Now that she was out of high school and had her own truck, Deem drove down to visit Erin once a month or so. The only downside to visiting Erin was driving through Las Vegas to get there. She hated Vegas.

Once Erin moved, it left a hole in Deem's life that Winn later filled. He was gifted too, and smart – and they worked together a lot of the time. Winn was almost ten years older than Deem, and she couldn't stand his approach to relationships and sex, but he had been a reliable ally in some scary situations they faced in the past couple of years since Deem's father passed away. And beggars couldn't be choosers – there weren't a lot of gifteds around in the downwind area. The River was too twisted and strange for most of them. Once they took a trip to California or Oregon and saw what normal ghosts were like, the gifteds moved. Deem counted herself lucky to have Winn and Erin around. She knew she could rely on them.

Deem emerged from the mine shaft and walked into the bright desert sunlight. She pulled her sunglasses from her shirt, put them on, and kept walking toward her truck. She checked her watch – ten-thirty. She told Winn she'd meet him at noon; just enough time to get home and get cleaned up.

■ ■ ■

Deem pulled her truck up to Winn's trailer and honked twice. Winn's trailer was on a four acre lot, and neighbors were scarce. There was an unfamiliar car parked outside the trailer next to Winn's Jeep. Deem knew what this meant; he was entertaining someone. She looked at her watch. She was ten minutes early, but she didn't feel like sitting out in her hot truck until Winn was finished, so she honked again, a signal to Winn that she arrived and would be knocking on the door in a few seconds. It gave him time to get dressed – and to get whoever was in there with him dressed as well.

Deem grabbed her Big Gulp from the cup holder and hopped out of her truck. She walked up to the door of the trailer. When she was ten feet from it, it burst open and a girl about Deem's age spilled out, pulling a t-shirt over her head as she walked down the steps.

"See 'ya," she heard Winn call from inside.

The girl adjusted the shirt on her body as she walked past Deem and toward her car. "Next!" she said as she passed, and began giggling.

Deem stopped walking and rolled her eyes. She hated that anyone might think she was visiting Winn for a fling. She liked Winn, and she respected him as a fellow gifted who knew his shit, but she hated how he ran his personal life, which seemed to be a perpetual stream of conquests. She considered yelling something back at the girl, like "I'm not here for that!" or "I'm just a friend!" but she knew it wouldn't matter, so she just kept walking to the door.

Winn appeared in the doorway, wearing nothing but a pair of thin Nike shorts. He propped his hands up against the top of the doorway and leaned out.

"Geez, can't you dress?" Deem said.

"It's a hundred degrees," Winn said. "Why should I?"

"At least a shirt?" Deem asked.

"Is my chest bothering you?" he asked her teasingly. He flexed his pecs.

"Stop," Deem said. "Just stop."

"If you'd hadn't shown up early," Winn said, "you wouldn't have had to see her leave and you wouldn't be so pissy. That's *your* fault."

"Please don't suggest I'm jealous," Deem said, putting a hand on her hip and staring him down. "Ever since Steven and Roy left, there's someone you're banging every time I come over."

"Banging?" he interjected. "You learned a new word for it."

"I realize you've lost St. Thomas as a project," Deem said. "But filling the void with cheap sex isn't very productive."

"Sez you!"

He walked from the trailer doorway and flopped into an outdoor chair next to an overturned cable spindle that served as a table. He lit up a cigarette.

"You gonna tell me why I'm here?" Deem asked, sitting in a chair next to him.

"Friend of mine in St. George," Winn said. "He runs a tour operation. He has an interesting little problem."

"I hate those outfits," Deem said.

"Hear me out," Winn said. "He shuttles groups from the tour office to wherever they're going for the day. Some days it's ghost towns, some days it's Native American ruins."

"All the more reason to hate them," Deem said.

"Twice now, driving back from Pipe Springs at night, he says they were followed."

"Followed?"

"By a man, running as fast as their bus, a hundred feet out in the brush. His eyes were glowing."

"Bullshit," Deem said.

"Twice, both times in the same spot. People on his bus saw it too."

"So what does it have to do with us?" Deem asked.

"He wanted to know if we'd figure out what it is."

"Does your friend drink?"

"Nope, straight-laced Mormon through and through."

"Why do I want to help a tour operator?" Deem asked. "They make money marching people all over sacred ruins."

"He was worried it might be something dangerous," Winn said, reaching into his shorts and adjusting himself.

"Would you please not do that in front of me?" Deem asked.

"I've got an itch."

"Can't imagine why."

"You've really got to lighten up," Winn said. "You're way too uptight about sex and stuff. People have junk, and they like to use it. Everybody does. Don't freak out over it."

"I'm not freaking out," Deem said. "It just seems to me you could wait to do that in private."

"I just do it naturally, I don't think about it. So, he invited us to come along, tonight. What do you say?"

"You go," Deem said. "I'm really not interested."

"Oh, come on!" Winn said. "It'll be fun. Bus leaves at three from St. George, we'll be back by ten. The bus is big enough for fifty, and Dave says there's not even ten reservations, so it won't be crowded. Maybe we'll get to see it!"

"See what?" Deem asked.

"The man who runs by the bus!" Winn said. "Weren't you listening? He said the guy's got yellow-green eyes, and they shine in the dark."

Deem had to admit it sounded intriguing, but she wasn't really inclined to help anyone who ran a tour outfit. The tourists were always interfering with the places where she tried to work, and she didn't like the idea of anyone profiting off ruins.

"Come on," Winn begged. "It'll be fun."

"If this is the best you can do to replace St. Thomas work, I'm not impressed," Deem said. "Seems kinda lame."

Winn furrowed his brow. "Don't be that way," he said. "I'll reach into my shorts and scratch myself again."

"Alright!" Deem said, a small smile cracking her lips. "Don't reach. I'll go."

"That's what I wanted to hear!" Winn said. He stood up and smashed his cigarette into an ashtray. "Be at their place on Bluff right at quarter to three."

...

As Deem approached the tour office, she saw Winn standing out front, looking for her. Winn's smile quickly faded when he saw that Deem was not alone.

"Mom, I think you know Winn," Deem said, making introductions. "Aunt Virginia, this is my friend Winthrop James."

Deem's aunt held out her hand to Winn. "Nice to meet you," she said. Deem could tell she was taken with Winn's good looks. He was tall and his hair was cut short in a military style. He had put on a t-shirt that showed every muscle in his chest.

"Guess we'll need two more tickets," Winn said, forcing a smile. "I only bought two, sorry, I didn't know you were coming."

"Oh, that's no problem," Deem's mother said. "I'll go get us another two." She stepped away and walked into the tour office.

"So," Virginia said, "Deem tells us we're going on a tour to some ruins?"

"Yes," Winn said, "it's Anasazi ruins in northern Arizona." He smiled, not really wanting to make small talk, and wondering why Deem had brought people along.

"Margie shouldn't have to pay for my ticket," Virginia said. "Let me go give her some money. If you'll excuse me."

Winn stepped aside and let Virginia walk into the tour office.

"What the fuck?" Winn asked Deem.

"She's visiting from Arizona," Deem said.

"So?" Winn asked. "Why are they here?"

"My mom asked me what I was doing tonight, and I told her about this tour," Deem said. "Next thing you know, they were coming along."

"You couldn't dissuade them?" Winn asked.

"I mentioned there were only ten reservations for a fifty-person bus," Deem said apologetically. "And I think my mom was looking for something to do with her sister. She's been in town for a week and they haven't done much. She insisted."

"Did you tell them I was coming along?" Winn asked.

"I did," Deem said, knowing where this was going. Deem's mom wasn't a big fan of Winn, and Winn knew it. Winn was a smoker, a swearer, a drinker, promiscuous, and, worst of all, non-Mormon.

"So she's here to keep an eye on me," Winn said.

"Yup, make sure you don't corrupt her daughter."

"Well, won't this be fun," Winn said sarcastically.

"Buck up," Deem said, walking to the tour office. "I think my aunt likes you."

. . .

They re-boarded the bus after a brief stop at Pipe Springs. No matter where Winn sat, Deem sat across from him, and Deem's mother and aunt sat behind them.

The driver of the bus, Winn's friend Dave, had chatted with Deem while they were letting the tourists explore the Windsor House at Pipe Springs. Deem asked him about the man they had seen running by the bus, and he became quite agitated describing what he'd experienced. He said it appeared twice, both times on the drive back to St. George, just after sunset.

"It wasn't a hundred percent dark yet, so you could see it was a guy, not an animal," Dave said. "And the thing that made him stand out was his eyes. They glowed. You might not have even noticed him out there if it weren't for the eyes, moving along so fast."

"How do you know they were eyes?" Deem asked.

"'Cause they blinked," Dave said. "Once you focused on them, you could tell it was a man. And the creepy thing was, he was running so fast, but it didn't look like he was struggling. I mean, I was going sixty down the road, and he's keeping up with the bus!"

"Other people saw it too?" Deem asked.

"The second time, yeah," Dave said. "They all took pictures, but nothing turned out. Too blurry."

Deem thanked Dave and walked to the dusty parking lot, waiting for the others to finish. She'd seen Pipe Springs many times, and didn't enjoy walking through it while rubbing elbows with other people. Eventually the stragglers made their way back to the bus and they departed for their next destination on the tour.

Deem listened as Dave spoke over the intercom. They were twenty minutes from their final stop, the Anasazi ruins. Deem leaned over to Winn, sitting across the aisle.

"Dave seems nice enough," Deem said.

"Told you," Winn said.

"Do you think the tour office might be rigging something?" Deem asked. "To build an audience for a ghost tour or something?"

"How do you rig a man running that fast?" Winn asked.

"You're right," Deem said. "I guess I just need to see it to believe it."

"Your aunt felt me up back there," Winn said, "when we were alone in one of those rooms at Pipe Springs."

"Eeww!" Deem said. "She did?"

"Yup," Winn said.

"You realize she's not a spring chicken," Deem said, "like your usual."

"She's what, in her mid-fifties?" Winn asked. "They're usually the horniest."

"Stop!" Deem said. "She's my aunt!"

"Grabbed my ass," Winn said. "Just telling ya."

"You will not have sex with her, do you understand?" Deem said. "I don't care if she throws herself at you. Promise me."

"Why?" Winn asked. "She's kinda hot."

"'Cause she's my aunt!" Deem said as she reached across the aisle and pushed his arm. "And I introduced you. I don't want to be blamed if she catches something."

Winn pushed her back. "Nothing to catch. I'm as clean as a virgin."

"Hardly. And I don't want my mom thinking anything is up."

Winn turned to Deem and gave her a big smile, widening it until Deem picked up on the innuendo. Her face contorted in revulsion. She saw him look back in the bus to where Margie and Virginia were sitting, then glanced back at her aunt just in time to see her give Winn a wink.

Bringing them along was a bad idea, Deem thought.

...

Deem felt Winn's hand on her knee, and she woke up. The sun had set and it was dark inside the bus.

"Wake up," Winn whispered to her, shaking her leg. She turned to look around the in the bus. Her mother and aunt were several seats back, napping. There were a few more people behind them, many of which had fallen asleep.

"Look!" Winn said, pointing out the window. Deem turned to look, trying to focus her eyes.

At first she saw only brush whizzing by at sixty miles an hour, hills in the distance. The landscape was dark.

"Is it out there?" Deem asked.

"A hundred feet straight out," Winn said. "Dave was right."

Deem struggled to find what Winn was looking at. She couldn't locate anything unusual. "I don't see it."

Winn sat next to her and pointed. "It's there. Keep looking right where I'm pointing."

Deem continued to focus out the window, searching the land-scape for any sign of movement.

Then she saw one speck of light become two as it turned to look at them.

Deem gasped and strained her neck to see better. Around the eyes she could see a shape, a head. Below it was the dark body of a man, moving incredibly fast. Now that she'd made out the man's outline, she could see it fine.

"I understand why the photos didn't turn out," Deem said.

"What?" Winn asked.

"Dave told me they tried to take pictures last time," Deem said, "and they didn't turn out. I don't think you could get a picture of that. It's too dark."

Deem watched as the man occasionally turned his head to look in their direction.

"How could anyone run that fast?" Deem asked.

"I don't think it's human," Winn said. "Or, not completely."

"It's getting closer," Deem said. "It's angling in toward us."

The silence of the bus was pierced by the scream of a woman in the back. Deem turned to look, and a woman sitting behind her mother and aunt was looking out the window, observing the running man. A woman sitting next to her raised her camera to try and take a picture. The flash from the camera lit the inside of the bus. People on the left side of the bus got up and walked to the right, trying to see whatever had caused the woman to scream.

"Please stay in your seats," Dave announced over the intercom. "We've got to have everyone seated for safety."

"Do you see that, Deem?" Virginia asked. "Do you see it?"

"Yes," Deem answered. "I do."

Virginia got out of her seat and moved into the seat directly behind Deem and Winn. "What is it?"

"It's a man," said Winn.

As they watched, the running man closed the distance between him and the bus by half. Now he was easier to see.

Deem's mother followed Virginia and moved up behind Deem and Winn. "Is he going to attack the bus?" she asked.

"I don't know," Winn said.

"How could someone run that fast?" Margie asked. "It's not possible. It's got to be a trick."

The man running beside the bus angled in again, and now was just ten feet from their window. They could see his face, which was dark and featureless. Deem gasped again as the man's eyes locked onto hers, and he lifted from the ground and moved toward the bus as though he was flying.

The woman in the back of the bus screamed again. Dave began to slow the bus.

"Don't stop!" Winn yelled. "Speed up!"

The man was hovering four feet off the ground and moving quickly to Deem's window.

"Get back from the window," Winn said to Deem. Then he yelled, "Everyone! Back from the windows!"

The man landed at Deem's window and pressed his face against the glass. Winn backed out of the seat next to Deem and pulled Deem with him. Virginia and Margie moved across the aisle, behind them.

The man's head passed through the glass without breaking it, his body attached to the outside of the bus. His head extended inside the bus, looking like a mounted trophy, but moving. He looked down at Deem. She saw his eyes center on her, felt his gaze deepen. Then it shifted its head and looked past Winn at Virginia and Margie. The woman in the back of the bus screamed again.

The head slid along the inside of the bus, its body moving on the outside. It stopped when it found the woman who had screamed. It studied her, staring at her as though it wanted her to scream again. She obliged and let out another piercing shriek.

Dave flipped a switch, and white fluorescent bulbs kicked on overhead. The light seemed to bother the head, and it pulled itself out of the bus. It continued to hang onto the outside, staring in. It moved back to where Winn, Deem, Virginia, and Margie were huddled further up the bus. It stared at them.

"What does it want?" Virginia asked.

Deem could feel something emanating from its eyes. It was a kind of heat, something that was making a connection. She felt it sink into her, and for a moment she felt light-headed. She lost her peripheral sight as tunnel vision took over and the only thing she could see was the man's head outside the bus, staring at her. She gripped the side of the seat, afraid she might fall over. Then she saw the man detach from the side of the bus, falling backwards into the dark.

The others in the bus rushed back to the right side, trying to see where the man had gone.

Deem turned and saw that Virginia had passed out. She was lying next to Margie in her seat, her head hanging. "Mom," Deem said, trying to get Margie's attention. Margie was straining her neck to see out the windows on the other side, along with the others in the bus. "Mom!" she repeated.

Margie turned to look at Deem, and Deem pointed to Virginia. "Help her!"

Margie turned and finally saw that Virginia was out. She grabbed Virginia's hands, then tried patting her cheeks. Virginia's eyes fluttered open.

"What happened?" Virginia asked.

"You fainted," Winn said.

"It was looking at me," Virginia said. "I felt it."

"Me too," Deem said.

"We'll be back in St. George in about twenty minutes, everyone," Dave said over the intercom. "Please stay seated."

Winn got up to talk to Dave. Deem joined him at the front of the bus.

"Did it come in like that, before?" Winn asked Dave.

Dave kept his eyes on the road as he answered. "Not that I saw," he said. "It just ran alongside us. Didn't come in."

"Did you see it this time?" Winn asked. "Its head? Inside?"

"I saw something," Dave said, "in my mirror. Can't say exactly what. Obviously someone's upset back there. Can you talk to the woman who screamed, make sure everything's OK?"

"I'll check on her," Winn said, and walked back into the bus.

"Did he say its head was inside?" Dave asked Deem.

"Yes," Deem answered. "Its head was inside."

"But none of the windows are open, are they?" Dave asked.

"No, they're closed," Deem said.

"That doesn't make any sense," Dave said.

Deem left it at that. Dave hadn't seen the head inside the bus, and she'd learned from her father not to relate stories that others might find crazy; it tended to make them think *you* were crazy.

"You might want to consider cancelling this particular tour going forward," Deem said, "until we figure out what this thing is. I think it's dangerous."

"Not my decision," Dave said. "That'd be for the owners to decide."

"Then you might want to ask for another route," Deem said.

"What do I tell them?" Dave asked. "Something jumped on the bus and stuck its head inside?"

Deem knew Dave wouldn't be relating that story to his boss. Winn rejoined them.

"She's fine, just shaken up," Winn said. "She's got a set of lungs on her, that's for sure."

"Deem says it's dangerous," Dave said, his eyes looking at Winn through his rear view mirror. "Do you think it is?"

"Might be," Winn said. "Hard to say. Don't know what it is, exactly."

"Can I talk to you for a second?" Deem asked Winn, pulling his arm as she walked back into the bus. Winn followed her to a seat that was several rows from the front, with no one around.

"It's dangerous," Deem said, "but not for any reason you can tell Dave. I felt it lock onto me. I nearly passed out, like Virginia."

"Lock onto you?" Winn asked. "Like how?"

"Our eyes were locked," Deem said, "but then everything on the edges began to black out until all I could see was his eyes. I got dizzy, thought I might fall over. It was some kind of attack. Did you feel it?"

"No," Winn said. "No tunnel vision for me. I didn't feel anything like that."

"Did you feel it was looking at you?" Deem said. "Like it was targeting you, specifically?"

"No," Winn replied. "It glanced at me, but I felt nothing."

"Well, it could be dangerous," Deem said. "I told your friend he should cancel the tours until we know what it is."

"He's just a driver, Deem," Winn said. "If he tells them what we saw, they'll just think he's whack, or drunk. Might lose his job over it."

"If that thing out there has appeared before, it obviously knows this bus and the schedule. It'll happen again." She was scratching her left hand with her right.

"But what came of it, other than a scare?" Winn said. "I don't know what harm it caused. It was kind of like seeing a UFO. Not a lot you can do about it."

"It was more than that," Deem said. "I'm sure of it. We'll need to ride this bus again tomorrow. Try the River next time...what the fuck is this?"

Deem raised her left hand where she'd been scratching. There was a round, quarter-inch bump in the skin of her left little finger, between the first and second knuckles.

"Looks like a bite," Winn said.

"It's not," Deem said, pressing on the bump with her right index finger. "There's something really hard inside, and it's sharp. It hurts when I press it."

Winn took over and tried pressing on the bump. It looked red and sore like a spider bite, but he could tell as soon as he touched it that it wasn't a bite. It was soft and squishy, like a pocket of liquid, but inside was something small and hard.

"Ouch!" Deem said. "Don't push on it!"

"How long have you had this?" Winn asked.

"No idea," Deem said. "I don't remember seeing it before."

Winn reached into his pants pocket and removed a pocketknife. He popped the blade open.

"Whoa, hold on!" Deem said. "What are you going to do?"

"Cut it open," Winn said. "I'll just slit the top open here."

Deem winced at the idea, but part of her knew the bump was abnormal, and she wanted whatever was inside it to be out of her. "It's gonna bleed all over the place."

Winn got up and walked back to Margie and Virginia. They talked for a moment, then Winn returned with a small white hand-kerchief.

"We'll use this," Winn said, "to wrap it up."

"Alright," Deem said.

Winn held Deem's little finger and slowly inserted the blade into the bump. Once he had the tip of it past the skin, he slid the blade sideways, making an eighth-inch cut. As he removed the knife, thin wisps of grey smoke emerged from the incision, and the skin collapsed as the gas escaped. Winn gently pulled the skin apart, and saw a small piece of something white.

"Hope that didn't hurt," Winn said.

"Didn't feel a thing," Deem said. "No blood, either. What is that?"

Winn gently inserted the blade of his knife back into the slit and pried under the object, lifting it out of the skin. He held it up for Deem to see. It was small, white, and jagged.

"What is that?" Winn asked, studying it. He held it for Deem to see. "Is it bone?"

"What the fuck?" Deem asked, looking up at him.

2

Deem stared up at the ceiling, suddenly awake. The first thing she felt was the bandage wrapped around her little finger. She felt it with her other hand, running her fingers over it in the darkness of her room.

Seems normal, she thought. *Isn't swollen again. Doesn't hurt. Should probably leave it alone. What time is it?*

She glanced over at her alarm clock on the nightstand – two-thirty. She felt wide awake.

She raised her hands to her face, rubbing it. She let her hands slide down to her neck, and then she slid each hand down her opposite arm. She could see a spot on the ceiling where the paint had come off when she'd ripped down a stick-on glow-in-the-dark star years ago. She stared at the spot as she rubbed her arms at the elbows, and she felt it.

Again? she thought. She stopped her right hand, pressing on the small mound of raised flesh just above her left elbow.

What the fuck is that? she thought. *It feels just like...*

She threw off the covers and walked to the adjoining bathroom. She flicked on the lights and waited for her eyes to adjust. Then she lifted her left arm and pointed her elbow at the mirror above the sink. She peered into the mirror, trying to see what she was touching.

Oh my god, she thought. *It's the same!*

She poked at the skin. It looked a little like a blister, but taller. The skin rose off her arm a good half inch. She pushed at it with the index finger of her right hand, watching it in the mirror. It wasn't hard like a bite, it was soft and squishy, just like the one Winn had cut open on the bus earlier that night.

Cut it open, she thought. *I'm going to see if it's the same.*

She rummaged through a drawer under the sink, looking for the sharpest thing she could find, and settled on the pointed end of a metal nail file. She poured a little rubbing alcohol over it and then held it up to the blister, using the mirror to guide her as she poked the sharp end into it.

There was no pain, and when the tip of the nail file pierced the skin, two small wisps of grey smoke emerged. The sack of skin collapsed around something hard inside.

She placed the nail file on the counter and pressed against the skin of the blister, forcing whatever was inside out through the hole she'd cut. It was another small piece of bone.

Then she heard steps above her, on the ceiling. Someone was on the roof.

She went back into her bedroom and slipped on some jeans and a t-shirt. Then she crept down the stairs to the main floor.

The house was dark and quiet. She listened again for the sounds from above, but the steps had stopped. She walked into the living room, looking out through the windows into the front yard. There was enough moonlight to make the yard very visible. Everything looked normal and still, like a painting.

She thought she smelled something strange – it smelled like the desert, after a rain – the smell of wet sage. She looked outside again – there was no rain. Just another hot Nevada night.

Then she noticed something in the yard. Movement, very slight. It was a dark figure, trying to stand still next to a tree in the distance. If she didn't know the yard as well as she did, she would have mistaken it for another tree. She walked up to the window to get a better look at it.

As she approached the window, the dark figure left the side of the tree and sped toward her. It met her on the other side of the window just as she approached it. The sudden appearance of the figure at the window made Deem gasp and she took a step back.

Then it opened its eyes, and Deem knew she was looking at the creature that had jumped onto the bus. Its features were dark and smooth. It raised its hands and pressed them against the window. Deem took another step back, afraid the glass might break.

Instead, the creature's arms passed through the glass and reached for her. The skin on its arms was dark and peeling, revealing a lighter tone underneath. Deem wondered if the skin had been burnt – it looked like it was peeling in big pieces.

Then it brought its head through the glass.

Deem had walked back into a couch. She stopped, and dropped into the River. From within the flow, the figure looked like an ordinary man, wearing the type of suit you might see someone wear to work at a law firm or a bank. He was Caucasian and bearded, balding on top. Completely normal – even boring.

The figure stopped halfway through the glass of the window when he realized Deem was in the River. His eyes widened, and he slowly began to back out, pulling his head and arms to the other side of the window. He stood for a moment in the front yard, staring at Deem through the glass. Then he turned and disappeared so quickly Deem couldn't see which direction he'd gone.

■ ■ ■

Deem walked into the kitchen. Her mother was seated at a small table tucked into a corner that had a view of the back yard. She was reading a church magazine.

"Good morning, dear," Margie said, looking up from her magazine. "Want anything to eat?"

"I'll just pour some cereal," Deem said, reaching for a cupboard and pulling down a box.

"Virginia is still in bed," Margie said. "She's not feeling well. I might run her in to the doctor later. I don't like how she looks."

"What's wrong with her?" Deem asked while pouring milk into her bowl.

"Well, she's very weak," Margie said. "And her tongue is black. I've never seen anything like it. I thought maybe she'd eaten something that discolored her mouth, you know, like blueberries or something, but she swears she didn't eat anything since dinner last night."

"Black?" Deem asked. "Her tongue is black?"

"And she smells a little funny," Margie half whispered, as though she didn't want Virginia to overhear.

"Funny how?" Deem asked.

"Oh, I don't know exactly," Margie said, "just funny."

Deem placed her bowl down on the counter and walked out of the kitchen.

"Don't you go and wake her up," Margie called after her.

Deem walked down the hallway to the guest room on the main floor. The door was closed. She knocked.

"Aunt Virginia?" she said.

"Yes?" came the reply from inside.

"It's Deem. Can I come in?"

"Oh yes, it's open."

Deem opened the door and walked into the room. Virginia was in bed, the covers pulled up to her neck. She looked pale and feverish.

"Mom says you're not feeling well," Deem said. As she walked up to the bed, she noticed the same smell she'd encountered the night before – wet sage.

"No, I'm not," Virginia replied.

"What feels wrong?" Deem asked, sitting next to her on the bed.

"I feel weak, like I don't want to move," Virginia said. "Doesn't hurt, I just don't want to get up."

"Mom said your tongue is discolored," Deem said.

Virginia stuck out her tongue. It was a solid black, and Deem pulled her head back in surprise. "Wow," she said. "She wasn't kidding. Can I get you anything?"

"No," Virginia said. "I don't feel like eating or drinking anything. Just sleeping."

"Alright," Deem said, standing up, "I'll leave you alone to sleep." She wished Virginia's arms were above the covers – she wanted to check her for a blister similar to the one she'd popped open the night before, but Virginia looked so tired she decided to just leave her in peace.

As she walked back into the kitchen, her mother chided her. "Now why did you go and wake her up when I asked you not to?"

"I want you to do something for me," Deem said, taking a bite of her cereal and joining her mother at the small table.

"What?" Margie said, lowering her magazine.

"I want you to check her for bites," Deem said. "Look for a blister that's soft but feels like there's something hard inside it, like a small stone."

"You think she was bit?" Margie asked.

"Maybe," Deem lied, knowing she couldn't share the full truth with her mother. Margie was a true believing Mormon and didn't like Deem's gift or anything she considered supernatural. She could believe in a God and Satan, but ghosts were a step too far.

Deem often felt herself walking a tightrope with her mother. Deem had stopped going to the church that her parents raised her in, finding it didn't meet her needs and took up way too much of her time. Margie wanted Deem to return to the church, but Deem told her in no uncertain terms that wasn't going to happen. They'd reached a sort of detente in the house, avoiding the subject of religion and the supernatural. Margie considered Deem's use of the gift to be evil, and Deem considered Margie's adherence to the church naïve.

What really threw Deem was that her father was also gifted but had remained an active Mormon until the day he died. He'd even been in the local leadership of the church. Deem never understood how he balanced the two; to Deem, they seemed very much at odds with each other. And Deem knew her father's passing hit Margie hard – not only had she lost her husband, but she was no longer the wife of a powerful stake president, overseeing the spiritual and temporal welfare of ten local wards. In the male-dominated LDS church, she was now just a widow, fit for making meals at funeral receptions, attending the temple, and little else.

At times it made Deem angry. But most of the time it just made her feel sorry for her mom, so she tried to be gentle with her when her mother pressed her to go back to church. The rest of the time she tried to avoid the subjects of the church and the gift when she was around her.

"What I'd like you to do is check her arms and hands," Deem said, "and see if you notice anything that looks like a bite."

"Would it cause her tongue to go black like that?" Margie asked.

"Could be," Deem lied. "I've got to go check on something this morning, but I'll be back in a while. Try and see if you can find a bite before then. It might help us figure out what to do for her."

"Alright," Margie said, standing from her chair and taking Deem's empty cereal bowl from under her. She walked it to the dishwasher and put it inside.

"When I come back, if she's not better, I'll help you take her in to the clinic," Deem said.

"Thank you, dear," Margie said, looking up at her from the dishwasher and smiling. Deem knew her mom appreciated Deem taking a leadership role in the house, now that her father was gone. She also knew her mom would never acknowledge that Deem was in that role. Margie was so used to doing what other people told her to do, following instructions just came naturally to her. Deem had filled the gap created by her father's departure, and Margie had been happy to let her.

■ ■ ■

"Are you alone?" Deem asked Winn over her cell phone. "Good. Drag your ass out of bed, I'll be there in a half hour."

She pulled her truck into the 7-11 at the west end of Mesquite and two minutes later walked out with a Big Gulp, sipping it through a red straw. She climbed into her truck and placed the drink into the cup holder adapter. Normal cup holders couldn't accommodate a Big Gulp, but Deem found an adapter at the D.I. that enlarged the hole for the cup perfectly. It would also hold Super Big Gulps on those occasions when she wanted extra caffeine.

She eased the truck out of the parking lot. It was filled with others walking out with their own Big Gulps.

A half hour later she pulled her truck into the dirt driveway by Winn's trailer. Winn came out as she walked up to it, and they sat together at the cable spindle table. Winn lit a cigarette.

"It followed me home," Deem said. "I saw it last night, in my yard."

"The creature from the bus?" Winn asked, surprised.

"Yes," Deem said. "It tried to come into the house, but it stopped when it saw me in the River."

"Back up and start from the beginning," Winn said. "How did you know it was there?"

"I heard it on the roof," Deem said. "I'd woken up around two. I found another blister with a piece of bone in it, just like the one you cut open on the bus. Then I heard it walking on the roof, so I went downstairs. I saw it in the yard. It saw me, and came up to the windows in the living room. It passed through them, just like it did on the bus. I dropped into the River, and that spooked it. It ran off."

"Interesting," Winn said. "We've got to figure out what this thing is, exactly. Now that it's decided to attach itself to you."

"Now you believe me," Deem said.

"Sure I do," Winn said, flashing her a smile. It was the kind of smile Winn used on women all the time. It usually worked on them, but it had little impact on Deem.

"It isn't a ghost," Winn said. "A ghost wouldn't physically latch onto the bus like that. Or go to the trouble to run next to the bus in the first place. What did you see when you entered the River?"

"A normal man," Deem said. "Middle aged, rather boring looking. Dressed in a suit, like he was going to work. Far from intimidating."

"Any idea what it might be? Or who?" Winn asked.

"I can't think of anything," Deem said. "Nothing I've encountered before."

"I'll post something on my forum," Winn said. "Someone will recognize what it is."

"I wish I had a book, like Roy's," Deem said. "His book had five generations of knowledge in it. Do you know how valuable something like that would be?"

Winn knew that although she was talking about a book, what Deem really wanted was her father back. He'd been her source for information and guidance, and with him gone she often felt helpless and isolated.

"Hey, my mom didn't leave me a journal, either," Winn said. "Apparently our parents didn't get the memo."

"What bugs me," Deem said, "is that Mormons are so keen on keeping journals. My dad was a stake president, probably told hundreds of people to keep a journal. Why wouldn't he have kept one himself?"

Deem took a sip of her Big Gulp.

"I wonder if he did," Deem continued, "and my mom hasn't given it to me. Or maybe he has it locked away somewhere."

"He never mentioned one?" Winn asked.

"No, never did," Deem said.

"Then maybe there isn't one," Winn offered. "It might be that simple."

"It's bugging me," Deem said.

"Seeing Roy's book got you all worked up," Winn said, crushing his cigarette into the red plastic ashtray on the table. "His was grand; all that history. But not everybody has that. Are you writing one?"

"Me?" Deem asked. "What would I write?"

"See," Winn said, "that's how it happens. Next thing you know, you're dead in a mine somewhere, with nothing to leave your gifted child. You should start writing now. What we learned in St. Thomas, for starters."

"I suppose you're right," Deem said. "I'll have to find a blank journal and start." She looked at Winn, who had propped his feet up on a plastic milk crate.

"Your mom never left you anything?" Deem asked.

"I don't think it would have been useful, if she had," Winn said. "Most of the time she was too drunk to speak, let alone write."

"She must have sobered up enough to teach you how to use your gift," Deem said.

"Hardly," Winn said, lighting another cigarette. "It was a buddy of mine named Chris. We both figured out we had the gift about the same time. I got most of my information from his father. Sometimes I'd ask my mom something and she'd try to answer me, but I think she hated that part of herself and she didn't have much to say about it."

"Is that why she drank so much?" Deem asked.

"I don't know," Winn said. "Probably. That and men. She wasn't very good with them. She couldn't keep one for more than a year. Always fighting."

"Geez," Deem said, "it's amazing you turned out normal. Well, as normal as you are, I guess."

Winn shot her a dirty look and Deem smiled back.

"How long before someone replies to your post?" Deem asked.

"No way of knowing," Winn said, putting his cigarette out and standing. "I'll get it posted and call you as soon as I hear something."

"Alright," Deem said, getting out of her chair and walking back to her truck. "Thanks," she called back over her shoulder.

"Don't mention it," Winn yelled back, walking back inside his trailer.

...

As Deem drove back to her house in Mesquite, she thought about her conversation with Winn. As sad as Winn's upbringing was, he turned out fine. *He's been a good friend to me,* Deem thought. *I should lighten up on all the shit I give him.*

She was still bothered by her father and the lack of a journal. It didn't sit right with her. She'd seen Roy's book, a collection of different hand-made volumes all bound together. A mess, but a beautiful mess, full of a hundred years of information. She felt stranded with just Winn for support. She had friends in Kingman, and now up in California and the Pacific Northwest, but they were so far away.

She considered trying to contact her father again. She'd tried multiple times since his departure, and on none of those occasions had he communicated with her. Deem felt he'd passed over, no longer available to communicate with the living. *He knows he left me down here,* Deem thought. *You'd think he'd hang around for a while, make sure I'm getting on OK after he's gone. But no.*

The last time she tried to contact him, she went so far as to break into the Mesquite cemetery at night and sit right on his grave for the séance. Even that hadn't worked. No, her father had moved on.

But the journal, she thought. *He must have kept one. He wasn't a hypocrite, telling people to do one thing while doing another. He must have had one.*

When she'd asked Margie about the possibility, Margie denied ever seeing her father keep one. *Maybe she's lying to me,* Deem thought. *Maybe she had a look at it, saw stuff about Dads gift, and thought it was evil. She'd hide that from me. I'll bet it's tucked away in the house somewhere. I'm going to look.*

...

After Deem returned from shuttling Margie and Virginia to the clinic, she started going through boxes in the basement. Margie had come down to ask her what she was doing, and Deem said she was looking for some items from her childhood. After Margie expressed concern that she not make a mess, she left her alone and Deem was plowing through box after box.

Why do we keep all this shit? Deem wondered as she opened another box, this one full of Tupperware. *Why keep a box of Tupperware?*

She made her way through half of the basement when she got a call from Winn. He'd found someone who claimed to know what the creature might be.

"He lives in Indian Springs," Winn said, "but he said he'd drive over here after work. I suggested Pete's, in Overton. Can you make it around six?"

"I'll be there," Deem said, checking her watch. That'd give her three more solid hours of box searching.

"Great, see you then," Winn said.

Deem worked through the boxes for a couple of hours more, then decided to take a break. She went upstairs to pour herself a Diet Coke from a bottle in the fridge. Margie was in the kitchen making a tray for Virginia.

"How is she?" Deem asked.

"The same," Margie answered. "She won't eat anything. I'm going to put the most tempting things I can think of on this tray and take it into her. I'm quite irritated with that doctor. We wait half an hour to see him, then he has no idea what's wrong with her."

"Did you find a bite on her?" Deem asked.

"I haven't looked," Margie said, arranging a vase with a flower for the tray.

"Will you please?" Deem asked. "It's important."

"The doctor didn't say it was a bite," Margie said.

"I'll check her myself if you don't," Deem said.

"Really, dear, what makes you think you know more than the doctor?"

Deem turned and left the kitchen, walking down to the guest bedroom. She knocked lightly, then entered.

Virginia looked worse. Her eyes had dark circles around them and her breathing seemed more labored.

"Aunt Virginia?" Deem asked, trying to wake her. "Aunt Virginia?" She shook her gently.

Margie came into the room behind her. "Leave her alone!" she said. "Let her sleep."

Virginia's eyes opened and she smiled when she saw Deem. "Oh dear, it's you!"

"Aunt Virginia," Deem said, "I need to check you for bites. I'm worried that what you have might have been caused by a spider bite or something like that. Have you felt any bumps on your skin? Anything like a bite?"

"No dear," she said weakly. "But I haven't checked. I feel too weak."

Virginia's arms were over the bedspread. Deem glanced them over, not seeing anything.

"Do you mind if I check you?" Deem asked.

"Oh, stop," Margie said.

"Well, if you think it would help, of course," Virginia said.

Deem moved closer to her and ran her hands under Virginia's arms, not feeling anything. Then she raised her hands to Virginia's neck and reached behind it.

"What's this?" Deem asked, feeling something strange.

"I don't know," Virginia replied, suddenly alarmed. "I don't feel anything."

"Would you roll to your left?" Deem asked. Virginia slowly rolled, exposing the back of her head.

Deem lifted Virginia's hair, and at the base of her hairline was a large red welt, about the size of a quarter.

"Oh!" Margie said, moving closer to see the welt.

Deem poked at it with her finger. It looked red and swollen. "This doesn't hurt at all, when I poke it?" she asked Virginia.

"Can't feel a thing," Virginia answered.

It was twice as big as the two blisters Deem had cut open earlier. She could feel something hard inside, just like the others.

"Mom," Deem said, "would you find me a small, sharp blade? Sterilize it and bring it to me?"

"What are you going to do?" Margie asked.

"And bring some tissues and bandages," Deem said. "We're going to drain this."

Margie didn't move. Deem turned to look at her, and she could see Margie wanted to argue.

"Mom?" Deem said. "Please?"

Margie gave in. She turned and left the room.

"Is it big?" Virginia asked.

"Not too," Deem said. "I think once we drain it you might feel a little better."

"I can't believe the doctor didn't find it," Virginia said.

"He must not have looked you over very thoroughly."

"I doubt he spent five minutes with us. Wrote a prescription and left."

Deem looked at the nightstand next to the bed. There was a yellow bottle with a prescription label. Deem picked it up and read it – it was for an antidepressant. *That's all these doctors down here know to give women,* Deem thought.

"Have you taken any of these yet?" Deem asked Virginia, who was still lying on her left side.

"No," Virginia said. "I was sleeping."

"Well, don't," Deem said.

Margie returned and handed Deem a paring knife from the kitchen.

"You sterilized it?" Deem asked.

"With rubbing alcohol," Margie said.

"Alright," Deem said. "Don't move, Aunt Virginia."

Deem placed the knife at the welt and pressed in. Immediately grey smoke rose from the welt as though it had been under pressure. The skin deflated, and Deem used the knife to widen the slit. Then she removed the white bone from the flesh. It was twice as large as the one she'd removed from herself the previous night. She held it up for Margie to see.

"Oh my!" Margie said, examining the white lump. "Those edges look sharp! I can't believe you couldn't feel that, Virginia!"

"Can't feel a thing," Virginia said, still on her side.

There was no blood, so Deem used a couple of bandages to cover over the incision, and she allowed Virginia to roll back.

"What was it?" Virginia asked.

"We don't really know," Margie said. Deem held the knife up for Virginia to see the bone fragment, still perched on its tip.

"Oh my god!" Virginia said.

"Language!" Margie chided Virginia.

"That doctor oughta be sacked!" Virginia said. "Thank you, dear," she said, looking at Deem. "I feel better already!"

"Would you like something to eat?" Margie offered. "I was making a tray for you."

"I'll get up," Virginia said. "Let me walk around for a bit and see how I feel."

Deem turned to Margie, and her mother gave her an appreciative smile. "I think you may have a future in medicine!" Margie said.

3

Deem sipped her hot chocolate while Winn drank a coffee at Pete's.

"What's his name again?" Deem asked.

"Awan," Winn said. "Awan Agai."

"Strange name," Deem said.

"You're one to talk," Winn replied.

"Did he say anything about it?" Deem asked.

"Nope," Winn said. "Just wrote that he knew what it was, and wanted to meet up."

"Indian Springs is a good hour and a half away," Deem said. "He must think it's serious."

"We'll see," Winn said. The waitress brought him a plate of French fries covered in brown gravy.

"That looks disgusting," Deem said.

"Deliciously disgusting," Winn said, smiling. "Want some?"

"No," Deem said, scrunching up her nose. "By the way, I cut a piece of bone out of my aunt just before I came here. Same thing I had, but twice as big."

"No shit!" Winn said. "That must be why she was sick."

"I'm guessing if I hadn't cut mine out, I'd be sick too."

"That's a good bet."

The chimes attached to the diner's door rang as a tall man walked into the room. He was wearing cowboy boots, tight fitting Wranglers, and a Yankees baseball cap on his head – dark black hair sticking out from under it. He had on a tight white t-shirt, tucked into his jeans. He looked lean and fit, and a few years older than Winn. He walked over to Deem and Winn's booth and stood next to them.

"Winn?" he asked.

"That's me," Winn answered.

"Awan," he said.

Both Winn and Deem slid further into the booth to allow Awan a place to sit. Awan looked at both open spots on either side of the booth and chuckled. He sat next to Deem.

"I'm Deem," she said, extending her hand.

"Nice to meet you," Awan said, taking her hand.

Deem felt a little flustered, which wasn't normal for her. She wasn't sure what she was expecting, but it wasn't this. Awan was disarmingly handsome. And now that he was sitting next to her, she noticed he smelled fantastic.

"So I read your post," Awan said, looking down at Winn's fries. "Can I have some of those?"

"Help yourself!" Winn said, shoving the plate closer to Awan, who grabbed several fries that were covered in gravy and stuffed them into his mouth.

Deem noticed that his teeth were perfect. *Not something you usually see around here,* she thought.

"Damn, those are good," Awan said. "I think I'll order a plate myself."

"So you think you know what we've run into?" Deem asked.

"I'm pretty sure," Awan said. "But tell me the whole thing, from start to finish."

Deem and Winn alternated telling Awan the story. They started with the bus trip and Deem ended with the removal of the bone from her aunt's neck.

"I'm pretty sure I know," Awan said. "The combination of it being on your roof and your aunt having a black tongue is what makes me think it's a mutated naagloshii."

"Skinwalker?" Winn asked.

"Not like any skinwalker you've heard of," Awan said. "This bunch has changed due to downwind radiation. They're different. Friends I know have been calling them skinrunners because they're not like regular skinwalkers."

"Bunch?" Winn asked. "You've seen more of them?"

"Lots of them in the past few months," Awan said, eating more fries. "They function only at night. Their ability to transform into animals is limited, but they gain the attributes of some animals without transforming."

"Like being able to run as fast as a bus?" Deem said.

"Exactly," Awan said. "The glowing eyes are another sign. And they target people, especially people who've seen their face."

"That would be me," Deem said. "And my aunt, too."

"What do you do to stop them?" Winn asked.

"That goes back to how they became skinrunners in the first place," Awan said. "The man who attacked you became a skinrunner by performing a ritual with the aid of a shaman. The ritual has changed from the traditional, in part because of a rogue shaman who is using downwind mutations to create more naagloshii than usual. Normally it's the shaman who decides to become a skinwalker, but this guy is spinning out skinrunners by the dozens, for a fee. Anybody can become one with his help, as long as they complete the requirements and pay his price. It's become a business to him."

"What are the requirements?" Deem asked.

"There's a ritual the shaman performs," Awan said. "It stops, halfway though. The person has to leave, and kill someone he loves. Then he returns to the shaman, and the ritual completes, and they become naagloshii. Skinrunners."

"Navajo?" Winn asked.

"He was Navajo until they kicked him out," Awan said. "Now he's practicing a blend of Navajo and Hopi medicine. I'm guessing the Navajos probably wish they'd put him down rather than exiled him."

"How'd you find all this out?" Winn asked. "Normally the Navajos won't talk about skinwalkers."

"I'm Paiute," Awan said, "and I've got some gifted friends who are Navajo. They know I specialize in tracking bad medicine, so they've been keeping me informed. It's nothing they'd tell a white man. And they're always cautious about saying too much. I think they're hoping I'll track this shaman down and take care of him for them. He was experimenting with things that bothered them, mutations especially. They exiled him years ago, but it's only been in the last few months that he figured out how to mass-produce these skinrunners. They know it's him, but for some reason they're not taking action to stop him."

"Are you going to track him down?" Deem asked.

"Wasn't my plan," Awan said. "I've got some trouble back home at the moment. I saw your post about the black tongue and thought I'd better warn you."

"Thanks for that," Winn said. "Any suggestions as to what we should try?"

"Well, he'll keep coming back," Awan said. "Stay up and watch tonight, get a spot where you can see the roof of the house clearly. I'll bet you see him up there, blowing corpse poison down your chimney."

"Corpse poison?" Deem asked.

"It's made from the bones of dead babies," Awan said. "Extra potent if they're twins. It's what's causing the blisters on your skin with the bone fragments inside. You can keep cutting them out, but he'll keep doing it, and you'll just keep getting them. And eventually you'll succumb, because the blisters will stop appearing on your skin and develop on the inside of your body instead. You've got three days after you develop black tongue to get it resolved, or you'll die."

"Great," Deem said sarcastically. "Any idea how to stop him?"

"Well, there's stopping the attack and there's stopping him," Awan said. "Two different things. If you want to stop the attack, there used to be a device that would remove the black tongue and permanently protect you from another infection. My grandfather used to have one, but it's long gone. He said it was stolen. Other than something like that, you can only keep cutting out the bones, until you can't find them anymore."

"Can you tell me more about this device, Awan?" Deem asked. "The object your grandfather said was stolen?"

"I never saw it," Awan said. "But I know he used it a lot. There's always been skinwalkers down here, and people trying to put them down. He'd use it on people with black tongue, and they'd be free of the attack."

"I wish we could find an object like that," Deem said. "Did he keep journals?"

"He did," Awan said, becoming more enthusiastic. "Good journals. He might have sketched it out. When I get home I'll check. If I find anything I'll take a picture of it and send it to you."

"Even if we knew what the object looked like," Winn said, "how would that help us? Where would we get one? I don't collect objects, and I don't know anyone who does."

"I might know someone who can point us in the right direction," Deem said. "Eliza. Remember her, when Steven and Roy were down?"

"Sure," Winn said. "She has objects?"

"I know she uses them in her work," Deem said. "She might have one, or be able to refer me to someone who would know. I'll reach out to her and see."

"I would also suggest," Awan said, "that you try to find out who this skinrunner is. A name and an address. Might come in handy if you can't get the object."

"Any ideas how to find that out?" Deem asked.

"We track him," Winn said.

"Exactly," Awan agreed.

"What, from my house?" Deem asked. "Tonight?"

"We'll never be able to do it ourselves," Winn said. "He's too fast. But I know someone who can."

"A Caller?" Awan asked.

"Yes," Winn said. "How'd you know?"

"They're the only ones who can keep up with them," Awan said. "But hard to use. They always want something in return."

"What Caller?" Deem asked Winn.

"I know one named Sagan," Winn said. "Lives in an abandoned house south of Mesquite. He works with a loser named Brett Jones, robbing liquor stores. He's not the sharpest crayon in the box, so I'll bet I can get him to track the skinrunner."

"How?" Deem asked. "Do you have a plan?"

"Kinda," Winn said, smiling. "It's a half plan. Might work."

"I hate half plans," Deem said.

"His big thing is corpses," Winn said. "Every time Brett finds some road kill, he scrapes it up and uses it to pay Sagan for his help. So, I'm thinking we offer Sagan something more juicy for his time. Real corpses."

"How are you going to do that?" Awan asked.

"Devil's Throat," Deem said, remembering the dozens of animated corpses they'd trapped inside.

"Exactly," Winn said. "I'll offer to tell him where to find them if he tracks the skinrunner and gets us his address."

Deem nodded her head slowly, in approval. "OK," she said. "Not a bad half plan."

"Sounds like we each have an assignment," Awan said. "I'll get headed back to Indian Springs and I'll let you know if I find anything in my grandfather's journals."

"I'll contact Eliza," Deem said.

"And I'll go see Sagan," Winn said. "Want to come with?" he asked Deem.

"Sure," Deem said, "as long as we can stop somewhere on the way back. Won't take long."

"And then we'll set up to watch your roof tonight," Winn said, "and see if we can spot this fucker."

■ ■ ■

Winn stopped his Jeep in front of a half dilapidated house several miles south of Mesquite. Deem stepped out of the passenger side and looked around. The nearest neighbor was a speck on the horizon.

The house appeared to have been abandoned for years. The front yard was overgrown with large sagebrush. Part of the roof had collapsed, and not a pane of glass remained in any of the windows.

"What a dump," Deem said.

"Perfect for a ghost, right?" Winn said.

Deem knew the ghost they'd be encountering wasn't just a ghost. Callers were more self-aware than most ghosts. They weren't trapped in some endless cycle, unable to move on. They *liked* being ghosts, and they made a life of it. They were created by being buried in a cave that housed a spirit in the rocks. The spirit granted them Caller abilities, provided they fed the spirit what it wanted. Most wanted blood.

Winn walked through the brush in front of the house. The door was boarded over. He walked around the side of the house, Deem following.

In the back, there was a set of stone steps descending to a basement. They were covered over by a piece of loose plywood. Winn pushed the plywood aside and descended the steps.

Once they were inside the basement, Deem looked up; there were holes in the ceiling which she could see through to the main floor. She pulled out her flashlight and turned it on. Seeing the structure made her even more nervous that it might collapse.

"Sagan?" Winn called. "Come out. I want to talk to you."

Deem felt something brush the back of her hair, and she turned quickly. Nothing was there.

"I felt something," Deem said.

"Sagan?" Winn called. "Don't fuck around, I've got something you want, and you don't want to piss me off."

Sagan materialized directly in front of Deem. It startled her and she jumped back.

"I told you not to fuck around," Winn said.

Deem saw Winn jump into the River. She took another step back from Sagan and then followed Winn into the flow.

Sagan looked like a twenty year old delinquent. He wore a dirty wife beater and a baggy pair of chinos. His arms were covered in tattoos. He leered at Deem, a small face peering out from around long hair.

She's pretty! he said.

Too bad you're a ghost, Winn said to Sagan.

Yeah, I'd love to tap that, Sagan said, moving around Deem.

You want some fresh meat? Winn asked.

Sagan turned from Deem to look at Winn. *Whatcha got?* he asked.

Human corpses, Winn said. *A nice supply. Would keep that cave spirit of yours happy for a long time.*

Deem saw Sagan respond like a dog. He ran up to Winn.

Where? Sagan asked. *I could use some!*

Well, this is a nice supply, would probably set you up for a long time, Winn said. *That's worth a lot, isn't it?*

If it's true, Sagan said, losing some of his enthusiasm.

Aren't you tired of working with Brett, living off the deer carcasses he drags back here? Winn said. *I thought you were destined for greater things.*

I got my application in with the St. Thomas crew, Sagan said. *They're gonna take me.*

They ain't gonna take ya, Winn said, *'cause there isn't a St. Thomas crew anymore. The place is gone.*

I don't believe you, Sagan said. *The St. Thomas crew is the greatest crew around here, and I'm gonna join them.*

Well, you keep telling yourself that, Winn said, *but in the meantime I was wondering if you were interested in something a little more significant than dead squirrels and rattlesnakes. Something that might demonstrate your ambition to a crew.*

Maybe, Sagan said. *What?*

I have a task I need done, and if you do it, I'll tell you where to find enough human corpses to last you for years. You might even be able to sell them and set up your own crew. How about that?

What task? Sagan asked.

I got someone I want you to track, Winn said. *I want you to find out where they live. You give me their name and address, I'll tell you where the bodies are.*

Why do you need me to track 'em? Sagan asked. *Why can't you track 'em yourself?*

'Cause they're faster than me, Winn said. *Are you interested or not?*

How many bodies? Sagan asked.

At least a dozen, Winn answered. *That'd last you how long, years? Imagine not having to feed anything to that cave spirit for a while. It'd be like you're a free man.*

Deem watched as Sagan began to get excited. She knew he probably transported an animal carcass to wherever he was buried several times a week to feed the spirit in the cave and keep himself a Caller. A human corpse would be worth far more to the cave spirit.

Tell me where they are, Sagan said, *and I'll do it.*

Nah, Winn answered. *You track the guy first, get me his address, then I'll tell you.*

How do I know you won't renege on your end of the deal, Sagan said, *once I've done my part?*

You'll just have to trust me, if you want those bodies.

Well, I have trust issues, Sagan said. *Brett told me I'd get ten animals for every store I broke him into, but now I only get one or two.*

Brett ain't part of this deal, Winn said. *This is between you and me.*

Yeah, but I find that humans lie, Sagan said, turning to walk away from Winn. *They tell you they'll do something, but then they don't.*

Deem watched Sagan as he walked back and forth, kicking at the ground. It made her smile; Sagan thought he was negotiating, but he obviously didn't know Winn.

I guess I'll see if Gale over in Littlefield wants the gig, Winn said, turning. *Let's go, Deem.*

Now hold on, Sagan said. *I didn't say I didn't want the job.*

Yeah, but you didn't say you did, and this place stinks, Sagan. I can barely stand to be in here with you. So make up your mind. I know Gale will do it, he's desperate to make some coin. I only stopped here because it was closer and I thought I'd let you in on something big-time instead of dog and cat corpses.

Winn turned again, and Deem followed him as he walked back toward the steps.

I'll do it! Sagan called after them. *Alright, I'll do it. But I want an oath.*

No oath, Winn said, turning back to face Sagan. *You do it, I tell you where they are. That's the deal.*

Fuck, you aren't being fair, Sagan said. *I ain't got no protection in this deal.*

That's because you're a white trash low life, Sagan. You were a degenerate when you were alive, and you're still a degenerate. I don't trust you at all. Degenerates don't get protection in deals. Take it or leave it.

Damn, you're kind of an asshole, Sagan said.

Come on, Deem, Winn said, turning again to head for the stairs.

No, wait, wait! Sagan said. *I said I'd do it, and I will. Who am I supposed to track?*

He'll be at Deem's house sometime tonight, Winn said. *You watch the outside of the house until he appears, then follow him. I want a name and an address, then you get your corpses. Oh, and under no circumstances are you to go inside the house, is that clear?*

Yeah, Sagan said. *Don't go in. How will I know the guy?*

He's dark and his eyes glow, Deem said. *And he moves fast, much faster than a human.*

So he's not human? Sagan asked. *What is he?*

That's none of your concern, Winn said.

It is if I'm supposed to track him! Sagan said. *What if he turns on me?*

Just stay back far enough that he doesn't know you're following him, Winn said. *I don't want him tipped off.*

I give you his address, you set me up with the bodies?

Name and address, Winn said, *and after I verify that you got the right guy. Then I set you up.*

Alright, Sagan said. *Where's the house?*

Deem relayed her address to Sagan. He seemed to be memorizing it, repeating it over and over. It didn't inspire confidence.

Can I ask you something? Deem asked Sagan.

Sure, he said, repeating the address under his breath.

How'd you get the name Sagan? she asked.

I drew a bunch of stars on my skateboard, he replied. *Constellations and shit. When my homies saw it, they started calling me Sagan.*

After Carl Sagan? Deem asked.

Who's that? Sagan replied.

Come on, Deem, Winn said, walking to the stairs. *This idiot doesn't even know who he's named after, and I gotta get out of here before I choke. Don't fuck this up, Sagan. You fuck it up, the deal's cancelled and I take it to Gale.*

Chill! Sagan said. *I'll do it, you don't gotta worry.*

■ ■ ■

"He's an idiot," Deem said, riding in Winn's Jeep. "Makes me a little nervous to have him working on this."

"Me too," Winn said, "since he's our only option."

"There's no Gale in Littlefield?" Deem asked.

"Nope," Winn said. "Sagan's the only Caller I know that's close. If he doesn't work out, the next closest I know of are in Ely."

"Damn, let's hope he gets it right," Deem said. "Are you going to tell him the corpses are animated?"

"Nope," Winn said. "He'll have to figure that one out. But he will, he's so hungry for them. He'll clean the place out."

"If he doesn't fuck it up," Deem repeated.

"Yeah, that," Winn said.

Deem felt her cell phone buzz in her pocket. She pulled it out and checked it – it was a reminder to visit Joseph Dayton, a friend of her father's.

"So this stop I need to make," Deem said to Winn, "is right in the middle of town. If you want, you can take me home and I'll drive there."

"How long will it take?" Winn asked.

"I don't know," Deem said. "I want to talk to him about my father. He was good friends with him. I think he's gifted, too, and won't admit it. I'm hoping to ask him if my father kept a journal."

"I'll take you there," Winn said, knowing this was of major importance to Deem. Anything that involved her father was major.

"I can't tell you for sure how long it will take," Deem said.

"I'll wait," Winn replied.

Deem gave Winn the address. She was grateful that he was coming along. She could use the moral support.

...

Winn watched as Deem left the house he was parked in front of and walked to his Jeep. She opened the passenger door and hopped inside.

"That was fast," Winn said.

"He wouldn't tell me anything," Deem said, fuming. "Wouldn't admit to having the gift, said he didn't know if my dad kept a journal. I dropped into the River and could tell he was lying. I think he knew I knew."

"Did you call him on it?" Winn asked.

"No," Deem said. "I just thanked him and left. I feel like a pussy."

"Want me to go talk to him?" Winn asked.

"No," Deem said. "It's just that...goddamnit, it's just how smug he was. There's all this judgment. I'm not active in the church, so the walls are up. It makes me angry. It's my father we're talking about, church or no."

"Yeah," Winn said, "I know what you mean."

"He and my dad spent a lot of time together," Deem said. "He was Dad's counselor in the stake presidency. They were both gifted, I know it. I'll bet he has gifted kids of his own, too. He should be more compassionate."

"I thought you said your father didn't leave a journal?" Winn said. "Did you discover something different?"

"It doesn't make sense," Deem said. "He advocated keeping a journal, he advised others to do it, as part of the religion. I can't believe he didn't keep one himself. My mom says there's no journal, but he may have hid it from her, or she might be hiding it from me. I spent most of today digging through boxes in storage at home, seeing if I could find something. I know it's there, somewhere."

"And you were hoping this guy would know something?"

"I thought maybe he could confirm if my dad kept one," Deem said. "But he denied any knowledge of anything. It was like he never knew my dad. And worse, he lied to me."

Deem was tearing up. Winn saw her wipe her eyes. "When I was younger," Deem said, "I thought he was a very nice man. Now he's just an asshole."

"You know, there's always been those rumors about Mormon gifteds," Winn said. "Maybe that's why."

"My dad told me they weren't true," Deem said.

"Yeah, well, he didn't tell you about a journal, either. Maybe it was something he was waiting to tell you, but he passed away before he could."

"He died a slow, agonizing death from leukemia," Deem said. "He had plenty of time to tell me anything he wanted to say."

"You could always go talk to Claude Peterson," Winn said.

Deem turned to look at Winn. "Crazy Claude? I'd be shot before I could knock on his door."

"The guy knows a lot about it," Winn said.

"It's all bullshit," Deem said. "He's a lunatic."

"He just knows some things he probably shouldn't have talked about," Winn said, "and it got him branded as crazy. It's the community here that's isolated him. I've always believed him."

"Well, you believe in UFOs, too," Deem said.

"This sudden interest in a journal is because of Steven and Roy, isn't it?" Winn asked. "Seeing Roy's journal?"

"It got me thinking, yes," Deem said. Deem felt her phone buzz once again. She slipped it from her pocket and scrolled through the messages.

"Awan found a picture," she said, turning to Winn and smiling.

4

"I told her I'd see what I could find," Eliza said, "but I didn't tell her anything about Eximere, of course."

"Good," Steven said, pouring himself a cup of coffee with his left hand while holding the cell phone with his right. "I'm going there tomorrow. I'll look for it. You'll email it? The picture?"

"As soon as I get it from Deem," Eliza said.

"This would be a nice way to return one of those objects, if it's there," Steven said. "I think we'll have a hard time returning the others without someone stepping forward like this."

"Is that Eliza?" Roy asked, walking into Steven's kitchen to get some of the freshly brewed coffee.

"Hold on, I'm going to put you on speakerphone," Steven said, removing the phone from his ear and pressing a button. He moved to the kitchen table and Roy sat next to him.

"Hello?" Steven said. "Can you hear me?"

"Yes, I can hear you," Eliza said.

"Hello, Eliza!" Roy said. "Nice to hear your voice."

"Yours too!" Eliza said. "How's things? How's Jason?"

"He's fine, doing fine," Roy said. "Well, fits and starts, but he's coming along."

"I had to pull back a little," Steven said into the phone. "I've been dumping a lot on him. I didn't want him to feel I was holding back anymore. I think it was too much too soon."

"Jason told him to slow down," Roy said into the phone. "Things were going too fast."

"Well, he got what he wanted," Eliza said. "At whatever speed. Any lingering issues with St. Thomas?"

"Doesn't seem to be," Steven said. "What do you think, Dad?"

Roy remembered the warning Deem had given him about Jason, the potential for something subliminal to reemerge. He hadn't seen anything along those lines yet, but he'd been watching.

"He seems fine," Roy said. "Nothing out of the ordinary."

"That's good," Eliza said. "So, you think we can give up one of those objects at Eximere, for Deem? If it's there?"

"I'd be happy to," Steven said. "We owe them. This would be a nice way to repay them."

"Alright, I'll just tell her I've got some friends looking for it. If you find it, let me know and I'll give her a call."

"Are they in trouble?" Roy asked.

"Yes, it sounded bad," Eliza said. "One of her relatives is under attack, at her house. A friend of theirs found this object in his grandfather's journal, they're hoping it will help. His grandfather claimed it was stolen from him."

"I wonder if he was one of Unser's victims," Steven said.

"Goddamnit!" Roy said, suddenly standing up. "Hot coffee in the crotch!"

Steven could hear Eliza laughing. "I'll let you go," she said. "Sounds like you need to clean up."

"He knocked over a full mug," Steven said. "Coffee everywhere. I'll call you if we find anything. Or if we don't, either way."

"Thanks," Eliza said, and hung up.

● ● ●

As Winn poured himself another cup of coffee from his thermos, Deem grabbed the Big Gulp from the cup holder in Winn's Jeep and took a long sip. Their car was parked a half block down from Deem's house, with a perfect view of the front of the house and the roof.

"You still drinking that shit?" Winn said. "The sugar'll kill ya."

"What you're drinking isn't any better," Deem said, replacing the Big Gulp in the cup holder.

"Of course it is," Winn said. "I drink it black, no sugar at all."

"I'm drinking a Diet Coke," Deem said. "No sugar."

"Just a ton of chemicals bubbling in carbonation," Winn said.

"Mmm, mmm," Deem said. "And it tastes so good!"

They'd been in the car for over an hour. It was one a.m.

"So you just don't like coffee?" Winn asked, bored.

"I love the smell of it," Deem said. "But drinking it sucks."

"That's because you want it to be sweet," Winn said. "They put chemical sweeteners in Diet Coke, you know. And coffee is good for you. Lots of studies on the internet."

"That's not what we were told in Sunday School," Deem said. "They had all kinds of stories about how bad it was for you."

"Well, you know that was a load of horseshit," Winn said, taking a sip.

"OK, let me try some," Deem said.

Winn passed his cup over to her. She smelled it, then took a small sip. She handed it back.

"That's nasty," she said. She reached for her Big Gulp to wash away the taste.

"Maybe you need to ease your way into it," Winn said. "With cream and sugar, like most girls drink it."

Deem knew he was trying to get under her skin with the "most girls" comment. She ignored him.

"Roy says I've just never had good coffee," Deem said. "He said in Seattle they'd make sure I got the good stuff."

"Hey, Roy liked *my* coffee," Winn said. "I think you just prefer your candy. That's fine, all little girls like candy."

"You're starting to piss me off," Deem said.

"I'm bored," Winn replied. He slid down a little in his seat, adjusting himself. Deem knew Winn had a reputation for being sizeable in the endowment department, and she couldn't help but notice how much of Winn was straining in the tight jeans. She glanced away before he could catch her looking.

Like everyone says, she thought. *He's hung.*

She'd considered becoming involved with Winn early on when they first met. He was charming and handsome, and at first she felt she'd met someone who understood her on her gifted level, and it appealed to her. But after a while she decided Winn was too much to handle as anything more than a friend. She learned he had a harem of both women and men who'd sleep with him whenever he wanted, and she found that irritating. He'd tried to seduce her early on, but she put the brakes on it and made it clear their relationship was going to be on a professional level only.

And it's going to stay that way, Deem thought. *Even if he's huge.*

"Look," Winn said, putting his coffee cup in the Jeep's cup holder.

Deem looked up, searching. She saw the figure as it crested the skyline of the house, a dark, crouched shape that was quickly moving along the top of the roof. It ran up to the brick chimney and placed its head into it.

"It's blowing the corpse poison," Winn said. "Virginia's gonna have another blister to take care of."

It pulled its head out of the chimney and looked around. Deem could see its glowing eyes as its head turned.

"Maybe it knows I'm not in the house?" Deem said.

"Maybe," Winn said, watching the figure.

They watched as the figure lifted off the roof. It hovered five feet above the chimney.

"It looks so creepy," Deem said, "a man just hovering in air like that. No flapping of wings, no jet pack strapped on his back."

"Yeah, very unnatural," Winn said.

Deem saw the man's eyes. They'd been centered in her direction for several seconds now, and she had the impression that he'd seen her, sitting in the car.

"I think it knows we're watching it," Deem said.

The figure above the roof drifted higher and began moving away from them. It flew rapidly, rising up and out of their field of vision.

"There's no way you or I could track that," Winn said. "Awan has pointed us in the right direction."

"As long as Sagan saw it," Deem said. "For all we know he's sleeping under a tree."

"He's a greedy little fuck," Winn said. "I don't think he'd want to risk me taking my business elsewhere."

"We'll see," Deem said, grabbing her Big Gulp and reaching for the door handle. "I'd better go check Virginia. Let's talk in the morning."

"Alright," Winn said, starting up his car. Deem jumped out of the passenger side, turned to wave at Winn, and began walking to her house. She heard Winn turn the car around behind her and leave.

As she walked back to the house, she thought about Winn's suggestion that she go see Claude Peterson. She hated the idea. Claude was known far and wide as a crazy, a constitutionalist gun nut who kept himself barricaded in his home in Ivins. She knew he'd been raided multiple times by Feds looking for illegal firearms and weapons. There was a rumor he'd laminated his permits and had them nailed to the side of his house.

Maybe I should see him, Deem thought as she walked into the house. *At least, rule him out.*

She walked to Virginia's room, and knocked quietly on the door. Her mother was sleeping in the master bedroom upstairs, and she didn't want to wake her.

"Virginia," she said, "it's me. I need to come in."

■ ■ ■

Deem called Winn early the next morning, asking him to meet her for breakfast in Mesquite.

"I've decided to go see Claude," Deem said, sliding into the booth where Winn was waiting. "And I'd like you to come along."

"Alright," Winn said.

"I'd go myself, but I'm afraid I might get shot," Deem said. "You can at least talk to him, if he has a problem with females and won't talk to me."

"You're assuming the worst," Winn said.

"Always the best approach," Deem said.

They ordered breakfast. Deem ordered a hot chocolate, which came with a large spray of whipped cream on top.

"See, more sugar," Winn said. "Are you noticing a pattern here?"

"Shut up and let me drink what I want," Deem said. "You're like my mother."

"I'm nothing like your mother," Winn said. "I can guarantee that."

"I cut open a blister on Virginia last night," Deem said. "A small one. Bone inside, like the others. She's beginning to freak out."

"Any word from Eliza yet?" Winn asked.

"She emailed me to say that some friends of hers are looking for an object like Awan's."

"I wonder if those friends are Roy and Steven," Winn said.

"She didn't say," Deem said. "I assume if it was them she'd have mentioned it."

"Unless there was a reason not to," Winn said.

"All I care about is getting the object," Deem said. "I don't care where it comes from."

"Well, you should," Winn said. "The history of the object matters. Tells you a lot about where it came from, and what it might do. Some of that shit is dangerous."

"You've had some experience with it?" Deem asked.

"My mom," Winn said. "She had a couple of items. She didn't do a good job of locking them up. One day when I was eight or nine I found this magnifying glass. Had a wooden handle and I remember the metal surrounding the glass had these little markings on it. So I'm thinking, great, let's take it outside and burn up bugs."

"Gross," Deem interjected.

"So I'm frying ants, and they're popping like normal, and then I see a lizard. It was about six inches long. I trapped it and put a brick on its tail so it couldn't move. Then I used the magnifying glass on it."

"That's cruel," Deem said.

"I know, I was stupid," Winn said. "And I was eight. So anyway, the lizard doesn't burn. There was no smoke like with the ants. It just sat there, and I remember thinking that maybe it was dead, or the magnifying glass was broken. Then it began to cough up its insides. I felt bad, so I took the magnifying glass off it, but it kept puking. Then all of it came out. Its tail pulled up into its body and came out its mouth. It literally flipped inside-out. Freaked me out. I put the magnifying glass back and didn't touch it again."

"That's a horrible story," Deem said as their food arrived.

"I asked my mom about the magnifying glass a couple of years later," Winn said, "and she wigged out on me, asking how I knew about it, if I'd been snooping. She told me never to touch it. Next time I looked for it, she'd moved it. I never saw it again, until she died and I went through her things."

"So you still have it?" Deem asked.

"Yes, but what am I going to do with it?" Winn asked.

"I wonder if it would work on something larger," Deem said.

"Like what?" Winn asked.

"Like a dog, or a person," Deem said.

"Now you're being gross," Winn said. "I have no interest in finding out. It was disgusting. I never tortured another living creature after that. I don't even kill spiders. Everything's got a purpose on this Earth."

"She had other objects?" Deem asked.

"Two others," Winn said. "I know they're special, because they change shape when I'm in the River. But I have no idea what they do."

"And she never said anything about them?" Deem asked.

"Are you kidding?" Winn asked. "She was completely freaked out that I knew about the magnifying glass. She didn't trust me with that kind of stuff."

"Because you were a juvenile delinquent," Deem said.

"That was a very brief part of my life that is long over," Winn said.

"But she didn't trust you?" Deem asked.

"No, not really," Winn said. "I mean, she was far from perfect. A bad mother by most standards. She changed when I got taken to juvie. She never really trusted me after that, scaled way back on the training."

"How old were you?" Deem asked.

"Sixteen," Winn said. "Just started driving."

"So she trained you before that?" Deem asked.

"Yes, from when I was ten," Winn said. "Probably not like most, though. She was drunk most of the time. Occasionally she'd show me things in the River. After sixteen, nothing. It was like a switch. My being in juvie really pissed her off."

"Sorry to hear that," Deem said. "At least you're a straight arrow now. Well, kinda straight."

"What's that supposed to mean?" Winn asked.

"You can't really call yourself straight if you have sex with men," Deem said.

"Everyone's got their vices," Winn said. "You like to drink liquid candy and swear, and I like to have sex with both men and women. And why shouldn't I, I'm damn good at it."

"So you keep telling me," Deem said.

"I can get you some testimonials if you want," Winn said.

"No need. I believe you."

"Wow, next thing you know, you'll be drinking coffee."

"I doubt that."

"When did you want to go see Claude?" Winn asked.

"Right now, if you're up for it," Deem said.

"I suppose we could try to call him," Winn said, "but I don't think he has a phone."

"Probably figures they'd bug it anyway," Deem said, finishing up her breakfast. She stood up and threw money down on the table. "I'm buying, and I'll drive."

"Love it when a woman takes charge," Winn said smiling.

■ ■ ■

Deem walked up to the gate in the chain link fence surrounding the small house on the outskirts of Ivins. There were three signs on the gate: "No Solicitors," "Beware Of The Dog," and "This House Insured By Smith and Wesson."

"Do you think he really has a dog?" Deem asked Winn, who was right behind her.

"Probably," Winn said. "I would if I was him. I think it's the Smith and Wesson sign you should worry about most."

Deem opened the gate and walked into the yard. A short cement path led to the front door. In the yard was a large board with papers stapled to it. It was covered in plastic to protect the papers from the elements. The writing on the papers had faded in the sun. Deem peered at the board, trying to read the documents.

"It's a copy of the Constitution," Winn said.

"Oh," Deem said. She noticed that under the Constitution board were two more signs, "This is Private Property" and "Keep Out."

"He likes signs," Deem said. She looked at the house; it had large antennas on the roof. They were much taller and larger than television antennas. "Do you see those?" she asked Winn, motioning to the roof.

"Looks like he's into shortwave radio," Winn said. "Lots of people on the fringe are."

Deem walked up to the door and knocked. A dog started barking loudly, and she could hear it jumping up against the door on the other side. As she waited she read more signs on the front door:

"I have spent over $3,512 fixing this door due to no-knock warrants. I have yet to be reimbursed."

"If you are selling or promoting something and you've ignored my 'No Soliciting' sign, don't expect a warm welcome."

"Jesus," Deem said. "I don't know if this was a good idea."

"We'll soon find out," Winn said. "I hear someone coming."

The door opened. Deem wasn't sure what she was expecting, but she was surprised to see a short man, thin, wearing a button down shirt and knee-length shorts. He was wearing sandals. He looked like he might be in his early sixties. He had his hand wrapped around the collar of a large pit bull which was barking and trying to leap out of his control.

"Stop!" the man said to the dog. The dog quit barking, but continued to strain against his hold. He turned to the visitors.

"Whatcha want?" he said, looking them both in the eye.

Deem stammered. She wasn't sure where to start. The man obviously wanted a quick explanation of why she was there, and she wasn't quite prepared to sum it all up in a short sentence.

"I urged my friend to come see you," Winn said, jumping in, "because I believe you may know some things that would help her."

"Help her how?" Claude asked, pulling back on the dog.

Winn waited for Deem to offer up the next answer, but Deem still seemed frozen. Winn elbowed her.

"I'm sorry," Deem said. "I was hoping to talk with you, but I'm really intimidated by your dog."

"That's why he's here," Claude said. "You selling anything?"

"No," Deem said, trying to hide her nervousness. "Was just hoping you might know something about people who have 'the gift.' Mormons, in particular."

"You a journalist?" Claude asked. "What do you do for a living?"

"I'm a student," she said. She knew this was half true; she'd was sitting out the current semester.

"I work in construction," Winn said, which was true – when he had a job.

"Anybody send you?" Claude asked.

"Nope," Winn said. "All my idea."

"Hold on a second," Claude said, and closed the door. The dog started barking again, and they heard him pulling it deeper into the house.

"This was a bad idea," Deem said, looking at the ground.

"Just breathe," Winn said. "He's putting the dog away. That's a good sign."

Within a minute Claude returned and opened the door. They could hear the dog barking in the distance. "I put Kimo in the back yard," Claude said. "He's very protective."

"Yes, he seems...protective," Deem said, feeling embarrassed.

"Why don't you two come inside before someone spots you on my doorstep," Claude said, stepping back and allowing them inside. "If I'd known you were coming, I'd have had you park further down the block, but no matter."

He escorted them into his living room, which was small and crammed with stacks of magazine and papers. In one corner of the room was a table filled with electronics. There was a large microphone on a stand. Deem assumed it was his radio station.

"Do you broadcast?" Deem said.

"KBUH, the Hour of Truth," Claude said. "Every night at seven p.m. Ever heard it?"

"No, I haven't," Deem said. "I've never heard that station."

"That's because you need a special radio to get the signal," Claude said, sitting in a large overstuffed chair. "Please, sit," he said, motioning them to a brown cloth couch. The tables on each end of the couch were piled high with stacks of magazines and papers.

"I am planning on putting the program on the internet if I can ever figure out how to do it," Claude said. "I've been broadcasting the Hour for more than thirty years. Lots of people listen to it, from all over the world."

"Sounds interesting," Deem said.

"How would you know?" Claude asked. "You've never heard it."

"You're right," Deem said. "But I suppose I'd be willing to give it a shot."

"Get yourself a shortwave radio," Claude said. "You'll be surprised what's on it."

"I'm Winn," Winn said to Claude, "and this is Deem. I suggested she come see you, since she's been trying to get some information on her father, and she'd being stonewalled."

"By whom?" Claude asked.

"Joseph Dayton," Deem said.

"Counselor in the Mesquite Nevada Stake Presidency," Claude said.

"You know him?" Deem asked.

"I do," Claude said. "But what are you trying to get from him?"

"Information about my father," Deem said. "Robert Hinton."

"Oh," Claude said. "You're President Hinton's daughter?"

"Yes," Deem said, surprised that Claude was using the Mormon title her father had before he died.

"My condolences," Claude said.

"Thank you," Deem replied.

"I have to tell you," Claude said, "most families of prominent Mormons wouldn't be caught dead anywhere near me. I'm persona non grata to them. To most people around here."

"I'm aware of that," Deem said.

"So I'm right to be suspicious when one shows up at my door step," Claude said.

"I suppose so," Deem said.

"Before we go any further," Claude said, "I have to know if you're carrying anything that might record me. A phone, a wire, a tape recorder, anything like that."

"No, I'm not," Deem said.

He turned to Winn.

"Me either," Winn said.

"I'll have to check," Claude said. He stood and walked to a metal filing cabinet and opened it. He removed an electronic wand with small LED lights on the handle. Deem recognized it as a metal detector, the hand-held kind they used at airports.

"You're going to scan us?" Deem asked, a little surprised.

"I can't take any chances," Claude said. "If you want to talk, I insist."

"Alright," Deem said.

"Please stand up, if you would," Claude said, turning on the device. He waved it over Deem, and it screeched as it passed over her front pants pocket.

"My phone," Deem said.

"Would you take it out please?" Claude asked.

Deem removed the phone as Claude proceeded to check Winn. His pockets set off another alarm from the device. Winn dug into them and removed his phone and his car keys.

"I have a box I'll put these in until we're done," Claude said, extending his hand to collect their phones. "It blocks all transmissions, and is soundproof. I promise you'll get them back when you leave."

Deem looked at Winn. He passed his phone to Claude, and Deem followed suit. Claude went back to his filing cabinets and replaced the metal detector, then opened another drawer and lifted the lid from a box inside. He placed the phones in the box, replaced the lid, and closed the drawer.

"Well, this is a first for me," Deem said. "I've never had my phone taken away before. Except once in school."

"You should try living without it for a day," Claude said. "The convenience is far outstripped by the loss of privacy. Now, tell me what you wanted from Brother Dayton that you didn't get."

Deem relayed the story of suspecting her father kept a journal, and confronting Dayton about it. Winn jumped in to mention he'd heard of Claude's stories about Mormon gifteds.

"So you're both gifted?" Claude asked.

"Yes," Deem said. "Are you?"

"No," Claude asked. "I've just been blessed with an ability to cut through bullpucky and see what's really going on."

"You're not a member of the church?" Deem asked.

"No, not for many years now," he said.

"But you obviously keep up on who's in charge," Deem said, "if you knew my father was a Stake President."

"The most powerful force around here," Claude said, "aside from the radiation fallout, is the LDS church. You can't know what's really going on if you don't know what it's doing. It's more powerful than all the politicians down here, 'cause they're all members. You don't get elected unless you're a Mormon, you know that."

"It's less that way in Nevada," Winn said, "but I know what you mean."

"Are you two LDS?" Claude asked.

"I never was," Winn said.

"I was raised LDS," Deem said, "but I stopped going a couple of years ago, after my father died. My mother is still very active."

"So then you must know what a unique problem you present to them," Claude said. "Your father was gifted too, right?"

"Yes," Deem said.

"I thought so!" Claude said. "And you think Brother Dayton might be gifted, too, am I right?"

"Yes," Deem said. "He and my father were great friends. They spent a lot of time together. I assumed that's why my father picked him as a counselor when he became stake president several years back."

"What did Brother Dayton tell you when you confronted him?" Claude asked.

"He said he never saw my father keep a journal," Deem said, "but that a journal was a personal thing, and if my father kept one, he wouldn't have seen it. When I started suggesting things about the gift and the River, he acted like I was from outer space. Went into complete church counselor mode, spouting the normal crap. It felt like he was lying."

"Your father's other counselor, Brother Linden, became State President when your father died," Claude said, "and Brother Dayton is still a counselor in the state presidency, now reporting to Linden. He's in a very powerful role. Do you think he'd jeopardize that by revealing to you that he's gifted?"

"Why not?" Deem said. "I'm gifted, I get it. He must know I am, I'm his friend's daughter."

"You are not very familiar with the kind of secrets Mormons keep, are you?" Claude said. "You dropped out before you went to the temple, am I right?"

"I went when I was twelve," Deem said.

"Baptisms for the dead," Claude said. "Yes, all kids do them. But you never went for your Endowment, am I right?"

"Right," Deem said. "I became heathen long before that."

"So you at least know that the Endowment is secret," Claude said.

"Well, they always told us in church that it was sacred, not secret," Deem said.

"Right," Claude said. "So sacred that it's kept secret. So it's secret, regardless. Every adult Mormon in good standing keeps secrets."

"If you say so," Deem said. "I don't really know the details."

"I won't get into them," Claude said. "I just want you to know what you're dealing with. Dayton has taken oaths to keep certain things secret. Keeping his gift secret is probably even more important to him, since it isn't something that normal Mormonism encompasses. If it were to get out that he's gifted, he'd certainly lose his title, and probably his membership. The church's rules have no accommodation for the gift. Those who have it must either suppress it, or find a way to use it that keeps it secret."

"That's the boat my father was in," Deem said. "I never understood how he balanced the two. He was obviously successful in the church, but he used the gift too, because he taught me all about it. If he thought it was bad or against the church, he wouldn't have shown it to me."

"Did you ever discuss how he managed that?" Claude asked.

"No," Deem said. "He died before we ever had that conversation. But he never once made me feel bad or ashamed for using the gift. Not once."

"I think I know why he never talked about it with you," Claude said.

"Why?" Deem asked.

"You're a woman," Claude said.

Deem knew instantly what Claude meant. In the Mormon world, Deem would never run in the same circles her father did – all the leadership roles went to men.

"Then he felt it was something I didn't need to know?" Deem asked.

"Because you'd never have to balance it like he had to," Claude said. "He probably hoped you'd get married and start pumping out the babies. Use your gift to keep track of the kids."

Deem lowered her head and felt like crying. She had always felt that her father wanted more for her, inspired her to go to college and do something great with her life. She never felt that he saw her as a normal Mormon girl; he had always told her that she was special and destined for big things. She remembered the day she had asked him why girls weren't allowed to hold the priesthood in the church, even though all of the boys got to. He looked pained, like it was a conversation he had hoped he would never have to have. And when he explained to her how God only gives the priesthood to men, she felt slapped in the face. She couldn't change her sex; by making her female, God had decided she would never be worthy, never as important as men. She knew in her heart, the moment she heard it, that it was wrong, and she saw that her father believed that too, although he was telling her the church line. He wouldn't look at her as he talked to her about it. He knew what it was doing to her, how his words were sinking into her, teaching her the first of many lessons that women were to be subservient to men, and she knew he felt awful for it, that it was counter to what he really believed about her. Ever since that day, she'd known he didn't always mean many of the things he said, especially when it related to the church and her sex. Others hadn't known that he felt this way, but she knew, and she held onto that knowledge whenever misogyny or cruel tradition reared its ugly head. Now, with him gone, she had to hold onto those small signals that he'd sent to her, telling her that she was as good, as worthy, as important as any boy. She had used those signals many times, at critical points in her childhood when she felt beaten down. It made her miss him terribly. She raised her hand to her face, not wanting the others to see her cry.

"I'm sorry," Claude said. "That was rather insensitive of me."

"No," Deem said. "I know where you're coming from. That's what every girl my age is expected to do. It's just that my father never said those kinds of things to me."

"I'm not being fair," Claude said. "I'm afraid I've let my prejudices against the church show through. Your father may not have talked about this balance between the gift and the church because you're a woman, but he had other reasons, too. Reasons that were probably more influential to his thinking."

"Like what?" Deem asked.

"I believe that local, influential, gifted Mormons like your father are part of a secret council," Claude said. "They operate in private, away from the eyes of Salt Lake – or anyone else, for that matter. Your father was likely part of this council. If so, he took an oath that would have kept him from talking to you about it."

Deem was stunned. She didn't know if Claude was spouting a crazy conspiracy theory or the truth.

"How do you know this?" Deem asked.

"I can't say," Claude answered. "I have to protect the people who keep me informed. But I have, in my files here, plenty of evidence that makes me confident."

"What do you know about this council?" Winn asked.

"It's made up of gifted Mormons who've achieved higher ranks in the church," Claude said. "There's not many of them, but they banded together years ago for support. They have their own organization, with their own officers. All men, of course. And they take an oath of secrecy. Just as none of them would ever break their temple oaths, these people would never break their council oaths, either. So Dayton was never going to tell you anything. He's bound not to. Don't take it personally."

Deem found it hard to process. Her father was part of a secret organization? It seemed incredible.

"It's very possible that his journals, if he kept them," Claude said, "are the property of the secret council. What he wrote in them might contain things you wouldn't be allowed to see, even though you're his heir and by rights you should have them. You're not part of the council. And because you're a woman, you never will be."

Deem sat stunned.

"I think I already know the answer to this question," Winn said, "but do you have anything to back this up? Any kind of proof?"

"Oh, plenty," Claude said. "But digging it out to show people is a waste of time. People believe what they want to believe, proof or not. I believe my sources. Whether or not you believe them is up to you."

"I just..." Deem said, halting. "...just find it so hard to believe."

"What, that there's a secret group of Mormons with the gift?" Claude said. "If you're gifted, as you claim, I expect you've seen some incredible things in your time, stuff that other people would find unbelievable. Am I right?"

"That's true," Winn said. "Stuff we don't discuss with other people because they'd think we're crazy."

"Welcome to my world," Claude said, rising up out of his over-stuffed chair. "Listen, this is going to bounce around in your head for a while. You'll decide it's true, then it's bullpucky, and back and forth. That's what always happens."

He walked to the filing cabinet and pulled their phones out of the box. "Once you realize that a group of secret Mormons isn't so implausible in light of the ghosts and other weird stuff you normally deal with, you'll want to talk to me again. So I'm gonna give you my phone number."

He handed Deem and Winn their phones and then walked to his desk, where he scribbled a number on a piece of paper. "If you decide that I'm not just an old man sitting here throwing crap against the walls, give me a call."

He handed he paper to Deem, who took it. She stood, and extended her hand.

"That just spreads germs," Claude said. "How about a pat on the back?"

Deem smiled and turned her back to Claude. He gave her three quick slaps. They walked to the door.

"You both be careful about telling other people what I've told you today," Claude said. "I don't broadcast about the secret council. Lots of people around here take oaths very seriously and I'm already in enough trouble with the town. And please don't share my phone number with anyone."

"I won't," Deem said. "I appreciate you taking the time to talk to me, even though I'm not sure what most of it means."

"Keep in mind," Claude said, "if you decide to pursue this, it's dangerous. It's worth some serious thinking before you go any further."

"Why do you do this?" Deem asked as she opened the door. "If it's risky, why would you help me?"

"'Cause you're being lied to," Claude said, "and I hate that. I don't call it 'The Hour of Truth' for nothing."

5

After leaving Claude's, Deem drove to the abandoned house south of Mesquite to see Sagan. She parked her truck just off the road by the house, and she and Winn walked to the back. The wind had picked up and was blowing sand. Deem tried to cover her face with her hand.

Winn lifted the plywood covering and descended into the basement. "Sagan!" Winn called, dropping into the River.

Sagan appeared, hunkered in a corner.

There you are, Winn said, walking over to him. *Well? Did you track him?*

Yes, Sagan said, *I know where he lives. But my price has gone up.*

What do you mean? Winn asked.

I mean, Sagan said, standing up to face Winn, *the guy you had me track was a fucked up skinwalker. You didn't mention that.*

What's his name? Winn asked.

I want double, Sagan said.

Don't be ridiculous, Winn said. *That wasn't our deal.*

I don't care, Sagan said. *If you want to know who it is, I want double.*

So I offered you a dozen corpses, Winn said. *You want two dozen?*

Yes, Sagan said, *and I want your word that if he or his creator decides to attack me, you'll defend me.*

Why would he attack you? Winn said. *Did you fuck up? Did he see you?*

No, Sagan said. *I don't think so. But I saw his place, and he's seriously twisted. And he doesn't act like a normal skinwalker, he's faster. Whoever made him is a powerful motherfucker, and I don't want to anger the guy.*

Alright, Winn said. *Two dozen corpses, but that's it.*

Sagan eyed him suspiciously. *No, I want protection,* he said. *If this comes back on me, I expect you two to help me out.*

You're a Caller, Deem said. *Why would you need our help?*

'Cause I like my life, Sagan said, *such as it is. I got this pad to myself, I get to scare little kids at the bus stop, peek in people's windows at night when they can't see me, go along on some good hum busts.*

Hum busts? Deem asked.

I'll tell you later, Winn said to Deem.

So I assume you're gonna take this guy down? Sagan asked. *If you do, whoever created him will know. They'll wonder if you're going to take down more. They'll hunt you down. I don't want to be part of that.*

You already are, Winn said. *If we run into trouble, yours is the first name I'm giving up, unless you tell me.*

That's not fair, Sagan whined. *That wasn't the deal.*

Oh, so now you want the original deal? Winn asked. *Fine, a dozen corpses. Give it up, Sagan, or I swear to god I'll find where you're buried and dig you up.*

You really are an asshole, you know that? Sagan said. *If you'd seen this guy's house, you'd know I'm right. You'd be paying me a hundred corpses!*

You went in his house? Winn asked.

Yeah, Sagan said. *Well, his garage. After I tracked him, I watched for a while. He left again, so I went inside. And I'm telling you, you'd best just walk away from this guy. He's seriously fucked up.*

Just tell me his name, Winn said. *Name and address. That was the deal. We're not leaving until you do.*

Sagan waited. *Three dozen,* he said.

Two, Winn said, *and you can contact me if you get in trouble. No promises about what I'll do, if anything.*

Alright, Sagan said. *He lives south of Hurricane on 59.*

Where on 59? Winn asked.

Don't know exactly, I didn't see a number on the house. Ten miles out, before Apple Valley.

What's his name? Winn said.

I don't know, Sagan said.

Goddamnit, Sagan! Winn said. *You're pissing me off!*

I can tell you which house, Sagan said. *You should be able to figure out his name from that. It's red brick and there's a large yellow garage in the back. A couple of pecan trees out front. Off 59 on the left side if you're going south.*

That's right on the tour bus route, Deem said to Winn.

Yeah, makes sense, Winn said.

So now, my corpses please, Sagan said.

I didn't get a name or an address, Winn said, *so no corpses until we find the place.*

There was a red Surburban in the driveway, Sagan said. *Yellow garage in the back, and a horseshoe pit. Two ATV's under a blue tarp next to the garage. And there was this cement lizard thing by the front door. You just drive south on 59, count off ten miles out of Hurricane, and keep looking to the left. You'll see it.*

OK, Deem, Winn said. *Let's see if we can find this place.*

Just don't say I didn't warn you, Sagan said.

■ ■ ■

Deem drove the fifty miles from Mesquite to Hurricane after stopping at 7-11 to get a Big Gulp. Winn smoked while she was inside. He asked her to buy him a bottled water.

The sun was pounding down as they started up the little highway that lifted behind the Hurricane fire station to go over mountains and down into a neighboring valley. Deem checked her odometer.

As Hurricane was falling away in her rear view mirror, her phone rang and she pulled it from her pants pocket.

"Oh, it's Eliza," Deem said, reading the caller ID. "Here," she said, passing the phone to Winn. "Take the call, would you?"

Winn took her phone and pressed a button. "Hello?...Oh, hi, Eliza!"

Deem listened, hearing a buzzing coming from the phone but not able to make out what Eliza was saying over the noise of her truck.

"It's good to hear your voice, too," Winn said, looking at Deem and smiling.

More pausing while Eliza spoke to Winn.

"Uh huh," Winn said. More pausing. "Uh huh."

Deem regretted not turning on the speakerphone before she handed it to Winn.

"What's your address, Deem?" Winn asked. "They're going to FedEx it."

"They found something?" Deem asked.

"Yes," Winn said. "What's your address?"

Deem gave Winn her address and he relayed it to Eliza.

"Thank you," Winn said. "No, we will...yes, I'll make sure she calls you...please thank your friends for us...alright. Bye."

"Well?" Deem asked.

"It'll arrive tomorrow. She said it looked almost exactly the same as your picture."

"What a relief!" Deem said. "At least we can stop the attacks." She looked down at her odometer. "Nine miles," she said. "Keep an eye out."

"He said left side, right?" Winn asked.

"Correct," Deem said. "Red brick house, yellow garage in back."

Although she was doing seventy-five, a car sped around her, passing on the left. She slowed to sixty so they wouldn't miss the house.

They could see Apple Valley ahead in the distance, with Smithsonian Butte rising behind it. Houses were sparse along this stretch of road. She saw her odometer cross the ten mile mark.

"That's it," Winn said, pointing to a house still too far in the distance for Deem to make out.

"You can see that?" Deem said.

"Yup," Winn said. "Yellow garage. Something under a blue tarp right next to it. That's it."

"Do I stop?" Deem asked.

"Nothing in the driveway," Winn said. "Sagan mentioned a red Suburban. Maybe no one's home."

"I don't want to alert this guy in any way," Deem said. "What do we need to figure out who it is?"

"A house number would be nice," Winn said. "Slow up as we pass."

Deem checked her rear view mirror – no one was there. She slowed the car to a crawl.

"13595 are the numbers on the house," Winn said. "That should do it."

"Looks completely ordinary," Deem said. "Who would suspect anything evil would be inside?"

"That's always the story, isn't it?" Winn said. "White picket fence outside, gruesome murders inside."

Deem let her truck roll slowly past the house. "Do you think he's got children's corpses in there?"

"He's got to be getting the corpse poison from somewhere," Winn said. "So, yeah, probably."

The windows to the house that faced the highway were covered on the inside with a drape, the backing of which was a bright white, reflecting the sun. As Deem was wondering what might be behind the drapes, she saw the left edge pull back slightly. Someone was looking out at them.

She pressed the accelerator and the truck sped up. "Shit," Deem said, turning her head back to face the road. "Someone is in the house. I think they saw me."

"You sure?" Winn asked, looking back over his shoulder. "I don't see anything."

"I saw the drape pull back," Deem said, "and I saw a face."

"Damn," Winn said. "So much for subtlety."

"We might as well just walk up to the door, now," Deem said. "Why not?"

"Could you tell who it was?" Winn asked. "Was it him?"

Deem pulled her truck off to the side of the road and then made a turn back onto the highway, going back toward the house.

"No, I couldn't tell," Deem said. "If it's him, we'll confront him. If not, we'll see who it is."

"And if it's him?" Winn asked. "What are you going to do?"

"Awan said the skinrunner can only transform at night," Deem said. "Now might be the perfect time to talk to him and explain he needs to stop."

"I'll be very surprised if that works," Winn said, becoming uncomfortable with Deem's plan.

"So what if it doesn't?" Deem said. "He's already targeting me. I can at least let him know I'm on to him. Might cause him to back off. He seemed wary when he saw me enter the River."

"And if it's not him?" Winn asked.

Deem pulled her truck into the driveway by the house and shut off the engine. "Then we'll play it by ear," she said, opening the truck door and sliding to the ground. Winn sighed and followed her.

She walked to the front door of the house. Winn was watching the draped windows, looking to see if there was any movement. He saw none.

She pressed the doorbell next to the front door, then she knocked.

"Mrs. Jones?" Deem said. "Your ride to the airport is here."

The door slowly opened to three inches. A small woman with long brown hair peered out at them.

"You have the wrong place," the woman said meekly. "This is the Braithwaites."

"Oh, I'm sorry," Deem said, checking her phone. "You didn't call for a lift to the airport?"

"No," the woman said meekly. She began to close the door.

"Says 13959 Highway 59 here," Deem said, scrolling on her phone.

"We're 13595," the woman said, opening the door a little more. "That'd be further down the road."

"Oh, my apologies," Deem said. "Could I ask you a big favor?"

"What is it?" the woman asked.

"I can't get any bars on my phone," Deem said, "and I need to call into the office to check on this. Could I use your phone?"

The woman's eyes darted left and right, trying to decide if she should let them in or not. Finally she stepped back and pulled the door open more. "Alright," she said.

"Thank you," Deem said, stepping inside. Winn followed.

"It's just in there," the woman said, pointing toward a kitchen.

Deem walked in the direction the woman was pointing and located a phone hanging from a wall. She picked up the receiver and dialed a fake number, and began a fake conversation.

While she was giving her performance, she looked around. Everything inside the house looked normal – nothing seemed odd at all. The woman had her arms crossed, with one arm raised to the side of her head. She seemed to be listening to Deem.

Winn looked at the walls in the entryway. They were lined with photographs. One showed the woman with a man and two small children.

"Oh, these must be your kids," Winn said.

"Yes," the woman said, "that's Jody and Jennifer. They're both off to college now."

Winn looked at the man in the picture. He was wearing a three piece suit from the previous decade. He had a slight comb-over and large glasses. He looked anything but frightening.

Deem concluded her fake call and hung up the phone.

"Thank you," Deem said as she approached the woman. "It was nice to meet you, I'm Danielle Smith." She stuck out her hand.

The woman took her hand and shook it. "Geraldine Braithwaite," she said. "My husband is John. Works at a bank in Hurricane."

"Oh, that's nice," Deem said. "I appreciate you letting me use your phone. Cell reception is kind of spotty out here."

"That's why we don't have one," Geraldine said.

"Have you lived here long?" Deem asked.

"Ten years," she answered. "Moved out from Toquerville. John wanted to have more room between us and the neighbors."

"Well, you sure achieved that," Winn said, and smiled at her. Winn's smile lit her up like a light bulb. She tilted her head looking at him, then a broad smile broke out on her face.

"Say, would the two of you like a pop?" Geraldine asked. "I've got cold pop in the fridge."

"Well, we do have to pick up that airport ride," Deem said.

"But, sure, I'd love a pop, if you have one," Winn said. "We're a little early for the pickup, aren't we Deem?"

Deem shot him a look, then turned back to Geraldine. "Sure, we've got a minute."

"Come in," Geraldine said, ushering them into her kitchen. She told them to sit at her kitchen table, and she went to the fridge.

"Fanta orange, grape, Sprite, or root beer," she said. "Which would you like?"

"Root beer," Winn said.

"Sprite for me," Deem answered.

"Alright," Geraldine said. She pulled the cans from the fridge and placed them on the table. "Would either of you like a glass?"

"No," they both answered simultaneously.

Geraldine went back to the fridge and pulled a root beer for herself. She sat across from Winn at the kitchen table.

"I don't get many visitors out here," Geraldine said. "Visiting teachers once a month, but that's about it."

"Lovely home," Deem said.

"Thank you, dear," Geraldine said. "It's a three bedroom house, built in 2002. We've got two acres. John's got a garage out back."

"Oh, I noticed that when we drove past," Winn said. "Bright yellow."

"It was yellow when we moved here," Geraldine said. "John always says he's going to paint it another color, but he's too busy. Between his work at the bank and his hobbies out in the garage he barely has time to breathe."

"Oh, he has hobbies?" Deem asked.

"Yes," Geraldine said. "I do too. I collect these little Christmas villages. When my youngest daughter moved out, I took over her room and unboxed my entire collection. I'll show it to you before you go."

"Wow," Winn said, smiling at her again. "That sounds fascinating. You did all the work?"

Geraldine seemed to melt as Winn talked to her. Deem recognized that he'd turned his charm to full blast.

"I did!" she said. "Took months to get everything just right."

"What kind of hobbies does your husband do?" Winn asked, smiling again.

Deem watched Geraldine's reaction to Winn's question. *God, he knows how to wrap women around his little finger,* Deem thought. Geraldine smiled back at Winn and actually batted her eyes.

"I think he just putters, really," Geraldine said. "To be honest with you, I don't know. He doesn't let me in the garage, he barred me from it years ago. Now it's his 'man cave.' I let it go, since he didn't object when I took over Jody's room for the Christmas villages."

"We should get going," Deem said. "We've got to find this pickup and get them to the airport."

"Of course," Geraldine said.

"Would you mind if I used your restroom before I go?" Winn asked.

"Not at all," Geraldine said. "It's just down the hall, first door on the right."

They all got up from the table and Winn made his way down the hall.

"Thanks again for the use of your phone," Deem said.

"Oh, it's no problem," Geraldine said. "So he's your co-worker?"

"Who?" Deem asked, pulling her phone out of her pocket. "Oh, him? Winn? Yes, he's the backup driver." She immediately regretted using Winn's real name.

"Quite a handsome fellow," Geraldine said.

Deem was looking at her phone, checking messages. "Yes," she said without looking up from the phone. "He is."

"Not such a bad job, riding with him all day," Geraldine said.

"Right," Deem said, wishing Winn would hurry up.

"I thought you said you couldn't get signal?" Geraldine asked.

Deem lowered her phone. "Looks like a text message got through. How, I don't know."

Winn came back from the restroom and thanked Geraldine for her hospitality.

"Stop by anytime," she said, smiling broadly at Winn as he and Deem stepped out the front door. "Come back and see my villages!" she called after them.

Once they were back in Deem's truck, Winn said, "Nice lady."

"Yeah," Deem said. "She sure was into you."

"And high as a kite," Winn said.

"What?" Deem asked.

"She's got an entire pharmacy in that bathroom," Winn said. "Every anti-depressant you can imagine, and sleeping pills up the wazoo. That's why she doesn't know her husband leaves the house at night. She's medicated to the eyebrows."

"You think she's got no idea her husband is a skinrunner?" Deem asked, backing the truck out of the driveway and back onto Highway 59.

"What do you think?" Winn replied.

"You're right," Deem said. "She hasn't got a clue. But honestly, neither do we. We've got no proof this is the guy. For all we know Sagan picked a house at random. Visiting with her didn't really confirm anything. And most housewives around here are self-medicaters. That's not uncommon."

"Well, I can think of three ways to confirm it," Winn said. "We could try going to the bank in Hurricane and confront the guy like you were trying to do here. We could wait until tonight and stake out the place, see if he comes and goes. We'd have to figure out how to make ourselves less obvious – there's little cover around here. Or, we could break into that garage and see whatever it is he doesn't want his wife to see."

"Break into the garage," Deem said.

"Best time to do that would be during the day, while he's at work," Winn said. "Too risky at night. We'll have to make sure Geraldine doesn't see us."

"We'll come back in a couple of hours," Deem said. "I'll hide in the truck and you'll go to her house. Tell her you just got off your shift and you wanted to see her again, that you wanted to see the Christmas villages. She's completely smitten with you, she'll let you in."

"And then what?" Winn said. "Seduce her?"

"Yeah, whatever it is you do," Deem said. "Find a way to medicate her. Slip some of her prescriptions into a drink, something like that. Once she's out, come out and tell me, and we'll search the garage."

"What if her husband comes back from work?"

"It's just after noon. We wait an hour, then you go in. Get her knocked out within an hour. We'd have another hour before it's three. Plenty of time. But we should leave by three, at the latest."

"The idea of staking out the place is starting to sound better," Winn said. "Less risky."

"I want to see what's in that garage," Deem said. "I want to know what we're dealing with, and something tells me that garage would explain a lot."

"Alright," Winn said. "We need to kill an hour before I go in."

"Let's go back to Hurricane. I want to refill my Big Gulp."

"And we'll need to pick up some bolt cutters to get in that garage. He's got it padlocked."

"You could see that from the driveway?" Deem asked. "Man, you must have some kind of super-vision."

"20/15," Winn said. "Plus I thought to check."

■ ■ ■

Deem had been hunkered down inside her truck for a long time, and she was getting antsy. She checked her watch – Winn had been in the house for almost an hour.

It must be working, she thought, *or he would have come back to the truck already.*

Just as her watch reached the one hour mark, Winn emerged from the front door of the house and gave her a thumbs up sign. She grabbed the bolt cutters, got out of her truck, and ran up to meet him.

"Took long enough," Deem said. "She's out?"

"Out," Winn said.

"You were in there a long time," Deem asked. "Tell me you didn't have sex with her."

"No," Winn said. "But I could have. She was sending all the signs. Drank a shitload of root beer."

They walked quickly back to the garage. Traffic on Highway 59 was sparse, but they didn't want to be seen.

Deem snipped the lock and Winn removed it from the door. Then he pushed the door open and they stepped inside, pulling the door closed behind them.

The room they were in housed an old, half rebuilt Ford Mustang, sitting on blocks. All of the car's parts were rusted and unpainted, and several panels were on a bench at the far end of the room. To their left, behind the car, was a set of double doors that looked as though they hadn't been used in a long time.

"Over here," Winn said. At the back of the garage was another door. He tried the handle.

"Locked," Winn said.

"Kick it in," Deem said.

"Really?"

"If you don't, I will. We've already cut off his lock. Come on."

Winn reared back and landed his foot near the door's handle. It burst open, slamming back on its hinges.

Deem walked through the door and searched for a light switch. Once she found it, long fluorescent lights overhead came on and dimly lit the room. It was as wide as the garage, but half the size of the room with the car. There were metal shelves along one wall filled with white banker boxes that all looked the same except for a small number label attached to the side of each box. Stacked in a corner were three large blue Coleman coolers. An old refrigerator stood in the opposite corner. A thin work table lined the remaining wall.

Deem wasn't sure what she had been expecting, but it wasn't this. There were no strange symbols drawn on the walls or projects half-finished on the work table. In fact, there was nothing on the table. The room looked like any organized garage, except for the oddity of the numbered boxes. The floor was clean. Nothing was out of place.

"Is it just me," Winn said, "or is this place creepier than I imagined because it's so clean?"

"Come on," Deem said. She walked to the banker boxes, pulled one from the shelf, and placed it on the table. She lifted the lid.

Inside was a mat of twigs and sagebrush, lining the cardboard. The bottom of the box had a thin layer of red dirt.

"Alright," Deem said. "Now it's starting to get strange."

Deem reached into the box and pulled out the sagebrush and twigs; they came out as a matted clump.

"Is that hair?" Winn asked, examining what Deem held. Deem looked more closely at the handful of dried weeds. There were, indeed, strands of red hair running around and through the twigs and delicate branches of the sagebrush. She looked back in the box and saw something green – it looked plastic. She removed another handful of twigs and dried sage, and found the handle of a brush. She pulled out of the box and showed it to Winn.

"A hairbrush?" Winn asked. There were several strands of red hair flowing from the brush. "Obviously used."

"There's nothing else in here," Deem said, poking through the box. "There's some dirt, and...wait," she said, shaking the box to shift the dirt.

She froze. "I don't really want to touch this," she said, stepping back from the box to allow Winn to look inside.

Winn stepped up to the box and looked in. Resting on the dirt was a piece of jaw, with three teeth attached.

"Looks animal," Winn said. "Put everything back in the box, like you found it."

Deem replaced the hairbrush and then covered it with the twigs and weeds. Then she put the cardboard cover back on the box. She slid the box back onto the metal shelf.

"If that was number five," Deem said, reviewing the small numbers on the boxes, "I wonder what might be in the last one, number nineteen here." She pulled that box from the shelf and placed it on the table, then carefully removed the lid.

A similar mass of sagebrush and twigs matted the top of the box. She pulled the weeds out and placed them on the table. Then she looked at what was under them.

"That's my bracelet!" she said, looking down. "I can't believe it!"

Winn reached into the box and pulled out a small charm bracelet.

"I recognize the charms," Deem said. "One of them is inscribed 'Happy Birthday Kiddo.' My dad gave it to me."

Winn examined the bracelet and found the charm she described.

"Where did you keep this?" Winn asked.

"In the jewelry box on my dresser," Deem said, "in my bedroom."

Deem looked at the intertwined twigs and sagebrush she'd removed. It contained strands of hair, similar to the hair she'd removed before. But these were colored brown.

"Is that *my* hair?" Deem said. "The fucker stole my hair!"

"You didn't notice any missing?" Winn asked.

"No," Deem said. "I didn't. He must have been in my room that first night, before I woke up and saw him."

Deem walked over to the metal shelves and pulled out box number eighteen. It was filled with similar twigs and weeds. "This looks like Virginia's hair," Deem said, inspecting the contents. Under the twigs was a white handkerchief.

"She gave me that on the bus," Winn said.

"I think we have our proof," Deem said, grabbing the handkerchief.

"Here," Winn said, handing her the bracelet. "If your dad gave this to you, I imagine it's pretty important."

"You have no idea," Deem said. She took it from him and looked at it. "My eleventh birthday. He started tutoring me a few months after he gave me this."

Winn walked to the refrigerator. He reached for the handle and pulled. Inside were two plastic tubs. He removed one of them and sat it on the floor. Deem joined him.

"Wait," Deem said, noticing another small label. She bent over and read it. "You may not want to open that," she said.

"Why?" Winn asked. "What's it say?"

"Limbs," Deem replied.

Winn looked at Deem, then he lifted the lid from the tub. They were knocked back by the smell.

"Oh my god," Deem said, turning away. "Those are children's."

"The bone supply for the corpse poison, I imagine," Winn said. He placed the cover back on the tub and returned it to the fridge.

"Wipe your fingerprints," Deem said, handing Winn Virginia's handkerchief. "When we turn this motherfucker in, we don't want trouble."

Winn took the handkerchief and began wiping down the areas he touched.

"Ready to go?" he asked.

"Yes," Deem said. "I'm taking these two boxes." She placed the lids back on the boxes and stacked them. "Would you wipe the light switch?" she asked.

Winn continued wiping as they left, getting the door handle. Then they left the garage and walked to the truck.

"I'm going to go back into the house and wipe a few things," Winn said.

Deem placed the boxes in her truck and waited for Winn, who emerged from the house after a few minutes. She backed out of the driveway and headed back to Hurricane.

"We could call the cops," Deem said.

"I might be wrong," Winn said, "but I think he can still get to you from jail. Awan would know."

"What about her?" Deem asked. "Geraldine?"

"She'll wake up in a few hours and be embarrassed that she passed out while I was there. She might hunt around to see if I stole anything. I gave her a fake name, and so did you. I doubt she'll say anything to her husband, and I doubt her husband is going to say anything about the break in."

"I have a confession," Deem said. "I slipped up and called you Winn in front of her when we were here, earlier."

"She might think it was a nickname," Winn said.

"Either way," Deem said, "there'll be little question as to who it was. He'll know it was me, taking those two boxes."

"He's gonna be pissed," Winn said. "Maybe we should have gone about this a little differently."

"Fuck him," Deem said, still smarting over the violation of seeing her father's gift lying in the skinrunner's box. "Maybe without these objects, he'll have a little less power over us."

"I think we should talk to Awan again," Winn said. "Tell him what we found. Maybe he'd have some ideas."

Deem thought about this for a moment. Although she was pissed, the gravity of the situation was beginning to sink in. She had no idea how the skinrunner might really respond when he discovered that they'd broken into his garage and disturbed his work.

"Call Awan," Deem said.

"And I guess I'll have to tell Sagan about the corpses at Devil's Throat," Winn said. "I'll go see him later."

"Be sure to tell him that Carl Sagan was a renowned astrophysicist," Deem said.

"He won't know what astrophysicist means," Winn scoffed.

Deem pressed the accelerator and began the descent into Hurricane.

They agreed to split the distance and meet Awan at a restaurant in a truck stop off I-15 in North Las Vegas. Awan was already waiting at a table when they arrived.

He looks a little more dressed up than last time, Deem thought. *Maybe he's trying to impress me. Or Winn.*

They related the events of the past day. Awan listened with interest.

"They often make little treasure piles," Awan said. "It's the bird in them. But I've never heard of using banker's boxes. That seems a little anal."

"He's a banker in Hurricane," Deem said. "His day job. Maybe it's just what he knows."

"Does it weaken him," Winn asked, "since we took the boxes for Deem and her aunt?"

"No," Awan said. "It'll just make him more determined. He'll try to get more hair and objects. Once they fix on you, they don't stop."

"Great," Deem said. "So I just pissed him off."

"Probably," Awan said.

"Well, I can stand watch tonight," Deem said. "And my friends found an object like your grandfather's, so that should be here tomorrow. Once we use it, we'll be permanently protected from him?"

"Supposedly," Awan said. "I never saw the thing myself. It was stolen from my grandfather before I was born. But his writings say it's a permanent protection."

"Well, that should solve it, then," Deem said.

"Have you decided if you're going to take down the shaman who created him?" Winn asked Awan.

Awan smiled at Winn. "I don't think I have the resources," he said. "I've taken down rotten belly shaman before, and they're tough. Everything I've heard about this guy, he scared the tribe so bad they exiled him. And he's unique; he's figured out how to manipulate the mutations to spin out these skinrunners quickly. It'd take some research and then a lot of firepower I don't have."

"How does he find candidates?" Deem asked. "Does he recruit them?"

"It's all word of mouth," Awan said. "Becoming a skinrunner means you don't die, at least not in a normal lifespan. So it attracts people who want to live forever, who aren't afraid to lose their souls in the process. There's plenty of people who fit that criteria. Once they've changed, they tell other people. So it kind of sells itself. The shaman charges them a ton of money to transform them."

"He had a tub of body parts in a refrigerator in his garage," Winn said. "If there's a lot of these skinrunners being made, where are they getting all the bodies for corpse poison?"

"No child grave anywhere near here is safe," Awan said, "even ones going back decades. They're only after the bones. And then there are abductions, which happen routinely."

"Horrible," Deem said.

"I wish I could take him on," Awan said, "but right now I'm trying to stop a group of extortionists who use Callers to scare innocent people into paying protection money."

"Maybe we could help you?" Winn said. "Pay you back for you helping us."

"It's dangerous work," Awan said. "Do you have much experience with Callers?"

Deem smiled. "We do," she said.

"So you know how they are," Awan said. "There's this half-gifted guy in my town, and his brother. They figured out how to manipulate some Callers. They started picking normal people in town to target. They'd go to their house and demand protection money. If they didn't get it, Callers would show up that night and scare the shit out of the family. Then the brothers would come around again the next day and tell them the hauntings would continue until they paid up. It's been going on for weeks now. They're preying on poor families who have little in the first place, demanding thousands of dollars, and getting it. Some people approached me about putting a stop to it."

"Sounds interesting," Deem said. "You know the brothers?"

"Oh yeah," Awan said. "Everybody knows them."

"Well," Winn said, "Callers get wrapped up in a lot of things, but the one thing it usually comes down to is blood. They must be paying the Callers somehow."

"That's what I haven't cracked yet," Awan said. "I haven't been able to locate the Callers to find out what the agreement is. I suspect you're right; the brothers are supplying them blood, probably by killing dogs and cats. If I could find the Callers, I could try making them a better deal, but I don't relish the thought of hauling carcasses from the slaughterhouse out to them on an ongoing basis. But I can't find them to make an offer anyway. So I'm taking a different approach, going after the brothers instead."

"How are you going to do that?" Deem asked, intrigued.

"I found something in my father's journals, something that might work if I can get the ingredients I need."

"What is it?" Deem asked.

"Blood souring," Awan said. "Ever heard of it?"

"No," Deem said.

"Once I do it to the brothers," Awan said, "the blood of any animal they touch will be tainted. Most cave spirits will reject an offering that's been soured. The Callers will stop doing business with the brothers if the cave spirits won't accept the corpses they're trading."

"What do you have to do to the brothers?" Winn asked.

"That's the hard part," Awan said. "I use this object my father gave me. It looks like a little thimble. You fill it full of the ingredients, then you place it upside down on the skin, right over a kidney. The stuff inside the thimble is drawn through the skin and into the organ. It permanently infects their blood, makes it go sour. They turn yellow and need dialysis for the rest of their lives. And any animal they touch, a little of the infection passes through the skin to the animal. It doesn't make the animal sick, but it sours their blood just enough that a cave spirit will reject it."

"What if they figure it out and work around it?" Winn asked. "Have someone else handle the animals?"

"Then I'd sour them, too," Awan said. "But I don't think they're that smart. They're both big and stupid, and the brighter of the two, he's the one I called half-gifted, he can barely enter the River. They're both high most of the time. I think if the Callers stop helping them, they'd drop the extortion tactics and return to being the bums they are. Plus they'll have the dialysis to contend with. Fair payback for the grief they've caused and the money they've stolen."

"What help do you need?" Winn asked.

"I'm missing two ingredients," Awan said. "One I haven't been able to locate, and the other will take a trip to get."

"What are they?" Deem asked.

"Alocutis and ghost chalk," Awan said. "Have you heard of them?"

"I know of them," Deem said. "I have a couple of people I could try, see if they have any."

"You won't be able to get the kind of ghost chalk I need from friends," Awan said. "It has to be harvested from a specific kind of ghost north of here. Hence the trip."

"Have you ever made ghost chalk?" Winn asked Deem.

"No, but isn't it just ghost matter that you condense and bake down?" she asked.

"Essentially," Awan said. "It takes a while. There's no problem making the chalk if we can get the matter. The hard part, according to my father, is that it's gotta come from ghosts at the Broken Hills mine."

"Why there?" Winn asked.

"Something about the mix of minerals there," Awan said, "makes it potent enough to work for this purpose. I suspect you could try it with other ghost matter, but I'd rather go with my father's recipe and not experiment. Needs to work the first time, especially since we'll have to capture the brothers and incapacitate them while the souring takes."

"Let me get started on the alocutis," Deem said. "When were you going to go up to Broken Hills?"

"It's a six hour drive one way," Awan said, "so I wasn't planning on going until the weekend. I got a full time job. I was gonna go up Saturday, collect it, stay in Fallon overnight, and come back Sunday."

"Want us to come with you?" Winn asked. "We could help you collect it, and help you administer the mixture to the brothers."

"That'd be a great help," Awan said. "Sure, if you want to come, I'd enjoy the company."

"You up for it, Deem?" Winn asked.

"We'd go up the day after tomorrow?" Deem asked. "Up on Saturday, back on Sunday?"

"Right," Awan said.

"Well, as long as the object from Eliza works tomorrow, I don't see why not," Deem said. "I wouldn't mind putting some distance between myself and that skinrunner, if even for a night."

"Alright, it's a plan," Awan said. "I'll email you directions to my place. Let's plan on leaving around nine a.m. Saturday morning. Can you make it that early?"

"Sure," Winn said.

"Yes, we'll be there," Deem said, looking forward to a change of scenery and an opportunity to leave the skinrunner problem behind.

■ ■ ■

Deem selected another movie on pay-per-view. She'd been up most of the night, determined to stand watch in the house. She considered trying coffee to keep herself awake, but decided against it, opting for chocolate and movies instead.

Earlier, after her mother and aunt had gone to bed, she duct taped a cardboard cover over the fireplace in the living room, using most of the roll to ensure it was a tight seal all the way around.

Deem checked her watch. It was three a.m. She stared at the television, trying to become engaged in the movie, but it wasn't grabbing her. She found her mind drifting to the skinrunner, wondering if he might be prowling outside the house at that moment. *He's going to try something,* she thought. *Thank god that object will be here tomorrow. Staying up late is a bitch.* She pulled up her phone and checked the time for sunrise – five forty a.m. Three more hours to stay awake. She was going to be useless tomorrow.

She awoke with a start. She knew she'd let her eyelids close, just for a moment, completely sure she would be opening them again in a few seconds, but they'd felt so good to leave closed. She checked her watch. Three-ten. *Better move around,* she thought, *or I'm going to fall asleep for good.*

She got up and walked to the bathroom. She sat on the toilet, resting her head on her hands.

She awoke and shook her head. *Damnit!* she thought. *Fell asleep again!* She finished on the toilet and washed her hands, splashing water onto her face. She examined her face in the mirror, thinking of ways she might keep herself awake. *Diet Coke,* she thought. *But there's none in the house - Mom won't allow it. I can't drive off to 7-11.*

She noticed something in the mirror above the sink. She turned to look behind her. The bathroom was small, and the wall behind her was only three feet away. Nothing there. The thing she'd noticed in the mirror had been near the top of the reflection. She looked at the ceiling – nothing. Everything looked normal.

She turned back to the mirror. The reflection showed something behind her. It looked like a tail. From her angle, standing in front of the mirror, she could only see a few inches of it. She wondered if it was a defect in the mirror that she'd never noticed.

Then the tail moved. She jumped.

There's nothing behind me! she thought. *I must be dreaming. I've fallen asleep.*

She lowered her head and looked in the mirror, trying to change the angle of her view so she could see higher in the reflection. The tail belonged to a large lizard, attached to the upper wall and ceiling behind her. It was watching her, hanging a couple of feet over her head.

She freaked. She bolted from the bathroom. Once outside, she turned to face the door, waiting to see if anything emerged. Nothing did.

She ran her hands over her arms and neck, and she felt it – just under her right armpit.

Goddamnit! She thought. *I should have tried coffee.*

She walked upstairs to her bathroom and turned on the lights. She checked in the mirror for any unexpected creatures, and finding none, began examining the blister under her arm. She used a sharp nail file to open it and remove the bone.

Eliza said the package would arrive by ten a.m., she thought. *I'll set the alarm for nine. When it arrives, I'll use it on myself, then I'll use it on Virginia.*

For all the angry scenarios she'd imagined the skinrunner might pull, he'd just infected them again the same way he'd done it the past few nights. He hadn't marched in with a machete screaming bloody murder. He just followed his pattern.

Except for the lizard, Deem thought. *Then again, the lizard might have been in the house last night, while I was asleep. Is the lizard how he plants the bone?*

She walked back downstairs and turned off the TV, then walked back up to her bedroom, set her alarm, and turned out the lights.

Awan was right, she thought as she drifted off. *He won't stop.*

■ ■ ■

Deem awoke to the sound of the doorbell. She checked her alarm clock – it was five to nine, and the alarm hadn't gone off yet. Three loud knocks on the front door.

It's here, she thought, throwing herself out of the bed and grabbing her robe as she ran downstairs.

She opened the front door and saw a FedEx sticker hanging near the handle. The delivery man was walking back to his truck.

"Wait!" she yelled, running out onto the walkway in her bare feet. The cement was already hot and she decided to step onto the grass instead.

The FedEx guy stopped, turned, and seeing her, returned to meet her on the grass. He handed her the package and the electronic signing board. She scribbled her name, thanked the driver, and ran back into the house.

She took the package back to her room, not wanting her mother or aunt to see her unwrap it.

The box was small, and she had it open within minutes. Inside was a thin piece of tin about six inches square. Symbols had been stamped into the corners. It looked exactly like the picture she'd sent to Eliza. She dropped into the River and looked at it again – it transformed into a thin piece of white linen, about the same size. There were two small black beads woven into the material on one side. It glowed a light green.

Awan said to wet it, she thought, *place it over my nose and mouth, and breathe through it.*

She took it into her bathroom and ran water over it, and shook it a little to remove the excess water. Then she walked back into her bedroom, lay down on the bed, and placed the linen over her face. She drew in a breath.

Hmm, she thought. *I don't feel anything. Maybe I'm not supposed to.*

She let the linen sit on her face for a while, breathing through the moist cloth. After several minutes, she dropped out of the River, and the cloth reverted to the square tin, sitting on top of her face. It began to slide off, so she grabbed it.

Let's try Virginia, she thought. She put on clothes and walked downstairs to the guest room. She knocked lightly on Virginia's door, then opened it.

Virginia was sitting up in bed, reading. She turned to Deem.

"Oh dear," she said. "I feel awful again today."

"Stick out your tongue," Deem said. Virginia complied and stuck it out – it was black.

"I think you've been bit again," Deem said. "Can I check your arms and your neck?"

"Certainly dear," Virginia said, putting her book down. "Margie should get the house sprayed. This is really quite annoying."

Deem checked her aunt's arms and found nothing. When she rolled to one side so Deem could check the back of her neck, she found the blister in the same place as the day before, right under the hairline. It was an angry red and the size of a half dollar.

"Roll back," Deem instructed. "I have a remedy I want you to try," Deem said. "It's a folk cure, but I think it'll help." She showed Virginia the tin.

"How does it work?" Virginia asked.

"I'll hold this over your face," Deem said, "and you breathe through it for a few minutes. That's all."

"Alright," Virginia said. "Seems strange, but sometimes the old cures are better than the new ones."

Deem placed the tin squarely against Virginia's nose and then dropped into the River. She saw the wet linen drop around Virginia's nose and mouth, and saw her aunt begin to breathe through the cloth. Deem held the tin in place for a couple of minutes. When she felt it had been enough, she dropped out of the flow and removed the tin from Virginia's nose.

"Let's check that blister again," Deem said. Virginia rolled over.

"Did I ever tell you about the time your Uncle Wayne tried to drink Mormon tea?" Virginia said as Deem examined her. The blister was gone.

"No, I don't recall," Deem said. "You can roll back, it's gone. Stick out your tongue again, would you?"

Virginia rolled back into position and stuck out her tongue. It was normal.

Worked! Deem thought. *Thank you, Eliza!*

"He'd picked the wrong bush in the desert," Virginia said, "and it nearly killed him. They pumped his stomach at the hospital. Mormon tea is supposed to settle your stomach. I don't know why he couldn't just use a Tums."

"Uncle Wayne was always trying new things," Deem said. "One of the reasons I like him so much."

Virginia turned wistful for a moment. "Yeah, he kept me on my toes," she said. "He thought the world of you, you know."

Deem smiled.

"And so do I," Virginia said, pushing the covers aside to get out of bed. "I feel so much better, I think I'll make breakfast for everyone. What do you say?"

"I think that's a great idea," Deem said.

"Any requests?" Virginia asked.

"Pancakes," Deem answered.

"Pancakes it is," Virginia said, grabbing her robe and heading to the bathroom.

Deem walked back upstairs and hid the tin in her dresser drawer. *My first object,* she thought. *I should find somewhere safe to store it. Nothing in this room is safe from my mother.*

She fell back on the bed and let her eyes close. It was a relief to be free of the skinrunner. After a few minutes, she heard Virginia calling from the kitchen. She rose up out of bed and walked downstairs.

"Will you get your mother up?" Virginia said as she rounded the corner into the kitchen. "These pancakes are ready!"

"Sure," Deem said, turning and walking back out of the kitchen. She walked past the guest room on the ground floor and to the closed door of the master bedroom. She knocked.

"Mom?" she said. "You awake? Aunt Virginia's made breakfast."

"Come in," she heard through the door. Deem opened the door and walked into her mother's bedroom. She could tell instantly that something was wrong.

"I don't want any breakfast," her mother said from the bed. Deem walked to her. She looked weak – a lot like Virginia had looked.

Oh no, Deem thought. *The skinwalker hit her, too.*

"Stick out your tongue, mom," Deem said. Her mother stuck out her tongue, and as Deem expected, it was black.

"You've been bitten by the same bug," Deem said. "You've probably got a blister on your arms or neck."

Margie turned her arms over and the blister was obvious, right in the crease of her left elbow. Margie poked at it with her right hand. "There's something hard inside," she said, looking up at Deem.

"We'll fix you right up," Deem said. "I've got the cure. I'll be right back. Don't move."

Deem left her mother and ran back upstairs to her room. She dug in her dresser drawer until she found the tin, took it to her bathroom for a quick re-wetting, and ran back downstairs.

"This may seem odd," Deem said as she walked into her mother's bedroom, "but it worked for me, and it worked for Aunt Virginia. She was in bed like you this morning with a bite on her neck, but after this she bounced out of bed and made breakfast. So it works."

Margie looked at the tin skeptically. "This isn't one of your...things, is it?"

"No," Deem said, knowing her mother would reject it if she thought it had anything to do with the River. "It's just an old folk remedy. Like Echinacea. You like Echinacea, right?"

"Yes," Margie said. "Oh, alright."

"I'm just gonna place this over your face for a minute," Deem said. "All you need to do is breathe, OK?"

"Alright," Margie said.

Deep dropped into the River. She saw the tin transform into the linen and fall around Margie's face. She saw the cloth suck slightly into Margie's mouth and nose as she breathed. Deem held the tin in place for a few minutes. *If she knew I was in the River, she'd be pissed,* Deem thought. *Normally I wouldn't around her, but this is for her own good.* After a while she dropped out of the flow and removed the tin.

"Let's check that bite," Deem said.

Margie raised her left arm. The blister was still there.

"Hmm," Deem said, puzzled. "Let's try it again."

Margie closed her eyes and Deem placed the tin over her nose once again, repeating the process. As the linen fell into place Deem studied it closely. The two tiny black beads that were woven into the fabric were gone.

Doses, Deem thought. *Each bead was a dose. I used it up on myself and Virginia.*

"Hold on just a moment, mom," Deem said. "I'll be back."

She left the master bedroom. As she turned to go upstairs, Virginia called to her. "These pancakes are getting cold!"

"We'll be right there," Deem called back.

Deem ran up the stairs and into her bedroom, searching for her phone. She located the email she'd received from Awan and opened the picture of his grandfather's object. It was a square piece of tin with markings. She zoomed in on the markings. There were a total of five, one in each corner and one along an edge. Three of the edges did not have markings. *Five doses on Awan's,* Deem thought.

She looked at the tin in her hands. The two markings in the corners were gone. She dropped back into the River and examined the linen again – no beads.

Damn, she thought.

She walked to her bathroom, grabbed her nail file, and wiped it with a cotton ball she'd soaked in rubbing alcohol. Then she ran back downstairs to her mother's room.

"We're going to remove the hard part," Deem said, "just like we did with Virginia. Then you'll feel better."

"What about the tin?" Margie asked.

"I think it only had two doses," Deem said, "and I used them up on myself and Aunt Virginia. Sorry."

Margie held her arm out for Deem to access. Deem poked into the blister and dug out the small white bone fragment, grey smoke rising from the incision.

"Did it hurt?" Deem asked, looking at the bone fragment she was holding in her fingers.

"Not at all," Margie said, smiling at Deem. "And I do feel better."

"Deem!" Virginia called from the other room.

"She's made pancakes," Deem said to Margie. "We'd better get in there."

"Tell her I'll be right in," Margie said.

7

"So we're not out of the woods," Winn said, backing away from the 7-11 where Deem had just purchased a Big Gulp.

"Nope," Deem said. "Virginia and I are safe, but I'll have to keep cutting bones out of my mother. I've got no way to cure her."

Winn drove out of Mesquite and onto I-15. They were headed back to Ivins. Deem had decided she wanted to talk more with Claude.

"I guess this means there's a box number 20 back in that garage," Winn said. "He must have stolen something of your mother's."

"I saw him in the house last night," Deem said. "He was a lizard, about four feet long. At least I think it was him. It was three a.m. and I was getting loopy from staying awake."

"You saw a lizard?" Winn asked. "In the house?"

"Hanging above me in a bathroom," Deem said.

"Ooo," Winn said, shivering. "That'd freak me out."

"I'm surprised I didn't scream," Deem said. "I didn't want to wake the house."

"So what now?" Winn asked. "You can't keep cutting the bones out of your mom forever."

"I know," Deem said. "When we go with Awan tomorrow, we need to talk with him about how to take down the skinrunner. He said it was hard, but I don't see what other choice I have."

"Are you OK with leaving your mom for a night?" Winn asked.

"Yeah," Deem said. "I'll talk to Virginia. She's got lots of energy now, and she can tend mom the way mom was tending her. I'll tell Virginia how to remove the bone. I think she'll be OK."

"It only had two doses, huh?" Winn asked.

"That's what I'm guessing," Deem said. "I didn't realize what the markings or the beads were at first, and I didn't think to check them between the time I used it and Virginia used it. Awan had never seen it, so I doubt he knew it was dose-based, either. We should remind him to amend his grandfather's journal."

They sat silently in Winn's Jeep as he wound through the Virgin River Gorge, twisting and turning, passing slow moving trucks. Winn knew Deem's reference to Awan's journals probably got her thinking about her own father's journals, which was the reason for their follow-up visit to Claude.

"What do you want from Claude?" Winn asked.

"More info on the secret council," Deem said. "If they have my father's journals, I want to figure out how to get them. It'd be helpful to know more about them. I can't just break into Dayton's house and start rummaging around."

"You could," Winn said.

"Bad idea," Deem replied.

"I thought it was interesting that Claude is obviously an apostate from the church," Winn said, "but he still calls people by their Mormon titles, like 'President' and 'Brother.' Wonder why?"

"It's ingrained," Deem said. "You get used to it when you're growing up and it stays with you. It seems like I still run everything through the Mormon filter I was raised with."

"Ah, that's why you don't drink coffee," Winn said, "even through you're an apostate yourself."

"You know," Deem replied, "you might be right. I was raised to hate it. What do you expect? No big surprise I don't like it."

"It was all that was available for breakfast in my home," Winn said. "My mom made a pot every morning, but that's all she made. She wasn't a breakfast person."

"She never made you breakfast?" Deem asked.

"Not once that I remember," Winn said. "If she didn't like it, she didn't do it."

"But she'd have cereal for you, so you could eat, right?" Deem asked.

"Nope," Winn said. "As far as she was concerned, I could drink coffee for breakfast, like her. I learned to like it, and I learned to skip breakfast, too."

"I'm sorry," Deem said. "I wonder whose upbringing was more screwed up, yours or mine?"

"Mine," Winn said. "I promise you."

After a few more miles, Winn pulled up in front of Claude's house and they both walked up to the door. Deem knocked, and a dog started barking in the distance. Within seconds they heard it slam against the other side of the door.

"That dog is something else," Deem said.

"I don't blame him for keeping it," Winn said. "I imagine he's got a few enemies."

The door opened and Claude smiled at them, pulling at the dog's collar.

"Come in!" he said cheerily. "I'll just put Kimo in the back. Please seat yourselves."

"You could leave him out to visit, if you want," Deem offered, trying to be accommodating.

"Oh no, my dear," Claude said, wrestling the dog into the back. "You'd lose a hand."

Claude disappeared with the dog and returned empty handed after a few minutes. Deem and Winn were sitting in his living room, the stacks of papers and magazines rising higher than their heads.

"So, you're back!" Claude said. He seemed genuinely happy to see them again.

"I am!" Deem said, smiling. "I was thinking about what you had said, like you said I would, and I felt I needed to talk to you again."

"You want to know more about the secret council," Claude said. "So you can get your father's journals back. Right?"

"It's that obvious?" Deem asked.

"It's what I'd do," Claude said. "Then again, I was never very risk averse. Not always wise."

"I have no idea how to go about it," Deem said. "But I want to try."

"I love when someone puts their money where their mouth is," Claude said. "Of course I'll help you. I'll tell you what I know."

"Do you know who is on the secret council?" Deem said.

"No," Claude replied, "that's one of their big secrets. They take an oath to never reveal that. But I do have some educated guesses. I thought your father was on it, and now I'm sure of that. It's a good bet Brother Dayton is on it. Don't know about the new Stake President, though."

"Do you know how many are on it?" Deem asked.

"Well, it can't be many," Claude said. "Remember, it's only gift-eds who are in high-level positions in the church. The local council probably encompasses everyone in southern Utah and Nevada, probably northern Arizona, too, and I'd be surprised if there's more than a half dozen men on it. There's another council up north, in Salt Lake. I know there's at least one General Authority on that one."

"Is the Salt Lake council in charge?" Deem asked, "of all the local councils?"

"No," Claude said. "It's not like the church, with Salt Lake always running things. The local councils don't take orders from anywhere else."

"Why are they organized like this?" Winn asked. "What do they do?"

"I think some of it is camaraderie and being part of a club," Claude said. "People like to be together with others who are like themselves. That's why you two work together, is it not?"

Deem nodded.

"I think some of them probably get off on the power of it, the secrecy," Claude continued. "But as for what they do exactly, what they accomplish as a group, I don't know. More secrets. There are rumors."

"Such as?" Winn asked.

"I've heard some say they control the Danites," Claude said.

"Danites?" Deem asked. "What is that?"

"A secret group that does the dirty work of the church," Winn said. "You haven't heard about them?"

"No, and it sounds like bullshit," Deem said. "Sorry for swearing."

"Oh, we've crossed another line, have we?" Claude chuckled. "Danites were very active in the late nineteenth century, when the church was still threatened by the United States government. The modern day Danites are the lobbying companies the church employs – far more effective than the Danites of old, and a lot less bloody. But I think it's just a rumor – I don't think the secret councils are involved with them. The Danites always took orders straight from the church in Salt Lake. The secret councils operate independently. There might be some crossover, but if there is, I think it's small."

"Then what?" Winn said.

"Like I said, rumors," Claude said. "Some think they were behind the Mountain Meadows Massacre. Some think they secretly fight against the fundamentalist polygamists. I once heard that they keep alive the folk magic traditions of Joseph Smith. Who knows? It might all be bullpucky. They might be up to something else altogether."

"If they have my father's journals," Deem said, "then they must have other people's journals, too. They must keep them somewhere."

"That they do," Claude said. "And your next question is, 'where'? Right?"

"Well?" Deem asked.

"No idea," Claude said. "That's another of their most tightly guarded secrets."

"If they're a council," Deem said, "then they must meet. Sometime."

"Yes," Claude said. "They do, occasionally."

"We could follow one of them," Deem said. "Dayton. See where he goes."

"If you could pull it off," Claude said, "that would give you the 'where,' but you'd have to monitor him continually to know the 'when.' That's going to get tiring."

"It's a start, at least," Deem said. "If we can find their meeting place, that might be where the journals are kept."

"You'll need to be smart about this," Claude said. "They're high-up in the church, which means they're shrewd. And they're gifted, which means they can employ some intimidating defenses against people like you. You need to be careful."

"I'm not afraid of them," Deem said. "Besides, what's the worst they could do, if they found me out?"

"Well," Claude said, "Danites used to cut their victim's throats from ear to ear."

"Brother Dayton wouldn't do that," Deem said. "I've known him since I was a little kid."

"What you don't know," Claude said, "is what oaths he's taken to protect their council. He'll treat those oaths seriously. You need to tread lightly."

"Any ideas on the 'when'?" Deem asked.

"It'll be something routine," Claude said, "so they don't have to communicate with each other about it between meetings. But what that routine is, I have no idea."

Deem thought about this. She remembered seeing something recently that fit in with what Claude was saying, but she couldn't remember what. Then, it came to her: she'd seen an old day planner when she was going through boxes two days ago.

"My father's schedule book," Deem said. "I saw it. It might have something."

"Maybe," Claude said. "It won't be obvious."

"I'll hunt through it," Deem said. "Anything else you can tell me about the secret council?"

"Just that I think you need to be a lot more cautious than I currently sense you to be," Claude said. "I get the feeling you think you can barrel into this and be successful. One of the council's goals will most certainly be to protect itself, and you're threatening that."

"If my father's journals are there," Deem said, "I'm going to get them. You can be sure of that."

"I admire your determination," Claude said. "But listen to me. I've been at this for a long time. I've seen some horrific things from people who claim to be upright Christians. The people who kick against the pricks are targeted. I've seen them get their throats slit, left as a warning for others – or they disappear, buried somewhere out in the desert never to be found. And if you're too high profile to just kill outright, they get to you in other ways. Destroy your job, your reputation, your family. Things that are important to you. I know you said Brother Dayton would never do anything like this, but I'm telling you he would. They're ruthless and effective, and you'll never be able to prove they did it. And if you try, you'll be considered crazy. Do you understand where I'm coming from?"

"Yes," Deem said. "I do."

"I want to show you something," Claude said. "Wait here."

Claude rose from his chair and walked into another room. He returned with a manila folder, which he handed to Deem. She opened it, then quickly closed it.

"Look at it," Claude said.

"I saw it," Deem said, handing the folder back.

"No, you didn't," Claude said. "There's some details I want you to notice."

"It's disgusting," Deem said. "If you're trying to gross me out to scare me, consider me grossed out."

"Deem," Claude said softly, "it's a picture of my father."

Deem dropped her head, embarrassed. "I'm, sorry," she said. She reopened the folder.

It contained a single 8x10 black and white photo. It was a picture of a barbed wire fence in a pasture. A man had been tied to the fence with wire at his feet, waist, and neck, his hands bound behind his body. His throat had been cut, and the blood had run down his chest, making the shirt he wore dark. The body had been left for some time before the picture was taken, and birds had removed the eyes.

"Found April 6, 1957, about a mile outside of Silver Reef," Claude said. "Back then, Silver Reef truly was a ghost town. No new houses, like now. Just old, abandoned buildings from the mining days. So they didn't discover the body for a while after he'd been murdered."

"I'm sorry," Deem said again. "How old were you?"

"Twelve," Claude said. "Do you want to know why this happened to him?"

"Why?" Deem asked.

"Because he told me he was on a secret council," Claude said, "and I told my friend Gale Stucki. My father had sworn me to secrecy, but I just couldn't keep it to myself. Gale told others, word got around, and this is what they did to him, as payback for violating his oath."

"So he really was on a secret council, like my father?" Deem asked.

"I believe so," Claude said. "And I believe his gift was inherited by my brother, Duane, who is now dead. The moment my father's death was discovered, the church stepped in and helped my mother keep things going. At the time I was so grateful for that. Later I learned how things really worked, and I realized that many of those same people who were offering help were the ones who had killed him. I guess that's why I do what I do. All of this," he said, waving his arms around him.

"Did you ever find his killers?" Deem asked. "Bring them to justice?"

"No," Claude said. "Which is why I'm telling you this. I would love to see these secret councils brought down. Nothing would give me greater pleasure. But I've shown you this," he nodded to the folder Deem was holding, now closed, "because you need to know what you're dealing with. I've been fighting the good fight for fifty years now, but I've never located anything that would implicate anyone in my father's death, and that's because they're careful and ruthless. You'll have to be more careful and ruthless if you want to interact with them and stay alive."

"Have you talked about the councils on your radio program?" Deem asked.

"Never," Claude said. "I talk about all kinds of other things, but I've never brought up the councils. Hits too close to home."

"I understand why you have the dog," Deem said. "You must have lived in fear for your life, doing what you're doing."

"I used to," Claude said. "I got alarm systems, cameras, you name it. Kimo, of course. And a ton of guns. But once they succeeded in marginalizing me, making me look crazy, I think they decided I was better off alive. They use me as an example. 'If you think the way Crazy Claude thinks, you're crazy too.' Works well for them. I can say most anything I want to say, and they just write it off."

"Well, we believe you," Winn said. "My mom used to listen to you. She had tapes."

"Oh yes, tapes!" Claude said. "People used to record my show and give tapes to their friends. I think more people have heard me on tape than have ever heard me on shortwave."

"I have a friend," Winn said, "who could help you get your program on the internet, if you're having trouble with that. You'd have a podcast going in no time."

"Really?" Claude asked. "Well, that's nice of you to offer. Would he do it for free? I don't have any money for that kind of thing."

"Maybe," Winn said. "I'll talk to him. I think once he finds out what your show is about, he'll want to do it."

"Send him here," Claude said, "and make sure he mentions you, so I don't shoot him on the doorstep." He smiled.

"Thanks for your time," Deem said, handing the folder back to Claude. "And for being so open."

"Do you promise me you'll be careful?" he asked Deem, taking the folder.

"I do," she said. "Your point has hit home."

"Good," Claude said. "I don't want to have a picture like this of you in my files."

■ ■ ■

Winn stopped at a 7-11 on Bluff Street in St. George so Deem could get another Big Gulp, then he drove her back to Mesquite, dropping her off at her house. Deem said she'd be at Winn's place by seven a.m. the next morning for their drive to Indian Springs to meet Awan.

Deem walked inside the house and sat down on the large white couch in the living room, sipping her Big Gulp. Claude had shared a lot with her, and she felt the need to sort it all out. *I've got to find that day planner,* she thought, looking around the room absently. *I know I saw it.*

She saw a piece of duct tape that was still sticking to the fireplace bricks from the makeshift cover she removed earlier that morning. She rose from the couch and removed the tape. She looked up, and saw the family picture that had hung over the fireplace for the past several years. Her father and mother were in the back of the picture, with her brothers in front of them, and Deem sitting alone in front of the brothers. She was fifteen in the picture, and had braces. *This was the last family portrait before Dad died,* she thought. *He looks so tall and handsome. And he always had a wise face, like he knew how to solve any problem. That's why so many people trusted him. That's why he became Stake President.*

She looked closely at her father in the picture, his torso rising behind his sons, his right arm wrapped around Deem's mother.

And you had secrets, too, didn't you, Dad? Secrets you couldn't tell me. You trained me. None of my brothers inherited your gift, just me. Did you want to tell me about the council, but couldn't because I was a girl? Was I not old enough to know? Did you know about Claude's father? Does the council keep a history?

She studied the lines in his face, his hair, his eyes. He'd always seemed so open to her, ready to share anything she asked. *Why keep this from me?* she wondered. *You always answered every question I had. You never held back. Why this? Why did you hide this side of you from me? Did you take an oath? Did you have a hand in killing people to keep your council secret?* Her father's face stared back at her, silent. Silent as the grave.

She turned from the photo, wiping a tear from her cheek, fearing the answers that were dawning to her questions. *I'm going to find that goddamn day planner.*

■ ■ ■

Deem spread out the materials she'd found, covering her bed. She locked the door to her room so her mother wouldn't barge in unannounced and discover what she was doing. She sat cross-legged on the bed, surrounded by papers and books.

She found three day planners along with a variety of other documents that intrigued her. Before, when she'd been hunting through boxes for her father's journals, she'd just been looking for bound books, the kind that looked like the blank journals you could buy at the store and start writing in. This time she'd been more meticulous, going through her father's papers and pulling out anything of interest. Most of what she'd collected didn't relate to what she was really looking for, but she wanted to go through it anyway, because it caught her eye. Most of it just helped her understand her father better. And some of it did no more than help her remember him, and that was a sufficient reason to pull it.

She opened the first day planner, for 2009. She scanned through it, looking for repeating patterns. There was nothing that stood out. Most of the appointments in the planner were for evening and weekend meetings, and most were typical Stake President tasks, like setting apart missionaries and high council meetings.

She moved to the 2010 and 2011 planners, flipping through the pages. She stopped when she reached July of 2011, when the appointments in the pages began to thin out abruptly, and their nature changed from church meetings to doctor and hospital appointments. By October the planner was virtually empty. There was nothing after Halloween. Her father had died on November 29th.

She turned the page and stared at December, two pages completely blank. She looked at Christmas, sitting on the page with no hint of how awful it had been. *The worst Christmas of my life,* she thought. She ran her finger over the day in the planner, wanting to rip it out. She noticed a small dot under the date, as though her father had lightly touched a ball point pen in that spot. It was a Sunday, the last Sunday in December.

She turned a page back. The last Sunday in November had a similar dot under the number. It was tiny, just a speck. If you weren't looking for it, you might think it was an error in the printing.

She turned back to October. The last Sunday had a dot under it. She lifted the planner and held the page up to the light. Was it made by a pen? She turned back another page, to September. There was an indent on the back side of October. *It was made by a pen,* she thought.

She flipped back to January. Last Sunday of the month, a dot under the number.

She picked up the 2010 planner and opened it to July. Same marking. She flipped through the rest of the months. For each final Sunday of each month, the same mark appeared.

She tried the 2009 planner. The marks were consistent.

This doesn't prove the secret council met on the last Sunday of each month, she thought, *but he did mark these dates. And there's nothing on the schedule for those evenings, like there are on other Sundays. And he marked all of 2011, probably at the first of the year when he got the day planner, since he knew in advance those would be the meeting dates, even though it wound up that he couldn't attend the final ones that year. This must be it.*

She checked her phone, pulled up a calendar for the current month. The last Sunday of this month would be the day after tomorrow, the day they were to return from Broken Hills with Awan.

She checked the 2011 planner in January. Her father's appointments on the last Sunday of that month ran until six p.m. She checked other days, and found the same thing – no appointments after six.

We'll be back from Broken Hills long before six, she thought. *And we'll track Dayton and find out where he goes.*

Deem drove to Winn's at six a.m. the next morning and left her truck at his trailer in Moapa. Winn drove them both in his Jeep to Indian Springs.

"We've got to make a quick stop in North Vegas to meet Erin," Deem told Winn as they started off. "Her mom had some alocutis and she's driving it up from Kingman to meet us this morning."

"Oh, I'd love to see Erin again," Winn said, smiling.

"Leave her alone," Deem said.

"It's not me," Winn said. "She's got a thing for me."

"Don't encourage her," Deem said. "She's naïve and doesn't know what bad news you are."

"'Bad news' is not how most people describe an interaction with me," Winn said. "They usually come away happy and satisfied."

"Ugh. Don't flirt with her, I mean it."

"We'll see. It'll have to be a quick stop if we're going to make Indian Springs on time."

"She knows it'll be quick. I told her we're on a timetable."

"How did looking for your father's day planners go?"

Deem related what she'd found to Winn. "I can't be one hundred percent sure the mark he made on those dates means a secret council meeting, but it's worth a shot."

"So we'll need to be back in Mesquite by four or five, at the latest?" Winn asked.

"Yes," Deem answered. "If we miss this opportunity, we'll have to wait a month to track him again."

"If you're right about the dates."

"If we watch him and he doesn't leave the house then I'll know to start over."

"We should be able to make that fine, provided we get the work done today. We'll want to leave Fallon early tomorrow to be safe."

"Have you ever collected ghost matter before?" Deem asked.

"No, but I watched my mother do it," Winn replied. "It's an unpleasant process, as I recall."

"I've never done it. This'll be educational for me."

They met Erin at a truck stop by the Speedway in North Vegas. Seeing Erin's car in the parking lot, Deem hopped out of Winn's Jeep and ran to give Erin a hug, then produced a small box wrapped in shiny green paper.

"Oh, my favorite color," Erin said. She was about Deem's height and slightly heavier, with black hair and a tattoo on the side of her neck.

"Happy birthday!" Deem said. "Another time I'll tell you what I went through to get it."

"Here's this," Erin said, exchanging the alocutis for the wrapped box.

"Thanks," Deem said. "I'm on my way to Indian Springs to give it to a guy there. Well, don't wait, unwrap it before I have to leave!"

Winn walked up to the two as Erin was unwrapping the box. Erin saw him coming and smiled. "Oh, hi, Winn!" she said.

"Hello, beautiful," Winn said, giving her a kiss on her cheek. "I understand it's your birthday."

"Yes," Erin said, a little embarrassed. "Deem has given me this!" She held up the box for Winn to see, then finished unwrapping it and looked inside.

"It's a powder," Erin said, a little underwhelmed. She looked up at Deem.

"Iridium," Deem said.

Erin mouth dropped. She formed her mouth into a large oval.

"From Tillburton," Deem added.

Erin's eyes widened and she let out a scream of delight.

"No!" Erin said. "How did you...?"

"Another time," Deem said. "I'll come down when the mess I'm in is over. And that's a birthday present to you, personally, not an exchange with your mom for the alocutis. I'll repay her for that separately."

"She'll be shocked you got me this," Erin said, staring down into the small box. "I can't believe it either."

Deem smiled, glad that her present was appreciated. *I guess it was worth what I went through to get it,* she thought.

"We've got to run," Deem said. "Say hi to your mom for me."

"I will," Erin said, still staring down into the box.

Deem leaned forward to give Erin a goodbye hug and walked back to the Jeep. Winn opened his arms to give her a hug too.

"Happy birthday again," he said as he wrapped her up in his arms. When he let her go she was a little flushed.

"Thank you," Erin said, smiling broadly.

Winn returned to the Jeep and they took off for Indian Springs.

"Well, that seemed to go over well," Winn said.

"You didn't grope her during that hug, did you?" Deem asked.

"So suspicious! You've really got to trust me more."

"I would if I didn't know you better."

■ ■ ■

An hour later they reached Indian Springs, a small town dwarfed by the air force base it sat next to. Awan's modest house was at the edge of town. As Awan saw them pull in, he came out of his house with a large backpack, threw it into the back of Winn's Jeep, and jumped into the back seat.

"You know the way?" Awan asked Winn.

"Straight up 95?" Winn asked back.

"Yes," Awan answered, "about two hundred and fifty miles. Then we turn off and go another fifty."

"So if we're lucky," Deem said, "We'll make it by two."

"Plenty of time," Awan said.

"You've been there before?" Winn asked. "Inside Broken Hills?"

"Once, many years ago as a kid," Awan said. "We should be able to get in and out within an hour once we're there."

"Broken Hills isn't downwind," Deem said. "Right?"

"Correct," Awan said. "No zombighosts, just the regular old fashioned kind."

"Refreshing," Winn said. "Haven't been around normal ghosts in a while."

"It's a different experience when you don't have to worry about your skin being ripped off," Awan said.

"We've got a couple of things we need to discuss with you," Deem said. "First, we need to head back as early as possible tomorrow. Some things that I need to get done tomorrow back home."

"We can leave as early as you want," Awan said.

"Second, how much do you know about how to kill a skinrunner?"

Awan furrowed his brow. "It's come to that?" he asked.

"Turns out the object Eliza sent us only worked twice," Deem said. "I used it on myself and my aunt. We're both fine, but now my mother has become infected, and the object is finished. So unless I want to spend the rest of my life cutting bone fragments out of her arm, we've got to find a way to shut him down completely."

"That'll be tricky," Awan said. "And dangerous. But there is a way."

"How?" Winn asked.

"Well," Awan began, "with a regular skinwalker, there were two traditional ways. If a victim could find out the skinwalker's identity, he only needed to speak the full name of the skinwalker to kill him, or to cause him to leave you alone. If you weren't a victim, they say you can kill one with a bullet dipped in white ash.

"But with the mutations this shaman is creating, things are different. You've already seen how fast he can run and fly while remaining a man. The way you kill him is different, too. Just saying his name isn't good enough. You have to get the loved one he killed to say his name. It's more powerful, and it seems to work."

"The loved one he killed to become a skinrunner in the first place?" Winn asked.

"Yes," Awan said.

"How the fuck are we going to do that?" Deem asked.

"You'll have to do some research and get a name," Awan said. "It's no good without the name of the person they killed."

"If we get a name," Deem said, "then what?"

"If you can find something that belonged to the killer or the victim, and you have the name, my sister can help locate them," Awan offered.

"I've got something he's touched," Deem said, thinking of the bankers boxes she'd taken from the skinrunner's garage.

"But even if we know who he killed, there's a bigger problem," Winn said. "They're dead. They can't speak. Not with a real voice."

"That's why I said it was tricky," Awan replied. "There's only two things I know of that can make a ghost corporeal. The first is whatever this mutation is that turns them into zombighosts. You won't be able to deal with the result of that, they're too irrational when they turn – they just want to attack. So that approach is out. The second way is something very rare. Have you ever heard of the Rivers of Statera?"

Winn looked at Deem. They both shrugged. "No," Winn said.

"There's a couple of places in the River," Awan said, "where these waters run. They're sometimes called blood rivers. They only exist in the River, you can't see them any other way."

"What are they?" Deem asked.

"No one knows for sure," Awan said. "There are gifteds who have tried to figure them out. Some people think they're a symbolic representation of the blood shed of innocent people, but no one's been able to prove that."

"How would this make a ghost corporeal?" Winn asked.

"When the waters wash over a ghost who was killed unjustly," Winn said, "the story of their demise becomes known. Some people think this gives them the knowledge they need to right the wrongs committed against them. It allows them to break their patterns, finish things up and move on."

"How does that help us?" Winn asked.

"There's only a couple of known blood rivers in North America. One of them happens to be here, downwind. As usual, it behaves a little differently than the others, due to the radiation. If the ghost drinks from the waters of the blood river here, they become corporeal, for a period of time. Presumably to seek vengeance upon those who wronged them. When they're in that state, they can speak. This worked for a friend of mine in Ely. Or so he said."

"So you've never seen it yourself?" Winn asked.

"No," Awan said. "Never really needed to before now."

"And that'll kill the skinrunner? When it speaks its name?" Deem asked.

"Slowly," Awan said. "First the skinrunner will lose its powers. Then it begins to decompose while still alive. Takes a couple of days to complete. But yes, it kills them."

"I'm in," Deem said.

"Me too," Winn said.

"Get the name and the things he touched," Awan said, "and then let me know. I'll hook you up with my sister. She lives in Littlefield. She'll be able to figure out where the victim is now, so you can communicate with him. Or her. You'll have to convince them to go with you to the blood river."

"We know the name of the skinrunner," Winn said, "so we should be able to dig up information about his friends and relatives. It's bound to be one of them, we just have to find out who."

"Look for anyone who went missing or died of any cause," Awan said.

"Where is the blood river?" Deem asked.

"He said it was in a cave somewhere between Panaca and Enterprise," Awan said. "He'd have to give us the exact location. I'll get it from him."

"The middle of nowhere," Deem said.

"Anything to worry about in the cave?" Winn asked. "Since it's downwind?"

"Don't know," Awan said. "Never been there. My friend might know."

Deem sat back in the front passenger seat and thought about the information Awan had shared with them. *It's all doable,* she thought. *We just have to find out who Braithwaite killed and convince them to go with us to the blood river. Doable.*

"What do you think, Deem?" Winn asked.

"I said I'm in," Deem replied. "You still in?"

"Hell yeah," Winn answered.

Awan laughed. "I like working with you guys," he said, leaning back and smiling.

■ ■ ■

Awan handed Deem a headlamp as they prepared to enter the mine.

"Shit," Winn said.

"What's the matter?" Awan asked.

"Winn's claustrophobic," Deem said.

"Then why did you volunteer to come?" Awan asked.

"We needed your help with the skinrunner," Winn said, "and for some stupid reason I thought I could handle it."

"Buck up," Awan said, giving Winn a slap on the shoulder.

"What's the story here?" Deem asked Awan. "You said it had to be this mine because of the minerals?"

"The ghosts have been here almost a hundred and forty years," Awan said. "There's a unique blend of gasses and minerals, both from the mine itself as well as The River. Makes them perfect for this recipe."

"So it's like they've been marinating?" Winn asked.

Awan chuckled. "Kind of."

"Do you know anything about the ghosts here?" Deem asked.

"No," Awan said, "I didn't see them when I came here as a kid. According to my grandfather's journal, the ghosts were settlers, and they are at the very back of the mine."

"Great," Winn said, looking pale. "You got a collector knife?"

Awan pulled a tube from his back pocket and handed it to Winn. Winn took it and turned it over. At the bottom were crystals that would act as a blade. When they found a ghost they could harvest from, the blade would be slid over the ghost, and like a wood plane sliding over wood, it would shave off matter, collecting it in the handle.

"Let's go," Awan said, taking the knife back from Winn.

The entrance to the mine was on the side of a sharp rise. It had been closed off with barbed wire, enough to keep animals out but not any human who was determined to enter. A sign on a stake by the entrance warned of falling into shafts.

Awan held the barbed wire open for Deem and Winn to pass under, then Winn returned the favor on the other side.

The entrance was cut square. As they walked into the adit, it began to narrow until they could no longer walk side by side, and Awan took the lead, with Deem in the middle and Winn in the rear.

After a hundred feet the angle of the adit began to rise slightly, and the walking became a little more labored. Wooden beams began appearing on the ceiling, connecting wooden posts on the sides. At first the beams were rare, but they increased the deeper they progressed.

"Guys," Winn said, stopping them. "I'm not doing well here."

Deem turned. "What, the claustrophobia?"

"Yes," Winn answered, looking around at the walls and ceiling.

"Stop looking around," Deem said. "Here, come get between us, I'll take the rear." She moved in back of Winn and pushed him forward. "Only look down, where you're walking. Concentrate on that."

Winn picked up behind Awan and the group continued on. Deem looked up to check on Winn frequently, and was met with his backside, which wasn't an unpleasant view. She couldn't help herself watch Winn's jeans, which moved and strained in just the right places when he walked. *Whatever he has in there,* she thought, *looks pretty good. It's no wonder he gets what he wants most of the time.*

The adit turned sharply to the left, and then again to the right, continuing on for several hundred feet. They stepped over an area where some rocks had collapsed from the ceiling onto the floor.

"That's disturbing," Winn said.

"Just keep walking," Deem said.

After several more minutes they came upon a shaft going down.

"Do we have to go down there?" Winn asked.

"I don't know," Awan said. "The adit we're in continues on, so I think we'll just keep going on this level."

"What's that smell?" Deem asked, peering over the shaft.

"I'm guessing bat guano," Awan said. "Let's hope they're all down there and not up ahead."

They carefully walked around the shaft opening and continued down the adit for another five minutes. The shaft widened out into an area about twenty feet across. There was no exit. They'd reached the end.

"Alright," Awan said. "This is where my grandfather's journal said to go. I'm going to drop into the River. You're welcome to join me, or not, up to you."

Awan sat on the ground cross legged and closed his eyes.

Winn looked at Deem. "You going in?" he asked her.

"Yeah," Deem said. "Walked all the way in here, might as well."

"Alright," Winn said, joining Awan on the floor. "Me too."

Inside the flow, Deem immediately noticed four graves against a far wall.

Help us! she heard behind her, and she turned. Nothing was there.

Did you hear that? Winn asked.

The ghosts are here, she thought.

Three figures slowly appeared over the graves. They were bound at their hands and feet, and there were blood-stained burlap bags over their heads. A light mist swirled around the figures. Deem felt a chill go down her spine.

Awan stood and walked to the apparitions. He removed the bag from one of them. Underneath was the frightened face of a woman, her eyes wide. As he looked down on her, he knew something was wrong with her face. She looked up at him, and Awan saw that her lower jaw was missing.

Awan removed the other two burlap bags. One uncovered a man in his mid-thirties with a short beard. The other was a young boy, about ten. The boy was trembling.

Help us, mister! the boy said. *He's coming!*

Who's coming? Awan asked.

Him! the boy wailed.

John Sorensen, said the man tied up next to the boy. *He owns this mine.*

Is this your wife and son? Awan asked, pointing to the other two.

Yes, the man said. *Please help us!*

Where is her jaw? Awan asked, pointing to the woman.

Sorensen removed it, the man said. *She screamed too much.*

What do we have here? came a low voice from behind them. They turned, and a large man dressed in old dusty clothes walked into the area from the adit. *Visitors?* the man said to Awan. *Come for a taste?*

The man walked past them and pulled the woman to her feet.

Leave her alone! the woman's husband shouted.

This is Sorensen? Awan asked the man on the ground.

That's him, the monster, came the reply.

Who wants to know? Sorensen asked, forcing the woman to bend at the waist. The boy began to cry hysterically.

Deem was about to ask Sorensen what he intended to do to the woman, when Sorensen raised the woman's dress and threw it over her back, exposing her backside and legs. He pulled down her underwear, exposing her flesh. Then he moved his head toward her. The woman thrashed, trying to break the bonds that held her, but she was no match for the much larger Sorensen. When he pulled his face away from her, Deem recoiled in horror. Sorensen had taken a bite of her, just below her buttocks on the right leg. The wound was bleeding, and Sorensen turned to face them, his mouth full of the woman's flesh. He chewed, staring at Awan, blood running down his chin.

Jesus Christ, Winn said, turning away.

Sorensen swallowed. *Tasty,* he said to Awan. *The thigh is my favorite.*

He eats you? Awan asked the man on the ground.

We're his neighbors, the man said. *We've been fighting with him about water rights. He settled it by kidnapping us at gunpoint last night, and brought us into his mine. Then he eats us, alive. Buried us where I'm sitting.*

The only thing around these parts worse than being a horse thief, Sorensen said to the man, *is being a water thief. You stole my water, you sonofabitch. So now I'm getting what's mine in return. In blood.*

Sorensen took another bite from the woman, enlarging the hole he'd already created. Then he stood and removed a leather canteen from his jacket. He opened the canteen and held it at the boy's mouth, forcing him to drink. The boy wrapped his lips around the canteen's spigot and drank hungrily.

This one's getting nothing but milk until I eat him, Sorensen said. *It'll soften him up even more.*

You bastard! the man on the ground shouted. *You'll rot in hell for this!*

They've been doing this for a hundred and forty years? Deem asked Awan.

Looks like it, Awan answered. Behind them, Sorensen returned to the woman and took a bite from her calf, pulling flesh and tendons.

Do we stop him? Winn asked.

I'm just after the ghost matter, Awan said to Winn. *This is going to be pretty distasteful, but I've got to keep focused on the goal here. So don't freak out over what I'm about to do. Remember, these people are long dead.*

Awan turned to Sorensen. *How much for a bite? Just one?*

Sorensen looked up at Awan and smiled. *A kindred spirit! Hungry, are ya? There's plenty to go around, just so long as you never tell. I get the woman and boy, you can have the man.*

Awan looked back at Deem and Winn. Deem, realizing what Awan was about to do, turned to look away.

Awan walked over to the man bound on the ground. *Sorry about this,* Awan said.

What are you going to do to me, mister? the man asked.

Awan pulled up the man's pant leg, exposing the flesh of the man's ankle and calf. Most of the man's leg was gone, already shaved away. He pulled up the man's other pant leg and saw the same.

So he's been eating you, too? Awan asked the man.

No, the man answered. *People like you did that to me.*

Awan swallowed his distaste and ripped the man's shirt open. His chest was intact. Awan removed the collector knife from his back pocket and placed the blade edge on the exposed chest. He slid the knife, pressing down so the blade would dig into the man and slice off part of his skin. The man screamed.

That's some fancy work there, Sorensen said behind them. *Me, I just like biting into them. I like to feel the flesh as my teeth passes through it; feel them twist under me in pain.*

Deem raised her hands to her ears to plug them. In the River it didn't block any noise.

Awan continued to scrape at the man's chest.

You're as bad as him, the man said to Awan, nodding at Sorensen.

I'm not a cannibal, Awan replied to the man.

You're worse, the man said. *You're taking what I have left. Just like the others who never help.*

After several more passes, Awan lifted the knife and inspected the container. It was full.

We're done, Awan said.

You gonna cook that up? Sorensen asked.

Yes, Awan said, wanting to leave the mine without further incident. *I and my friends are going to fry it later, and have it for dinner. Thanks for sharing.*

You're welcome, Sorensen said. *But remember, if you tell anyone what's going on here, I'll hunt you down and have you for dinner myself.*

Your secret is safe with me, Awan said. He dropped out of the River, Winn and Deem following him. Deem rose from the floor and walked over to where she'd noticed the graves in the flow.

"My god," she said. "They're buried here. You can see where the ground has been dug up."

"And now he eats them, over and over," Winn said. "I think I'd prefer zombighosts."

"And it sounds like people have been harvesting the man," Deem said. "At some point down the road, he'll be gone. Used up."

"Let's head out," Awan said, placing the collector knife carefully into his backpack and lifting it to his shoulder. "I need a shower."

...

In Fallon, they rented two rooms, one for Awan and Winn, and the other for Deem. Then they went for food at a Mexican restaurant. Deem sat in a booth, and Awan and Winn sat opposite her.

"Thanks for the support," Awan said. "I guess I could have done it myself, but it was nice to have you along."

"That poor man," Deem said. "Not only does he have to watch his wife and son get eaten over and over again, he occasionally has to put up with visitors like us who carve off part of him. It's sad."

"Sad is how I'd describe most ghosts outside of the downwind area," Awan said. "Sounds like you haven't run into many like this."

"No," Deem said. "Most of the ghosts I know are the kind that chase you and rip into you if they catch you. I'm not used to normal ghosts with a story."

"They're all a lot like the ones in the mine," Awan said. "Something is keeping them here. Sometimes you can figure it out and help them move along, but most of the time they're set in their ways and they keep performing the same routine over and over."

Deem watched Awan as he spoke. Although he couldn't have been more than a couple of years older than Winn, he seemed to have a deeper level of wisdom than either of them, and she found that when he talked, it calmed her, not unlike when her father would counsel her. She liked the sound of his voice, the calm and measured way that he spoke. And his facial features were handsome, especially when he smiled at the end of a sentence.

She looked at Winn, who was staring at Awan as well. He seemed taken with Awan too.

138

"Pardon me," Awan said, rising from the booth. "I need to get that cave washed off my hands before the food arrives." He walked back into the restaurant, looking for the restroom.

"Is there one or two beds in your room?" Deem asked Winn, once Awan was out of earshot.

Winn smiled at Deem. "It's gratifying that you're always so interested in my sex life. What do you say we just get it over with, and just do it, you and I? Then you'll know and won't have to be so obsessed."

"I'm not obsessed," Deem said, "I just saw how you were looking at him."

"He does have a way about him," Winn said. "You gotta love a guy who's both handsome and smart. I wouldn't say no."

"You're disgusting," Deem said.

"And you're too laden with your Mormon sexual repression," Winn said. "Sex is a good thing, not disgusting."

"If you sleep with him and it screws up him helping us, I'll be really pissed," Deem said.

"More like jealous," Winn said. "I saw how you were looking at him. If *you* sleep with him and it screws things up, *I'll* be pissed."

"Back," Awan said, sliding into the booth next to Winn. "Did you miss me?"

Winn saw Deem blush, and decided to distract Awan so she wouldn't be embarrassed. "We were just discussing what your next steps would be, back in Indian Springs. You've got the ingredients for the blood souring. When do you plan on kidnapping the brothers? Will you need help?"

"First I have to make the ghost chalk," Awan said. "I'll start on that tomorrow, as soon as I get home. It'll take several days to bake and condense down. If you don't mind, I'll give you a call to help plan out how to incapacitate the brothers once that's ready to go."

"Sure," Deem said, the blood in her face having returned to normal. "We'll do what we can."

"So you need to get back early tomorrow?" Awan said. "I hope you don't mind my asking."

"I don't mind," Deem said, but a part of her did mind. The issue of her father's journals was deeply personal, and she had only spoken to Winn and Claude about them. Now she was about to open up to Awan. She decided he was trustworthy.

"It has nothing to do with the skinrunner," Deem said, "it's something else. You mentioned your father's journal. I assume it's important to you."

"Very," Awan said, a serious look crossing his face as he replied.

"Well," Deem said, "I suspect my father kept journals as well. He was gifted, and he died a while back."

"Sorry to hear that," Awan said. "It's tough when you lose a father, I know. Especially one who trained you. It leaves a big hole in your life."

Deem instantly knew Awan had gone through the same loss, and she realized it was safe to tell him more. She felt tears start to form, but she fought them back.

"He was a high-up in the Mormon church in Mesquite," Deem said. "So all the more reason to keep a journal, right? Well, I'm beginning to think he was part of a secret group of gifted Mormons who are holding onto his journals."

"If he kept journals," Awan said, "they should go to you."

"They won't give them up," Deem said, "because they think the journals would break the secrecy of the group. And I can't join their group because I'm a woman. And I'm not a good Mormon, that too. So I plan on finding the journals and stealing them."

Their food arrived, and all three of them began eating.

"What's happening tomorrow?" Awan asked.

"A meeting of this secret council, I think," Deem said. "Last Sunday of each month; that's why I need to be back early. I'm going to follow one of them, see where they go."

"You need to be careful," Awan said. "Make sure they don't know you're following them. Mormons with secrets can be very dangerous. Are you going with her?" he asked Winn.

"Yes," Winn said. "I was planning to."

"If they meet somewhere remote," Awan said, "it will be easy for them to figure out if they've been followed. You can't risk that. I have something better. We'll stop at my place on the way back tomorrow and I'll give it to you."

"What is it?" Deem asked.

"A GPS tracker," Awan said. "Just stick it under the guy's car. You only need to be within ten miles of it to track it. Much safer."

Deem smiled at Winn, pleased that she'd confided in Awan. Winn smiled back.

"Thank you, Awan," Deem said. "I appreciate that."

"You should have your father's journals," Awan said, slipping a forkful of enchilada into his mouth. "There's things in there he wrote just for you, as my father wrote just for me."

"That's the feeling I can't shake," Deem said. "There's something in them that's intended for me, I just know it."

"Not just intended," Awan said. "They're part of your future. What's in his journals will change you. Part of your future self is missing until you get them."

"Hadn't thought of it that way," Deem said.

"Trust me," Awan said, "I know. My father's journals changed me. I'm a different person. They will change you, too."

Deem took another bite of her chile relleno and thought about Awan's words. It made her double her commitment to locate her father's writings.

Winn followed Deem back to Mesquite, offering to drive her around town as she looked for Dayton. Deem was worried that Dayton might recognize her truck, but he'd not give a moment's notice to Winn's Jeep.

They arrived at Dayton's house mid-afternoon. It was in the middle of a large subdivision of new houses. There was an SUV in the driveway.

"That's his wife's," Deem said. "Uses it to haul their five kids around town. He won't take that to wherever he's going, he'll have to leave it here for her to use in case she needs it in an emergency. He's driving his BMW."

"It's not here," Winn observed.

"Of course not," Deem said. "It's Sunday. It'll be at the stake center. That's where he spends most of Sunday."

Winn followed Deem's directions to the large Mormon church that served as a gathering place for several of the local congregations. The parking lot was full and no one was outside. Winn slowly maneuvered through the lot as Deem turned on the two devices Awan had given her.

"Where's your cigarette lighter?" Deem asked Winn, who pulled the lighter out of the center console and dropped it into his cup holder. Deem plugged the cord from the flat panel display into the outlet and turned on the unit. A map popped up with a blinking blue dot exactly where they were driving.

The second part of the unit was a square plastic box about the size of a pack of cigarettes. It was magnetized along one side and had a three inch plastic antenna coming out of one end.

"Hope this works," Deem said.

"Awan said it'd stick to the underside of the car and not fall off?" Winn asked.

"That's what he said," Deem answered.

"What if he goes through rough terrain? Can it be knocked off?"

"If something hits it on the underside, I can't see why it wouldn't fall off," Deem said. "We'll just have to hope that doesn't happen."

"Wait," Winn said. He placed the Jeep in park and jumped out of his door, running around to the back, where he rummaged through some items. When he returned to the driver's seat, he handed Deem a roll of duct tape.

"Insurance," he said. "There's no one out here. Once we find the car, you should have plenty of time to tape it into place, just to be sure."

"Thanks, Winn," Deem said, scanning the cars in the lot as they slowly moved up and down the aisles.

"What color is it?" Winn asked.

"Black," Deem said. "And I'll bet it'll be around back, by the back entrance. All the offices are back there. Since he's in the stake presidency, he gets here early and I'll bet he goes for the closest parking space to that entrance."

Winn turned into the back parking lot of the building and sure enough, the black BMW was parked next to a cement sidewalk that led straight into the back entrance of the building.

"Park in that empty space there," Deem said, pointing to a vacant spot a few cars away. "Then I'll go plant it."

Winn pulled into the parking spot and turned off the motor. He rolled down his window. "If someone comes out, I'm going to whistle," he said. "Stay under the car until I give you an 'all clear,' alright?"

"Good," Deem said. "I'll be fast. If we're close to a meeting letting out, a hundred people could come streaming out those doors."

Deem jumped out of the passenger side of the Jeep, tracking device in one hand, duct tape in the other. She walked over to the BMW and looked under it. The hot pavement was reflecting the day's heat and she felt it intensify the closer her face got to the ground. She stretched out and slid under the car, looking for a spot to attach the tracker. She tried a couple of places, but it didn't sit flush. She finally found a spot that seemed flat enough to hold it, not perfectly, but the best she was going to get. She ripped off piece after piece of duct tape, pressing the long strips against the metal surrounding the device. Soon the entire device was covered, with duct tape radiating out in all directions, the small three inch antenna poking out. She tested the tape, tugging slightly on the device. It seemed firm.

Winn whistled.

She slid further under the car, looking around to see if she was as covered as possible. She tilted her head up and saw several sets of feet walking toward her. A child was screaming hysterically. The feet marched up to the minivan parked next to the BMW. Deem could see a woman's shoes and at least five sets of children's feet of various sizes. One by one the feet lifted from the ground and into the minivan. The woman's feet circled the vehicle, arranging the children inside.

Leaving early, Deem thought. *Sounds like one of the kids threw a tantrum and she had to take them out.*

It seemed to take forever for the woman to finish packing in all the kids. One of the children kept screaming at the top of their lungs the entire time.

Finally Deem heard the sliding door of the minivan close. Instantly the screaming muffled. The woman walked around to the driver's side. She paused at the door and sighed before she opened it, releasing the sound of the tantrum once again into the parking lot. She slid into the vehicle and closed the door.

I'll never have kids, Deem thought to herself.

The minivan roared to life and slowly backed out of the parking space. Deem slid a little more to the side opposite, hoping the woman wouldn't be able to see under the BMW when she had the minivan pulled all the way back.

She probably is too busy dealing with the kids to notice anyway, Deem thought.

The minivan pulled away and the parking lot returned to normal. She heard Winn say, "All clear!"

Deem slid out of the BMW and stood up. She walked over to Winn's Jeep and jumped back into the passenger side. The moment she closed the door to the Jeep, the doors of the church opened and a stream of people began to emerge.

"Just in time," Winn said, watching as men in white shirts and ties emerged. Some of them tugged at their ties the moment they stepped out of the building, loosening them and unbuttoning the top of their shirts. Women emerged with them, all in knee length dresses. Children swarmed around both, and as family after family emerged it became impossible to tell whose kids belonged to whom.

"Jesus Christ, that's a lot of kids," Winn said. "Do you think Dayton will be coming out? There's too many people behind my car right now for me to back out. Too many kids, I'm afraid I might hit one."

"No," Deem said, "he'll be one of the last ones out."

As the words came out of her mouth, Deem saw Dayton walk through the door and into the sunlight. She shrunk down in her seat.

"That's him!" she said to Winn.

146

"Who?" Winn asked, looking at the crowd.

"The guy in the suit!"

"They're all in suits!" Winn replied.

"Brown suit, red tie, balding," Deem said.

"That narrows it down by half," Winn said. He watched to see which of the men would walk to the BMW.

"Shit!" Deem said.

"What?"

"The duct tape! I must have left it under the car!"

"Are you sure?" Winn asked.

"That woman with the kids distracted me," Deem said. "I think I set it down and I forgot to take it with me when I slid out."

"Let's hope he doesn't notice it when he backs out," Winn said. "He's started his car. He can't really leave yet, too many people walking behind it. He seems to be in a hurry."

Winn watched as Dayton tried to pull out. People moved away from his car as it slowly slid from the parking space. Parents wrangled their children, taking them by the hand so that they wouldn't dart into the path of the slowly moving car.

As Winn watched, a family began to load into the car that was parked on the other side of the BMW. A boy of about twelve noticed the duct tape on the ground. He bent to pick it up.

"Damn," Winn said. "A kid found the tape."

The child looked up at the BMW, which had finished backing out and was starting to move forward down the parking lot.

"President Dayton!" the boy yelled, holding up the duct tape.

The BMW continued to pull away, moving through the crowd. People in front of the car stepped aside to let the BMW through, most of them recognizing the occupant and deferring to authority.

The boy ran behind the BMW, desperately trying to return the duct tape, calling "President Dayton! President Dayton!"

The boy's father yelled for him to come back, and the kid stopped in his tracks, turning to look back at his father.

"Get in this car!" the father called.

"President Dayton forgot this!" the boy said to his dad, returning to the family vehicle. The BMW was now on the other side of the parking lot, nearing the exit.

"You can give it to him the next time you see him," the father said. "Get inside."

The boy got into the backseat of the car, and the father got into the driver's seat and began backing out.

"Crisis averted," Winn said. "The kid has the duct tape. Dayton is gone."

Deem sat back up in her seat and turned on the flat panel. She watched as the blue dot moved on the screen.

"Half the people can't get out of the parking lot fast enough," Winn observed. "The other half are standing around shaking each other's hands like they have nowhere to go."

"That's what they do," Deem said.

"Is it working?" Winn asked, trying to see the screen Deem was holding.

"Seems to," Deem said. "It looks like he's headed home."

"Let's find out," Winn said. There were fewer people walking in the lot now, and he carefully backed out of his parking spot. They exited the lot and drove back to Dayton's home, Winn asking Deem for directions a couple of times once they entered the subdivision. As they neared the house, they both observed the BMW in the driveway.

"Yay, it works," Deem said. "Thank you, Awan!"

"What now?" Winn asked.

"We wait," Deem said. "I have no idea what time the meeting will be."

"Are you hungry?" Winn asked. "I could use something."

"7-11 first," Deem said. "I'm dry."

As Winn turned the Jeep around and left the subdivision, Deem kept her eyes on the blue dot. For the first time she began to think she might actually be able to locate her father's journals. It seemed within reach. Until now, it had just been an idea. *This little blue dot is going to lead me to them,* she thought. *I might have them today. Tonight.*

She watched the blue dot remain stationary at Dayton's home as they moved throughout the town, picking up her Big Gulp and then going through a fast-food drive thru.

"He's still there?" Winn asked.

"Yup," Deem said. "Hasn't moved."

"Want to double check it?" Winn asked.

"Yeah," Deem said. "Why not."

Winn drove back to the subdivision and past Dayton's house. The BMW was still there in the driveway.

"Can't be too sure," Deem said.

"It's not like we have anything else to do," Winn said.

"Let's find a place to park in the shade," Deem said. "And we'll wait him out."

...

"Where is he now?" Winn asked, speeding his Jeep through Snow Canyon. The red rock on either side of the road would occasionally break open into wide spaces where small communities of homes were being developed, then enclose again.

"Ahead a couple of turns," Deem said.

"This road twists enough that he won't notice us if we stay back. But I don't want to lose him, so let me know if the distance increases."

"I wonder who that was he picked up in St. George?" Deem asked. Dayton had stopped at a house in the older part of St. George, near the college. An older gentleman in a suit and tie had come out of an extremely well maintained home and jumped into the passenger seat of Dayton's BMW.

"Probably another member of their secret council," Winn said. "Carpooling. I wonder how far away this meeting will be."

Deem kept her eyes glued to the blue dot pulsing on the screen. It slowly progressed up Highway 18, winding its way over hills and through small canyons. Soon they passed the turn off to the Mountain Meadows monument.

"How appropriate," Winn said as they sped past it. "Some things never change."

"We don't know that this secret council was as bad as the people who committed that massacre," Deem said.

"Giving them the benefit of the doubt?"

"My father was one of them, so yes, I'm trying to."

"But what if they were, Deem? What if they operate on the wrong side of the fence? Claude sure made it sound like they were formidable."

"Formidable doesn't mean evil," Deem said, watching as the blue dot on her screen moved slowly toward Enterprise. "There's every possibility that they use their gifts for good. They're leaders in the church, for god's sake."

"Then why all the secrecy?" Winn asked. "And don't you start defending the church all of a sudden. You're usually much harder on it than I am."

Deem sighed. "I guess I'm dreading what we might find. I don't want to discover that these people I've respected all my life are not what I thought they were."

"Your father included?" Winn asked.

"Yes," Deem said, "him too."

The significance of this seemed to soften Winn a little. "I hope you're right. I really do."

"But be prepared for the worst, right?" Deem asked.

"I've always found that to be a wise approach."

They slowed down through Enterprise and soon found themselves at the junction of Highway 56. The locals called it Beryl Junction.

"Take a left," Deem said. "He's headed back into Nevada."

"Not much out there," Winn said. "I wonder if they meet in a cave or a mine."

"In suits and ties?" Deem asked. "Not a chance."

A train mirrored their progress, travelling along the side of the road as they approached the Nevada border. After they crossed, the train split off southward.

"That line leads to Caliente, doesn't it?" Deem asked.

"Yeah, it does," Winn said. "Wouldn't it be funny if that's where they're meeting?"

"Why funny?" Deem asked.

"Just the whole fundamentalist thing," Winn said. "You know, the Warren Jeffs marriages."

"No, I don't know," Deem said.

"When they were trying Jeffs for marrying off underaged girls to fundamentalist Mormons, it came out that they held a lot of the secret marriages at a motel in Caliente."

"Ugh," Deem said. "Creepy."

"So, wouldn't it be interesting if this secret council meets in Caliente?"

"Doesn't mean anything," Deem said.

"Who was it said 'there are no coincidences'?"

"I don't see how they can be connected," Deem said.

"Maybe the secret council includes some fundamentalists?" Winn said. "Why not?"

"Because the regular LDS despise polygamists," Deem said. "They think they give the church a bad image. They root them out and excommunicate them, when they find them."

"You don't seriously consider this secret council to be regular LDS, do you? They're rogue."

Deem watched the blue dot speeding along on the screen. What Winn was saying was right, but she wasn't fully prepared to accept it. Being raised Mormon, it was hard to kick the patterns of thinking that had been drilled into her from a young age. And she didn't like thinking about what it meant so far as her father was concerned.

She remembered a time when she was fifteen, and she learned that friends of hers who she'd grown up with, the Halworth family, neighbors just down the street, kids she'd played with for years, were discovered to be polygamists. Her first reaction was that it didn't matter, but as she watched the family become ostracized from the rest of the community, she began to feel betrayed. How could the Halworths have lied to her all these years? She had sleepovers at their house when she was younger. She babysat for them on occasion. All the while, they'd been secretly practicing polygamy. Deem's mother was insistent that she cut off all communication with them, and her father, as stake president, was involved with excommunicating the family.

Then she began to feel annoyed, that the reaction to the discovery was overkill, and the public shunning was unjustified. She knew the family to be good people. They were the same kids she'd played with last year. They hadn't changed. But the community's reaction to their outing had been decisive and swift. They were ignored, no longer invited to functions. They were not welcome in other people's homes. The kids were teased endlessly at school. Deem remembered her mother making a point of purging all of the Halworth family contacts from her email lists. Deem felt it was wrong, and it began to feed her sense of rebellion against the way she'd been raised. Soon she was finding ways to skip church, and backing out of invitations she used to accept.

She knew her father sensed the rebellion when it began. He'd always been careful not to throw gasoline on the fire – he'd never confronted Deem directly about her growing disinterest in the normal religious routines of the community. He'd always seemed supportive, regardless of how active Deem had been in the church. But Deem knew her father had played a role in excommunicating the Halworths. He was part of an organization that was the reason they were being treated like trash. She resented it. She thought it was cruel.

Then again, what she learned about the fundamentalists bothered her too, especially the forced underage marriages. She didn't have a problem with adults practicing their religion the way they wanted, and she didn't have a problem with people having more than one wife, if that's what they wanted. Live and let live. But she abhorred the idea of a fourteen year old girl being forced to marry a sixty year old man, just because some self-proclaimed "prophet" somewhere decreed it.

Which was worse? she wondered. *My father's church, which would cruelly ostracize and shun an entire family, making their life hell? Or a prophet who would marry off underage kids?*

The latter, she thought. *Definitely the latter.* But it didn't make what her father had done any more palatable to her. She knew that if her father hadn't excommunicated the Halworths, higher-ups in Salt Lake would have forced the issue, so he had no choice.

That just means he was willing to do awful things in the name of religion, Deem thought. *Am I sure I want these journals? I may not like what I find.*

She suddenly felt incredibly sad as she watched the blue dot moving further into Nevada and turning south toward Caliente. Part of her wanted to give up and just abandon the whole attempt.

Then another part of her emerged, the part she knew well – the rebellious part. *No,* she thought. *No burying heads in the sand. No caving in to these religious nuts. I want the truth, whatever it is. My father's journals are mine, not theirs.*

She focused down on the blue dot, pushing out all feeling of doubt and sadness. The dot was the goal, it was going to be dealt with. She was not one to start something and not finish it.

"You may be right," she said to Winn. "A secret council might be capable of anything."

Winn knew something was going on with Deem. He decided to let her comment sit, and they rode on in silence.

■ ■ ■

"How long has it been?" Winn asked.

Deem checked her watch. "Just over an hour and a half."

Winn adjusted himself and tried to stretch out in the driver's seat of his Jeep. They were parked half a block from an old, abandoned church in Caliente.

Earlier, they had followed Dayton to a side street where he'd parked his car and walked two blocks to the church. The others who had met him there had followed the same procedure – there were no cars parked in front of or around the building. It still looked as silent and vacant as it had before Winn and Deem had seen half a dozen men enter the back of the church.

"Why way the fuck out here?" Winn asked, looking around.

"Based on what Claude indicated," Deem said, "I'm guessing the group is spread out. Caliente might be central for all of them."

Earlier, after they'd watched the men entering the building, Deem had asked Winn to drive around the streets surrounding the old church, two blocks in each direction. She'd taken pictures of every parked car, and noted license plate numbers. She had about twenty cars on her list. She knew some of them probably didn't belong to council members, but she figured a good number of them did.

"They're coming out," Winn said. "Well, at least one guy."

Deem raised her camera as discreetly as she could and began taking pictures. She was using the zoom, and because it was dark, she wasn't sure the pictures would turn out to be useful, but she took them anyway. The first man left the back exit of the church and walked away into the night. It was a couple of minutes before the next man emerged.

"They don't want to draw attention by leaving all at once," Winn said. "They've got this down."

After twenty minutes it appeared they'd all left; no more men came out of the building.

"Come on," Deem said, grabbing a small duffel bag. "We're going in."

Deem jumped out of the car and Winn followed her. They walked the half a block to the old church along a tree-lined street. There were no streetlights, and only the light coming from the moon made them able to see their way.

The old church was small and well over a hundred years old, built by Mormons in the early 20th century. Needs of the local congregations had long ago exceeded the capabilities of the tiny building, and it was replaced by modern brick structures in other parts of town. Deem was surprised this old church hadn't been torn down. Then it occurred to her that the church might have been serving the needs of the Mormon gifted for many generations. Although it appeared abandoned, it was still in use.

As they approached the back door, the security system sticker reflected the moonlight.

"That looks relatively new," Winn said, observing the warning not to enter.

"Hold on," Deem said, leaving Winn and circling around the side of the building. She searched the sky for wires, and soon found the box where the phone lines entered the building. She pulled wire snips from her bag and cut every wire that emerged from the junction box, then she returned to Winn.

"That's done," Deem said. She retrieved Winn's lock picking tools from the duffel and handed them to him. "You can pick it?"

Winn studied the lock. There were two, a deadbolt and a separate lock on the handle.

"No problem," he said, pulling the thin tools out of a sheath and inserting them into the keyholes. "Give me a minute."

Deem waited patiently while Winn worked. She looked around, hoping they'd avoid any cars or passersby. The back of the church faced a row of short trees and shrubs that separated the property from the next street, which contained a couple of industrial structures. She could see why the council members used this entrance – it was quiet and private.

"Yes!" Winn said as the door opened, and he let Deem take the lead. She pulled a flashlight from her duffel and entered the building. Winn followed and pulled the door closed behind him.

They were in a short hallway, with small rooms branching from each side. "Classrooms," Deem said, shining her light in each and quickly moving on. "For Sunday School."

After a bend in the hallway she came upon a locked door. "We'll come back to this," she said, continuing on.

After another turn, they emerged into the chapel. The pews were still in place, and a raised podium made of wood was still at the end of the room. Deem walked down the aisle, amazed that the elements of the chapel were still intact. She had expected that something this old might have been vandalized. When she reached the podium she walked up the dais and looked out over the small room. There were fifteen rows of pews, divided into a left and right side. There was nothing on the walls, but she didn't expect there to be – Mormon churches were strictly utilitarian with no ornamentation.

"Do you think they met in here?" Winn asked.

"Probably," Deem said, searching around the podium for any signs of use. There were none.

"There's nothing here," Winn said. "Or back in those rooms."

"Except for that locked door," Deem said. She walked down from the dais and back through the pews. "Let's get it open."

Winn followed her back to the locked door and he knelt, examining the lock. "Alright," he said. "This should only take a second."

Winn had the door open quickly, and Deem stepped inside. It was a sizeable room. The walls were lined with open, free-standing metal shelves that contained cardboard boxes.

"Hmm," Deem said. "Remind you of anything?"

"Yeah," Winn said. "The skinrunner's room."

Deem pulled one of the boxes off the shelf. It was heavy. She opened the lid and looked inside. It was filled with green hanging file folders, each stuffed with multiple manila folders. She pulled one out and looked at it – she recognized the church logo in the upper right corner. It was filled with handwriting. As she read it, she realized it was the notes from a church service long ago. She looked at the top right and saw a date: September 17, 1972.

"These are just old church records," Deem said. "Nothing as interesting as the skinrunner's."

She replaced the folders and put the box back on the shelf. They scanned the room. There didn't appear to be anything unusual or out of place, just a room full of boxes.

She examined the writings on the face of each box. They all seemed to be minutes from various church meetings.

"Do you think they kept minutes of their secret council?" Winn asked, joining Deem as she searched.

"Maybe," Deem said. "Mormons love to take notes. But these all appear to be minutes from old sacrament and priesthood meetings."

Winn could tell from Deem's tone that she was beginning to feel disappointed.

"Your dad's journals might be in here somewhere," Winn said. "These boxes might be mislabeled, might have been re-used."

Deem pulled another box at random. She inspected the documents inside and compared them to the notes on the box. They were the same. Even the handwriting was the same, from box to box.

"Damn," she said. "I was really hoping they'd be here."

She tried a succession of boxes. Each time the papers inside were merely meeting minutes, syncing with the dates that had been noted on the exterior of the box. Winn assisted her, checking several boxes. When he replaced the box he had just checked, he noticed that the box met with resistance as he pushed it back. He assumed the box had hit the wall behind the shelving, but something didn't seem right. He removed the box and shined his flashlight into the empty space.

"Deem," he said. "Come here."

Deem replaced the box she had been looking through and joined Winn.

"Look," he said.

"So?" she said, seeing nothing.

"The backing," Winn said. "This set of shelves has a back on it."

Deem looked inside again and saw the wood that lined the back of the shelves. She walked to the set of shelves to the left and pulled out a box. She shined her flashlight into the hole and saw the wall behind the shelves. "No backing on this one."

Winn did the same with the set of shelves on the right. "None here, either."

"So just this one set of shelves has it?" Deem asked. She pulled more boxes from the shelves, exposing more of the wooden backing. Once they'd removed all of the boxes, the backing was obvious.

"Help me," Winn said, grabbing the shelving on one side. Deem went to the other side and lifted. With the boxes removed, the shelving slid easily. They pulled the shelves back until they could easily get around it.

"Ha!" Winn said, seeing the door in the wall behind the shelves.

"It doesn't even have a handle," Deem said. "Just a lock."

"A handle would have kept the shelves from sitting flush against it," Winn said, bending over to examine the dead bolt lock. He removed his tools and began to pick it.

Within moments he had the door open, and they looked inside. It was a wooden stairwell leading down.

"A basement!" Deem said. "Something tells me we've found it!"

She started down and was at the bottom of the stairs within moments, searching for a light switch. She found one, and a hanging fixture suspended in the middle of the room popped on. It was hanging directly over a large round table that had a dozen chairs around it.

"This is where they meet," Deem said, stepping off the stairwell landing and onto the floor of the basement. Winn was right behind her.

She walked to the table and touched it. It was made of exquisite wood and inlaid with a fine pattern. It looked very old. She touched one of the chairs, letting her hand run over the headrest. It was leather. It was slightly worn. It, too, looked old.

"Deem," Winn said. "There's something down here. With us."

Deem dropped into the River immediately. She saw the figure looking up at her from a side table against the wall. It was a man, dressed in a suit and tie. The style of his clothes looked very old. He stared at Deem over a set of small glasses. As she watched, he placed a pen down on top of some papers at his table, and stood.

You're not supposed to be in here, he said.

Deem thought quickly. The man had been writing – perhaps he was keeping minutes? Were all those writings upstairs his?

I'd report you to Brother Dayton right now, except I can tell you both have the gift, he said. He drifted closer to Deem without walking. He seemed to be examining her.

And I know you, don't I? he asked.

You probably knew my father, Deem said. *President Hinton.*

You're his daughter! the man said, circling her. *How nice it is to meet you.*

Likewise, Deem said. *But I didn't get your name?*

Brother Hester, he said, extending his hand. She shook it, feeling nothing. *I'm the ward clerk for the third ward.*

Well, you're doing an excellent job, Deem said. *Your record keeping is exemplary. And well organized.*

He beamed. There was no higher praise for a ward clerk, Deem knew.

Thank you, he said, continuing to drift around her. *I'm supposed to report anyone coming in here to Brother Dayton, but you're President Hinton's daughter. So I suppose it's alright. And who's this?* Hester said, drifting over to Winn. *He's not righteous. He's a backslider.*

Deem suppressed a smile. *He's an investigator,* Deem said, using the common Mormon term for someone who wasn't a member of the church but was trying to find out more about it, to see if they'd like to join. Mormons were always on their best behavior when an "investigator" was around, hoping to set a good example and not give the potential convert any reason to think negatively about the church.

Oh, that's wonderful, Brother Hester said, drifting back from Winn and facing him head on. *I'm Brother Hester,* he said, extending his hand. Winn reached out to shake it, unnerved by the lack of feeling when he attempted to grab it.

The third ward is a wonderful ward with outstanding members. I know you'll enjoy it, Hester said, trying to impress Winn.

Winn looked at Deem. He was completely flustered. He saw Deem mouth the words "go with it!"

I'm sure I will, Winn stammered.

Brother Hester smiled and drifted back to Deem. *I have a great deal of respect for President Hinton,* Hester said. *A better leader the Lord couldn't have selected. Under his leadership attendance increased by sixteen percent!*

Deem smiled. She knew her father had been well liked in the community, but she had no idea he'd been popular with the ghosts, too. She decided to try and use this to her advantage.

My father used to tell me about your good work, Deem said. *He told me you were the best ward clerk he'd ever known.*

Hester seemed shocked by Deem's words. *Oh!* he said. *Did he, really?*

Yes, Deem said, *and he told me if I ever needed help, Brother Hester was the person to talk to.*

He did? Hester asked. *Me?*

Yes, Deem said. She decided to pull out all of the stops. *And I just knew he was full of the spirit of the Lord when he told me that. I felt it, right in here,* she said, placing her hand over her heart, *right out of Moroni.*

Any remaining doubts Hester might have had about Deem's presence in the room seemed to vanish. He beamed at her with adoration.

And such a pretty daughter, too, Hester said. *I imagine you'll be married soon. Perhaps to this young gentleman? Is that why he's investigating the church? So he can convert, and you two get a temple marriage?*

Deem did her best to not spit up. She needed to keep Hester on her side for as long as possible.

Maybe, she said, smiling, holding back a strong desire to laugh. *We'll have to see how things go. You know, if he converts and all.*

Oh, yes, well, I'm sure he will, Hester said.

I was explaining genealogy to him the other day, which is why I'm here, Deem said to Hester. *He seemed interested in it, so I thought I'd show him my father's journals. You know how important it is that we follow the Lord's instructions and keep journals.*

Indeed, Hester said. *People don't always do it like they should, and they thereby miss out on the blessings. I write in mine every night. Er, well, I used to.*

Deem began walking around the room, looking for more boxes. *Since my father came here so often, I was hoping my father's journals might be here, somewhere,* she said. *Do you know if they are?*

I don't think so, Hester said. *Most people keep their journals at home.*

But my father, he was part of this council, Deem said. *I just assumed they kept their journals here.*

I've never seen any, Hester said. He began following her as she rounded the table and walked to the back of the room.

What do they do down here? Deem asked Hester.

Well, they meet, of course, Hester said. *I offered to keep minutes, but they don't want minutes.*

But they want you to guard the place, Deem said. *To alert them if anyone shows up.*

Yes. Otherwise, I just work on the ward's business. There's a lot to do.

Are they all gifted? Deem asked.

The council? Yes, I think so, Hester said.

Are you gifted? Were you gifted? Deem asked.

No, Hester said. *I was not so blessed. But these men of God who were chosen by the Lord called me to stay here, and keep the ward minutes, and let them know if anyone came in. That's reward in itself for me.*

Has anyone ever come in? Deem asked. *People without the gift?*

No, no one's ever come down here outside of the council, other than you. You're the first.

No one's ever broken in upstairs? Deem asked.

I don't know, Hester said. *I don't go up there. Well, I do go up to the filing room. That's where all my minutes are kept. But that's as far as I go. Since they called me to serve in this position, I've tried to follow their instructions precisely.*

I remember my father telling me how impressed he was with you and how you performed your calling, Deem said, knowing she needed to keep the ruse going. *How long have you been in this calling, Brother Hester?*

How long? He asked. *I'm not sure. It seems like a long time.*

Well, I'm sure the Lord will release you, soon, Deem said. *That is, unless you're doing such a good job they just can't do without you!* She turned to look at Hester and smiled.

That is the burden of those of us who take our work seriously, Hester said. *We're sometimes too good at it, and it goes on forever as a result.*

The council met today, didn't they? Deem asked. *They meet around this table, don't they?*

They do, Hester said. *Once a month.*

Do you attend the meeting? Deem asked.

No, I'm not a member of the council, Hester said. *I just sit over at my ward clerk's table. I've got minutes from last Sunday's meeting I've got to transcribe so I can file them. It's important that they get done on schedule; otherwise I'll have a backlog.*

Do you ever listen to their meeting? Deem asked. *You're sitting so close to them, you must overhear what they're talking about.*

Sometimes, Hester said. *I try not to, because it ruins my concentration and I make a mistake on the transcription. Then I have to start all over. I don't like mistakes of any kind on the page.*

My father always appreciated that, Deem said. *He said your minutes were always the cleanest, well-written minutes.*

I just loved your father, Hester said. *A man of God.*

Did the council distract you at all, today? Deem asked. *Did you happen to hear anything they said?*

Yes, they kept talking about the problem in Ivins, Hester said. *I have an uncle who lives in Ivins. He's an apostate and a drunk, and I assumed they were talking about him. So it distracted me, and ruined my transcribing.*

Did they say your uncles name, specifically? Deem asked. *Did they say what the problem in Ivins was, exactly?*

No, Hester said, *they just referred to it several times as 'the problem in Ivins.' I just assumed it was about my uncle.*

What else did they talk about? Deem asked.

Oh, there was some new directive from Salt Lake, Hester said. *They didn't agree with it. They took a vote to reject it, which passed with ten in favor of rejecting, and two abstaining.*

Sounds like you really got distracted on that one! Deem said, smiling at Hester.

I supposed I did, Hester said. *You're not supposed to reject things from Salt Lake. I don't think you're even supposed to vote on them. You just accept the counsel, and follow the brethren.*

Do you know what the directive was? Deem asked.

Something about all councils following a new set of guidelines. They felt the directive wasn't practical, since they're dealing with the downwind River, and things are different here as a result. You can't correlate and standardize this area. Too many oddities for that. Or so they were inspired to feel.

Anything else? Deem asked.

There was a new initiate from Toquerville. He'll be taking his oaths at the next meeting.

So they add new members? Deem asked.

Occasionally, Hester said, *whenever there's a new gifted in a position of authority within the church.*

Do people leave the council if they're released from their church calling? Deem asked.

Depends, Hester said, *on how high up they are. If they're Stake Presidency or higher, they usually stay on. But anything lower than that they kick out. They don't usually admit Bishops in the first place, unless they really like them.*

Are they following bylaws? Deem asked. *Who makes the rules?*

Well, I suppose they do, as a group, Hester replied. *There's no rulebook that I know of. You know, you have your father's eyes and nose. Did I mention how much I admired your father?* Hester drifted very close to Deem, and it made her take a step back.

You're very kind to say so, Deem said. *So, just to be sure, there are no documents of any kind here? Other than your minutes, upstairs?*

No, Hester said. *Just my minutes for the third ward.*

And you don't keep minutes for the council?

No, I don't. They don't allow minutes.

That's it then, Deem thought to herself. *Dead end.*

My father would be very appreciative for the help you've given me, Deem said to Hester.

If you see him, please pass along my best wishes, Hester said. *And to Sister Hinton. I imagine his passing has been hard on her. And you.*

Yes, Deem said. *It has been hard. We really miss him.*

I do too, Hester said. *He was truly chosen of the Lord.*

Deem turned to leave the room.

I just think it's a shame, Hester said, half to himself.

What's that? Deem asked, turning back around. *What's a shame?*

What they're going to do to you, Hester said, returning to his desk.

Deem felt anxiety suddenly materialize within her, and become so pronounced it shot up her body and out the top of her head. She took a step toward Hester, wanting to be sure she heard what the man was saying.

What they're going to do to me? Deem asked, trying to mask the fear in her voice. *What are they going to do to me?*

They're going to destroy you, Hester said, picking up his pen and beginning to write. *It's a terrible, terrible shame.*

And with that, Brother Hester vanished.

Brother Hester? Deem called. *Brother Hester!*

The basement room was silent. She turned to Winn and dropped out of the River.

"Did you hear that?" Deem asked.

"Yes," Winn said. "He said they were going to destroy you."

"That's what I thought he said."

"He must have heard them discussing it."

"But kill me?" Deem asked. "Seems a bit extreme. What have I done to them?"

"Broken into their inner sanctum for starters," Winn said. "It's like Claude said – they're all about the secrets. You're uncovering too many of them."

"Yes, but kill me? I'm twenty, and I'm a girl. To them I'm just marriage bait. I can't possibly be a threat to them."

167

"There's nothing down here," Winn said. "Let's get out."

Deem walked to the stairwell and turned off the light. They walked back through the storage room, sliding the shelves back into place and replacing the boxes. Then they left the church and returned to Winn's Jeep.

Winn pulled out and began weaving through the streets of Caliente, back to the main road. The light from the tracking panel lit up the inside of the Jeep, bothering Winn's eyes.

"Can we disconnect that thing now?" he asked Deem, who was sitting silently, staring out the window. "We don't need it anymore, do we?"

Deem turned and picked up the screen. She reached for the cigarette lighter adapter and pulled. Just as the screen faded out, she saw the blue dot, moving. Then it was blank.

"Wait a minute," she said, plugging the adapter back in. The unit took a moment to come back on.

"Come on, come on!" Deem said, shaking the screen.

"What did you see?" Winn asked.

"I can't be sure but..." she said as the screen lit up once again. She studied it for a moment. "It's behind us."

"What's behind us?" Winn asked.

"The blue dot. Dayton. He's following us."

Winn looked in the rear view mirror. There were headlights in the distance. "How far back, can you tell?"

"A quarter mile or so," Deem said. "What if he's following us so he can..."

Winn looked at Deem. She looked sick to her stomach. Winn turned back and pressed his foot on the accelerator, increasing the speed of the Jeep to twenty miles per hour over the speed limit.

"When we get to Beryl Junction," Winn said, "I'm going to keep going straight. He should turn to go back to St. George. If he doesn't, we'll have reason to worry. Until then, let's not assume the worst."

"He obviously waited for us to leave the church before following us," Deem said. "He knows. Maybe Brother Hester turned me in somehow."

They sped through the hills east of Caliente, back toward the Utah state line. They covered the distance in half the normal time.

"How far behind us, now?" Winn asked.

"Same as before," Deem answered. "He's keeping right with us. There's too many turns in this road for you to see him back there."

"I could slow down and let him catch up," Winn said. "Make him go around us. We'd see him then."

"Too risky," Deem said. "I like your Beryl Junction idea better. How far to it?"

"Another twenty minutes," Winn said.

"Alright," Deem said. "Let's keep going, full speed."

Once or twice the road straightened out long enough for Winn to get a glimpse of car headlights behind them, in the distance.

"Even if he turns," Deem said, "it's too much of a coincidence. We were in that church for half an hour, at least. I can't believe he just happened to wait in his car for exactly that long before he started home. And he's carpooling! No way. They were waiting for us to leave."

"To, what, trail you?" Winn asked. "Why bother? He knows where you live. He doesn't need to trail you."

"You're right, it doesn't make sense," Deem said, "unless he intends to kill me now, on the way home. A lot less people around, out here, than in Mesquite."

Winn could tell Deem was really getting worked up. He could count on one hand the number of times he'd seen her this panicked. "Or maybe it's just to scare you," he said, trying to calm her. "We don't know if Hester knew what he was talking about or not. He just drops this comment and blips out. He didn't stick around for us to clarify what he meant. Let's see what happens at Beryl Junction."

Deem watched the blue dot on her screen as they approached the junction. It remained constant behind them, never varying in distance.

"It's up ahead," Winn said. "I'm going to slow down and let them catch up a little, so we can see them turn."

"I've got this map," Deem said. "I'll be able to see if they turn."

Winn slowed down his Jeep nonetheless, and passed the turn to St. George, continuing straight. The road ahead didn't have any curves. He slowed to twenty miles per hour and watched his rear view mirror.

The lights from the car behind them covered the distance rapidly.

"They're not turning," Winn said. The lights were approaching at a great deal of speed. Winn was afraid he was going to slow and would be hit.

"They passed the junction," Deem said. "They're still following us."

Winn pulled his Jeep off the road. The car behind them was barreling down on them, not slowing. Just as he got the wheels of the Jeep off the asphalt and onto the gravel, the car behind them sped by. Deem felt the Jeep shake from the wind turbulence.

They both watched the tail lights of the car passing away from them down the road.

"Was that him?" Winn asked. "I didn't see what kind of car it was. I was trying to get off the road so it didn't hit me!"

"They're still behind us," Deem said, observing the map.

"Impossible," Winn said. "There's nothing back there."

Deem showed him the screen. "It passed the turn off, still following us. He's back there."

"How far back?" Winn asked.

"I don't know," Deem said. "A thousand feet? A quarter mile? I'm not sure. There's no scale on this thing."

"Is it moving?" Winn asked.

"No, it's still," Deem said. "Not moving."

Winn made a U turn and drove back down the highway. "Is it still there?" he asked.

"Yes," Deem said. "We're coming up on it. Slow down."

"There's nothing here, Deem."

Winn looked in his rear view mirror. No cars – the road was empty. Late on a Sunday night, cars should be few and far between on this desolate stretch of highway. He let the car drift forward.

"It says we're on it," Deem said, reading the screen. "It's right here."

"There's no car here," Winn said.

"What the fuck?" Deem asked. "It's got to be!"

Winn squinted at the other side of the road and stopped the Jeep, turning the wheels a little toward the other lane of traffic, the one they'd sped down just moments before. He put the headlights on high beam, and stepped out of the car. He was assaulted by a dry wind.

Deem looked at the window of the Jeep in disbelief. At first she thought it was a bird, but then she realized a bird couldn't remain stationary off the ground. There, floating about four feet off the as-

phalt, in the middle of the road, was the tracking device. A few pieces of duct tape still hung from it, flapping in the wind. She watched
as Winn walked up to it and grabbed it. Then he got back into the
Jeep. He handed it to Deem.

"They're fucking with us," Winn said.

She turned it over in her hand, examining it, becoming angry. It
looked exactly the same as when she'd placed it under the BMW.
"We're gonna fuck back," she replied.

10

"Are you sure about this?" Winn asked as he pulled his Jeep into Dayton's driveway, parking directly behind the BMW. "It seems a little reactionary."

Deem opened the door to the Jeep. "Come on," she said. "I need you as a witness." She slammed the Jeep's door closed and began marching up to the front door of Dayton's house.

"A witness?" Winn asked, following her.

"I'm not going to be intimidated by these people," Deem said. "They need to know that."

Deem pounded on the door. It opened, and Deem was ready to start laying into the person opening it. Then she realized it was a small boy, maybe five years old.

"Hello?" he asked.

"Is your father here?" Deem said. "I need to speak with him."

The boy turned and ran away, leaving the door open. "Dad!" he yelled as he disappeared deeper into the house.

Deem pushed the door open and stepped into the entryway. Winn remained outside.

"Come on," she said. "They won't know the kid didn't invite us in."

"You're scaring me a little," Winn said.

"You love it," Deem answered.

"Yeah, I kinda do," Winn replied.

A woman emerged from around a corner and walked toward them. She was tall, lean, and pretty. "Deem?" she said as she approached. "Is that you?"

"Hello, Sister Dayton," Deem said, trying to tamp down the anger in her voice. "I need to see Brother Dayton. Is he home? It's urgent."

"I think he just got back from a meeting," she said, eyeing Deem and then giving Winn a once over. "How are you? I haven't seen you since the funeral. I hope you're doing well."

"Well enough," Deem said.

"I haven't seen you at church in a while," the woman said.

Always watching, Deem thought. *Nothing ever slips by these people.*

"That's what I need to speak to Brother Dayton about," Deem replied.

At that moment Dayton arrived in the room, the small five-year-old boy in tow.

"Sister Hinton," Dayton said, approaching Deem. He extended his hand for the customary handshake. Deem took it, playing along.

"Can I speak with you?" Deem said. "I really need to talk to you for a moment."

"It's late," Dayton said. "I'm on family time at the moment. Can I schedule an appointment with you for tomorrow?"

"It's urgent," Deem said. "Ten minutes, and I promise I'll be done." She turned to Dayton's wife. "I'm sorry for the interruption at home, Sister Dayton. It's just..." Deem looked like she might break into tears.

"Joe, you'd better see her," Dayton's wife said, grabbing Dayton by the arm. "I'll keep the kids downstairs." She grabbed the five-year-old's arm and they left the entryway, disappearing deeper into the house.

"Do we have anything to talk about?" Dayton asked. "Really?"

"We do," Deem said.

"Then come into the living room," Dayton said, waving them to the right. "Have a seat."

Deem picked a couch where Winn joined her. Dayton sat across from them in a leather chair.

Winn looked around the room. It was expensively furnished. Above the fireplace was a large picture of the St. George temple, in a gilded, ornate frame.

"What can I do for you?" Dayton asked.

"You'd like me to stop following you," Deem asked. "Fine. I will. You give me my father's journals, and you'll never hear from me again."

"I don't have your father' journals," Dayton said.

"Then where are they?"

"I have no idea."

"I don't believe you."

"Doesn't change the fact that I don't know where they are. Usually a person keeps them at home. Have you checked at home?"

"I'm not some stupid kid you can condescend to," Deem said.

"I don't think you are. It's late. Is there anything else?"

"We both know you're part of a secret organization," Deem said. "I'd hate to have to spill the beans about it to people. Spread the secret around."

"I think you're misunderstanding something, Sister Hinton, and I would strongly advise you against this course of action."

"What was all that up in Caliente?" Deem asked. "We talked with Brother Hester. He said you intend to kill me."

"Brother Hester? In Caliente? He died thirty years ago. I think you must be mistaken."

"How can you lie like this?" Deem asked. "You just go repent to yourself and call it good?"

"Sister Hinton, I think something's gone wrong. You used to have the spirit in you. I remember you bearing your testimony as a little girl. You were so sweet, but more than that, you were always dynamic, a real powerhouse. But something has happened. I suspect it has to do with losing your father, who was a righteous father in Zion, a man I greatly respected. Now you seem to be filled with the spirit of contention. I think you might be in need of care, some kind of mental help. The things you're saying – well, they seem delusional; I don't know what else to call it."

"How dare you bring my grief over my father into this," Deem asked. "It's all a game to you, isn't it? Pretend to be just a counselor in a Stake Presidency, when we both know you're much more than that. Something every normal member of the church around here would find evil."

"I take my calling very seriously, young lady," Dayton said, standing. "I realize something has upset you, but I assure you there's little I can do about it. Or need to do about it. Our meeting is over, it's time to go."

Deem sat on the couch, fuming. Things hadn't gone with Dayton how she'd imagine them going on the ride back into town. She stood and turned to Winn.

"We'll find another way to locate his journals," she said to Winn. "Then we'll expose these motherfuckers." She walked out of the living room and to the entryway.

"Sister Hinton," Dayton said, "I do not allow that kind of language in this house."

"What are you going to do?" Deem repeated, turning to Dayton. "What exactly are you going to do, you so-called man of God?"

Dayton's calm exterior had broken, and his eyes betrayed his anger. "I'm not going to do anything," he said, measuring each word. "The Lord will take care of you. He's got plans for you."

Deem walked up to Dayton and stuck her face in his. "You gonna kill me?" Deem said. "You and your little band of gifteds who meet in the dark, in secret, like criminals? Like Gadianton robbers? How are you going to do it? Blood atonement style? Are they going to find me in my bed, my throat slit from ear to ear? Is it going to be you? Are you going to slide the knife? Or are you going to hire a Danite to do it?"

Dayton pushed Deem back.

"Take your hands off her!" Winn said, stepping between the two of them and pushing Dayton away from Deem.

"We're not going to do anything," Dayton hissed. "You're targeted by a skinwalker. You're dead already."

Deem looked at Dayton, examining his face. He was angry, but truthful. "You guys are a piece of work," Deem said. "Do you monitor everything around here?"

"Everything," Dayton said, staring back at her. "*Everything.*"

"I'm not some powerless little member who needs the help of the church to get by," Deem said. "I can deal with the skinwalker on my own."

"Not this one," Dayton said. "I know what you're capable of. You're punching above your weight, with both me and the skinwalker. It's a shame to lose you, because of how much I respected your father. But unless you repent, you'll be used up soon."

"Did my father behave this way?" Deem asked. "When he was part of your secret club? Was he as reprehensible as you?"

Dayton pressed his lips closed and stared back at Deem. He was refusing to answer.

"He was? He was as evil as you?" she asked.

She stared Dayton down for a second more, then turned. "Come on Winn, I gotta get some air. The stink of hypocrisy is choking me."

She opened the door to the house and walked outside.

"If you harm her," Winn said to Dayton as he turned to follow Deem, "I'll kill you."

"The skinwalker isn't my doing," Dayton said. "You two started that on your own."

"I was in that bus, too, with Deem and her mother and aunt," Winn said. "Why hasn't it targeted me? It's funny that it only targeted Deem's family."

"What you don't know could fill the world," Dayton said. "You don't even know yourself."

"You really are a hypocrite," Winn said.

"The Lord works in mysterious ways," Dayton said. "I don't expect a sodomite gentile like you to understand it. You're a far bigger threat to her than me, corrupting her spirit, destroying her chances at the celestial kingdom. She'd be better off if you'd just crawl back under that rock you came from."

Winn turned and left Dayton standing alone in the entryway. Deem was already in the Jeep. Winn jumped into the vehicle, started it up, and backed out of the driveway.

"What was that about?" Deem asked.

"I wanted to threaten him," Winn said. "So I did."

Deem smiled. "It won't work with him," she said. "I know these people. They think they're above everything. Including the law. Everything I said to him in there was a waste. I shouldn't have come here."

"Well, it felt good to say it," Winn said. "He called me a sodomite gentile."

"Ha!" Deem said, laughing so hard spit flew from her lips and landed on the dashboard. "In their world, that's the best insult they can come up with!"

"Yeah, 'motherfucker' had much more panache," Winn said.

Deem laughed even harder, slapping her hand against the dash.

"Did you see him recoil when you said it?" Winn asked. "It was like you'd slapped him."

"Oh god," Deem said, trying to breathe. "I really shouldn't think that's funny, with all that's going on. But I can't help it."

Winn watched her laugh. It made him smile to see her let loose for a moment. "It's been hours since you've had a Big Gulp," Winn said. "I'll bet you're really jonesing for one."

"God, yes," Deem said. "And some food."

"How about we just go to Home Plate and you can load up on soda there?"

"Sure," Deem said, still giggling, struggling to breathe normally. "Sodomite gentile!" she repeated, and burst into another round of laughter. "Oh, I am *so* going to use that!"

■ ■ ■

"What was all that about robbers?" Winn asked Deem as they sat in a booth at the restaurant. He was guzzling a beer and she was sipping on Diet Coke.

"Oh, you mean at Dayton's?" Deem asked.

"Yeah. You called the secret council 'gaddy-something robbers'. And Danites. What is all that?"

"I knew it would bother him," Deem said. "Gadianton Robbers. They're characters from the Book of Mormon. They were considered an evil, secret organization that would extort governments. Kind of like an organized crime syndicate, but really big."

"It did bother him," Winn said. "I saw the look on his face when you brought it up. And Danites?"

"When the church was still in Missouri, before they moved to Utah, they were under heavy persecution from the locals. To fight back, Joseph Smith organized a secret group of people to do the church's dirty work. They operated in secret, and they were called Danites. The name comes from the book of Daniel in the Old Testament. Anyway, they'd fight back against the Missourians. It's what led Missouri to issue their extermination order."

"Extermination order?" Winn asked. "Extermination of what?"

"Mormons," Deem said.

"A U.S. state issued an order to exterminate all Mormons?" Winn asked. "I find that hard to believe."

"You weren't paying attention in history class," Deem said. "Missouri hated the Mormons. Especially when a Danite shot the Governor."

"You're making this up!" Winn said as the food arrived and he dived into a patty melt.

"No, I'm not!" Deem said, pouring ketchup over her fries. "The order wasn't rescinded until 1976. Anyway, when the Mormons moved to Utah in 1847, the Danites came with them. People think they took orders from Brigham Young, but since they operated in secret, no one knows. The rumors have always persisted though. Many people think they're still active today, controlled by the church. They clean up problems, put pressure on enemies of the church, that kind of thing."

"Like Men in Black?" Winn asked.

"I guess, if Men in Black are even real."

"Oh, they're real."

"Here we go with the UFO shit again."

"It's not shit, Deem."

"Well, whatever. I have no idea if they exist or not. But think about this, Winn. We're both gifted, right? And we got it from our parents. My father was gifted, so was your mom. They got it from their parents, and so on. This goes way back. Who knows when it first started? Maybe it's existed from the very beginning. That means, throughout history, there have been gifted people operating in society, including the Mormon church, right? It's not just Dayton and my father. They've existed all along. This secret council that Dayton is part of might have been formed in the earliest days of Mormonism, and there's probably similar groups in other religions. Maybe that's what parts of Opus Dei are, to the Catholics. We just have to deal with it here because there's so many Mormons, kind of like how we have to deal with the mutations in the River because we're downwind. If we were back east, it might be a group of secret Catholics, or in the south, secret Baptists. When someone finds out they're gifted, and they're also part of a religion, they've got to balance it somehow. Make both halves work. The leaders of the regions wouldn't sanction it, that's for sure, so they operate in secret. Having the gift doesn't mean you ditch all of your religious beliefs."

"You seem to have," Winn said.

"Well, I'm different," Deem said.

"Really?"

"Yeah, I always thought it was bullshit. It was easy to stop going. But it wasn't for my father."

"Well, you obviously knew what to say to upset Dayton," Winn said. "He was furious."

"Good, he pissed me off," Deem said, taking a bite of her hamburger.

"Do you think he had anything to do with the skinrunner?" Winn asked.

"I don't see how," Deem said. "You were turned on to that by your friend who drove the bus. I think the council just monitors things very closely. They might have a device that tells them if something paranormal occurs within a certain area. I don't know what the purpose of their secret council is, what they actually do. But part of it involves keeping an eye on anything unusual going on. We should talk to Claude about it, maybe he knows more."

"We've got to finish off that skinrunner first," Winn said. "Your mother can't keep digging bones out of her skin forever."

"Dayton talked like it was going to finish *me* off," Deem said. "I don't see it. Based on everything Awan has told us, I've got the thing on the ropes already. We just have to deliver the knockout."

"Maybe it's got more tools to use against you than Awan knows about," Winn said. "They're mutations; they change constantly. I think the best thing we can do is eliminate the skinrunner as quickly as we can, especially now that we know Dayton considers it a threat to you."

"We've got to figure out who the skinrunner killed," Deem said. "When I get home, I'll get on the computer and start researching."

"Let me know when you have a name," Winn said, "and I'll call Awan so he can hook us up with his sister."

"Speaking of Awan, did you two do anything in that motel room?" Deem asked.

"If we did, I wouldn't tell you," Winn said. "It'd just get you upset."

"Maybe not," Deem said, trying her best to be cavalier about the subject. She resented that Winn thought she was a prude.

"I'm not falling for that," Winn said. "You would get upset, I know you."

Deem knew he was right. She decided to let it drop and finish her meal quickly, so she could return home and start researching.

■ ■ ■

"So your sister is gifted, too?" Deem asked, sitting in the front seat of Awan's car. They were bouncing down a dirt road about a mile outside of Littlefield, headed to a small trailer in the distance. The sun was starting to go down.

"A little," Awan said. "Not as much as me. I think her personality didn't mesh well with her ability."

As Deem wondered what that meant, Winn leaned forward from the back seat and pointed out the window ahead of them. "Are those cop cars?"

"Shit," Awan said. "She's always in trouble."

Two police cars were heading back down the dirt road toward them. Awan edged his car to the side of the road so they could pass. He observed who was in the back seat of one of the cars.

"They took Theron," Awan said.

"Who's Theron?" Deem asked.

"My sister's boyfriend," Awan said. "Wonder what happened. Well, we'll find out. I should warn you, my sister is a little strange. It might be a good idea to let me do most of the talking."

Deem looked back at Winn, concerned. Winn was just smiling, as though meeting Awan's sister was something he was looking forward to.

At the end of the dirt road was an old trailer. Awan pulled his car up next to it and they all got out. There were junked cars and piles of metal garbage surrounding the trailer. Deem thought it reminded her of Mad Max.

"Aggie?" Awan called as they approached the trailer. The trailer door opened, revealing part of a woman – just the part that the doorway could reveal. There was obviously much more of her beyond.

"Aggie, these are my friends, Winn and Deem," Awan said, walking toward the trailer. "What was that all about with the police?"

"Theron was pissing me off," Aggie said from the doorway. "So I cut myself and told them he'd done it. They hauled his ass away for domestic abuse."

She turned, the doorway revealing her side and then back. There was no seeing past her into the trailer. She was immense.

"Aggie, I need you to find out something for me," Awan said.

The figure in the doorway turned, and sat. Aggie still filled the doorway, even five feet back from it. Deem realized they were not going to enter the trailer.

"What?" Aggie said.

"Deem here has got a skinwalker on her," Awan said. "We need to know who the skinwalker killed, where he's buried."

"Oh, I don't like skinwalkers," Aggie said, shaking her head. Large pockets of flesh on either side of her face continued to jiggle after she'd stopped shaking it.

Awan produced a bottle of Johnny Walker Red and placed it on a wooden picnic table.

"Just the one?" Aggie said, eyeing the bottle.

"I'll bring you another for your birthday," Awan said.

"These new skinwalkers, Awan, they're bad news," Aggie said, snorting a little. "You sure?"

"We're already down that road, Aggie," Awan said. "She's got to get rid of it. Talk to Bune."

"Name?" Aggie asked.

"Evan Eugene Braithwaite was the victim," Awan said. "John Carl Braithwaite is the skinwalker."

"You got something he can smell?" Aggie asked.

Awan walked to Deem and took the banker box from her, then walked up to the trailer's door and handed the box to Aggie. She stood up and took the box, then turned and slowly waddled deeper into the trailer.

Awan returned to the picnic table and sat. "This might take a while," he said. Deem and Winn joined him at the table. Deem felt little pieces of peeled paint crush under her butt as she sat down on the bench.

"So what's she doing in there?" Winn asked.

"The only way Aggie has ever used her gift," Awan said, "is with Bune. He lives in an abandoned well under her trailer. When she discovered Bune, she moved out here to be next to him. Placed the bedroom of her trailer right over the well."

"Bune is a ghost?" Deem asked.

"Something between a ghost and a demon," Awan said. "The radiation has actually mellowed him out. He killed the people who dug the well, years ago."

"How did Aggie find him?" Deem asked.

"She was dating a guy who lived in Littlefield and was obsessed with metal detectors," Awan said. "She was much thinner back then. He'd take her all over these parts, looking for coins and metals. She found this well when they were out here, and she struck up a relationship with Bune. Eventually she moved this trailer out here to be next to him. Like I said, it's the only way she knows how to exercise her gift. They've come to some kind of mutual arrangement. They help each other out. I think, over the years, they've come to really like each other. Aggie's put on a lot of weight, as you can see. She's got the diabetes. I don't think she'll live much longer. But she'll stay out here with Bune until her last day."

Deem stifled a cry of shock as a figure materialized across the table from her. It had the body of a man, nude, but the head of a dog – it looked like a pit bull. In a flash it climbed on top of the table and the dog's head pressed itself against Deem. Its nose slid down between her breasts. She fell back off the bench, onto the ground. The man, on all fours, leapt off the table onto her, and ground its dog-nose into her crotch.

Awan and Winn shot to their feet. All of the windows of the trailer were open, and from inside they could hear Aggie. "No, Bune! No!"

The dog head continued to sniff Deem. She wanted to swing at the dog, but wasn't sure if that would just anger the creature. *Dogs stick their noses on people all the time,* she thought, *but this one has the body of a man. What the fuck do I do?*

Winn moved to pull the creature off Deem but Awan stopped him. "You don't want to touch it," Awan said.

The dog lifted its head and moved up Deem's body. When it got to her face, it began to lick her. The man part of the creature was now positioned over her body. The body was big, lean, and muscular. Deem could feel its erection pressing against her.

"Goddamnit, Bune!" they heard from inside the trailer. "Get off her. Bune! No!"

The dog lifted its head to look at the trailer. As quickly as it had appeared, it faded away and was gone.

Winn raced to Deem's side and helped her up.

"What the fuck?" Deem said.

"Sorry about that," Awan said. "I forgot he can be a little exuberant around females. I've never seen him that excited."

"It's 'cause she's gifted," they heard Aggie say from inside the trailer. "You didn't tell me she was gifted, Awan."

"Oh," Awan said. "I didn't realize it mattered."

"Of course it matters," Aggie bellowed. "Bune goes for us girls with the gift, don't you, boy?"

Deem shuddered, sitting back down on the picnic table bench.

"You OK?" Winn asked.

"I'm fine," Deem said. "Just feel a little violated."

"I'm sorry," Awan said. "It didn't occur to me he might do something like that, or I would have warned you."

"So he's a dog?" Deem asked, brushing herself off.

"No," Awan said. "Just a dog head. He's much more than that. You know how, if you trance, you can get at information you normally can't see?"

"Yeah," Winn said.

"Well, you and I need proximity to do that," Awan said. "I can't just trance and start observing Paris or London. I can only observe around here, where I'm at."

"Bune can go further?" Deem asked.

"If he has a scent," Awan said. "If you give him something someone has touched, he can follow the scent anywhere. Including the past."

"Like a dog," Deem said.

"I think he was originally a rock demon," Awan said. "Let loose by the people who dug the well. There's a reason there's no one else out this way; for years he terrorized the place. Somehow Aggie was able to communicate with him. He won't talk to anyone but her."

"So she's Bune's master, in a way?" Winn asked.

"Kind of," Awan said. "He's nice enough to her. But he can be trouble if he's angry. That's why I didn't want you to touch him. I know a guy who lost an arm that way."

Winn gulped.

"So Aggie has never done anything more with the gift?" Deem asked, her voice lowered.

"No," Awan whispered back. "Her whole life has been Bune, ever since she met him. It's one of the reasons she let herself go. She really doesn't care about anything else."

"Not even her boyfriend?" Winn asked.

"The one she just had falsely arrested?" Awan said.

"Point taken," Winn said.

"How long will this take?" Deem asked. "And do you think he'll attack me again?"

"I don't think he will," Awan said. "Aggie's got a hold of him now. I'd give it twenty or thirty minutes."

Deem watched as the bats began to fly overhead, rapidly collecting the day's bugs. She remembered when she was a little girl and thought they were "night birds," fast little birds that flew only at dusk. She remembered a day when she was about ten, and one of them had gotten inside the house somehow. It flew rapidly from room to room, including her bedroom. At first she thought it was a bird, and she was delighted. Then it landed on her bedspread, a few feet from her face, and she saw its wings and little mouth, opening and closing, exposing sharp little teeth. She screamed, and her father came running. When he entered her room, he grabbed the first thing he could find – a large, thick bible that Deem had been given in Primary. He swung at the bat, and it fell to the ground in Deem's bedroom doorway, stunned. Her father pulled the bedroom door over it and trapped it under the edge of the door. Deem hopped out of bed and examined the bat while her father went to get a bag to put it in. Having been whacked with a five pound bible, it didn't have much fight left in it. Deem could see its eyes move and its mouth open and close. Suddenly she felt bad for it. It wasn't the bat's fault it had gotten inside the house. It didn't deserve to die, just because she'd screamed when she saw it. She got closer to the bat, intending to pet it with her finger, maybe make it feel better. As she got close to it, it snapped at her and she screamed again. Her father told her to leave the bat alone, scooped it into a paper bag, and took it outside, where he dumped it onto the lawn. It sat there for hours. Deem would check on it every few minutes, waiting to see if it would regain its senses and fly away, like a trout that's been caught and released but hadn't yet started to swim. Eventually she forgot about it. When she checked on it the next day, it was gone. She worried the bat would remember her and hunt her down. Now, whenever the bats came out at dusk, she had a faint fear that they'd seek revenge for the one she'd harmed.

"Alright," Aggie said, reappearing at the doorway. "Here's the scoop."

They all turned to face her. She sat in the doorway as before, filling all available space.

"Somebody write this down, I ain't gonna repeat it," she said.

"I'll remember it," Deem replied.

"Alright," Aggie said. "He took his brother down to an old mining shack south of Devil's Throat. His brother was allergic to bee stings. He trapped him inside the shack, then he took a log and banged on the walls of the shack to stir up a hornet's nest. His brother was stung hundreds of times, and died from the poison. Once the hornets died down, he buried him about fifty feet from the shack. That's your guy."

"Can you tell me where the shack is, exactly?" Deem asked.

"Well," Aggie said, "you know the road that goes south from Devil's Throat? Not the one that goes east, but the one that goes south?"

"Yeah, I know it."

"Well, you take that road. It's gonna go a ways. When you get near the end of it, it's gonna jog a bit to the left," Aggie raised her hands to illustrate the jog, her arm flesh reverberating from the hand movements. "Well, you go past that, and there's another jog to the right. You go past that, and there's a wash you drive over. You walk up that wash about a quarter mile, then go up a hill on the right."

"Sounds like the Hardesty Mine," Deem said. "Is that it?"

"I don't know the name of it, honey," Aggie replied. "But at the top of the hill is a rock. You go around it, and there's the mine. Go further up the hill, and there's the shack. You trance at the shack, you'll find him."

"Thank you," Deem said. "I really appreciate it."

Aggie extended her hand, wiggling her fingers. At first Deem thought she might be wanting to shake hands, but then she realized Aggie had her hand pointed at the bottle on the picnic table.

"Awan," she said. "I'll take that Johnny Walker now."

11

Deem heard Winn honking in front of her house. She'd just removed a bone fragment from her mother's arm, with Aunt Virginia looking on.

"I've got to go," Deem said. "Keep an eye on her," she said to her aunt. "She should improve quickly, just like before."

"We've got to call the exterminator," Virginia said. "Really Deem, we can't go on like this."

"I'm working on it," Deem said. "Trust me." She left her mother's bedroom and raced to the door. Winn was waiting in his Jeep.

"Morning," he said as she jumped in.

"7-11, then off to Devil's Throat," Deem said.

"Good morning to you, too, Winn," Winn said.

"Sorry," Deem said. "I've been rushing around. Mom's still under attack by the skinrunner. My aunt thinks its spider bites, at least that's what I've told her. I'm worried she'll get sick of digging the bones out and try something else instead. We've got to shut this guy down."

Winn pulled into the 7-11 and they both went inside. Winn returned with a coffee, and Deem with her usual Big Gulp.

"You should get one of those refillable mugs," Winn said. "At the rate you go through pop, you'd save money."

"I'm not middle aged yet!" Deem said. "Please!"

"What, you're saying only middle aged women use refillable mugs?"

"Yes, haven't you noticed?"

"So you use a new cup each time, even though it'd be cheaper to do the refill, just because you think it would make you look old?"

"I'm not carrying around a nasty old mug."

Winn shook his head. "Whatever."

They drove toward Bunkerville and then down the small roads to Devil's Throat. It was slow going, but they were used to the route.

"I wonder how Jason is doing?" Deem said as they passed Devil's Throat, remembering the events that had occurred there.

"You should give Eliza and Steven a call and find out," Winn said.

"Or you could," Deem said. "Been kinda busy."

"I wonder if Roy has tried out the EM gun yet," Winn said. "He told me he'd let me know how it worked."

"I don't know about you," Deem said, "but Jason didn't seem a hundred percent to me when they left. I mean, I don't know the guy, so I don't know what he was normally like, but he just seemed a little off."

"He'd just been ripped out of St. Thomas," Winn said. "And then all that with Michael. He was bound to be a little off."

"It's not that," Deem said. "Something else."

"Oh, the residual stuff?"

"Yeah. That's why I'm wondering how he's doing back in Seattle."

"Are you sure you're not just wondering if he remembers you?"

Deem shot Winn a skeptical look.

"Hey, he's a good looking guy," Winn said. "I can see why you'd be interested in him."

"I didn't say I was interested in him," Deem said. "Really Winn, you always assume everything's about sex."

"I said 'interested in him,' not that you wanted to fuck him."

Deem winced when Winn said 'fuck.' Winn noticed.

"What, I can't say 'fuck' now?" Winn said. "You say it all the time."

"Not in that context."

"So it's alright to say as a swear word, but not if it refers to sex?"

"Right."

"That's really kind of fucked up, no pun intended."

"You'll never understand because you're so crude," Deem said.

"And you're just hung up on it," Winn said.

"No, quite the opposite. I merely think that sex is more personal and private. Doesn't need to be discussed the way you do."

"You're the one who always brings it up!" Winn said, a little exasperated. "And you say 'fuck' ten times more than I do!"

"In context."

"Yeah, you said that already. Fuck is fuck in my book, context be damned."

"I was just wondering if Jason had returned to normal, that's all. You're the one who brought up the sex."

"So you think something was embedded in him? Do you think Steven and Roy are in danger?"

"Don't know," Deem said. "I did warn Roy about it, before they left. You've seen it before, did you think he was embedded?"

"The safe bet would be to assume that he was," Winn said. "No way to know for sure until something emerges. At least, there's no way to know that I've discovered. No test or anything."

"What happens when it emerges?" Deem asked.

"Every embedding is different," Winn said. "I knew one girl who became depressed and killed herself. There was another in Henderson, authorities caught her trying to poison the town's water supply."

"Damn," Deem said. "Steven and Roy really could be at risk."

"Well, you warned Roy. He's a smart old man. He'll be on the lookout."

"I like Roy," Deem said. "He was fun to be around."

"Me too. We should go see them sometime. They did invite us up."

"I'd be willing to go when this is all over."

"Do you know this mining shack Aggie was describing?"

"I think so. Her directions were screwy, but if it's the one I think it is, we'll see the wash in about ten minutes."

Deem directed Winn off-road once they reached the sandy wash, and Winn drove around boulders in the dry streambed. They climbed slightly, and Deem had Winn stop the Jeep when she noticed the hill that led to the mine.

"That's it," she said. "Let's take water. I'm not taking any lights. I don't see any reason to go into the mine here. We only need to contact Evan in the shack."

"Well, I'm bringing a flashlight just in case," Winn said.

They trekked up the side of the hill. As they crested it, Deem saw the outcropping of bushes that had grown over the mine entrance and the small white sign placed there by authorities to warn people away.

"Around this way," she said, circling past the mine entrance and further up the hill. "Shafts used to lead from the shack into the mine, but they were sealed over years ago."

They rounded the hill and the shack came into view.

"Can't believe it's still standing," Winn said. "It looks like it's one storm away from collapsing."

Bushes had grown up around the shack, but the door to it was still accessible. Deem walked up to it and pushed it open. It creaked as it swung back. She bent down and looked at the door's hinges.

"These are new," she said. "He made sure he could trap his brother in here before he brought him up."

"And there's a new gate lock on the door itself," Winn said, walking past Deem and into the building.

"Careful," Deem said. "Hornets."

Winn turned on his flashlight and pointed up to the ceiling of the shack. "Look!" he said to Deem, who walked over to join him. They could see several hornets buzzing around the nest.

Deem scanned the rest of the shack. There was no way out, no windows or back doors. Only the one door they'd come in.

"So he must have died right here, on the floor," Deem said, looking down.

"Then John dragged him outside to bury him," Winn said. "Where do you want to try to contact him? In here, or outside?"

"Outside," Deem said. "The hornets make me nervous."

They walked out of the shack, and Deem looked for an area of open ground where they could sit. She located a spot behind the shack.

"You'll watch over me?" Deem asked Winn.

"I will," Winn said. "Go ahead and start. I'll make sure you're safe."

Deem sat cross-legged on the dirt, the warmth of the earth radiating up through her jeans and into her skin. She closed her eyes, and let herself fall into the River. Then she focused on the shack, on the inside floor where she imagined Evan had died. She kept the focus until she felt the trance form around her and become solid. Once the trance was complete, she felt free to walk around.

Evan! she called. *Evan Braithwaite!*

She listened, hoping she'd hear a call back. Nothing came.

Within her trance, she stood and walked to the shack. The door was shut, the gate lock thrown. She could hear a loud buzzing sound inside, and screams.

She passed through the door of the shack, and saw Evan on the floor. He was twisting back and forth, rolling on the floorboards of the shack, attempting to squash the dozens of insects that were on him. His face was already grotesquely swollen. He was struggling for air.

Evan! she called.

If Evan heard her, he didn't respond. He kept rolling back and forth on the floor, screaming. She watched as he struggled to breathe and his body began to shake, anaphylactic shock setting in. Eventually the shaking stopped, and he lay still on his stomach, face down. The hornets disappeared.

He won't come in for another half hour, Evan said. *He waits until he's sure the hornets have calmed down and returned to the nest.*

Who? Deem asked, already knowing the answer.

John, my brother, Evan said meekly into the floor below him. *Somehow the door locked. He was too far away to hear me. He forgot I was in here.*

Evan began to cry, still facing down.

Deem hadn't had much experience with normal ghosts. She was used to the kind that transformed and chased her. Evan was different. He was playing out a pattern, as Awan had said. *He doesn't realize his brother killed him,* Deem thought. *He thinks it was an accident.*

When he comes in, Deem asked Evan, *after a half hour, what does he do?*

He buries me, Evan said, *outside.*

Why doesn't he take you back into town? So you can have a proper burial, with a funeral?

Evan didn't respond.

Normally that's what people would do, especially a brother, Deem said.

Evan began crying again. *It hurts so bad,* he said. *I can't breathe. I need my EpiPen.* He rolled over to face Deem. His skin was blue and covered in hives. She tried not to respond to the horror of it, but she wasn't sure Evan could even see her – the flesh around his eyes had nearly swollen them shut.

Can you take me to where you're buried? Deem asked.

It's outside, Evan said. He rose from the floor and drifted through the walls of the shack. Deem followed him. There was Winn, watching over her body. She passed by him and followed Evan as he made his way through brush. He stopped at a barely perceptible mound.

Here, he said, staring down.

Why did he bury you here? Deem asked.

I don't know. I was dead, I suppose. Evan's breathing consisted of loud wheezes at he tried to pull air in and out through his swollen throat.

But he should have taken your body back to town. Had a funeral, so your wife would know where you are. Your wife thinks you've gone missing, just like the rest of your family and friends. Your brother John knows you're not missing, doesn't he? He buried you out here in the middle of nowhere so they wouldn't find you.

He did, Evan wheezed, wiping tears from his swollen face.

Why did he do that, Evan? Deem asked. *There must have been a reason. Why didn't he let you out of the shack, when it was full of hornets?*

I don't know, Evan said, frustrated. *I don't know why. He was too far away to hear me. I couldn't breathe – I needed my EpiPen.*

Because he killed you, Deem said. *He left you in that shack so you'd get stung. He knew you were allergic, didn't he?*

Yes, Evan said. *He's bringing it to me.*

Bringing you what?

My EpiPen.

But he didn't bring you anything, did he? And he buried you out here, so people wouldn't know he'd killed you.

No! Evan said, wailing. *He wouldn't do that! He was my brother. He loved me.*

He killed you so he could become a skinwalker, Deem said. *He had to kill someone he loved. He chose you. He planned all of this. He led you out here, trapped you in the shack, made sure the hornets stung you, and then he buried you. He let your family think you'd disappeared. They're still wondering what happened to you.*

No, no! Evan cried, trying to suck in air. *That's cruel. He wouldn't have done that.*

He did, Deem said. *That's why you're buried out here in the dirt, instead of a nice cemetery back in town. What other explanation is there?*

Evan raised his eyes from the grave to look at Deem. *He went to get my EpiPen. He's bringing it.* Evan looked down at his grave, then back up at Deem. *He killed me?* he asked.

Yes, Deem said. *I didn't see it happen, but I talked to someone who did. They told me you were here. That's why I came. We have to stop John. He's hurting more people since he killed you.*

I can't believe he'd do that, Evan said. *It's not like him. He's bringing me my EpiPen. He just needs to hurry. He can't hear me.*

How else do you explain why you're buried out here, Evan? Deem said patiently. She was beginning to become frustrated, but she knew she had to remain calm with Evan, convince him to work with her.

And now he's trying to put other people in the ground, too. Innocent people, just like you. He's sick, Evan. Your brother has become a monster, preying on people. Meanwhile, you stay here, getting stung by hornets until you swell up and die, over and over again. Aren't you tired of it?

It hurts so bad, Evan said, clutching his chest. *I can't breathe.*

Evan? Deem said. *Evan? Are you listening to me?*

He can't open the door, something must be stopping him. Maybe he doesn't know I'm in here. Maybe he can't hear me. John! I need my EpiPen! I can't breathe!

Urrgh! Deem thought to herself. *I can't get through to this guy.*

Evan! she said. *He killed you. He knew the hornets would kill you. That's why the door never opens. He comes in after you're dead, and buries you, to hide you, to cover up the fact that he killed you!*

That's not like him, Evan said, a fresh round of crying starting up. *He loved me. John! I can't breathe!*

Deem abruptly left the trance. She stood up in front of Winn.

"Arrrrgh!" she growled at Winn, raising her hands into claws. "I would strangle him, but he's already having problems breathing."

"Who?" Winn said, taking a step back. "Evan?"

"Yes, Evan!" Deem said, pacing. "The idiot won't listen to me. He keeps babbling on, saying the same things over and over."

"Did you explain that his brother killed him?" Winn asked.

"Of course I did!" Deem yelled.

"Hey, don't take it out on me!" Winn said.

"Sorry," Deem said, calming down. She kept pacing. "I explained the whole thing to him, several times. He seems happy to just keep getting stung until he dies, and complaining about how his brother doesn't open the door to the shack. I asked him why he thought his brother buried him out here in the middle of nowhere, but he never came up with an answer. I told him it was because he killed him, and he's trying to hide the body. He just started wheezing and saying he can't breathe. It's like he doesn't want to know. What do we do?"

"I don't know," Winn said. "I usually just shoot them."

"If we can't convince him to come with us to the blood river, we'll never get rid of the skinrunner."

"Maybe we need to try a different approach," Winn said.

"Yeah, but what?"

"I don't know. I'm not an expert. We should talk to someone who knows how to handle these kinds of ghosts."

They both paused for a moment, then they turned to each other. They both said "Roy!" at the same time.

"Drive me back to somewhere with cell phone coverage," Deem said.

...

Winn stopped in a spot where Deem was able to get a single bar of signal on her phone. She called Steven to get Roy's phone number, but it turned out Roy was at Steven's house, so Steven just passed Roy the phone.

She explained the situation and how she'd tried to get Evan to see that he'd been murdered.

"I could really use some help," Deem said. "Some idea of what to say to the guy to get him to work with us."

"You're trying to use the truth and be rational," Roy said. "It'll never work. These ghosts don't suddenly have some change of heart. They're locked into their patterns, and their patterns are irrational. They don't know anything else. He'll stupidly insist that his brother loves him and wouldn't have done this to him from now until the end of time. You'll have to get him to come along with you some other way."

"How?" Deem asked.

"Well," Roy said, "you've got to leverage what you already know to construct a lie, and lure him with something he wants more than his pattern. You said he can't breathe, right?"

"Yeah, he must have complained about it a dozen times. And he kept talking about an EpiPen, whatever that is."

"It's a shot that delivers a dose of epinephrine. People who are allergic to bee stings usually carry one with them wherever they go, in case they get stung and need to use it. It opens up the airways so they can breathe."

"Well, he kept saying he needed it. He thought his brother was going to bring it to him. Of course, he wasn't."

"You're going to use the promise of the EpiPen to lure him to the blood river," Roy said. "Tell him that if he'll follow you there, you'll give him the shot. That's what he wants, so use it."

"That seems a little dishonest."

"It's completely dishonest!" Roy said. "But what's more important, saving yourself and your mom? Or maintaining integrity with some ghost buried out in the desert?"

"I suppose you're right."

"Of course I'm right."

"It just never occurred to me to lie."

"That's one of the things I like about you, Deem. Despite that potty mouth you've got, you're one of the most innocent and naïve people I've ever met. People lie all the time to get what they want. I don't advocate it with humans, unless they're pricks. But I do what I have to when ghosts are involved."

"I understand," Deem said. "It makes sense."

"Of course it makes sense."

"I guess I'll give that a try."

"Deem, listen to me. You be careful. Some ghosts get angry if they figure out you've lied to them. And down your way, angry ghosts are deadly."

"Oh, great."

"Not all ghosts. The stupid ones rarely figure it out. He sounds stupid."

"He is, kinda. But I can't tell if he's really stupid or just wrapped up in his pattern."

"Does he say the same things over and over again?"

"Yeah."

"You've got a good shot, then. Go for it."

"If he's going to be flesh for a moment, after drinking from the blood river, I really could give him the shot. It might make him feel better. And then he wouldn't think I was lying."

"That's up to you. You've just got to get him to say his brother's name during the process."

"Thanks, Roy. I was at my wit's end."

"Well, don't lose your wits! Stay sharp until it's all over. We want you and Winn to come up and visit, and that'll be hard to do if you get ripped up by some zombighost or what not."

"I will. Thanks again Roy. Bye."

"Goodbye."

She slipped her phone into her pocket and turned to Winn. "OK, let's head back to town. I think I know what to do."

. . .

Winn and Deem split up for the rest of the morning. Deem need-ed to round down a friend of hers who was allergic to bee stings and see if she could borrow one of her injection kits since they weren't available over the counter. She wanted to have the epinephrine in hand when she went back to talk to Evan. Winn said he had a few things to take care of, and that he would contact Awan for the exact location of the blood river. If the shot was enough to lure Evan to go with them, they wanted to go directly to the blood river and get it over with. They agreed to meet up just after lunch and go back out to the mining shack.

The friend Deem contacted worked at a uniform supply story in Mesquite. She hadn't seen Molly since graduating from high school, and they were only acquaintances, so Deem wasn't sure Molly would hand over her EpiPen just because Deem asked for it. So, Deem made up a story about a friend from out of town needing one to go camping with her, and that her old one had expired, and she was unable to get one locally for insurance reasons.

"They want almost five hundred dollars at Walgreens!" Deem said. "I remembered you were allergic and was wondering if you could help us out so we could go camping."

"Sure, I have one in the car," Molly said, standing behind the counter at the shop. "I have to pay about $50 for mine, can you pay me that?"

"Sure," Deem said. She fished out her wallet, hoping she had the cash on her. "Oh, it just occurred to me, if I take this one, what if you get stung?"

"No problem," Molly said. "I have another at home. I doubt I'll get stung between now and then."

"But if you did?" Deem said. "I'd feel horrible."

"I live five blocks down the road," Molly said. "My mom would have it here in two minutes. It won't happen."

"OK," Deem said, guilt washing over her. Not only had she lied to Molly, now she felt she was putting her at risk.

Molly walked out from behind the counter. "Keep an eye on things, will you? I'm the only one running the store at the moment."

"Will do," Deem said. Molly stepped out from behind a glass case counter, and walked out of the store. Deem examined the items in the case. She was surprised to see colored handcuffs. They looked hard and soft at the same time.

Molly returned with the injection kit and handed it to Deem. Deem gave Molly the fifty dollars and opened the kit.

"Just for my own benefit," Deem said, "in case I need to use it on my friend, how does this work?"

"It's simple," Molly said, taking the EpiPen from Deem. "You remove this cap. Then you aim this end at the thigh. Don't hit an artery, you could kill them. Just go for the fleshiest part. Push it down hard and hold it for ten seconds. That's all there is to it."

"Have you ever had to use it?" Deem asked.

"Once," Molly said. "Thank god I had it. I thought I was going to suffocate." She handed it back to Deem.

"I was wondering," Deem said. "About these handcuffs in the case?"

"Oh, you saw those?" Molly asked. "Smith and Wesson."

"How much are they?" Deem asked. "The colored ones."

"Thirty plus tax," Molly said.

"I'll take one!" Deem said, surprising herself. She had no idea what she would do with a pair of handcuffs, but she enjoyed the thrill her impulse buy gave her.

Molly looked at her and smiled. "The pink ones?"

"Oh, god no," Deem said. She hated pink. "Let's go with the orange ones."

Molly opened the case and removed the handcuffs for Deem. She inspected them and said, "Ring me up!"

■ ■ ■

Evan? Deem said, within her trance, searching the empty mining shack. *Evan? Are you here? It's me again.*

Deem heard a faint sound that began to slowly grow louder – the hornets. They were buzzing around her by the hundreds. She fought an impulse to run.

Evan? Evan? I have your shot! I have the EpiPen!

Evan's body materialized on the floor of the shack, lying face down, as she'd seen him before.

I can't breathe! He said, struggling for air. *Give me the shot, quickly!*

I can't give it to you here, Deem said. *Come with me, and I'll give you the shot. Look, I've got it right here.*

No, *I can't breathe,* Evan said, rolling over on the floor and looking at Deem. Once again Deem fought back the urge to recoil at Evan's swollen features.

You don't have a body, Deem said. *There's nothing to stick the needle into. Come with me to a place where you can get your body back, and I'll give you the shot. Can you do that?*

Evan sat up and looked at her. She extended the injection kit toward him, showing him that she had it.

You have the EpiPen! Evan said. *Please give it to me. I can't breathe.*

It won't work unless you come with me, Deem said. *I'm going to go to a place north of here. Inside a cave. If you follow me there, I can give you the shot. Will you come?*

Yes, Evan said. *I need the shot.*

I have the shot here in my hands, Deem said. *Attach yourself to it so you can follow it. When we get to the cave, I'll give you the shot, and you'll be able to breathe.*

Alright, Evan said.

It's a long ways, Deem said. *A couple of hours. You won't lose me, will you? You'll follow me, so I can give you the shot?*

I won't lose you, Evan said. *I'll follow you. I'll follow the EpiPen.*

Deem dropped out of the trance and stood, brushing the dirt from her jeans as she walked with Winn back to the Jeep.

"It worked," she said. "Come on. I don't know how long he'll really follow us. I'll trance as you drive, and make sure he's still coming."

Winn took the old road to St. George, avoiding the gorge through Arizona. The old road was seldom used, and he felt it would give Deem and Evan less distractions. Once they reached Enterprise, Winn turned onto old road 219, and headed west into US Forest land.

"He still with us?" Winn asked, looking at Deem, who nodded.

About thirty miles outside of Enterprise, Winn saw Awan's car parked off the road. He stopped and rolled down his window. Awan walked over.

"You got the ghost?" Awan asked.

"Deem says yes," Winn said. "She's trancing to make sure he follows us. So far so good."

"The turnoff is just past my car," Awan said. "Why don't you follow me."

"Alright," Winn said. "Lead on."

Awan returned to his car and took the turnoff, going slowly down a dirt road. They continued for several minutes until Awan pulled into a small clearing and parked his car. Winn parked next to Awan, then went around to assist Deem as she exited the Jeep.

"Keep trancing," Winn said to Deem. "We don't want to lose him this close to the finish line."

Deem nodded and extended her hand. Winn took it and held onto her as Awan strapped lights onto their heads. "Follow me," he said.

Winn guided Deem behind Awan, who walked down a small incline and into a densely wooded area.

"It's not far," Awan said. "Watch your step."

Winn had his arm around Deem's shoulder and was holding one hand as they moved forward. Awan looked back frequently to make sure they were keeping up.

The air was colder here, at least twenty degrees colder than the hot desert they were used to. It was late afternoon, and flies and mosquitoes were abundant. Winn saw several land on Deem, and he tried to shoo them away without disturbing her trance.

"Here it is," Awan said as the trees ended a few feet from a steep rock rise. The cave entrance was thin and tall.

"Animals?" Winn asked.

"Not according to my friend," Awan said. "Still, we should look for droppings."

Awan walked into the cave opening. He turned sideways to enter.

"Fuck," Winn whispered to himself. He thought he saw Deem smile.

"Come here," Awan said, his arms extending from the opening. "We go sideways for a while, then it opens up. Put Deem between us."

Winn led Deem to the opening and turned her sideways. Once Awan got a hold of her hand, he was able to guide her into the entrance. Winn made sure she stayed turned sideways as they shimmied through the opening.

"Oh god," Winn said, seeing the rock wall inches from his face.

"It's not far," Awan said. "Focus on Deem."

Winn felt his feet unable to remain forward as they walked, stepping over small rocks and boulders. He had to twist his feet right and left in order to get them to land correctly. It heightened his claustrophobia. His headlamp scraped against the rocks in front of him, twisting slightly on his head.

"Awan!" Winn called. "How much more?"

"Not much," Awan said.

"No, how much? Seriously? I gotta know."

"Maybe twenty feet. Take deep breaths."

Winn felt rocks jutting from the wall of the passageway, rubbing against his back. It was slow going, making sure Deem was stable.

Once they emerged from the tight entryway, Winn stopped and bent over, his head between his legs. Awan walked over and placed his hand on his back. "It's over," Awan said. "Just breathe."

"We still have to go back out through that," Winn said. "So it's not over."

Deem lifted her head and looked around the room they were in. It was large, but there was no water.

"How much further?" Winn asked, raising back up and adjusting his headlamp.

"A ways," Awan said. "Through there." He pointed to an opening at the far end of the cavern.

"Let's go," Winn said. He grabbed Deem's arm again and they began walking.

Once they reached the opening, Winn saw that they'd need to climb a little. The hole was about five feet off the ground.

"How are we going to do this?" Winn asked.

"I'll go first," Awan said. "You help her into it, and I'll help her down on the other side."

Awan crawled up and through the hole, leaving Winn with Deem.

"Alright," Winn said. "Deem, we've got to go up through that hole. I can boost you, but you've got to use your arms."

Deem left the trance and looked at Winn. "I think he'll be fine if I drop out for a few minutes."

"He's still here? Following us?" Winn asked.

"He hasn't been more than five feet from the EpiPen since I showed it to him," she said.

Winn leaned down to give Deem a boost, and she scuttled up and over the opening. A short slide, and she landed at Awan's feet. He grabbed her and pulled her up.

"Thanks," Deem said.

"You left the trance?" Awan asked.

"He's still following me," Deem said. "We're good."

Awan extended a hand to Winn as he slid down from the hole, and they all looked into the new cavern they'd entered.

"This is it," Awan said.

"I don't see anything," Winn said. The cave was a large, open room, at least a hundred feet wide and just as long. The floor of the room looked flat, with an occasional boulder.

"Jump into the River," Awan said.

They all entered the flow, and there before them was the blood river – water moving rapidly in a stream at least twenty feet wide. The water emerged from a hole in the wall on the left, and flowed past them to a place on the far right, where it disappeared. It looked dark, like water always looked in caves.

"It's not water, is it?" Deem asked, stepping forward to its bank.

"No," Awan said. "It's blood."

Deem placed her hand into the water and withdrew it. She held her hand up to her headlamp. The liquid running off her hand was dark red. She smelled it, and the unmistakable copper odor hit her nose.

Deem felt a wave of nausea. Her brain hadn't constructed a literal river of blood when Awan had described it. She'd imagined a river of water that was just named 'blood river,' like all the other euphemistic names given to places downwind. Devil's Throat wasn't a literal throat of a devil. Mollie's Nipple was just a mountain with a tiny butte at the tip, not a real woman's breast.

"You need to get the ghost into the river," Awan said. "And he needs to drink from it."

Deem sat on the ground about ten feet from the bank of the river. She dropped into the flow and then reentered her trance.

Evan?

She turned and saw Evan standing near the river's edge.

This is it? Evan asked.

Yes, Deem said. *That's it. Walk into it, and drink some. Then I can give you the shot.*

Evan turned to look at her. His cheeks were swollen, appearing red from the stings and swelling, and blue from lack of oxygen to the tissues. His mouth was open as he tried to pull in air.

It's hard to breathe in here, Evan said. *I can't breathe.*

Step into the river. Just do as I say, and you'll soon have your shot.

Evan turned back to the flowing liquid in front of him. He placed a foot into it.

It's cold. And it's thick.

Go in. All the way. You'll feel better. And you need to drink some.

Evan took another step. The river wasn't moving as rapidly near the bank as it was in the middle, and he was able to take two more steps with ease. He was up to his knees in blood.

Do you feel your feet? Deem said. *You should be able to feel your feet now.*

It hurts! Evan said. *They're swollen.*

Be quick, Deem said. *Just jump in and drink some. The sooner you do it the sooner I can give you the shot.*

Evan turned back to look at her. Even though his features were almost beyond recognition and his eyes almost completely shut, Deem thought she had never seen a more pleading and desperate look on any face. He turned back to the blood, and submerged himself, lying down in it.

Deem saw the dark liquid washing over his figure. It bubbled over and around him. For a moment, it reminded her of a baptism. She performed baptisms for the dead at the Mormon temple in St. George when she was fourteen, dunked into water a good thirty or forty times, each time for the name of a dead person. As she watched the blood wash over Evan, she realized it was a real baptism of the dead – performing a kind of resurrection.

Evan? Deem called. *Evan, can you hear me?*

Evan sat up, his torso rising up out of the blood. As the liquid drained from his face, Deem saw he'd changed. Everything was solid – he wasn't a ghost.

She dropped out of her trance, but remained in the River, observing Evan.

Give me the shot! Evan said, still struggling for air. *I can't breathe!*

Deem looked at him. *Evan, tell me the name of your brother. Say his name. Say John Carl Braithwaite.*

Give me the shot! Evan repeated. *You promised!*

I will, just as soon as you say his name.

Evan stood, more blood flowing down off his frame. He looked like a nightmare, a grotesque figure rising from a grave of liquid. He held his hands out from his body, in front of his face.

I'm alive! he said.

Say his name, Evan. Say his name, and I'll give you the shot.

I'm swollen, Evan said, looking at the rest of his body. *Oh, god, it hurts! I can't breathe. I need the shot!*

Say John Carl Braithwaite, Evan. Say it. Say it and I'll give you the shot, and the pain will stop. She felt horrible the moment the words left her mouth. Now she was using his pain to force him to kill his brother.

You promised! Evan said, taking a step toward her. His blood-drenched image frightened her a little, and she stepped back from him. *You said you'd give it to me. If you won't give it to me, I'll take it myself!*

He took another step, the blood of the river now at his ankles. Awan and Winn, both in the flow, stepped between Evan and Deem.

Say your brother's name and you get the shot, Winn said. *That's the only way. We won't let you take it from her.*

Why? Evan said, looking at Winn. *She promised me the shot. I can't breathe. I need it now!*

Just say his name, Awan said to Evan. *Three words.*

Is this a trap for my brother? Evan asked, barely able to force the words through his throat.

You won't be able to breathe in a moment, Winn said. *If you don't say your brother's name before your throat swells shut, you'll be gone. If you say your brother's name, he'll come, and he'll bring the shot. Remember? He's outside the shack. He can get the shot from the car.*

He can save you. Call to him. He'll come, and you'll be able to breathe. That's all you have to do. Call him. Say his name.

Evan looked at Winn. *He'll get the door open, and save me,* he said, falling to his knees. *John, save me! I'm dying.*

Say his entire name, Winn said. *Say John Carl Braithwaite.*

Why doesn't he come in? Evan said, dropping his head to his chest and crying. *He must know I'm dying in here. He must know. Why isn't he coming in?*

Say his full name, see if he will come in! Winn said.

Evan gave in. *John Carl Braithwaite!* he called. *Bring me the shot, John! I can't breathe!*

Deem, unable to bear Evan's cries any longer, dropped out of the flow and walked between Winn and Awan, pushing them aside. Immediately the blood river disappeared, and the blood she'd seen dripping off Evan was gone. He was just kneeling there, sobbing. She pulled the cap off the EpiPen and stabbed it into his thigh, holding it firmly.

Evan fell forward. Winn and Awan lifted him up and turned him over. He was still covered in hives.

"Evan!" Deem called, kneeling next to him. "Evan! I gave you the shot."

"It hurts," Evan said. "I can't breathe."

She looked up at Awan and Winn. "Do you think it worked?"

"It should have," Awan said. "He's obviously corporeal, and he said the name."

"Why doesn't he come in?" Evan moaned, his body twisting on the cave floor. "I called for him!"

"I hope the shot helped somewhat," Deem said. "I mean, he dies regardless, I know, but maybe it eased the pain."

"What do we do with him?" Winn asked.

"You can leave him here," Awan said. "When the effect of the blood wears off, his body will disappear."

"And what will become of him?" Deem asked.

"He'll either move on," Awan said, "or go back to what he was doing before you met him. If he is smart enough, he'll realize the blood river righted the wrong his brother did to him. But it might take his brother dying and moving on for him to fully understand and move on himself. Injustice keeps a lot of ghosts alive."

"He was a nice enough guy," Deem said, "I'm sorry I had to lie to him."

"You did what you had to," Winn said. Deem smiled a little. *Winn's got my back,* she thought. *I'm lucky he works with me.*

"Let's go," Awan said. "We can make it back to town before dark."

They left, Winn struggling through the tight entrance but knowing he had no choice if he wanted to exit the cave. Once they reached St. George, they stopped for food.

"I've never seen anything like it," Deem said. "All that blood, moving so quickly. Where does it all come from?"

"The legend is that it's the blood of those killed unjustly," Awan said. "Legends are sometimes true."

"You said they're rare?" Winn asked as they looked over menus.

"Extremely," Awan said. "According to my friend in Ely, there's only two others in North America. And this one is special, because it's downwind. He wouldn't have been able to speak at the other two. So, in a way, our blood river is a one-of-a-kind."

"So much blood," Deem said. "There's times when I just can't handle blood. Even the color red turns me off."

Winn and Awan looked at each other, unsure how to respond.

"Never mind," Deem said. "So the skinrunner will lose his powers now?"

"Yes," Awan said. "Check your mom tomorrow. There's a good chance she'll be fine. If not by tomorrow, then the next day."

"And did you say he slowly rots?" Winn asked.

"Yes," Awan replied. "Takes a couple of days. Do you know where he works?"

"At a bank in Hurricane," Deem said.

"You could check on him," Awan said. "I'll bet you he calls in sick tomorrow. Once he realizes what's happening to him, he'll hole up at home until it's over."

"I can't thank you enough," Deem said. "It was bad enough with him attacking me, but when he went after my aunt and mom, it really pissed me off. If you hadn't helped us I'd still be digging bones out of them and myself."

"You're welcome," Awan said.

"How's the ghost chalk coming?" Winn asked. "We're ready to help you tackle the extortion brothers whenever you're ready."

"A couple more days," Awan said. "Have you ever made it? Ghost chalk?"

"No," Deem said. Winn shook his head.

"You have to bake it in a kiln. It collapses as it dries. Then you add a liquid to it, infused with thistle and alocutis. It bubbles up, so you have to let it settle back down for a day before you bake it again. Takes five or six times before it becomes powdery enough that you can spoon it into the contraption you hold over their kidneys. A couple more days and it'll be ready. I'll let you know. How'd things go with your father's journals?"

"Not so good," Deem said. "We followed the guy to Caliente, where they met in an abandoned church. We went inside but the journals weren't there. Somehow they knew we'd been there, and they found the tracking device. I've got it in my car to give back to you."

"So you're back to square one?" Awan asked.

"Kind of," Deem said. "I think I'm on their hit list now. I confronted the guy we tracked, and he told me they were planning on the skinrunner taking me down. He knew about the attacks."

"That is very troubling," Awan said, furrowing his brow. "More troubling than the skinrunner."

"I don't know," Deem said. "They're a bunch of old white guys, higher-ups in the church, who like to go to a lot of meetings and throw their weight around. They're not use to someone standing up to them. Especially not a girl."

"All the more reason to be concerned," Awan said.

"I was thinking we should go back to Claude and see if he'd be willing to share everything he knows with us," Winn suggested. "He said he had a lot on the secret council in his files."

"Who's Claude?" Awan asked.

"He's this guy Deem's been talking to about the secret council," Winn said. "I think he knows more than he's sharing, because he's unsure if we believe him or not. He's a little paranoid. He might open up more if we assured him we're on his side of things."

"He's paranoid with good reason!" Awan said. "Is this the 'Hour of Truth' guy?"

"You've heard of him?" Deem asked, surprised.

"Every non-Mormon has heard of him," Awan said. "People think he's a crackpot, like Art Bell, but they listen to him regardless."

"Hey, Art Bell's no crackpot," Winn said. "I like him."

"I'm just saying people know about him," Awan said.

"Claude told me everything I know about the secret council at this point," Deem said. "Without him, I wouldn't have known what to do."

"Maybe you should pay him another visit," Awan said. "Convince him you're sincere. He may share more with you."

"It's as good an idea as any," Deem said. "I need an ally in this cause, and he seems to know the most."

"Why don't we go over to his place when we're finished?" Winn said. "Awan, you should meet him. He's a good contact."

"Sure, I'd like to meet him," Awan said. "My brother-in-law listens to his show every night. I'll bet he'd let me borrow his riding mower if I got him an autograph."

"What do you say, Deem?" Winn asked.

Deem knew Winn was just trying to help. She thought she'd been as honest and sincere with Claude as she could possibly be. Skepticism came naturally to her, and perhaps it showed. But with everything she'd learned about the secret council and Dayton in the past few days, she was no longer skeptical. Things had risen to a new level. Maybe Claude would sense that and share more.

"Sure," she said. "He's gonna get sick of us just dropping in."

"We'd call first," Winn said, "but he doesn't trust phones."

12

It was dark when they arrived at Claude's. Deem walked up to the door to knock, Awan and Winn right behind her.

She raised her hand but stopped when she noticed the door was ajar.

"Winn," she said, whispering. "No way he'd leave it open like this."

Winn stepped forward and examined the door. "Whoever it is, they may still be inside."

"Who can enter a trance the quickest?" Deem asked. "It takes me about two minutes."

"A minute," Winn said.

"Twenty seconds," Awan said.

"Really?" Deem said, surprised. "OK, you do it."

Awan closed his eyes and entered the River. Once he constructed the trance, he drifted into Claude's house. After a few seconds he left the trance and returned to the others.

"One man, all in black, face covered, in the living room. He's holding a knife."

"Claude?" Deem asked.

Awan shook his head.

"Fuck!" Winn said. "What do we do?"

Awan pulled a gun from under his shirt and held it up. "We go in."

"Where the fuck did that come from?" Deem asked. "You've had that the whole time?"

"Yes," Awan said.

"And you know how to use it?" she asked.

Awan looked hurt. "Of course I do. I'll go first."

Awan pushed the door open and walked inside, following the path he'd seen in the trance. The house was dark, no lights were on. When they had all entered Claude's living room, Deem could see the man dressed in black, leaning over someone seated in a chair.

"Stop right there!" Awan shouted. The man whirled around, knife in hand. He immediately bolted into the kitchen, out of sight. Awan ran after him.

Deem looked at the figure in the chair. It was Claude. At first she thought he might still be alive, but as her eyes adjusted to the dim light, the truth of what had happened to him began to sink in.

"Oh god," she said, turning away from the sight. She looked at Winn; he opened his arms and she buried her face in his chest.

Awan returned from the kitchen. He flipped on a light switch, and the living room illuminated. "He's gone, out the kitchen door. There's a dead dog in the back yard."

"Could you tell who it was?" Winn asked. "Anything about him?"

"I don't even know if it was a 'him,'" Awan said. "He was completely covered."

Winn looked down at Claude. He was tied to the chair. The intruder had used the knife to disembowel him, and had grotesquely pulled his intestines out from the wound and strung them up and over Claude's shoulder.

"Look what he did to him," Winn said, shocked. "It's sick."

Awan stepped over to them and examined Claude. "That's a message."

"A message?" Deem said, turning back to the grisly scene. "What message?"

"The bowels removed," Awan said. "A penalty. For violating an oath. A Mormon thing."

"The secret council?" Winn asked.

"This is because of me," Deem said. "They knew he was talking to me. They killed him because of it."

"You don't know that," Winn said.

"They're watching everything!" Deem said. "They knew we followed them to Caliente. They knew I was being attacked by the skinrunner. They must have known I'd met with him."

"Now you're becoming paranoid, like him," Winn said.

"He'd been talking about strange things on the radio for years," Awan said. "But he never talked about this secret council, at least not on his radio program. I guess speaking to you about it crossed a line."

"So they killed him, for talking to me," Deem said, angry. "They didn't have to mutilate him like this."

"He violated an oath," Awan said. "That's what the disembowelment is about."

"What oath?" Deem asked.

"It used to be a temple oath," Awan said. "It isn't anymore. But old timers remember the original oaths, which had penalties for

221

breaking silence. Being cut open and having your bowels removed was one of the penalties."

"He left the church long ago," Deem said. "When you leave, those oaths no longer apply, do they?"

"To some old timers," Awan said, "they still apply, whether you leave or not."

"Maybe it doesn't have to do with the temple at all," Winn said. "If Deem is right, and this is in response to him talking to us, then it's all about the secret council. Maybe he took an oath with them. Maybe he was part of it, at some point. This has to be their work."

Deem left Winn's side and walked to Claude. "I'm so sorry," she said to him.

"We need to get out of here," Awan said. "This is a crime scene, and I don't think any of us want to get wrapped up with the cops."

"He had a security system," Winn said. "There might be tapes of us coming in."

"I'll find it," Awan said. "I know something about security systems." Awan left them and began searching.

"Wait," Deem said, staring at a stack of boxes to the right of Claude. "This stack of boxes wasn't out when we were here last time."

She opened the top box and pulled out some of the paperwork inside, leafing through it.

"It's all council stuff," she said. "Maybe they made him collect it like this before they killed him."

"When we startled the killer," Winn said, "he ran off without them."

"We're taking these," Deem said.

"What if someone sees us?" Winn asked.

"His nearest neighbor is two blocks away," Deem said, grabbing the first box and walking out. "It's a risk I'm willing to take. Are you going to help me?"

Winn grabbed the next box in the stack and followed Deem out of the house. They piled the boxes into the back of Winn's Jeep, then went back inside for the rest. Once they finished, there were six boxes of documents in Winn's vehicle.

They looked for Awan, and found him in a back room. He was reviewing video footage on a small black and white monitor. "This guy was old school, used tapes that he'd rotate. The tapes in the machine go back about a week. When did you first visit him?"

Deem tried to remember their first visit. "A week ago, maybe?"

"The date at the beginning of this tape is last Monday," Awan said, ejecting the tape and placing it in his pocket. "Let's hope that covers it. It looks to me like he locked his older tapes in that." Awan pointed to a small safe sitting on a counter behind them.

"We've taken some of his boxes," Deem said. "I think the intruder made him collect everything he had on the council before he killed him. Intended to take it with him before we interrupted."

"That's a very dangerous move," Awan said. "They'll know you took them. They'll want them. They'll hunt them down."

"Guys, we've got to get out of here," Winn said. "We can talk about this after we've left."

"Go back through the house," Awan said. "Wipe fingerprints. Remember everything you may have touched."

They methodically walked back through the rooms they'd entered, wiping switches and door handles. Finally they left through the front door.

"Leave it ajar, just as we found it," Awan said. Deem pulled the door so that it caught in the door jam, but not until it latched closed. Then they walked to Winn's Jeep and got inside.

"Should we call this in, anonymously?" Deem asked.

"There's no such thing as anonymous," Awan said. "You'll have to leave it be."

"He deserves better than being left like that," Deem said.

"He does," Awan said. "But you must not do it. They would track down anyone who called that murder in. Of greater concern are these boxes. If they were willing to kill Claude for them, they will certainly kill you for them."

"I need time to go through them," Deem said. "I need to store them somewhere."

"You can't take them home," Winn said. "You'd be putting your mother at risk."

"Would they really do that?" Deem asked. "Wouldn't that draw too much attention?"

"Please don't be offended, Deem," Awan said, "but you've under-estimated these people from the beginning, giving them the benefit of the doubt when they don't deserve it. I know they were associates of your father's, but you need to start thinking of them as cold blooded killers and assume the worst, because they'll do whatever they think they have to, including burying you in a hole in the de-sert."

"How can they justify this?" Deem said. "It goes against every-thing. I can't believe they would take it this far. Don't they have some kind of conscience?"

"They think God is on their side," Awan said. "That makes them the most dangerous of all, because it overrides everything else. You cannot take these boxes home. You and your family will be in enough danger as it is."

"Well, they've got to go somewhere until I can read through them," Deem said. "Winn? Any ideas?"

"My trailer is too obvious," Winn said. "They know I'm with you on this. It'll probably get searched tomorrow."

"And they monitor everything," Deem said. "I've got to store them somewhere they can't see."

"Transfer the boxes to my car when we get back to St. George," Awan said. "I know a place. I'll take them there."

"Where?" Deem asked.

"I have an aunt in Leeds," Awan said. "She lives in an old house, from pioneer days. It'll offer some protection for the boxes, if we make a deal with Lyman."

"Who's Lyman?" Deem asked.

"It's a long story," Awan said. "But the boxes will be safe. Trust me."

"It's better than taking them home, Deem," Winn said. "Safer for your mom."

"I don't know," Deem said. "I can't afford to lose them. I feel like they've fallen into my lap for a reason, and I need to read what's inside. What if your aunt loses them? Or Dayton tracks them there and intimidates her into giving them up?"

"Tell you what," Awan said. "Come with me to Leeds and drop them off yourself. Meet my aunt, and Lyman. See if you're comfortable leaving them there."

"What if we're being followed?" Deem asked. "They'll know where the boxes are."

"It won't matter if they know they're at my aunt's," Awan said. "If Lyman agrees to watch over them, there's nothing they can do."

"They could kill him," Deem said, "like they killed Claude."

"He's already dead," Awan said.

"Oh," Deem said. "Well then. Alright. But I want to talk to him, to be sure."

"Of course," Awan said, smiling. He turned to Winn. "She can be very insistent."

"You have no idea," Winn said.

"Then we don't need to go to your car, Awan," Deem said. "Let's just go straight out to Leeds now, and we'll bring you back to St. George after. Alright, Winn?"

"Yes," Winn said. "Let's do it."

"I'll call her," Awan said, pulling his phone from his pocket, "to tell her we're coming."

...

Winn pulled up to the old home situated at the dead end of a flat street in Leeds. Newer homes lined the street that led to the house, but there was a comfortable distance between the last houses on the street and the old one at the end. It was surrounded by a white two beam fence and had a large front lawn. A hill rose up steeply behind it, the reason for the dead end. Winn drove into the driveway. Deem noticed a large sign that said "No Visitors – No Trespassers – No Solicitors – No Missionaries" posted on a stake just inside the fence. Winn parked next to an old green Ford station wagon that had wood paneling on the side.

"Carma is gifted," Awan said as they walked to the door, "but her practice is a little different." Awan knocked on the door. It flew open and Carma rushed out, extending her arms to Awan, who allowed her to wrap him in them. Carma was thin and tall, just over six feet, and had perfectly manicured hair – she looked as though she'd just left a beauty parlor. A thin cigarette dangled from one hand.

"You don't visit enough," she said in a slightly raspy voice, which Deem assumed was due to the smoking. She hugged Awan until Deem thought he would pop. Then she abruptly released him and turned to Winn and Deem.

"Your companions?" she said.

"Deem and Winn," Awan said. "Good friends."

"I am so pleased to meet good friends of Awan's," she said, transferring her cigarette from her right to her left hand, then extending the right to each of them. When Deem shook Carma's hand she thought she could feel every bone in it, and she was afraid of using too much pressure and breaking it.

"It won't break," Carma said, smiling at her. "I take calcium pills. They do a number on my stomach, but my doctor insists. Didn't drink enough milk as a child apparently."

She whirled around in a perfect one-eighty and walked back into the house, motioning for them to follow her.

Deem looked at Winn. He smiled at her, and she smiled back. They both seemed to approve of Carma.

"Now, this house is over a hundred and forty years old!" Carma said as they walked into a hallway and down it to a back room. The hallway was lined with pictures of the house from different eras and the surrounding area. Deem recognized pictures of abandoned buildings at the nearby ghost town, Silver Reef.

"Built by a Mormon pioneer named Hosea Hamblin, a revered name in these parts. He was a favorite of Brigham Young until he sided with John D. Lee and apostatized. They killed apostates in those days, but Hosea had built himself a nice homestead here and he had some resources as well as friends, so the local church decided to leave him alone rather than slit his throat. Anyone like some iced tea?"

They emerged into a back room that had a comfortable sitting area with more pillows than Deem could count. It had large glass windows that looked over the back yard.

"I'd like some," Winn said. "Thanks."

"Awan?" Carma asked.

"Not for me, thanks."

"How about you, dear?" Carma asked Deem. "You look like you could use something right about now."

Deem looked out over the beautiful back yard, lit by small lights placed here and there, and a larger light that lit part of the large hill rising at the end of the lawn. It was beautiful. The day had been brutal, and for the first time in a long time, she felt peace wash over her. She felt a release coming, and lowered her head to her chest, fighting the urge to cry. *I will not let Winn and Awan see me cry,* she thought.

She felt Carma place her hand on her back. "I have a Diet Coke with your name on it, my dear. Does that sound good?"

Deem shook her head yes.

"Good," Carma said, walking away. "I'll be right back with drinks, you all make yourselves comfortable."

"Nice place," Winn said to Awan. "That yard is amazing."

"You OK, Deem?" Awan asked.

"I'm fine," Deem said, looking for a place to sit down, and finding a large overstuffed chair she flopped into. It was soft and enveloping, and she instantly felt the tension that had built up in her body seep out and into the chair. "It's been a long day."

"That it has," Winn said, joining her by sitting on a nearby couch. Awan joined him.

"Here we are," Carma said, entering the room with a tray. "Now, take what you want and leave what you don't. I've brought some of these little Asian crackers you might want to try. I've fallen in love with them. Not everyone likes them, because of the seaweed. If you don't like them, just ignore them."

"Thank you," Winn said, standing up and pouring himself a glass of iced tea from a pitcher. He took the can of Diet Coke from the tray and handed it to Deem, who popped it open and took a long swig.

"The boxes!" Deem said, pulling the can away from her lips. "They're in the car!"

"We have some boxes of documents," Awan said to Carma. "We were hoping we could keep them here for a while. They're..."

"Dangerous?" Carma said, cocking one eyebrow.

"Yes," Winn said.

"Delightful!" Carma said. "How are they dangerous?"

"It's a long story," Deem said.

"Short version," Carma said, "so you can bring them inside."

"I think they have information about a secret council of gifted Mormons," Deem said. "Higher-ups in the church."

"How high up?" Carma asked, a smile spreading across her face as her eyes widened.

"Stake presidents and up," Deem said.

"Delicious!" Carma said.

"We think they killed a friend of mine to get them."

"Killed?" Carma asked. "Who?"

"Claude Peterson."

"Claude is dead?" Carma said in horror, pressing her palm flat against her chest.

"Yes," Deem said. "Eviscerated, in his home."

"And his files are in your car?" Carma asked.

"Yes. Awan said we might be able to store them here, to keep them safe."

"Awan," Carma said, "take this handsome man with you and the two of you go bring those boxes inside immediately."

Winn put down his iced tea and stood up as Awan made his way out of the room and back down the hallway. Carma turned and followed them, and Deem followed her. When Awan returned with the first box, Carma directed him to a side room, where he began stacking them. Deem started to walk out of the house to help them, but Carma stopped her. "Let the boys do it, dear," Carma said. "You've had enough excitement for one day. You relax." Carma took a long drag off her cigarette and blew the smoke into the outside air.

Once they'd all been moved inside, Carma led them back to the sitting room where Winn picked up his iced tea and returned to the couch with Awan. Deem sat back down in the large overstuffed chair. Carma seemed content to remain standing behind them.

"Really, Awan, leaving them outside like that," Carma chided.

"I thought the whole property was protected," Awan said. "Isn't it?"

"The house is stronger," Carma said. "Not as strong as the basement and the cave, but much better than the driveway, for heaven's sake."

"It sounds to me like you knew Claude," Winn said. "From the radio? Or personally?"

"Claude and I go way back," Carma said. "Before St. George got so built up, all the non-Mormons around these parts knew each other. We had to, to survive." She took a long drag off her cigarette and exhaled, deftly aiming the smoke behind her. "I can't believe he's dead. Then again, I can. He waded in turbulent waters, that man. Wasn't protected. I tried to get him more protection, but he thought alarm systems and surveillance and a good dog was enough. It was bound to catch up to him. He'd angered the higher-ups around here for years. Poor man. You said eviscerated?"

"Belly cut open," Awan said, "intestines pulled out."

"Damn Mormons," Carma said. "They really make me angry sometimes with their ridiculous penalties. I can't tell you how many people have died in this state with either their throats cut or their guts ripped out due to that crazy temple stuff. Are any of you hungry? Would you like something more to eat? I noticed none of you tried the crackers."

"We ate just before we went to Claude's place," Awan said. "Maybe two hours ago. I'm not hungry, but thanks."

"Me either," Deem said. "Just tired."

"Awan mentioned someone named Lyman," Winn said. "He said we'd need to make a deal with him."

"That'll be an easy deal," Carma said. "If those boxes have dirt on a secret Mormon council, he'll say yes without hesitation."

"He lives here?" Deem asked.

"Almost," Carma said. "He lives in a cave in that hill back there," she said, pointing through the windows to the hill that rose up at the end of the lawn.

"Awan said the boxes would be safe here," Deem said. "I need to read through what's inside. I gotta be sure they'll be OK if I leave them with you. And I'm worried that they'll make you a target of the council. That's why I couldn't take them home, I didn't want to put my mother and aunt at risk. It seems unfair to do the same to you."

"Don't you worry about that," Carma said, smiling at her. "They'll be safe here, I promise you. And we're under no threat from your council."

"Awan said you are gifted," Deem said. "You've protected the house?"

"Not me," Carma said, pulling another hit from her cigarette and exhaling. "Him!" She pointed out the window toward the hill.

"Is it strong enough to keep the council away?" Deem asked.

"They know better than to come here," Carma said. "The boxes will be safe."

"I'm sorry to keep asking," Deem said, "but I have to be sure. So many things have gone wrong recently. What keeps them away?"

"Lyman has slaughtered every high ranking Mormon who has set foot on this property for more than a hundred years," Carma said. "They stopped coming years ago. He's too dangerous to them."

"The sign out front?" Deem asked. "Warning people away?"

"It keeps the right people away," Carma said. "Rank and file don't need to worry, as long as their intentions are good. But I guarantee you, a Bishop or Stake President knows why that sign is there, and they respect it."

"Lyman hates church authorities?" Deem asked. "Why?"

"Tell you what," Carma said, taking the empty can of Diet Coke from Deem and placing it back on the tray. "I'll let you ask him that yourself, when you meet him tonight. He'll be out around four-thirty, and we'll go down. Why don't you all just sleep here for a while, and I'll wake you when it's time."

"Alright," Deem said. "Winn? What do you say?"

"I've got nowhere to be," he said. "Awan?"

"I'd rather sleep here than drive back home tonight," Awan said. "It's a long haul."

"Alright, it's settled," Carma said. "There's plenty of rooms upstairs. Go pick the one you like. I'll set the alarm for four-thirty and wake you up then."

"Why four-thirty?" Deem asked, rising from her chair.

"It's all moon-driven," Carma said. "He's always around, but he only materializes and talks when the moon is at its zenith. It's a little inconvenient, but I'm use to reading the almanac. A lot easier when it's during the day, but Lyman makes the rules around here."

Awan led the group upstairs, Carma following to check on each of them. Deem found a nice room with a large queen bed, and sat on its edge as Carma stood in the doorway, asking her repeatedly if she needed anything.

"Thank you again," Deem said. "It's really great of you to help us like this."

"Oh, I'd do anything for Awan. He's my favorite nephew. There, I've said it. Probably isn't fair to my other nephews and nieces, but it's true. He was always so empathetic as a child. I don't think he has a mean bone in his body. And he's turned into such a wise young man. Sometimes I think there's a very old soul in him. So he could ask me for a million dollars and I'd find a way to give it to him." She took a drag off her cigarette and blew the smoke into the hallway behind her.

"He's been very helpful to Winn and me," Deem said. "We owe him."

"I have so many questions for you," Carma said, turning and grabbing the bedroom door handle. "But I'll ask them all in the morning, after you talk with Lyman. At least, the ones I remember to ask. Get some sleep, I'll come wake you when it's time."

"Thank you," Deem said. The door clicked closed, and Deem fell to her side, out before her cheek hit the pillow.

13

Most of the lights in the house were off as Carma led them to the basement door.

"The neighbors aren't right next door," Carma said, "but I don't like people thinking I'm up in the middle of the night, like a nut case, so I leave the lights off when I'm up like this. So I guess what I'm saying is, watch your step!"

She led them downstairs, where she turned on the overhead lights. It was fully furnished. In one corner were ping pong, pool, and foosball tables, and at the opposite end was a large projection TV, surrounded by oversized chairs and bean bags. Between the two was a built-in bar. A "Pabst Blue Ribbon" neon sign hung behind it, currently off. Deem thought it was as comfortable and inviting as any play room she'd seen.

Carma walked past the pool table to a door, which she unlocked and opened. Inside was a closet, lined with boxes. At the other end of the closet was another door, also locked. Once Carma opened it, they walked into another part of the basement that was unfinished. Carma turned on an overhead light, and Deem saw the hole, angling down into the ground. It was about ten feet wide, and there were wooden steps and a handrail.

Carma walked to the steps and started down. Deem followed her, taking care with each step, but Carma practically ran down the steps as though she'd gone up and down them a thousand times, and was familiar with their placement. The distance between Deem and Carma was increasing. Winn and Awan were behind her, going as cautiously as she was.

"Come along!" called Carma. "I don't want to miss him!"

Deem picked up her pace. Soon she reached a level surface and was able to speed up and reach Carma. Deem looked up and saw light bulbs hanging from a wire that had been run overhead and tacked into the rock. It was unusual to her to be walking through a cave without having to hold a flashlight or use a head lamp.

After fifty feet the passageway opened into a room about twenty feet wide. The ground was bare and nothing was in the cave except a small table, a chair, and an occasional rock. She noticed an opening in the far end of the room.

"This is it," Carma said. "Underwhelming after all that lead up, isn't it." She noticed Deem observing the opening. "It continues into the hill for quite a ways, it's very deep. Lyman keeps an eye on it, so I don't go back in there, but I suspect it's never been mapped out. There's a few deep holes back in there that I wouldn't want to fall into. LYMAN!"

She pulled a candle and a lighter out of the pocket on her dress and placed the candle into a candlestick that sat on the table. Then she lit it with the lighter. "LYMAN!" she yelled again.

Carma dropped the lighter back into her pocket, and removed a pack of Capris. She removed a long, thin cigarette from the pack and lit it from the candle on the table.

"LYMAN!" she bellowed. "We need to talk to you! Now, come on."

Deem could feel Lyman enter the room from the entrance in the back. She dropped into the River and saw him walking toward the table. She was surprised to see that he was young – she guessed sixteen. He was handsome, with brown hair and sideburns. His shirt showed sweat stains from manual labor, and it clung to his torso, revealing the muscles of someone who worked hard. His pants looked homemade, and were too short for him, ending several inches above the ankles on his bare feet.

Carma, he said, walking toward them. Deem saw his feet move, but he moved faster than his feet, and he didn't step around the boulders on the floor, he passed through them.

Lyman, you remember my nephew Awan, Carma said, extending her arm to point at Awan behind her.

How could I not? Lyman said. *You talk about him incessantly.* He turned to look at Awan and nodded. *Awan,* he said.

Lyman, Awan nodded back.

These are friends of Awan's, Carma said. *Winn and Deem. Gift-ed.*

Pleasure to meet you, Lyman said, turning to each of them. He lingered on Deem.

Deem, he said, studying her. *That's a pretty name. I've never heard it before. Is it short for anything?*

I had a great aunt who was named Adeema, Deem said. *I was named after her, but they shortened it.*

Good thing they did, Carma said, *or your name would sound like an ailment!*

What can I do for you, Deem? Lyman asked.

Deem looked at him. Somehow he knew that it was her who had the need. He had classic features, strong, handsome, youthful. But he seemed sad, tired.

In my attempt to locate my father's journals, Deem said, *I've run afoul of a secret council. My father passed away a few years ago, but I've discovered that he was on that council when he was alive. I believe they have his journals, but they won't give them to me because they might contain things about the council.*

She stopped, and, out of habit, took a breath though she didn't really need one in the River. Lyman seemed to be hanging on her words.

Last night, we came across several boxes of documents that might help me find them. But I also think they might contain secrets about the council that they don't want divulged. They killed a friend of mine last night to get them, and it was dumb luck that we happened to acquire them.

You think it was dumb luck that you had the idea in that restaurant to go visit Claude? Lyman asked.

Deem pulled back, startled. Did Lyman know about that, or was he just reading her mind? *Proceed with caution,* she thought to herself.

At the time, Deem slowly said to Lyman, *I thought it was luck, yes. Are you telling me it wasn't?*

It wasn't, Lyman said. *Please, continue.*

Deem was a little thrown off her game. She began to wonder if Lyman already knew the whole story. If so, asking her to continue seemed condescending.

If you already know why I'm here, Deem said, *what's the point of me telling you?*

Because I love the sound of your voice, Lyman said.

Deem began to heat up, irritated. *There's no sound in the River,* she said. *You're toying with me.*

Drop out, Lyman said.

Deem left the River, feeling its waters recede. There was Lyman, standing behind the table as though he was flesh and blood.

"That's impressive," Deem said. "Winn, are you out of the River? Do you see him?"

"I do," Winn said. "I don't know that I've ever seen a ghost who can manifest that strongly outside of the River."

"For the longest time, I couldn't," Lyman said. "About fifty years ago, things changed. I got stronger and stronger."

"The radiation?" Winn asked.

"Probably," Lyman said.

"You're lucky it didn't turn you into a zombighost," Deem said. "That's what it did to most of the ghosts around here."

"Maybe there's something in the rocks here," Lyman said, looking up. "Or maybe it was my sense of purpose. It just made me more powerful. You do have a lovely voice, you know. Sweet and cheerful. Reminds me of Sarah."

"Sarah?" Deem asked.

"Love of my life," Lyman said. "The girl I intended to marry."

"What happened?" Deem asked.

Lyman turned away from her. "The boxes are in the side room upstairs, correct? I'll make sure they stay safe. No one will bother them. You can come and inspect them any time you like. On one condition."

"Name it," Deem said.

"That you come visit me down here, once in a while," he said.

"Alright," Deem said hesitantly. "I can do that."

Lyman picked up on Deem's hesitation. He turned back to her. Again, she was startled by how young he looked. "I only want to hear you talk, that's all," he said. "You sound so much like her."

"Just come down here and talk to you?" Deem asked. "Sure, no problem."

He smiled weakly. "Thank you," he said. "And I hope you find your father's journals."

Deem smiled back. "I know there's something in them that I need to read."

Carma jumped in. "Good, it's settled. Lyman, before you blip out on me, I need to talk to you about the Jeppsens next door. Their dog keeps breaking into the pecan orchard."

"I like that dog," Lyman said, still looking at Deem.

"Yes, but he shits all over the orchard and it makes irrigating a nasty affair."

"Think of it as fertilizer," Lyman said, cracking the first real smile Deem had seen him give.

"Why, that's a disgusting idea, Lyman," Carma said, becoming animated. "I do not want dog doodoo as fertilizer for the pecans! I think it would ruin their taste. Can't you make it so it goes back on to the Jeppsens yard if it needs to do its business?"

"Alright," Lyman said. "Anything else?"

"The fuses you wanted are going to take a little longer to arrive than I thought," Carma said. "The government tracks that kind of thing now, so to get them without a paper trail, it'll take some fancy footwork."

"I don't care how long they take," Lyman said wearily. "As long as we get them."

"Alright," Carma said.

"Anything else?" Lyman asked.

"No," Carma said, shaking her head. "Anything else I can do for you?"

"No," Lyman said, "but thank you for bringing them down to meet me. It seems like a long time since I've met other gifted people." He turned to Winn and Awan, telling them goodbye. They each nodded back at him.

"Deem," he said, turning to her. "You're kind to agree to my terms. It's a little pathetic, I know."

"I don't mind," she said. "You like my voice, and I think you're easy on the eyes. So it'll work out."

"Easy on the eyes?" Lyman asked.

"It means you're handsome," Carma interjected. "You're not hard to look at. She's flirting with you."

"Oh," Lyman said. Deem could swear he blushed a little. "Well, thank you. I guess I'll see you the next time you come around?"

"Yes," Deem said.

Lyman turned and walked back through the opening at the far end of the room, and was gone.

"Well," Carma said, turning to Deem, "that's a first."

"What?" Deem said.

"You're the first woman he's asked to come visit him," Carma said, turning to walk back down the passageway that led to the house. "He might actually be getting over Sarah. Never thought I'd see the day."

"That seemed like a touchy subject," Deem said, following her.

"Let's get back upstairs," Carma said, "and I'll tell you the story."

．．．

"Coffee?" Carma asked Deem. She'd just filled Winn's mug and was working her way around the table, where everyone was seated eating breakfast.

"No, thank you," Deem said.

"Ah, there's a little bit of Mormon left in you yet!" Carma said, moving on to Awan and filling his mug without asking.

"I like how it smells," Deem said, "but not how it tastes."

"Oh, if I had a dime for every time I've heard a Mormon say that," Carma said.

Deem thought for a moment that she should be a little offended at Carma's comment, but she found it impossible to go there. Carma was too warm, and even when she said something marginal, it came out more as entertaining than as insulting. Deem expected Winn to jump on and make a comment about the coffee, but he surprised her.

"Please don't take this the wrong way, Carma," Winn said, "but Deem's not in any danger coming here to visit Lyman, is she?"

"Well, if Lyman didn't like her," Carma answered, "I'd say maybe. But since he's enamored with her voice, I'd say not."

"And he's enamored with my voice," Deem said, "because I sound like Sarah?"

"Or so he thinks," Carma said. "Sarah was a hundred and fifty years ago. I think he over-romanticizes her."

"Tell them the story," Awan said, eating.

Carma sighed and sat down at the table with a mug of coffee. "Back in the 1860s, Utah wasn't a state, but it was the gathering place for all Mormons worldwide. Lyman's parents converted in London, and traveled to America. They pulled a handcart across the plains from Nebraska to get here. They settled in Manti.

"Polygamy was big at the time, with Brigham Young declaring it was the only way to get to heaven, and the local church leadership in Manti enjoyed marrying pretty young girls as soon as they were able to breed.

"Lyman was young, as you saw, and fell in love with a girl his age named Sarah, and she loved him back. Unfortunately, the Bishop in Manti at the time had his sights set on Sarah for years. He informed Sarah and her parents that she was to be sealed to him, which in those days was considered a bit of an honor, having an older church authority select you and all. Sarah didn't want anything to do with the old Bishop and told him so.

Carma took a sip of her coffee and continued. "Eventually it came out that the reason Sarah wouldn't agree to the sealing was because she was in love with a young boy in town, Lyman. The town found Lyman one Saturday morning, lying in the middle of the street with no pants on. He'd been castrated in the middle of the night, and left to bleed out right there on the main thoroughfare of town. His parents scooped him up and nursed him back to health.

"When the locals went to church the next day, they were in for a surprise. Lyman's balls were nailed to the wall inside the chapel. The Bishop gave a fiery talk during sacrament meeting. He pointed at Lyman's privates, and said, 'That's what comes from disobeying authority!'

"One of Lyman's friends overheard others in the ward talking about the incident. He heard that the Bishop had directed Danites to do the deed. The Bishop reasoned that once Sarah learned that Lyman was no longer a man, she'd lose interest in him and consent to the sealing."

Deem stared down at the bowl of cereal she'd been eating. She suddenly lost the urge to eat anymore.

"Lyman's parents were furious, but they knew they couldn't take on the Bishop and ward, so they left, moved down here to Leeds. Supposedly Brigham Young learned of the incident and was pissed. But he left the Bishop in his post, never did anything to him."

"What happened to Sarah?" Deem asked.

"After a couple of months she relented. Lyman's family was gone. It was easier to just give in, so she married the Bishop. Wife number nine."

Carma paused, took another sip of coffee.

"The story I've just told you isn't uncommon. It happened a lot back in those days. It still happens today, without the castration, in fundamentalist communities. The old men force the young men out, so they can have the young girls for themselves. They're called 'lost boys.' They dump them hundreds of miles from home and let them fend for themselves. They tell them if they ever come back into the community, they'll kill them."

"So Lyman was one of the first lost boys," Winn said.

"But he was gifted," Deem said.

"Something he didn't really understand at the time," Carma said. "His mother suppressed it, in both herself and Lyman, when they converted. She didn't think it was acceptable in light of her new faith. But after they left Manti and moved to Leeds, she decided her new faith might not be all it was cracked up to be, so she went ahead and told Lyman about the gift, and began teaching him how to use it. He naturally hated the Mormon leaders for what they'd done to him. He never really got over Sarah, and he spent the last year of his life using the knowledge his mother had passed to him to ensure he'd come back as a ghost so he could monkeywrench them from the other side. He died soon after from complications caused by the castration. The moment he died, he began working against the Mormon leaders in the area. He hates the fundamentalists as much as he hates the regular Mormons. He was particularly angry with Warren Jeffs and caused that man no end of trouble. It got a lot more serious when the nuclear testing brought all that radiation and he got more powerful."

"So that's how he knew about Claude?" Winn asked.

"Yes," Carma said. "And I suspect Claude knew about him. And he knows all about the secret council. It has remained his goal to keep making life hard for higher-up Mormons, and he's become really good at it."

"The secret council must know about Lyman, then," Deem said.

"I don't know," Carma said. "Lyman excels at staying under the radar. They must know there are forces at work here, laboring against them. They call it 'Satan,' but it's really just what it always is with the Mormons – problems of their own making coming back to haunt them. They are so wrapped up in their own world – you know how insular they are – that I'm not sure they've identified Lyman specifically. Even if they did, at this point they'd have a hard time doing anything about it. Lyman has spent the last thirty years building up a fortress here. For as long as I've lived here, he's been adding layer upon layer of protection. If they knew he was here, they'd have a very hard time rooting him out."

Deem smiled. "He's an ally, then," she said, regaining her desire to eat and shoveling a spoonful into her mouth.

"One of the best you could ever have, my dear," Carma said, smiling at her.

14

Deem stayed at Carma's for the rest of the morning, chatting with her and the others. Hanging out at Carma's was like staying at a really good friend's house – comfortable, relaxed, and fun. Before she knew it, it was ten a.m. and she felt the need to check on her mom.

They all packed back into Winn's Jeep and left, Carma standing at the threshold, waving to them as they left.

"I think she asked us to come back at least fifty times," Deem said as they rode back to St. George.

"That's her," Awan said. "And she means it. She obviously likes you two. You should drop in there anytime and visit her. You don't need me around to do it."

"That story about Lyman was a trip," Winn said. "Fucking barbaric."

"He seemed really sad to me," Deem said.

"That's because you reminded him of Sarah," Awan said. "Usually he's just angry. Very angry."

"Carma seems to know how to deal with him," Winn said.

"They've been a team for years now," Awan said. "She doesn't put up with bullshit, as you probably figured out. And he needs her to do things that he can't do himself, physically. So it works out. That's how she got the house."

"From Lyman?" Winn asked. "He gave her the house?"

"Yes," Awan said. "They struck a deal, way back."

"But since he's a ghost, how could he control the ownership?" Winn asked.

"I don't know," Awan said, "but for some reason, the documents always say what Lyman wants them to say."

They stopped at the restaurant parking lot where Awan had left his car the night before. "You'll call us when that chalk is ready?" Winn asked as Awan hopped out of the Jeep.

"I will," Awan said. Deem left the Jeep too, and ran to Awan, throwing her arms around him and giving him a long hug.

"Thank you," she said. "I owe you."

"You'll help me with the brothers in Indian Springs," Awan said, "and we'll call it even."

Awan walked to the open window where Winn sat inside the Jeep. Winn extended his arm, and said "Thank you, Awan."

Awan grasped his arm just below the elbow, and they held each other's arm for a moment. "You're welcome, my brother," he said, then dropped Winn's arm and walked to his car. Winn and Deem watched as he left.

Deem got back into the Jeep. "He called you brother," Deem said. "I don't think he meant it in the Mormon way."

"No, he meant it in the Paiute way," Winn said. "So he really meant it."

■ ■ ■

Deem checked with her mother as soon as she walked in the house. Her mother was vacuuming the stairs, something she only did if she felt good.

"No bite this morning?" Deem asked her above the roar of the vacuum cleaner.

"No!" her mother shouted back. "No bite!"

"That's good!" Deem said. "Aunt Virginia still here?"

"She's going back tomorrow," Margie shouted. "It'd be nice if you'd come with us to dinner tonight. I thought we'd drive into St. George and eat at that place in Santa Clara that serves fresh pasta."

"Sounds good," Deem shouted back. "What time?"

"Let's leave here at four," Margie yelled.

"Alright," Deem said. *That means we'll be eating at five,* she thought. *Old people.*

She went up to her bedroom and saw her father's day planners, lying in a stack on her dresser. She closed the door to her bedroom, cutting down the sound of the vacuum enough that she could make a phone call. She dialed the number for the bank in Hurricane.

"Hi," she said once a voice picked up on the other end. "I need to speak to Mr. Braithwaite. It's about my loan status."

"I'm sorry," the voice said, "but Mr. Braithwaite is out sick today. Could Mr. Bennett help you instead?"

"No, that's OK," Deem said. "I'll try back tomorrow. Thanks."

It's working, Deem thought. *Just as Awan said.*

She wondered what Braithwaite looked like right about now. Was his flesh falling off as he rotted? Maybe he tried to pick up something, and he felt the skin of his fingers slide off?

Deem shivered from grossing herself out, but then laughed to herself, feeling good at the sense of victory.

Maybe I should ride out to his house and see what's going on, she thought. *No. He still may have some power. Too dangerous. But I would love to see the look on his face.*

She spent the rest of the day getting cleaned up and regaining her strength. She thought she'd go visit Carma after dinner and begin looking through the documents they'd stored in the side room.

I should get those documents copied or scanned somehow, she thought. *I'll talk to Carma about it tonight, see if she has any suggestions.*

The idea of seeking Carma's advice sat well with her, and she knew Carma would be open to it. Carma was one of the most immediately approachable people she'd ever met, and even though she'd known her only a short time, she liked her immensely.

A couple of hours before four, she placed on headphones and listened to some music while lying on her bed, but she quickly fell asleep. She'd had an early morning on the heels of a long, tiring day, and it caught up with her. When she rolled off her bed after her nap, she saw it was time to go to dinner with her mother and Aunt Virginia.

Dinner had been pleasant and the pasta was very good. She saw other people with wine glasses at their table, and she wondered how it tasted. She'd never tried any alcohol, in accordance with her Mormon upbringing. When the waitress had asked her mom if she wanted to see the wine list, her mother laughed at her as though she'd asked if the sky was green. "Of course not!" she'd replied, with the air that said "I'm Mormon, I don't drink wine, and how dare you think I might!" Deem hated when her mother acted like that in public, but she didn't say anything to her about it. Her mother had developed this heightened attitude ever since her father had become stake president, and she knew her actions would be more heavily scrutinized by local members.

Deem noticed that the waitress did not offer coffee at the end of the meal, even though she'd seen her offer it to other tables. *Proba-*

bly doesn't want to get attitude again, Deem thought. *This meal needs to get over, so I can get out to Leeds.*

Deem was answering questions that her aunt was lobbing at her and picking at a dry piece of tiramisu when her she felt her phone vibrate. She pulled it out. It was Winn.

"Sorry," she said, standing up. "Gotta take this."

She walked to the back of the restaurant where the restrooms were located, and answered the phone.

"Winn?" she said.

"Yeah, it's me," Winn said. "We've got a problem."

"What?"

"Awan just called me. He's got a friend who's wired into the whole skinrunner thing, knows people who know the shaman, that kind of thing."

"Yeah?"

"Word is, the shaman is pissed. Braithwaite called him when he noticed he was losing his powers, demanding his money back. The shaman's in the process of figuring out how it happened. Presumably to put a stop to it for future skinrunners."

"Does he know it was us?"

"Awan didn't know. But Awan thinks we need to take the guy down."

"Who? The shaman?"

"Yes. He says if the shaman doesn't know it was us already, he will soon. And then he'll come after us, since we're a threat to his business."

"Jesus Christ!" Deem said. She could feel all of the relaxation of the day quickly evaporate. "How do we take down a shaman? Does he have any ideas?"

"He thinks we should meet up in North Vegas again. If I tell him eight, do you think you can make it?"

"No, make it nine. I'm in St. George at a goodbye dinner for my aunt, she's going back to Arizona tomorrow. So I'm not back to Mesquite for at least an hour."

"I'll tell him nine. Keep me posted if that changes, OK?"

"Will do."

"Here we go again," Winn said. Deem could almost see him shaking his head on the other end of the phone.

■ ■ ■

"We can't ignore him," Awan said. "He will track us down, I guarantee it."

Deem sat at the restaurant inside the truck stop in North Vegas. She'd been trying everything she could think of to avoid going after the shaman, but Awan had shot down each idea.

"We're in this up to our necks," Awan said. "Dealing with the shaman was always a potential thing we'd have to do. If I'd heard from my friends that he was blowing off the skinrunner, I wouldn't be saying we need to act. We could let it sit. But he's hunting, trying to figure out how it happened. He'll figure it out eventually."

"Even if he does, what's to say he'll come after us?" Deem asked. "We're gifted, he'll know that. I assume taking down a skinrunner will be viewed as substantial, powerful. Maybe he'll cut his losses and move on."

Awan shook his head. "I don't think so."

"Winn?" Deem asked. "What do you think?"

"I think Awan knows more about it than we do, and we have to listen to his advice."

Deem looked at Winn, upset. She was expecting him to back her up.

"Deem," Winn said, "why are you so resistant? Awan wouldn't feel this strong about it if it wasn't a threat. Normally you'd be all over it. What's up?"

Deem paused for a moment, thinking of the best way to phrase her reluctance. "To be honest with you, I thought we were free of the skinrunner, and I wanted some time to go through the documents we got from Claude. I had my heart set on it, was looking forward to it. The person I really want to bring down is Dayton. But if we have to do this, then we have to."

"After we deal with the shaman," Winn said, "we'll take down Dayton. He's next."

"I think you've both got your expectations out of whack," Awan said. "Dayton and the secret council are a much bigger threat than the shaman, and will take longer to fight. They're a network. They'll have lots of people to deal with. You don't even know all their names yet."

"That's what I'm hoping I'll find in Claude's files," Deem said. "That's why I want to start reading them."

"I agree with that," Awan said. "But I don't think you'll be taking Dayton down anytime soon. Even after we kill the shaman."

"Why not?" Winn asked. "He deserves it, for killing Claude."

"Let's say you're able to piece together the names of some or most of the council," Awan said. "These will be prominent people, right? What are you going to do? Pick them off, like assassins? That's not going to work, you'll be caught and tried as murderers. And I guarantee you there's a support structure, another group of people who do the bidding of the council, who don't even realize there IS a council, but they're loyal and do what they're told, and you'll have to deal with them, too. That wasn't a council member in

Claude's house, it was one of their followers. They're careful. They won't kill directly. When they come after you, it'll be one of their underlings, not them. You don't have a plan, and you'll need a plan to deal with them."

"Then the documents might help devise a plan," Deem said. "Right?"

"They might," Awan said. "And they might not. But suppose they do. The plan might be, at best, co-existence with the council. You might be able to find a way to neutralize their desire to take you down, and that's it. I'd be very surprised if you come up with a way to bring down the whole organization. I think you'll find that it's old, complex, entrenched, and very good at protecting itself."

"You're really bringing me down, man," Winn said.

"I'm just saying you need to be realistic," Awan said. "I don't like the IRS, but the best I can do is deal with my tax return. I can't bring them down, they're too big. I have to live with them, even though I don't like them."

Deem knew the moment Awan explained it that it was true. She didn't want it to be, but it was. The shaman was the immediate threat; the secret council was going to be a much bigger nut to crack. She might never crack it.

"Alright," Deem said. "I see your point. We need to deal with the shaman first. And I'll adjust my expectations on the council. But they have to pay for killing Claude."

"Of course," Awan said. "Lyman can help you with that."

"What do we do about the shaman?" Deem asked. "I don't even know where to start. With Braithwaite?"

"No," Awan said. "Braithwaite is doomed. He'll be gone in a couple of days."

"I called the bank, by the way. He did call in sick," Deem said.

"Good," Awan replied. "OK. What we've got to do is find the shaman and then figure out what his weaknesses are. Finding him is probably the easy part. My friends tell me when the Navajos exiled him, he moved to Kanab. The rumor is that he operates out of the old Indian school there."

"That's the school where they'd bus native American kids from the reservation?" Winn asked.

"Up until about twenty years ago," Awan said. "It was originally a hospital for vets. Lots of World War II soldiers were treated there. After the war they turned it into a school. They'd bus them in from all over, mostly Navajo. The kids stayed on campus for the school year, then went back home. Their big goal was to drive the Indian out of them, make them like white kids. Accelerate the Book of Mormon prediction."

"What was that?" Winn asked.

"That they'd eventually turn white," Deem said.

"You gotta be shitting me," Winn said.

"Nope," Deem said.

"There was a lot of abuse at the school," Awan said. "A lot of the staff thought of the kids as animals needing to learn white man ways, and they treated the kids accordingly. Eventually budget cutbacks shut it down, that and the fact the Navajos would rather teach their children on the res than have them bussed away for a year at a time.

"So the school is just a collection of old buildings now, slowly deteriorating. There's a fence around the place, but people break in all the time. Lots of graffiti. It has a reputation for being haunted, and it is. You can find videos on YouTube of kids exploring the place, but they never make it as far as the basements and the underground tunnels that connected the buildings. That's where my friends say the shaman is living. Set up shop in one of the sub-basements. Keeps the kids away by scaring them."

"Why there?" Deem asked. "Why not in a house somewhere?"

"The place is full of bad mojo," Awan said. "Years of vets going through constant pain. There are stories of an amputation pit, where they'd dispose of the limbs. Then add to that the abuse the kids went through, ripped from their families and forced to do things a certain way, the white way, or be punished. Whippings, confinement, sexual abuse. Lots of bad mojo. Then add fallout. A perfect vortex for his skinrunner ritual."

"Sounds like a horrible place," Deem said. "I don't relish the idea of going there."

"But that's where we'll need to start, right?" Winn asked.

"Right," Awan said. "At least, that's the only lead I have on him."

"Does he have a name?" Deem asked.

"He's known as Ninth Sign," Awan said.

"What do you suggest we do?" Deem asked. "Just walking right into his home base seems like a bad idea."

"I think we can get the Navajo to do the work and get rid of him," Awan said. "He came from them, so he's their responsibility. I have a Navajo friend who is already pressuring the tribe to do the work. They've told him they'll do it, but they don't know where he's at. Right now it's only a rumor that he's at the school, so we need to be sure. If we can tell the tribe his exact location, they'll feel obligated to go in. So, go tomorrow, during the day. See if he's there. I'd go with you, but I have to be in Vegas for my mom. She's having an operation."

"We could wait for you to come with us," Deem said. "Until after your mom is out."

"Waiting is a bad idea," Awan said. "You should do this before he figures out how Braithwaite was killed. He's still on the defensive, which is good. He won't know you. Once he moves to offense, it'll be a lot harder."

"So, we go in and make sure he's at the school?" Winn asked. "That's all?"

"Take a video camera with you," Awan said. "Go in as kids, just exploring the grounds for fun. See if you can locate exactly where he's at. The more specific you can be, the better, so note which building he's in, which tunnel, that kind of thing. Once you know, leave. Don't confront him. Call me as soon as you get out, and I'll call my friend. He'll pass the info on to the Navajos, and they'll go in and finish him off."

"Alright," Deem said. "Winn and I will leave for Kanab first thing tomorrow."

"Good," Awan said.

"Is he gifted, like you and me?" Winn asked.

"Yes," Awan said. "But when he became a shaman, it turned into more than that. He took on the ancient knowledge, and he carries it with him. When the tribe kicked him out, they stripped him of his right to that knowledge, but by that point he'd stolen the parts of it he wanted for his purposes. I think he used the radiation to twist and warp some of the tribe's processes. That's why kicking him out wasn't enough, and now they're going to need extreme measures to neutralize him."

"Your Navajo friend," Winn said, "he'll be able to get the tribe to finish him? They've agreed to do it?"

"I think so," Awan said. "I think the tribe thought they could kick him out, and he'd lose his powers, and disappear. So it's embarrassing to them that he's still operating. They don't want him out there, rogue, giving them a bad name. The Navajo keep that kind of thing to themselves, they don't like it to be known by outsiders. Most Navajo won't even *say* the word 'skinwalker,' so they're not likely to allow him to keep making them, even if he's off the res. Especially these fucked up skinrunners, attacking white people. Not what they want. I think they'll clean him up, quick. The tribe will be far more of a threat to him than us. We screwed with one of his skinrunners, but the tribe can screw with his entire operation."

"This may not be as hard as I thought," Winn said. "Thank god we've got the Navajo nation on our side."

"Don't let me mislead you," Awan said. "You'll need to keep your wits about you. It's important that he not detect who you are."

"Should we use protection, going in?" Deem asked. Protection was a liquid Deem used when exploring caves and mines. It offered a general protection against mental attacks, but she'd found it also helped repel creatures in the River.

"Yes, drink protection. And use this," Awan said, removing two items from his pocket and handing one to each of them. Deem took the item and examined it. It was a beaded emblem in the shape of a circle, about an inch wide. The beads formed a spiral pattern. "It'll keep the parts of your memory you don't want him to read locked away in the back of your brain," Awan said. "Wall off all of that stuff before you go in, and this will make it appear that it's not there. If you run into him, he'll think you're just two gifteds, out for a thrill, making a video like other kids. He won't pick up anything about the skinrunner or why you're really there. Think of it as insurance."

Deem dropped into the River, and the beaded circle in her hand transformed into a small snake that twisted between her fingers. It had a large blue head. She felt its tongue dart out, scratching at her palm. She screamed and dropped out of the River, dropping the beaded circle on the table.

"It moved!" she said. "It's a fucking snake!"

"Yes," Awan said, smiling at her reaction. "Just before you go in, hold the emblem to your forehead, like this." Awan picked up the beaded circle Deem had dropped, and placed it squarely above his eyes. "Then drop into the River. The snake will enter your head."

"Oh, fuck no," Deem said. Awan looked at her. "Fuck no!" she repeated.

"When you want to remove it, hold the emblem at the back of your head, here," Awan said, moving it to the back side of his head and pressing it against his hair. "It'll come back out."

"Goddamn it, Awan," Deem said, letting her head drop toward the table. Winn began to chuckle.

"She hates critters," Winn said to Awan, smiling.

"Why a snake?" Deem said, raising her head.

"Trust me, you'll be glad you had this," Awan said. "My grandfather made these. They work. Try it. Go ahead."

"Here?" Deem said, looking around the restaurant.

"They won't notice anything," Awan said. "Just hold it there for a second and drop in."

"You promise me it'll come back out?" Deem said, a panicked look on her face. Winn laughed and smacked the top of the table with his hand, delighted with her anxiety.

"Yes, it'll come back out," Awan said. "Before you do it, think of the things you want walled off, so the snake will know what to do."

"Oh, god, creepy," Deem said, shivering. She held the emblem up to her forehead, thinking about the skinrunner and the shaman, and their experiences over the past few days. She thought of Braithwaite's house, cutting the bone fragments out of her aunt and mother, and of the bus ride back from Pipe Springs. Then she pressed the circle against her forehead.

She fell forward, her head hitting the table with a bang. It flipped a spoon that flew up into the air and landed on Winn. He let out a loud laugh.

People at nearby tables looked over, and their waitress came running. "Is everything OK?" she asked.

Winn was trying to conceal his laughing. "She's fine," Awan said to the waitress, raising Deem's head from the table and hiding the emblem in his palm. "She's narcoleptic," Awan said. "Happens sometimes. She'll come around in a moment."

"Do you need anything?" the waitress asked, worried.

"No, everything's fine," Awan said. "We're used to it. Maybe a water refill?"

The waitress furrowed her brow, then turned to retrieve the water. After she'd walked away Winn said to Awan, "Did you know that would happen?"

"No," Awan said back. "It never does that to me."

Deem's eyes fluttered open, and she found herself leaning on Awan's shoulder. She slowly righted herself.

"Oh, that was fucked up," Deem said, holding the table.

"You passed out," Winn said, still snickering. "You flipped silverware all over. The waitress is coming back to check on you."

"I told them you were narcoleptic, so play along," Awan said.

The waitress returned with a water pitcher. "Oh, you're back, I see!" she said to Deem.

"Sorry about that," Deem said, looking up at her sheepishly. "I really can't control it."

"No problem, hun," the waitress said, pouring refills. "You just relax. Is there anything I can get you?"

"No, I'm fine, really," Deem said. *Other than having a snake crawling through my mind, that is.*

"Alright, you let me know if you do," the waitress said, turning away. She noticed a man at the next table staring at Deem. "What are you looking at?" she said to the man as she passed him, and he lowered his gaze back to the food at his table.

"What did it feel like?" Winn asked, running his fingers over the beads on the emblem Awan had given him. "Can you feel it moving around?"

"It felt like being swallowed," Deem said, "then nothing. Blackout. Now I just feel dizzy, like things are moving around me."

"That'll pass," Awan said. "Give it a couple of minutes, and you'll be fine. You'll want to plan for this before you go into the school. Give yourself ten minutes to get past the blackout and the dizziness."

"I want to try it," Winn said, raising the emblem to his head. Awan reached out and stopped him.

"I don't know how we'd explain two narcoleptics to the waitress," Awan said. "Wait until you're in the car, please."

"Alright," Winn said.

"You want to remove it?" Awan asked Deem.

"I do, but I want to let it stay in there for a while, so I know what it's like. Is there any harm to it being in there?"

"I don't think so," Awan said, "The longest I've ever known of it being in someone was my Uncle Barry. He had it in him for five years. Long story."

"So I just put it on the back of my head, like this," Deem said, holding it to the back of her head through her hair, "and drop? It'll come right out?"

"Right out," Awan said.

"What if it doesn't?" Deem asked.

"Then I guess you'll have an extra friend riding around with you," Awan said, smiling.

"I'm not kidding, Awan," Deem said. "I want it out of me."

"It'll come out," Awan said reassuringly. It wasn't enough for Deem.

"How will I know it's out?" she asked.

"Drop and look at the emblem, both of you," Awan said. They did, and Deem saw that her circle was still a circle. Winn's turned into a snake, and he jumped.

Winn's is out of him, Awan said. *You can see it. You'll know it's out of you when you can see it instead of the emblem, in the River.*

They dropped out of the flow, and Winn looked tense.

"It's only a snake, Winn," Deem said, unable to resist teasing him.

He let his body relax. "I know that," he said. "Doesn't bother me."

"Right," Deem said, smiling at him.

"Alright, I need to get back home," Awan said, rising from the table. He pulled out his wallet and tossed some money on the table. "My mom goes into surgery early tomorrow morning. You'll call me when you're done at the school?"

"We will," Winn said. "And thanks for this," he said, holding up the emblem.

"I hope your mom will be OK," Deem said. "What's the surgery for, if you don't mind my prying?"

"Gallbladder," Awan said. "She's been in pain for a while, so it's time to come out. She's never had surgery before, so she's scared. I promised I'd be there with her."

"Of course," Deem said. "I hope it all goes well."

"Thank you," Awan said. "Call me." He turned and walked out of the restaurant. Deem sat across from Winn, both of them holding the beaded emblem.

"So we're going to go into the lion's den?" Deem asked.

"Sounds like it," Winn said. "But I'm excited to try this." He held the emblem up and shook it. "Sounds like fun."

"I can't feel it now," Deem said. "The dizziness is past."

Winn placed the emblem to his forehead and pressed it there, surprising Deem. His eyes rolled back in his head. Deem reached forward, ready to catch his head if he fell forward. Instead, he slowly removed the circle from his head. His eyes rolled back into position, and he looked at Deem.

"That IS a trip," Winn said.

"It's hard to describe how it feels, isn't it?"

"Yeah. Kind of like...well, no...like..."

"Hard to describe, I know. Did you think about anything? What were you walling off?"

"Nothing. Didn't think about anything."

"Great. Maybe it'll wall off everything, by default."

"Or nothing. How would we know, unless someone who can read minds tested us."

"We could try it with Carma," Deem said. "I think she can read minds. A little, at least."

"We could stop there on the way out to Kanab tomorrow, and see. Do you want to leave them in, until then?"

"God no!" Deem said. She placed the emblem at the back of her head and pressed. Her head fell forward onto the table, making the dishes jump.

"Fuck," Winn said, sliding out of his side of the booth and back in next to Deem. He raised her head off the table and laid it on his shoulder. The waitress walked by again, and gave Winn a patronizing look that seemed to say, "I'm so sorry it happened again, but I'm glad I don't have that fucking disease!"

Winn smiled at the waitress as he patted Deem's cheek, trying to revive her. After a moment she opened her eyes.

"Please don't do that again in public," Winn said.

"I passed out again?" Deem asked.

"Yes."

"And you came to my rescue," she said, noticing how close he was sitting next to her. She patted his leg under the table. "I'm OK now, big boy. Thank you."

"Did it come out?" Winn asked.

They both dropped briefly into the River. Deem's emblem turned into the small snake, twisting in her palm and rising its head to slide around her little finger. Winn's emblem remained a beaded circle.

"Apparently so," Deem said.

"How'd it feel?"

"The same. Blackout. Now I feel like I have a headache growing deep in there."

"I imagine pulling a wall out of your head would be a little painful. I'm leaving mine in until later tonight." He slid out of the booth from Deem and back to his original side. "I've got someone coming over tonight, and I want to see what it feels like while having sex."

"That's so stupid," Deem said. "It walls off memories. It's not extascy."

"How would you know about extascy?" Winn asked, smiling at her.

"We learned about it in health class," Deem replied. "If you think that snake in your head is going to make you have a more intense orgasm or something, you're crazy. It just walls off memories."

"I was thinking more about having it wall off memories about the best sex I've ever had," Winn said, poking at a couple of lingering French fries on his plate. "It would make even shitty sex seem great."

Deem rolled her eyes. "Let's go," she said, sliding out of the booth. "It'll be after midnight before we get home. And we've got a big day tomorrow." She slipped the emblem into her pants pocket and pulled out her phone.

"Texting mommy?" Winn said as he stood up and paid the tab.

"She worries about me," Deem said. "And I worry about her, since Dad died. Pick me up tomorrow? For the drive to Kanab?"

"Sure," Winn said, pushing open the doors to the restaurant and walking outside. "Kanab will take two hours, so I'll be to your place around nine."

They walked out to Winn's Jeep, Deem texting as she walked. Winn stopped when he saw the Jeep, and Deem bumped into him.

"What the fuck, Winn?" Deem said. She saw him standing still, staring at the Jeep. She walked around him, and saw what he was looking at.

On top of the Jeep was a large animal with black hair. It was lying on its side, its head draped over the windshield. Its throat had been cut, and the blood had drained down the windshield and under the hood. Someone had used their finger to write two words in the blood: SUFFER. ATONE.

"Fuuuuck!" Deem said, turning to Winn. He stared at the car, unmoving. She turned to look around the parking lot, scanning for who might have done the act. Aside from a dozen other cars spread throughout the lot, she saw nothing.

"Who would do this?" she asked, walking up to the car. Winn slowly followed her. She could see that the animal was a large dog, a black lab.

"Suffer?" she said, turning back to Winn. "What the fuck? Why?"

"I don't know," Winn said. "But I can guess."

15

Deem swung at the alarm clock, hitting the snooze. After removing the dog from the Jeep, they'd driven to a car wash. She'd told Winn to take an extra hour, and pick her up at ten. She wanted to sleep in.

Now the extra hour didn't seem enough. It was nine-thirty, and she had just enough time to get up and shower before Winn would arrive. She groggily dropped one foot out of the bed and onto the carpet in her room, then swung herself up and used the momentum of the swing to propel herself into the bathroom.

After cleaning up and dressing she walked downstairs. Her mother was in the kitchen.

"Good morning, dear," Margie said.

"Aunt Virginia get off OK?" Deem asked.

"Yes. I wish you would have gotten up and said goodbye to her."

"I said goodbye last night, mom. Six a.m. is way too early." Deem removed a box of cereal from a cabinet and poured a bowl.

"She wanted to get an early start. Oh, some mail came for you this morning."

"I never get mail," Deem said, walking over to the envelope her mother had set aside for her.

"It's from the church," Margie said, watching over her shoulder as she opened it. "So it must be important."

Deem read the letter. Before she could get past the first sentence, she heard Winn honking outside.

"Gotta go, Mom," Deem said, folding the letter back up.

"What did it say?" Margie asked, following her as she walked to the front door.

"I don't know," Deem said, opening the door and running out. "I'll let you know. Bye!"

She shut the door and ran to Winn's Jeep. She could still see some blood caked below the windshield wipers.

"You gotta get another car wash," Deem said as she got in.

"Yeah, I saw that this morning once it was light," Winn said. "What's that in your hand?"

"Oh, a letter I just got," Deem said, strapping the seat belt around her as Winn took off. "It's from the church."

"The church?" Winn said.

"Yeah," Deem said, turning the envelope toward him. She pointed her finger at the logo in the left corner of the envelope. "Official."

"What's it say?" he asked.

"Don't know, haven't read it yet," she said, opening it up once again. She unfolded the stationery. Winn could see another logo at the top of the page. He let her read silently for a minute.

"They're excommunicating me," Deem said, dropping her hands to her sides. "I'm being called to a Bishop's Court."

"So what?" Winn said. "You hate it anyway."

"This is to hurt my mother," Deem said. "This will devastate her. To her it means I won't be in heaven with her, in the next life. This is Dayton's doing, to get back at me by hurting her. What an asshole."

"What's a Bishop's Court?" Winn asked.

"They haul you in front of a group of men and grill you," Deem said. "I heard my father talk about it, since he sat in on many of them. It's usually reserved for criminals, adulterers, and apostates."

"Well, you're certainly an apostate," Winn said.

"Not really," Deem said. "I'm just a jack Mormon. I don't go to church, I'm not active, but they don't excommunicate inactives. Half the church is inactive, they'd be half as big if they did that. They only excommunicate when they want to make a point."

"Are you going to go to the Bishop's Court?" Winn asked.

"Oh, hell no," Deem said. "That's playing by their rules. I'm not going to sit there and defend myself while the fix is in. They'll ex me in absentia. And excommunicating the daughter of a former stake president is a big deal, this'll be talked about. I don't care, really. It's my mom. She'll bear the brunt of it. Dayton knew it would hurt her. The fucker."

"She'll survive," Winn said.

"I don't know," Deem said, looking out the window. "You don't know how hard they make it. Her whole social structure is the ladies in her ward. An excommunicated daughter means she was a bad mother. Some of them will shun her, others will treat her differently. She's used to a certain level of respect because my father was a stake president. That'll all be gone now. That will be hell for her."

"After we take care of this shaman," Winn said, "we'll figure out how to get back at Dayton. We'll make him pay for hurting your mom like this."

"Tit for tat," Deem said. "I wonder what the charges are."

"Charges?"

"Oh, they have to accuse you of something in order to do this," Deem said, shaking the paper between them in the car. "They've trumped up something. It would be interesting to hear what."

Winn wound his way through the gorge, slowing for trucks and watching out for cops. Deem looked up at the steep mountain faces, some natural, others carved for the freeway. Whenever she drove through the gorge, she always thought she saw small cave openings in the rocks, high up on the sides of the mountain. It looked like hundreds of places to hide. As a little girl, she'd considered hiding in those imagined caves when she contemplated running away after fighting with her parents. Now she wanted to climb up into one of them, and just leave all of the turmoil behind. The shaman, the journals, Claude, the skinrunner, the excommunication, her mother, Awan, and Winn – just hole up in one of those caves up there with a supply of food, and ride it out, wait for it all to pass. But she knew that wasn't going to happen. She wasn't a little girl anymore. She'd fought alongside Winn as they tackled zombighosts and other creatures over the years, but meeting Claude and learning of her father's involvement with the secret council had caused her to grow up fast. The adults she trusted as a child were turning out to be false, untrustworthy, cruel. *Can't run away from this,* she thought. *Time to woman up.*

"You OK?" Winn asked.

"I'm alright," Deem said. "I guess having your history ripped out from under you makes more of an impact than I thought it would."

"That's how they want you to feel," Winn said. "Your history is still yours. You just have a more honest perspective on it now. That's better. That's healthier. Maybe they did you a favor."

"That's why they call it a 'Court of Love,'" she replied.

"You're shitting me," Winn said.

"No, really," Deem said. "They call this excommunication court a 'Court of Love.'"

"Oh, that's funny," Winn said. "And kinda creepy at the same time!"

"I know!" Deem said. "I always thought it was strange when I heard someone call it that."

"Don't let these fuckers get you down, Deem," Winn said. "That's what they want."

"I'll be OK," she said. "It's just a little jarring. I didn't think they'd go there. But they're really capable of anything, aren't they?"

"You saw what they did to Claude," Winn said. "What makes you think they won't do that to you?"

■ ■ ■

They arrived at Carma's and she welcomed them in with open arms. "Awan with you?" she asked.

"No," Winn said as she released him from a hug. "His mother is having surgery today."

"Oh, I didn't know," Carma said. She grabbed Winn's upper arm right at the bicep and gave him a squeeze. "You don't need his permission to come 'round, either of you! You can stop by anytime. I was thinking I might see you last night, Deem." She pulled Winn by the bicep into the house.

"I was planning to," Deem said, "but we had something come up, and I had to meet Awan in Vegas. We're having some trouble with a shaman that we need to do some research on later today."

"Does this have anything to do with the skinwalker epidemic?" Carma asked as they walked down the hallway to the sitting area with the view of the back yard. "Sit down and I'll get you something to drink."

Deem fell into the soft chair she'd enjoyed at their last visit, and looked out over Carma's backyard. *I suppose it's Lyman's back yard, too,* she thought. In the daytime she had a better view of the trees and bushes, and the beautiful lawn. The hill rising behind the yard made it all seem so private. There were occasional outcroppings of red rock on the hill, giving it an interesting range of color. Set against the deep green of the lawn and the trees, it looked beautiful.

Carma returned with a Diet Coke for Deem and an iced tea for Winn. "Now tell me about this shaman," she said, taking an iced tea for herself and joining them in the sitting room.

Deem relayed the story of the skinrunner and how they'd managed to neutralize him. When she mentioned the blood river, Carma's eyes went wide and she interrupted Deem.

"Oh, you didn't!" she shrieked. "Tell me you didn't!"

"Didn't what?" Deem said, confused.

"Tell me you did not walk into that awful place," Carma said.

"The blood river?" Deem asked.

"Yes," Carma said. "You didn't go in, did you?"

"I stuck my hand in it," Deem said. "And my feet."

"Oh no," Carma said, shooting up out of her chair. She began to wring her hands. "Well, Awan didn't know. He thought he was helping you. He should have talked to me first." She disappeared into another room.

Deem looked at Winn. "What the fuck?" she mouthed to him. He shrugged and took a sip of his iced tea, looking in the direction Carma had gone. "I don't know!" he mouthed back.

"Here," they heard Carma say before she entered the room. "Here!" She had a book in her hand, and she handed something to Deem in the other. Deem opened her hand and Carma dropped three small, round yellow balls in her hand. They looked like peas.

"Eat them!" Carma said. She opened the book and began reading from it, chanting in a strange language. Deem was beginning to feel freaked out, and she turned to look at Winn. He gave her another shrug, and she turned back to look at Carma, her face in the book, struggling to pronounce the words. Carma looked up, and saw the peas still in Deem's hand.

"You have to eat them while I'm saying it, dear," Carla said. "Or it won't work."

"What are they?" Deem asked. "What are you doing?"

"Cleansing you," Carma said. "You may have washed the blood from your hands and feet, but you're still tainted by it. Not all of it comes off by washing. Go on, they won't hurt you."

Deem popped the peas into her mouth. They were hard and she had to bite down on them with her molars for them to pop. Once she had them chewed down small enough, she swallowed them and chased them with a gulp of Diet Coke.

Carma continued chanting, watching as she drank. She completed the chant and closed the book, then returned to her seat next to Winn.

"Now promise me you'll not go near the place again," she said, looking pleadingly at Deem.

"We needed to," Deem said. "It was the only way to deal with the skinrunner."

"There's other ways, Awan just didn't know," Carma said. "The other blood rivers are fine, but that one is polluted."

"Its mutation is what made the ghost corporeal," Deem said. "That's why it worked. Because of the radiation."

"But what else does it do?" Carma asked. "What else is different about it?"

"I don't know," Deem said. "We were just operating off what Awan said."

"He didn't know," Carma said. "Just promise me you won't go there, again. Will you do that?"

"I suppose," Deem said.

"Sure," Winn said. "We have no reason to go back."

"And I want you to keep an eye on that hand," Carma said. "Which hand was it?"

"My hand?" Deem asked. "You mean the one I put in the blood river?"

"Yes," Carma said. "Was it your left, or your right?"

"My right," Deem said, holding it up.

"I want you to wrap it in a brown paper bag every night for the next week," Carma said, looking stern. "Spray the bag with a mixture of distilled water, Epsom salts, ground thyme, and a drop of rabbit urine. Do you have a little bit of rabbit urine at home?"

Deem saw Winn successfully control a spit-take of his tea.

"No," Deem said calmly, "I don't have any rabbit urine at home."

"Well, I'll give you some before you go," Carma said, leaning back in her seat. "It won't work at all if you don't use the rabbit pee. Now tell me about the letter you received."

Deem was dumbfounded. Carma moved from one thing to the next at breakneck speed. Further, Deem hadn't mentioned anything about the letter to her. *She* can *read minds,* Deem thought.

"You've been thinking about it since you got here," Carma said. "That and the windshield and the mindwalls. Start with the letter. What was it?"

"Bishop's Court," Deem said. "Excommunication."

"Delicious!" Carma said. "For who?"

"Me."

"Oh, that's wonderful!" Carma said, rising from her chair and extending her arms to Deem. Deem stood up and let Carma hug her. "Congratulations, my dear."

"Thanks, but I'm afraid it will not be a congratulatory thing for my mother."

"She doesn't know it yet," Carma said, "because she's brainwashed. But when she comes around, she'll realize it was the best thing for you."

"That might take a long time," Deem said, dropping back into her chair.

"Is your mother one of those Okazaki kind of sisters or is she more a jello and funeral potatoes kind of sister?"

"The latter," Deem said.

"Well, then yes, it might take a while," Carma said. "But you rest assured, my dear, it will all work out for the best." Carma's head drifted to the right, staring out the large windows. "I remember my excommunication just like it was yesterday. I sat in that Bishop's Court, looking at all those old white men staring back at me, accusing me of immorality, and I could sense that most of them were imagining the act, picturing me as their partner! I knew right then and there it was all bullshit – please pardon my language – and I felt the spirit of the Lord wash over me, the Holy Ghost filling me with the most wonderful sense of calm and peace, and I knew – I knew, I tell you – that everything was going to be alright and that the right thing was happening. They didn't want me around them, and I didn't want them around me. And there hasn't been a day since that I haven't been happier and more full of joy and peace than any day before that, let me assure you."

"Did you join another religion?" Deem asked.

"Opiate of the masses, my dear," Carma said. "You don't need religion to be full of joy and peace. I found it usually just gets in the way of the joy and the peace. Now, about the blood on your windshield last night. Winn?"

"Huh?" Winn said. He'd been tuning out the joy and peace stuff.

"Your windshield last night?"

"Oh," Winn said. "Someone killed a dog, drained its blood onto the windshield. They wrote the words 'suffer' and 'atone' in the blood."

"Do you know what it means?" Deem asked Carma.

"Yes, well, context is everything," Carma said, shaking her head. "They're messages. The 'atone' is a disgustingly literal reminder of 'blood atonement.'"

"You accused Dayton of that!" Winn said to Deem. "Remember?"

"I was just trying to upset him," Deem said. "I didn't think he'd actually do it. That was before he had Claude killed, of course."

"What exactly is it?" Winn asked.

"Blood atonement is a doctrine that was popular with Brigham Young," Carma began. "The idea was that some sins you might commit were so grievous, the blood of Jesus Christ couldn't atone for them, so your own blood had to be shed if you were to receive forgiveness for them. Murder was one of the sins that required blood atonement. More sins were added to the list as it became convenient, to scare and control people. Apostasy, mixing of races, things Brigham didn't like. They did away with the concept recently, but the idea of it lingered on in these parts. When the state executed Ronnie Lee Gardner in 2010, he said he wanted the firing squad because of his Mormon heritage. Supposedly it's only valid if blood is shed and spilled on the ground. Doesn't count if you're hanged or die of lethal injection. So it's still around, even to this day. That's why all the throat slitting."

"I've lived here for twenty eight years and this is the first I'm hearing of it," Winn said.

"Well, they don't teach it in history class, my dear," Carma said. "It's a part of history they'd rather forget."

"What about the word 'suffer?'" Deem asked. "I assume they mean us. Are they saying Winn and I should suffer by atoning with our blood?"

"Not exactly," Carma said. "It's more subtle than that. I think, in this context, 'suffer' refers to the penalty for the old blood oaths, in the temple. After making each oath, they'd agree to a penalty that went with the oath. You're familiar with the penalties; slitting the throat. Disembowelment. The penalties were to keep the oath secret, and the person was agreeing to have the penalty executed upon themselves if they ever divulged it. The words they would use were, 'rather than do so, I would suffer my life to be taken.'"

"You've got to be kidding," Winn said.

"They did away with the penalties in the ceremonies in 1990," Carma said, "but there's plenty of older people who remember them, who said those words. Just like blood atonement, they linger on. And all those people believe those penalties were the word of God, so they take them seriously. When the crazies and the religious freaks get involved, watch out – cross a line where they think you've broken an oath, and they're happy to execute the penalties on you. Remember the Lafferty boys? Slit that poor woman's throat from ear to ear, and her fifteen-month-old baby, too. Blood atonement for failing to follow a blood oath. Execution of the penalties."

"But Winn and I haven't taken any oaths," Deem said. "That I know of."

"Never went through the temple?" Carla asked. "Either of you?"

"No," Deem said.

"I'm not Mormon," Winn said. "Never was."

"Then I think the messages on your windshield were really intended for others," Carma said. "You were meant to relay them. Which you've just done, so they were intended for us, I guess. For me and Lyman. And any others they think are helping you. It's a reminder that they'll execute the penalties on us, just like they did on Claude."

"So Claude had taken oaths?" Deem asked.

"He had," Carma said. "He was Mormon, way back before he apostatized. Took those old oaths and penalties right there in the St. George temple. And he took other oaths, too, the secret oaths that people like Dayton take. Oaths you take when you join a secret group."

"Claude was a member of the secret council?" Winn asked, surprised.

"He was," Carma said, "a long time ago. When he apostatized, he lost his church membership and his church calling, and that kicked him out of the council by definition. But the oaths transcend the membership, they all know that. When he decided to talk to you about the council, he violated his oaths of secrecy. That's why they executed the penalty on him."

"You knew Claude?" Deem asked.

"I did," Carma said. "And he knew Lyman. Lyman considered him an ally."

"If Claude had been part of the council, he must have been gifted," Deem said. "He told me he wasn't."

"Well," Carma said, "he wasn't being completely honest with you. He was gifted, back in the day. Not a lot, mind you, but he had it. It left him, for some reason, over the years. I think from lack of use, but who knows, it might have been the radiation."

Deem sat in silence, letting what Carma had told her sink in. Things ran much more deeply than she had imagined.

"When we're done with the shaman," Deem said, "I'll have some time to come back and start reading the documents in the boxes we brought the other night. I was thinking it might be a good idea to scan them, digitize them, so we have a copy."

"Oh, that is a good idea!" Carma said. "Run each one right through a scanner after you read it! Smart child."

"Would you mind if I brought in a scanner and my laptop so I could do that?"

"Not at all!" Carma said. "Of course you may. Aren't you the polite child asking in advance and all! Oh, I could just eat you up, you're so cute!"

Deem smiled awkwardly. Sometimes Carma said the strangest things.

"It might take a while to go through them," Deem said. "I hope you don't mind."

"You take as long as you want," Carma said, rising from her chair. "That can is empty, let me get you another." She held her arm out to Deem, waiting for Deem to hand her the Diet Coke can. Deem passed it to her and she walked out of the room.

"That stuff about the penalties," Winn said, "is freaking me out."

"When this is over," Deem said, "I'm going to do some serious research. Utah history, that kind of thing. I wasn't paying much attention to history in high school."

Carma returned to the room with a replacement Diet Coke, which she handed to Deem.

"How long have you been excommunicated?" Deem asked her.

"Must have been thirty years ago," Carma said. "It was just after I was sealed to Lyman, so yes, that would be about thirty years."

"You and Lyman are married?" Deem asked.

"Yes," Carma said, smiling. "He proposed when I was just twenty, and I accepted immediately. He is so handsome, don't you think? And intelligent. Smart as a whip."

"I've never heard of anyone marrying a ghost before," Deem said.

"What do you think they're doing in that big temple in St. George, my dear?" Carla said. "Sealing dead people, all day long!"

"You have a point," Deem said. She knew Mormons went there to perform proxy sealings for the deceased.

"Lyman and I were sealed by the ghost of John Taylor. Not many people can say that. Some gifted fundamentalists, that's about it."

"The third president of the church?" Deem asked. "He's a ghost?"

"I think he was part gifted, myself," Carma said. "He's hung around for years. Some say he haunts the temple itself, in Salt Lake City. I contacted him at his gravesite in the Avenues and he agreed to do the sealing. He's sealed Lyman to a couple of other women over the years. He's a big polygamy advocate."

Deem leaned back in her chair. "You'll have to forgive me," she said, "but this is kind of blowing my mind."

Carma laughed. "It's OK, I'll stop. Too much for one morning, eh?"

"I guess I'm feeling overwhelmed," Deem said. "Awan told me last night to alter my expectations around the secret council, and I'm starting to think he was right. He believes they're going to take much longer to deal with than I was anticipating."

"Well, what were you expecting?" Carma asked.

"I was hoping to find something in the documents that I could use against them. Something damaging that might destroy their group."

"I think Awan is right," Carma said. "You might find something you can use, but destroying them might take much longer. Lyman's been fighting them and other groups like them for a hundred and fifty years, and he's much better at it than you. More experienced. He and Claude couldn't bring them down."

"Awan made it sound like I'd have to live with them," Deem said. "Coexist."

"And so you may," Carma said, "once you find a way to show them you won't be trifled with. I remind you, my dear, that your original goal was to locate your father's journals, not to take down the secret council. The former is an achievable goal, while the latter is probably not."

Deem tilted her head to one side, considering this. *She's right,* she thought.

"I don't mean to rain on your parade," Carma said, perking up. "Not on the jubilant day when you're learned you're to be excommunicated! We should be celebrating, not moping. Why don't you two run along and take care of that shaman, and come back here tonight for a dinner. I'll make my special pot pies, and we'll toast the Bishop's Court!"

Carma was so enthusiastic about the idea of the dinner that Deem couldn't help but smile and agree to come. "Sure," she said. "Why not?"

"And you, Winn, you'll come celebrate your friend's departure from the clutches of old while men who want to run everyone's lives, won't you? Say yes."

"Yes," Winn said, smiling at Carma's expository. "As long as we toast with booze."

"Oh, how agreeable!" Carma said, clapping her hands together. "I'll have to run to the store to get a few things. I want you to call me when you're on your way, so I can pop the pies in the oven. I don't care how late it gets, alright? We can eat and drink at two a.m. for all I care!"

"Sure," Winn said, rising from his chair. Deem stood too, knowing it was time to go.

"I'll call Awan and see how his mother is doing," Carma said as she walked them to the door. "I hope she'll be well enough that he can join us. Now, you two be sure to use those mindwalls Awan gave you. You'll be safe if you do. Well, mostly safe. I don't know how powerful this shaman is. I'll see if Lyman can lend a hand too. You said the school is in Kanab?"

"North side of town," Winn said.

"Well, I know his influence reaches at least as far as Colorado City," Carma said, "and it grows every day, so he might be able to help you in Kanab. I'll talk to him as soon as you push off."

Deem gave Carma a hug and Winn followed. Then they got into Winn's Jeep and Winn drove them back to the interstate.

"I'm not sure how to describe that visit," Deem said. "Carma just blows my mind."

"I'm still creeped out by that oath and penalty stuff," Winn said. "You Mormons are fucked up."

"This is a million miles removed from the average Mormon," Deem said. "Most are so nice you can't believe it. They'd be appalled by all of this. Anyway, I won't be a Mormon for long. By next week, I'll be off the rolls. Exiled. Denied the celestial kingdom in the next life. But you know what? If I wind up in the same place that Carma winds up, I think I'll be OK. She'll keep me entertained, at least."

"I wonder what will be in the pot pies? She didn't say."

"Let's hope it isn't rabbit pee."

16

Winn handed Deem his whiskey flask, filled with protection. "Here," he said. "Drink some."

"Damnit," Deem said. "I forgot to bring my own."

"What's wrong with mine?"

"The alcohol burns."

"You don't make yours with alcohol? I can't believe it works."

"It was a recipe my dad showed me. They figured out how to make it without alcohol."

"Mormons," Winn said, rolling his eyes. "Well, you'll be excommunicated soon, so you can drink this."

Deem took the flask and gulped down two large mouthfuls.

"Ack!" she said, gasping for air. "Why do people think alcohol tastes good?"

"They don't," Winn said. "That's why they mix it with things like orange juice."

Deem wiped her mouth and removed the beaded emblem from her pocket. "Time for this, too," she said.

"Lean over on me before you do it," Winn said. "I don't want you to crack your head open on the dash."

Deem summoned every thought she could invoke regarding the skinrunner and the shaman, and pressed the emblem against her forehead. She slumped against Winn, the emblem falling from her hand. Once she regained consciousness, Winn helped prop her back up.

"You dropped it," Winn said, pointing to the emblem on the floor of the Jeep. "You'll need that to get it back out."

"What about you?" Deem asked.

"I put mine in this morning," Winn said. "It's been squirming around in there for a while."

Deem shuddered. She still felt dizzy. She held the car door handle to steady herself.

They were parked in front of a chain link fence, and fifty yards beyond that was the cement face of one of the buildings in the school complex. The school was on the outskirts of town, and there were no houses close to it. Winn had chosen a side of the school that seemed quiet and abandoned, where no one would notice their car.

"Ready?" Winn asked, strapping a light onto his head.

"Give me a minute more," Deem said. "Still dizzy."

"No rush," Winn said. "It's early afternoon. We have plenty of time."

"What's the game plan, exactly?" Deem asked, rummaging in her backpack for the video camera Awan had told them to bring.

"Let's start with this building here," Awan said, "and work our way through the complex. From the pictures I saw on the internet last night, there's at least a dozen buildings."

"Connected by underground tunnels," Deem said.

"Yes. Awan said he's in the sub-basement of one of the buildings."

"Since he's drawing power from this place," Deem said, "would it make sense that he's in one of the central buildings, as opposed to one on the outskirts like this?" She pointed to the building in front of them.

"Possibly," Winn said.

"I'm going to trance," Deem said. "See what I can see, before we go in. Maybe I can find him without us setting foot in there."

Deem closed her eyes and dropped into the River. She immediately saw a green hue at the fence, rising up and over the building beyond.

Winn joined her in the flow. *That doesn't look good,* he thought, observing the glow at the fence.

Deem moved over to it and extended her hand. She pressed against the glow. It passed through a couple of inches, then stopped. *Some kind of barrier,* she thought. She dropped out of the River.

"Well, that won't work," Deem said, back in the car. "I guess we have to hoof it."

"Feeling good enough to walk?" Winn asked.

"Yeah, I'm fine now," Deem said, opening the car door and stepping out.

They walked up to the fence. There were plenty of spots where the fence was compromised. Winn chose one and held the fence open as Deem passed through, then she turned and held the fence for him.

Inside, they walked toward the first building. There was graffiti here and there on its face at the ground level. It looked like it was three stories tall.

"Did you look at any of the YouTube videos of this place?" Winn asked.

"Didn't have time," Deem said. "How do you get into it?"

"There's got to be a door or a window," Winn said, starting around the side of the building. There were no windows they could reach. Once they turned the corner around the edge of the building they saw the other structures of the complex. There were six or seven in sight, similar in height and construction, spread out in front of them. Cement walkways connected them all. Weeds had grown up between cracks in the walkways. Grass that had once grown between the buildings had long since burnt and dried out, and tall weeds had invaded.

"Wow," Deem said. "So quiet. And desolate."

Each of the three story buildings in front of them had broken windows and graffiti. In large letters on the one closest to them, someone had sprayed in large black letters: "Indians Go Home!"

Deem dropped into the River. It was hard to make out in the bright sunlight, but she saw figures moving along the cement sidewalks. As she focused in on them, she saw they were kids – Native American kids, carrying books.

Winn joined her in the flow. *We're downwind, Deem. It's dangerous if you're seen. They'll change and attack.*

Deem scanned he buildings. The largest one in the center was wrapped in an additional layer of green. *That's our building,* Deem said, dropping out of the flow.

"That one," Deem said, pointing to it. It was larger than the others.

"You sure?" Winn asked.

"No, but we've got to start somewhere," Deem said, "and that building has extra protection. So it's a good bet."

They walked toward the central building. It had been painted yellow years before, but the sun and the elements had turned the yellow into a peeling pale color, streaked in places where rain had carried minerals from the roof down onto the sides of the building. The doors to the structure faced a small circular cement pad, where

Deem imagined some benches or a statue might have once sat. The faded wooden sign over the double doors read "Administration."

Deem walked up to the doors. She tried the handles, which were hot. The doors didn't budge.

"Window," Winn said, stepping to the right. The lower half of a ground floor window had been broken out. It was about six feet off the ground. Winn bent over to give Deem a boost. She slid up and through the window, then turned and extended her hand to Winn, pulling him up.

They were in a small room with no furniture, but plenty of graffiti on the walls. Deem noticed a light fixture dangling from the ceiling, the glass of the fixture and the bulb smashed, lying on the ground below it. There was a wooden door with a glass window, also smashed, leading out of the room.

Winn walked out the door, and Deem followed. They were in the lobby of the building. Behind them were steps leading down to the double doors they'd tried to open. In front of them was a reception window, and hallways led to their right and left.

Deem dropped into the River again, and saw a woman sitting behind the reception window. Her head was turned away from them. She looked like she was typing. Deem dropped out.

"I wish you wouldn't do that," Winn said. "There could be hundreds of them in here, and if they see you, we're fucked," he said.

"You brought your EM gun?" Deem asked.

"Yes," Winn said, "but we're supposed to be exploring in here as kids, normal people making a YouTube video, not gifteds. That'll give us away."

"I gotta know what we're dealing with," Deem said. "I'll be careful, and I won't stay in long."

"Which way?" Winn said. "Right or left?"

"Well," Deem said, "I was raised to choose the right. So let's go left."

"Left it is," Winn said, starting down the left hallway. They passed doors, some closed, others open, exposing rooms inside.

"We're looking for a way down," Winn said. "Gotta find the basement before we can go to a sub-basement."

They poked their heads into some of the rooms they passed. They were all the same, mostly empty, some with junk. Spray paint here and there, light fixtures destroyed, glass on the ground.

The hallway reached a corner and turned right. They continued down the passage. Two large doors were open to their right, and Deem popped her head inside.

"Wow," she said, stepping into the room. "The auditorium."

They were standing at the back of a large open room. At the far end of the room was a raised stage. Deem let herself drop into the River, and saw the room filled with students. There was a group of teachers, sitting along a table on the stage. Most of them were looking down, but Deem saw one begin to look up in her direction. She dropped out of the River quickly.

"It's full of them," Deem said. "Don't drop here."

"Damnit, Deem!" Winn said. "Did they see you?"

"I don't think so. There's at least a hundred kids sitting in chairs, and teachers up on the stage. Someone speaking at a podium."

"Stop dropping!" Winn said. "It's not helping. I don't want to get chased out of here!"

"Alright," Deem said. They turned and walked out of the auditorium.

Deem saw the staircase directly across from the auditorium entrance. A wide set of stairs led up, and a smaller set led down. They walked down the stairs and found a closed metal door at the bottom, locked.

"Did you bring your picks?" Deem asked Winn.

"Of course," Winn said, setting down his backpack and retrieving his tools. He turned on his head lamp to light up the lock on the door.

"This is a no-go," Winn said. "Look."

Deem observed the lock that Winn had lit. Someone had smashed at it repeatedly, trying to get through the door. The lock itself looked so damaged it couldn't be picked.

"Great," Deem said. "Doesn't look like we can kick it in, either. Would probably already be open if you could."

"There might be another stairwell," Winn said. "Maybe on the other side of the auditorium."

Deem walked back up the stairs, Winn behind her. As she reached the top, she felt something pass by in front of her. She'd felt this kind of brush of air many times before, in caves and mines, and her experience told her it wasn't a draft. Her first reaction was to drop into the River and see what it was, but she knew that would expose her and Winn, so she resisted.

"What?" Winn said behind her. "Why'd you stop?"

"Something in front of me," Deem said. "Significant."

Deem strained to detect what was moving in the hallway in front of her. It wasn't a normal ghost, but it wasn't a zombighost either. *A different mutation?* she wondered. She focused as intently as she could – one step away from slipping into the River, which would betray them. She felt the air again. Whatever it was, it was turning in front of her, receding.

"You felt that?" Deem asked.

"No," Winn said. "I didn't feel anything."

"It's moving away," Deem said. "I want to drop in for just a second and see what it is. It'll be facing away from us."

Before Winn could object, Deem dropped into the flow and stared down the hallway. She saw a creature that was huge, lumbering away from her. It looked like a bear, but it was twice as big as any bear she'd ever seen. It was so large it nearly filled the hallway. As it walked, she noticed it left wet footprints behind. *Blood*, she thought. The footprints dried and disappeared after a few seconds. She dropped back out of the River.

"Bear," Deem said, turning to Winn. "Huge bear. I mean huge, not normal size."

"Spirits of animals he's trapped here?" Winn asked.

"Or a new breed of skinwalker?" Deem said. "Awan said he'd been experimenting, right?"

"I seem to remember that, yes."

"Then who knows what's in this place," Deem said, a little panicked.

"As long as we stay out of the River, we should be fine," Winn said. "That was the plan, remember? Let's just find the subbasement and locate the shaman, alright? No more dropping."

"Alright," Deem said, not entirely sure she could honor the promise. She'd learned, over the years, to resist the urge to drop in front of zombighosts and avoid the chase. But this place felt different, and the entities felt different. She wasn't sure if her fear would win out over her curiosity.

They walked through the auditorium, toward a pair of double doors on the other side of the room. Deem knew the room was filled with spirits. She resisted the urge to drop and examine them.

When they reached the far side of the auditorium, they went through the doors. Winn was right; there was another set of stairs. They went down.

Winn turned his head lamp back on and lit up the lock on the door at the bottom. This one was intact. He removed his tools and began picking it. Deem waited patiently, listening for sounds in the distance. She could hear a rumble that increased in intensity, then diminished. Then she thought she heard a scream, far in the distance. It was just loud enough that she wasn't sure she'd heard it.

"Hurry up," she said to Winn. "It feels like things are shifting in here."

"Shifting?" Winn said as he moved a torsion wrench in the lock. "What do you mean?"

"I mean something is building," Deem said, "and when it reaches a certain point, things are going to shift. We need to get out before that happens."

The lock gave in to Winn, and as he replaced his tools, Deem pushed the door open.

She turned on her headlamp, and they made their way through a dark hallway that opened after twenty feet into a large room. There were a number of passages leading out of the room in all directions.

"The tunnels," Deem said. "This is the central point."

"I remember seeing this on the YouTube videos," Winn said. "I remember those spray-painted arrows on the walls."

"People must have gotten in here somehow, even with that door locked," Deem said.

"Probably from one of these passageways," Winn said, walking to the entrance of one of them and looking down it. He could see ten feet before his headlamp illuminated a pile of junk blocking most of the tunnel. "Some of them must be passable. Maybe not this one."

Deem walked to another tunnel entrance and looked down into it. It went off into the darkness, further than her headlamp could reveal. "This one looks like it goes a ways," she said.

"This is the basement," Winn said. "But we're after the sub-basement. If these tunnels just run to the other buildings, they're not what we're looking for."

Deem paused, hearing the rumbling sound once again. A faint scream accompanied it.

"Did you hear that?" she said.

"No, I didn't."

"Sounds far away, but it was louder than last time. Something's coming, and it's coming fast. That's the shift I was talking about."

"I still don't know what you mean by a shift."

"It's like when the pressure builds in your ear, before it pops. You know it's going to pop at some point."

"Any idea what happens when this pops?"

"Not exactly, but it feels like something bad. There it is again. You don't hear it?"

"No! I can't hear anything."

Deem bent over, holding her hands to the side of her head. "It's so loud!" she yelled at Winn. "We gotta get out of here!"

Deem struggled to keep conscious. The sound was overpowering and rapidly increasing. She looked up at Winn and was confused that he just stood there, apparently not hearing the noise or feeling the pressure. It was building quickly, reaching incredible volumes. It was so loud she couldn't think straight, and it was painful.

Deem did the only thing she could think of to do; she screamed.

Like the effect of an ear popping, there was immediate relief. Deem opened her eyes, and saw Winn standing in front of her, bathed in a blue light.

"Oh my god," she said. Winn looked confused. She turned to inspect the room, looking for the source of the light. It was coming from one of the tunnels.

"Deem?" Winn asked. "Are you OK?"

She walked to the tunnel where the light emanated, and looked into it. About ten feet ahead, the floor of the tunnel gave out, dropping down into a room below the tunnel. The light was coming from the room.

Deem turned to Winn. "That's it!" she said, pointing.

"What's it?" Winn asked, confused. "Are you alright?"

"I'm fine now," Deem said. "Come on, let's check it out."

"Check what out?"

Deem stopped. "You don't see that?"

"See what?" Winn asked, becoming irritated.

"The hole in the floor? The blue light?"

"No, I don't. I see a tunnel running off into the distance. No hole. No light."

"You didn't hear that sound? The sound that built up until it shifted, when I screamed?"

"You didn't scream," Winn said, walking to her and grabbing her arm. "Deem, you're scaring me. Whatever you're seeing, I'm not seeing it. This room looks the same to me as when we came into it."

Deem looked at Winn and could see he was confused and worried. He wasn't lying. *Why can I see these things, and he can't?*

"Winn, I think this is the sub-basement," Deem said. "I think we've found him. Down that hole in the tunnel."

"Well then, good, I'll take your word for it. Let's leave, and we'll call Awan and tell him."

"But why can't you see it?"

"I don't care why, if that's it, I believe you. Let's just get out of here."

The blue light from the sub-basement lit their way back to the stairwell door for Deem, but Winn seemed reliant on his headlamp. When they emerged from the stairwell, Deem stopped.

"Winn, I want you to pop your head into the auditorium and try something," Deem said.

"What?"

"Drop into the River, for just a second. Tell me what you see."

"No!" Winn said. "Are you crazy?"

"If you stand in the door well, they won't see you. I need to know if you can see them like I can."

Winn relented, and walked to the double doors of the auditorium. He angled himself so he could see a thin sliver of the room beyond, and dropped. After a couple of seconds, he came back.

"Ghosts on the floor, in chairs," Winn said. "Kids."

"You can see them?" Deem asked, surprised.

"Yes, now let's go!"

Winn turned and walked down the hallway, back to the reception area. Deem followed him, puzzling over what he'd told her.

Once they had jumped out of the window and were outside of the building, Winn removed his cell phone. "One bar," he said, checking the reception. He pressed a button and held the phone to his ear as they began walking in the direction of their car.

"Deem found it," he said into the phone. "The Administration building, right in the middle of the school. Go down the right stairwell, and it's about twenty feet down one of the tunnels."

Winn paused as Awan talked on the other end. Deem scanned the complex for the building they'd walked around when they came in. She located it and guided Winn forward as he listed to Awan.

"Alright," Winn said. "Bye." He lowered the phone from his ear and hung up. "He's calling them."

"Good," Deem said, leading the way. "I'll be glad to hear when they've got him."

They made their way around the corner building and through the chain link fence. Once in the car, Deem reached for her Big Gulp.

As Winn got into the driver's seat, his phone rang. "It's Awan," he said, and he answered it.

"Hello?" Winn said to Awan. After a moment he said, "They what?"

Oh no, Deem thought, hearing Winn's tone. *Something's gone wrong.*

"But that wasn't the plan, Awan..."

She strained to hear the faint buzzing coming from Winn's phone. It was impossible, she'd have to wait until he relayed things.

Winn sighed. "I suppose...alright. Tell them we're parked on the north end of the school...alright. Bye."

"What?" Deem asked.

"There's three elders driving up from Kanab, right now. They want us to wait."

"To wait?"

"That's what Awan said. Wait."

"What, until they get here?"

"Presumably."

"I thought Awan was going to call people on the reservation. In Arizona."

"Apparently they sent three people up to take care of it, and they've been in Kanab, waiting for the call."

"Did Awan know about this?"

"It sounded like he didn't. He seemed surprised, too."

"Well, I guess they want us to show them the spot, exactly?"

"Your guess is as good as mine," Winn said, sliding down in his seat. "Kanab is only five minutes away, so I don't think we'll have long to find out."

Deem took another sip of her Big Gulp. "You know, it was Awan's idea that we do this. If the elders are powerful enough to take him down, why aren't they powerful enough to find him, too? Why did we have to do it?"

"I don't know. But I am beginning to feel a little shanghaied at the moment."

They waited until an old brown Chevy Impala pulled up next to the Jeep. Winn watched as two large Navajos got out of the front seat. One of them opened the back door for an old woman, who slowly got out and stood up.

"I'm guessing the old woman is the one with the power," Winn said.

"I thought it was an old man," Deem said.

Winn looked again; now he wasn't sure it was a woman. One of the large Navajo men walked up to the Jeep.

"You Winn?" he asked.

"That's me," Winn replied.

"This is Sani," the man said, introducing the old woman, who walked up to Winn's window.

"Will you come with me?" Sani said in a frail voice.

Winn turned to look at Deem. She shrugged her shoulders. Winn opened the car door and stepped out. Sani took his hand and they walked about thirty feet away, on the other side of the Impala.

Deem sat in the Jeep, wondering what was going on. When she looked out at the Navajo men, she saw them staring back at her, expressionless.

"Hi!" she said, raising her hand halfway to wave.

"Hello," one of them said back, his face quickly returning to its neutral state.

Deem turned to look at Winn, who was talking with Sani. Sani was pointing at his chest, as though she was accusing him of something. Winn was talking back to Sani, but Deem couldn't hear any of the conversation. *They went just far enough away that I couldn't hear them,* Deem thought. *Irritating, and a little insulting.*

After five minutes, Winn walked back with Sani. He talked to Deem through the open window of the driver's side.

"We're going back in, with them," Winn said.

"Why?" Deem asked.

"They need our help," Winn answered. "Strength in numbers, that kind of thing."

Deem was skeptical. "What did he tell you?"

"He? Oh, Sani? He just told me the game plan. We lead them until we reach the spot, then they take over."

"Why couldn't he tell me that?" Deem asked. "Particularly since I'm the one who knows where it is. You couldn't even see it."

Winn could see she was a little peeved; she'd been sitting in the car the whole time he was talking with Sani, stewing that she wasn't part of the conversation.

"I think she...he thought I was in charge," Winn said. "Probably a native protocol thing. Don't be pissed, Deem. We need you along. You *are* the one who knows where it's at."

"Goddamn it, Winn, I don't like being left in the dark," she whispered to him.

"I know!" he whispered back.

Deem hopped out of the car and walked around to the other side, where the others all stood. "Fine," she said.

Sani walked up to Deem and put his hand on her arm.

"Help us, child," Sani said, "and we will remove this curse from you. Show us."

Deem felt a good amount of her irritation melt away at Sani's words. "Alright," she said. "Follow me."

Deem led the group back through the chain link fence, around the corner building, and back to the central area.

"It's that one, there," Deem said, pointing to the Administration building.

"Show us," Sani said, following Deem by holding the arm of one of the Navajo men.

Winn boosted Deem into the broken window of the building, and then followed her. Deem wondered if Sani would have trouble getting through, but one of the Navajo men jumped into the window and between the two of them, lifted Sani inside.

Once inside, Sani began chanting. Deem stopped to watch him. He seemed to shuffle as he chanted, stepping lightly to his side and back again. Deem found the sounds he was making to be soothing.

"Lead," one of the Navajo men said. "We will follow."

Deem and Winn walked back through the building, taking a right turn at the reception area to avoid crossing through the auditorium. They led them down the stairwell and into the area where the tunnels connected. Sani's chanting continued the entire way, and as they approached the tunnels, it became louder.

"There was something that shifted when we were here, earlier," Deem said. "I could see an opening in the floor down this tunnel. There was a blue light coming from it. I assumed that was it." She pointed down the dark tunnel, a little embarrassed that the light and the hole couldn't be seen.

Sani's chanting grew in volume until Deem began to feel pressure building, the same pressure she'd felt when they were there earlier. It quickly rose in intensity, much faster than before.

She felt something rip all around her, and blue light washed into the room from the tunnel. Sani stopped chanting.

The two Navajo men began walking down the tunnel, toward the hole. Sani continued to hold the arm of one of the men, keeping himself steady. Winn walked with them.

"Winn?" Deem said. "Winn? What are you doing?"

"I'm going with them," Winn said. "I have to."

"You don't have to," Deem said. "You can't even see it."

"I'm following Sani," Winn said. "She told me to follow her, until it was over. I agreed to do it."

"Why?" Deem asked, confused. She didn't like being out of the loop, especially on something this important.

"You don't have to come, Deem," Winn said as Sani began to descend into the hole. "You can stay out here if you want."

Winn followed Sani down the hole, then the other Navajo man followed Winn. She watched as they walked out of her sight.

Stay up here? Deem thought. *Fuck that.*

She walked down into the hole, quickly catching up with the group.

The light was much stronger here, emanating from a large blue star on one of the walls. Deem saw Kachina figures drawn everywhere. The room was large, about forty feet square. She looked for other exits, but couldn't see any.

Sani's chanting resumed, once again growing in intensity. Deem sensed movement, and she looked up – the ceiling was moving, covered with something. She couldn't see with what, but she could sense it. The group continued to walk forward, reaching the middle of the room. Deem could tell that Sani was in the River, so she concluded that it would be save for her to drop as well.

She jumped into the flow. The ceiling was covered with large bats, all moving, crawling over themselves. She looked up and saw them, five feet overhead. They were large, much larger than normal bats in the area. She saw them looking down at her, snapping their mouths open and closed the same way she'd seen the bat her father had killed with the bible, trapped under the door. She wanted to lie flat on the ground and slowly crawl back out of the room.

Sani's chanting grew loud. This chant was different – it was punctuated with an occasional grunt that seemed to come from Sani's depths. He was shuffling from foot to foot, increasing the volume of his chant. He suddenly stopped and gave a final grunt.

Two large bears appeared in front of them. Deem recognized the bears as the ones she'd seen in the hallway upstairs. They were huge, their shoulders standing ten feet high.

Between them stood a man, wearing a Hopi mask and headdress. Colorful spikes emerged from the headdress, each ending in a sharp tip. The mask was white, with red lines running through it.

One of the bears tried to rise up, but was stopped by the ceiling. It lowered and opened its mouth, letting out a large and loud growl.

"Shilah," Sani called. "It is over."

"Far from over, Shilah," the man in the mask called back. "It's just beginning."

They both have the same name? Deem wondered, watching their exchange closely.

"No," Sani said. "You still hurt the tribe."

"The tribe hurt me!" the man called back.

"You are perverted, Shilah," Sani called. "Your medicine is rotten belly, and your twisted naagloshii are killing innocent people, innocent children desecrated for their corpse powder."

"You kicked me out, and I left," the man in the mask said, removing the headdress and mask from his head. He was dark skinned, and old. He smiled as he talked, confident Sani's visit would come to naught. "I'm off tribal lands. Go back home and run your kingdom. Out here I play by white man rules."

"The white man doesn't know how to deal with you," Sani said, "but we do."

"You can't do anything to me, Shilah," he said. "We both know that. I'm too powerful for any of you. I'm old, but I still have the ancient knowledge. And I bring the Ninth Sign."

"Shilah," Sani said, laughing. "You're not even Hopi! You think you can make a blue star here in this place of horror, and bring about the end of the world? You are deluded."

"When I have the right skinwalkers," the man said, advancing toward Sani, "they will stop your ceremonies, and the prophecy will be fulfilled."

"Is that why you're making so many?" Sani asked. "Looking for an army? We will never stop our ceremonies. If the Hopi legend is to come true, it will not be by you, Shilah."

"My name is Ninth Sign!" the man yelled at Sani.

"Your name is Shilah," Sani said. He started chanting again, and shuffling. Deem watched as he moved his hands in the air, up and down, as he shuffled. The air around him seemed to tighten somehow, as though it was condensing.

"You old fool," Ninth Sign said, walking closer to him, examining Sani's motions. "That won't work."

Sani didn't stop. He kept chanting, shuffling, and moving his arms. The air developed a thickness that radiated out from Sani. Then it began to move, slowly, toward him, as though it was being folded up. Deem felt her lungs drawn in his direction, but she held her spot. She took slow, deep breaths.

"I would know if you had the compass, old man," Ninth Sign said. "You can't divide the elements on your own. You'll die trying."

Deem heard a sound overhead and felt wind as a bat descended from the ceiling and flew past her. She ducked. Then she felt the wind from them all descending, leaving their perches overhead. Deem threw herself on the ground, and looked up at the others. They were all still standing, even as the bats flew around them, creating an incredible wind. Sani continued to chant. Winn was on the ground, lying on his back. The Navajo men stood at Sani's side, ready to hold him if necessary.

Eventually the bats thinned out – Deem realized they were leaving the room, going up through the hole. But the wind didn't stop – in fact, it was increasing. She raised back up on her knees and felt the wind pushing her toward the left wall of the room. It was so strong that she decided to lie back down on the ground, raising her head to see what was going on, but not able to keep her eyes open for very long before the wind blew dirt and dust into them. She raised a hand in front of her face to shield it from the wind, but it didn't help much.

She heard a rushing sound from behind her, and turned. It looked like water, pouring in from the floor above, falling down through the hole and into the room. There were thousands of gallons coming down – Deem braced herself for the feeling of cold water to hit her any second.

He's summoning the elements, Deem thought. She looked at Ninth Sign – the smug look that had been on his face when he removed his mask was now gone, replaced by concern. He was tracing the path of the oncoming water. He knew exactly what Sani was doing, but he didn't seem to believe that it was happening.

A flash of light accompanied by a crack of thunder caused her to turn back and look behind the bears. A fire had broken out, and within seconds it was raging along the north wall as if the entire are had been doused with gasoline. The flames lit the room in a pattern of dancing yellow and orange. The bears were caught in the fire, unable to escape it. Deem watched as Ninth Sign turned to see the fire, and his bears burning within it. When he turned back, he was panicked. Deem could feel the heat from the fire and knew it had to feel more intense where Ninth Sign was standing.

She wasn't sure it was the Navajo men or Ninth Sign first, but suddenly there was movement between the two. The Navajo men moved in front of Sani, physically blocking him just as Ninth Sign appeared to bend over and pick up something from the floor. Deem saw it was a spear, with two feathers attached near the tip. Ninth Sign blew on the feathers, and they began to glow a bright blue. He reared back, and threw the spear at Sani and the Navajos with all of his might.

One of the Navajo men reached forward as the spear approached, and grabbed it by the shaft mid-air, just inches below the sharp tip and feathers. Deem watched as the spear dissolved into a large snake, rapidly wrapping its body around the man's right arm. It opened its mouth wide, exposing two large fangs, and sank them into the flesh of the man's hand between the thumb and the index finger.

The other Navajo man reached over to the snake. It was a quick move, so fast that Deem wasn't sure she'd seen it. The coils of the snake instantly loosened from the man's hand and slipped to the ground. The head remained buried in the soft part of his hand.

Just as quickly, the second Navajo man returned his focus to Ninth Sign, while the first man reached over with his left and removed the snake head from his right. He cast the snake head aside. Deem saw it hit the floor and roll.

Behind the two men, Sani's chanting had increased to a frantic pace, and Deem felt as though everything was coming apart. The wind continued to blow against her, she heard the rushing of the water to her right, and the fire was consuming the walls ahead of her, subsuming the blue star and causing the paint of the Kachina figures on the walls to melt and run. The whole thing seemed surreal and hallucinogenic.

Once again she felt the air around her condensing, folding in toward Sani.

The water, wind, and fire raged around her, slowly approaching, slowly trapping her and the others. Deem hugged the earth, watching as Ninth Sign stood before Sani. He seemed most effected by the change in the air, his body arching slightly toward Sani, as though he was being pulled from the inside.

The ground began to shake, and Deem instinctually spread her fingers, trying to grab something to hold. Between Sani and Ninth Sign the ground began to split open. The look on Ninth Sign's face changed from panic to horror. "You don't have it!" he yelled above the roar of the element. "You don't have it!"

Deem saw Sani stop his shuffling in front of her, and raise his right hand. He was holding something, but it was turned away from Deem. Whatever it was, Ninth Sign saw it, and reacted. His face turned angry.

Long arms of the fire flashed out toward them and though Ninth Sign. Deem could see black marks across his body where the fire had struck him. The attack caused him to fall to his knees, but even before they reached the ground, Deem could see that he was collapsing upon himself, becoming wrinkled and shriveled, as though all of the moisture in his body had been sucked out. Within a moment, the life in his eyes had left, replaced briefly by a dead stare before his eyes collapsed inside his skull. Fire struck out again, and what was left of Ninth Sign turned to ash. Deem watched as the wind blew his ashes into the open hole in the ground in front of them. Slowly Ninth Sign's body was dissolved. As the last of the ashes were lifted by the wind, the fire extinguished. Deem realized she'd never been hit by water; it had all stayed to her right, waiting to receive that part of Ninth Sign that it had been called to receive. The ground rumbled beneath them all once again, the hole slowly closing, sealing up what was left of Ninth Sign. Once it closed the wind began to die down until you could no longer feel it against the skin.

Then, silence.

Sani collapsed, and one of the Navajo men grabbed him, scooping him up in his arms. They walked back toward Deem, who was still lying on the ground. Winn walked over to her to help her up.

"Now we leave," one of the Navajo men said as they passed her. "Come."

"Let's get out of here," Winn said, grabbing her arm. "I'll tell you everything."

...

At the car, Deem watched as the two Navajo men placed Sani in the back seat, lying down.

"Will he be OK?" Winn asked one of them.

"He's breathing, so I think so," the man replied. "We're done here. Thank you." He extended his hand to Winn, and he shook it. Then he got in the Impala and they drove off.

"Goodbye to you, too," Deem said as their car disappeared in the distance. She grabbed her Big Gulp and took a sip. "Ugh. Warm."

"Let's get a cold one," Winn said, starting up the Jeep and driving them back into Kanab. "No 7-11 here, how about Walker's?"

"I'll take it," Deem said, waiting for him to park in front of the store. She jumped out of the Jeep and ran inside. Winn followed. They both bought drinks and snacks.

Winn began the drive back to Leeds. "You want to call Carma, let her know our ETA?"

"Sure," Deem said. She pulled out her phone and gave Carma a call. She told her they'd be about an hour.

"Wow, it's later than I thought," Deem said, checking her watch. "How long were we in there?"

"Longer than it seemed," Winn said. "Couple of hours."

"I think I've been pretty patient," Deem said. "Let you take me to the store, get me all caffeinated up, get something to munch on for the ride back. My sugar's all balanced now. Are you gonna tell me what the hell happened in there?"

Winn smiled. "I'm a blank," he said, looking at her.

"A what?"

"A blank," Winn said. "That's what Sani called it."

"What's a blank?"

"I thought it was odd that you, your mother, and your aunt all were targeted by the skinrunner, but not me."

"True."

"And then, once we were inside the school, I couldn't see any of the things you saw."

"You saw the ghosts in the auditorium."

"Those were just normal, downwind ghosts, naturally there," Winn said. "Not put there by Ninth Sign, like the bear. When it came to him, things that used his power, I was a blank. Like the sounds you heard, the animal in the hall, the blue light, all of that."

"Did you see him? Ninth Sign? When Sani confronted him?"

"I saw a man. They talked back and forth."

"You didn't see the bears? The fucking bats?"

"No, none of that. Just a man, standing there talking to Sani."

"Is that what Sani was talking to you about, by the car, before we went in?"

"He had me swallow something," Winn said. "A small, round, flat rock. It was hard to get down. He called it a compass."

"Ninth Sign said something about a compass," Deem said. "He told Sani what he was doing was a waste of time, because he didn't have a compass."

"Sani hid the compass in me," Winn said. "All those green barriers, all over the complex? They were to alert Ninth Sign if a compass came through. He knew it was the only thing powerful enough to threaten him. Hiding it in me was Sani's way of keeping it hidden from Ninth Sign long enough to get close to him, so he could disperse him."

"Is that what he did? Disperse him?"

"Sani told me Ninth Sign was too powerful to simply kill. He had to split him into the four elements, to weaken him. He needed the compass to be able to do that. Then he scattered what was left, underground."

"Why not tell me?" Deem asked. "Why keep me in the dark while it was going on?"

"Sani said you'd already been tagged by Ninth Sign from when we went in earlier. If you had known about the compass, Ninth Sign would have picked it up in your thoughts and tried to take it out of me. Sani needed the element of surprise."

"I saw you duck when the bats flew," Deem said. "But you couldn't see the bats, could you?"

"No. I fell over when Sani removed the compass from my stomach. I'm guessing if he caused bats to fly at the same time, it was to create a distraction."

"How did he get the compass out of you?"

Winn raised his shirt. There was a two inch scar in the center of his chest, just below his pecs. It was bright red, and looked sore. "He warned me it would leave a mark," Winn said, lowering his shirt.

Deem remembered seeing Sani point at Winn's chest when they had been talking before they went in. Now that she had the whole picture, she felt a little sheepish for being upset.

"I guess I owe you an apology," Deem said. "For being so snippy before."

"I couldn't tell you," Winn said, "or you would have had to wait outside the fence. And I knew that would have *really* pissed you off."

"True," Deem said, sucking on her straw. "I would have been angry if you'd said, 'wait in the car,' and then the four of you went in without me. Did you see the snake? The spear Ninth Sign threw?"

"I saw the spear, and I saw the guy catch it. Which was pretty cool."

"It turned into a snake in his hand," Deem said. "Bit him. The other guy cut it off him, but I thought for sure he was poisoned."

"I'm pretty confident all three of them were full of some kind of protection," Winn said. "Probably drank a gallon of it before they came."

"So you're a blank?" Deem said. "I wonder exactly what that means. If it means more than just being impervious to Ninth Sign's creations."

"Don't know. I'm not too happy about this scar though."

"Worried it might screw up your love life? All the little sexpots in Moapa will run away screaming from the ugly scar? Like you're the Beast?"

"I'll have to make up a story, like a battle scar," Winn said. "Something that will make them want to sleep with me even more." He turned to Deem and gave her his widest, most charismatic smile.

"I guess you earned it," Deem said.

17

Carma sat at the head of a large dining table that was made of rough-hewn, polished wood planks.

"Deem, another?" Carma asked, motioning to her tray of pies on a nearby antique buffet.

"No, I'm stuffed, thank you!" Deem said, trying to speak through her laughter. She'd been listening to a story Awan was telling, and she'd been laughing for almost a minute straight. It was cathartic.

"Awan? How about you? You look hungry still."

"No," he said, still laughing as well. "Thank you. I can't."

Winn picked up his wine glass and drank the remaining half inch of merlot. "Awan, there's one thing I don't get."

Carma, seeing the empty wine glass, hopped up from her spot at the table and brought a new bottle over from the buffet. She corked it as Winn talked.

"How did Sani know about me?" Winn asked. "When she arrived…"

"By the way," Deem interrupted, "is Sani a 'he' or a 'she'? We couldn't figure that out."

"He," Carma said, pulling the cork from the bottle. "He's been gender bending for years."

"When HE arrived," Winn continued, "he knew all about me. He didn't ask, he just started telling me what the plan was, what to do. How'd he know I was a blank?"

"Lyman," Awan said. "Lyman picked up on it when you were first here. He told Sani. When I told them that you were going to go into the school, they traveled up from the reservation to be ready once you came out. Sani realized you were the opportunity they needed."

"Why did we have to go in first?" Deem asked.

"Sani's old," Awan said. "But he was the one with the most experience at dividing elements, which they knew was the only way they would be able to bring down Ninth Sign. They were worried Sani could handle it, at his age. They wanted to be sure they could go straight to Ninth Sign and finish him off, without searching the whole school. Letting you find him first helped with that."

"I was kind of disappointed they didn't stop to talk more after it was over," Winn said. "They said nothing as we walked out. We got back to our cars, they loaded Sani into theirs, and they took off. It makes sense that Sani was wiped out. But I would have liked to know more about them."

"The Navajo have never been comfortable talking with white people about medicine," Awan said. "Most Natives aren't. You have to understand. They don't even *say* the word 'skinwalker,' let alone have conversations about it. It was nothing personal."

"Sani called Ninth Sign 'Shilah', and Ninth Sign called Sani the same thing," Deem said. "A Navajo name?"

"It means 'brother'," Awan said.

"As in tribal brother?" Deem asked. "Or were they related?"

"I don't know," Awan said. "But since Ninth Sign had been expelled by the tribe, I doubt Sani called him Shilah because they were tribal brothers."

"Deem?" Carma said, holding the merlot bottle. "A sip?"

Deem hadn't been drinking during the meal, but she'd been enjoying how relaxed and uninhibited the others had become as they had imbibed. Her whole life she'd said no to alcohol, in accordance with her religion. *Now I'm losing my religion,* she thought. *The wine doesn't seem to have hurt these three people. And in a few days, I won't be a member anymore, anyway. What the hell.*

"Sure," she said. "A little."

"Whoa!" Winn said, pushing himself back from the table and laughing. "You're going to do it?"

"A sip," Deem said. "Don't get all worked up."

"I've been trying to get her to taste a beer for the last two years," Winn said to Awan, smiling. "No go."

"You don't tempt a woman with beer," Carma said. "Wine, especially a good one like this."

Deem raised the wine glass to her lips. She smelled the bouquet, and it surprised her. She was expecting it to smell like grape juice. *I'll bet it doesn't taste like grape juice, either,* she thought. *Brace yourself.*

Everyone was silent and all eyes were glued on Deem as she let the wine pass her lips and rest in her mouth. She swallowed.

"Yea!" Winn cheered.

Deem scrunched up her face as the alcohol hit. "It's a little bitter," she said.

"Not this wine!" Carma said. "No, my dear. This is the good stuff. If you want to taste bitter, try some bad wine."

"She's used to sugar drinks," Winn said. "Hot chocolates and Diet Cokes."

"Deem," Carma said, "I want you to try something. Take that last bite of pie you left on your plate, and wash it down with the wine. Right on the heels of it, OK?"

Deem did as instructed, and after she swallowed, a smile slowly spread across her face.

"Oh, I see," she said. "That's why people drink wine with food. I get it now."

"Oh, Deem," Carma said, reaching out to hold her hand. Deem almost laughed; Carma looked like she might cry.

"Pour her another glass!" Winn said.

"No!" Carma said. "She said a sip, and that's all. You just want to get her drunk and take advantage of her. Don't lie to me, young man!"

Awan started laughing, and so did Deem.

"You watch out for that one," Carma said to Deem, smiling. "He's after you, I can tell."

"He's after half of southern Nevada," Deem said.

Awan started laughing again, and Carma joined him.

Carma offered dessert, but everyone turned it down, too full. Carma said she'd save it for later, and they all moved into the sitting room overlooking the back yard. It seemed to be the favorite place to hang out in the house. Deem flopped into her favorite chair. The wine started moving through her, and she felt warm.

"Now to deal with your extortion brothers," Winn said to Awan. "That ghost chalk ready yet?"

"Still working on it," Awan said. He'd brought his wine glass with him, and was sipping from it. "But they've skipped town, so even if it were ready, we've got to wait until they come back."

"Something scare them off?" Deem asked.

"Don't know yet," Awan said. "They're not at their home, and they haven't been seen in town the last two days. So I'm in a holding pattern."

"Well, let us know if they come back," Winn said. He dug into his pants pocket, and pulled out the mindwall. "I suppose we should return these to you."

"Nah," Awan said. "Keep them. I have several, and my grandfather's book shows how to make more."

"Thanks, Awan!" Winn said, replacing the beaded emblem back into his pocket. "I find they come in very handy, in all kinds of circumstances." He looked over at Deem, and smiled. She rolled her eyes.

"Carma told me about the excommunication," Awan said to Deem. "Are you going to fight it?"

"No," Deem said. "There's no point. The fix is in. I'll just have to help my mom through it. She's the one I'm worried about."

"You know," Carma said, "you could confront Brother Dayton about it. You may have some incriminating information you could hold over him, force him to drop the proceedings."

"Nah," Deem said. "I'm OK with it. I'm more worried about what else he might do, or instruct others to do."

"If he's the one who had Claude killed," Winn said, "he needs to pay. Somehow."

Deem sat in her chair, contemplating. She agreed with Winn, she just didn't know how to approach it.

"I have something for you," Carma said, walking out of the room. She returned with a manila folder, which she handed to Deem. "A gift from Lyman. He wanted me to use it in another manner, but after meeting you he asked me to give it to you, so you could use it."

Deem opened the folder. It contained a single picture of a teen boy. His sleeve was rolled up, and a needle hung from the skin around the inside of his elbow. His head was leaning back, a wide smile on his face.

"This looks like Johnny Dayton," Deem said. "He's shooting up?"

"Taken by a friend of his while they were high," Carma said. "Lyman lifted the photo from the boy's iPhone when he conveniently lost it at the county rodeo."

"Lyman can do that?" Deem asked.

"Well, I say Lyman," Carma answered, "but I really mean one of the people in Lyman's network. They're always looking for trash on the higher-ups. And it usually isn't too hard to find."

Deem knew exposing Dayton's son as a drug addict wouldn't cause him to lose his position in the church. But it would cause people to talk, and Dayton would be viewed as a bad father, the same way her mother would be viewed as a failure for having an excommunicated daughter. It might make it hard for him to receive another position of power when he was released from the stake presidency. Might be fair play for the damage Dayton was about to do to Deem's mother.

Carma saw the thoughts swirling around in Deem's mind. "You don't have to use it, my dear. Only if it comes in handy. You might have far more powerful leverage in those boxes in the other room, once you get a chance to go through them."

"Thank you," Deem said to Carma. "Thanks for looking out for me. And please thank Lyman, too."

"You can thank him yourself," Carma said. "He's sitting right over there. He can hear you."

"Thanks, Lyman," Deem said, turning to the empty chair Carma had pointed at. It felt a little weird. She dropped into the River.

Lyman was faintly visible in the chair. It gave Deem a shiver, just as it did whenever she realized ghosts were in the room that she hadn't been aware of. She smiled, hoping Lyman might see it.

■ ■ ■

"Sister Hinton," Dayton said, opening the door. "I hope this will be a cordial visit, unlike last time."

"It will," Deem said, taking a deep breath and walking into Dayton's home. She was determined to keep a calm composure. "Is your wife home? The kids?"

"No one's home," Dayton said, leading her into the living room and sitting down. "And I see you're alone this time, too. Please, sit down. What can I do for you?"

"Did you kill Claude? Or have him killed?"

"Yes," Dayton said.

Deem was shocked. She was expecting him to act in stake president-mode, pretending he didn't know what she was talking about. It took her by surprise to see him admit it.

"He violated his oaths," Dayton said. "So his life was taken."

"It looked to me like whoever you sent to kill him was also supposed to retrieve some of Claude's things, too. Some documents."

"Yes. That's correct."

"Then you know he didn't succeed at that."

"Yes."

"And you know who has the documents now?"

"Who? You?"

"Yes."

Dayton laughed. "I don't think so."

Deem resisted every urge in her body to argue with Dayton. It irritated her that he was so cocky, so sure that she didn't have them. She wanted to rub it in his face, but she knew it was better to let it drop, to let him think she didn't have them.

"I see you've started excommunication proceedings on me," Deem said.

"That wasn't me," Dayton said. "That was your Bishop."

"Influenced by you," Deem said. "I know how these things work."

"I don't think you do," Dayton said.

"My father was part of your council," Deem said calmly, keeping control of her tone. "We both know that. You won't confirm it because membership is part of your secret oaths, but I know he was. I'll never be part of your council, I know that. I'm a woman, for one. Plus you're a little angry at me right now. I'm angry at you, too. Killing Claude was unnecessary."

"The Lord works in mysterious ways, Sister Hinton."

"I don't understand how you can say that, when you don't believe it. It's phony."

"That's where you're wrong, Sister Hinton. It's not phony to us. Not to any of us. We're all true believers, through and through. So was your father."

"You know I'm gifted," Deem said. "And I know what I'm doing. I don't sit at home, waiting for a returned missionary. I'm out there, doing things. I see things. I'm in touch with this area, all the strange places and people. I already know all about your council, and I'm learning more, every day."

"What's your point, Sister Hinton?"

"I know you won't take me on the council because I'm a woman and because I'm not active. But I am my father's daughter, and I know he was a good man. I know if he was on your council, there was a reason, a good reason. So I'm here to offer you a deal. Détente."

Dayton looked at her. He stayed silent.

"I don't care about the excommunication, personally. I'm a jack Mormon, I admit it. I know you're only doing it to hurt my mom. But you knew her, too. She's my father's wife. So I'd like you to drop it, for her sake."

Dayton continued to stare at her.

"In exchange, I'll be your ally. I can't be on your council, like my father, but I can do what I can to help your causes. I know you have people who work for you, that do the things the council can't or won't do directly. I would be a good candidate for that. And I come across information all the time. Things you might find useful. I was thinking, if we work together, we'd both get further."

"Frankly, Sister Hinton, your actions of late would suggest otherwise. Tailing me to a meeting. Causing Brother Peterson to violate his oaths. Threatening me in my home. It would seem we're on opposites sides of the fence."

Deem put on her best poker face and played her best card, the one she knew befuddled old men the most. She lowered her head and started to cry. "I miss him so much!" she squeaked out between sobs. She grabbed the sides of the chair she was sitting in, steadying herself. She forced herself to cry even more, thinking of her father's face in his casket at the viewing. "I want to honor his name. He was my father, and I owe him that. I didn't mean to get Claude killed. I was only trying to find my father's journals. You have to believe me. That's all. That's all it was, nothing more. That's something a child should want to do, right? Read their parent's journals? I'm so sorry, President Dayton. I hope you'll forgive me." She sobbed some more, letting the tears flow down her cheeks.

Dayton stood and handed her a box of Kleenex from the table next to his chair. *It's not the first time he's had someone crying in his living room,* Deem thought. She took one. He sat back down.

"I'd like to believe you, Sister Hinton," Dayton said. "Your father and I were great friends. He would want us to get along. I watched you grow up from an infant. I was in your blessing circle, you know that? I remember all those great barbeques your father invited us to, every summer. We used to really enjoy each other's company, being around each other's family. It's just that now – well, I question your sincerity."

"I understand," Deem said, hurling words out though the tears. "I was rude to you the other night. Things I said – completely uncalled for. I apologize, from the bottom of my heart. I was wrapped up in an obsession. I know you're on his side – my side. I know my father considered you a great man and a friend. I was hoping we could start over. I was hoping you'd give me a chance."

"But how, Sister Hinton? How can I know you mean what you say?"

Deem pulled the picture from her satchel, and handed it to Dayton. He looked it over, and his face slowly washed from concern to horror as he saw the picture of his son.

"Where did you get this?"

"A friend of mine had it," Deem said. "She was going to scan it and post it on Facebook. I didn't want any harm to come to you or your family, so I stole it from her before she could do any damage. I wanted to give it to you personally. It's the only copy that I know of. I'm sure this comes as a surprise to you. I'm so sorry to bring you this news! I thought, if I brought it to you, you might forgive me, and begin to trust me." She burst into a fresh round of tears.

Dayton let the picture drop and stood up. He sat next to her on the couch. He placed his arm around her and held her.

"There, there," he said reassuringly as she heaved heavy sobs. "You've done a good thing, and I want you to know I appreciate it. There's a special bond between those of us who have the gift. Your father was so proud of you. I know he thought you were a strong, powerful daughter of Zion. He wouldn't want this for you, all of this running around, fighting against authority. He believed in the church, in the council. If you're willing to meet me halfway, I'm sure we can come to some kind of arrangement. If I can count on your discretion, and you're willing to do exactly as I tell you, I'll talk to your Bishop about the excommunication. Are you willing to do that?"

"Anything!" Deem cried, sucking in air and using it to sob some more. "You name it. I want to help the council, not be against it. I'm on your side. I want to make my father proud."

"Here, stand up," Dayton said, standing next to her. Deem rose from her seat, wiping tears from her face with the Kleenex.

"Let's shake on it," he said, extending his hand. "I'll talk to your Bishop. You agree to help me out, when I need it."

"Deal!" Deem said, letting a smile break through her tears. "I so appreciate this, President Dayton. You can count on me."

"I hope I can," he said, leading her to the front door. "We're serious about deals, as you know."

"Yes, I know," Deem said, letting him escort her to the door. She opened it and walked out. She turned back to him.

"Thanks for giving me another chance," she said, wiping the remaining tears from her eyes. "I really appreciate it."

"Of course," Dayton said, smiling at her as he prepared to close the door. "Everyone deserves a second chance, especially a sister with gifts such as yourself."

As Deem turned to walk away from him, he closed the door, and the performance was over. Deem walked to her car, wiping the remaining tears from her face. She got inside, closed the door, and began to drive. She drove until she reached a bluff overlooking Mesquite. It was a hot evening, and the stars were just beginning to come out. She turned off the car and opened the windows. It was hot, but she wanted to feel real air on her face.

A slight breeze came through the windows, and gently rocked the orange handcuffs she'd attached to the rear view mirror. *Why'd I buy those things?* she wondered. *Some deep-seated bondage desire I don't realize I have? Or maybe some psychological thing, like a symbol – a symbol of being free, or a symbol of being trapped?*

She reached for her Big Gulp and took a long sip. It tasted good, really good. She thought about her father's journals, and realized she may never get them, if they even existed. They had propelled her into a confrontation with powerful forces that manipulated and controlled life in the area where she lived. She was playing with the big boys now. *If I never find them,* she thought, *at least they brought me here. Exposed this all to me. So I could open my eyes, and stop being a little naïve kid.*

When I was a child, I did childish things, she remembered from Sunday School. *But when I became an adult, I put away childish things.*

She thought about Carma and Lyman, and all they'd done to help her. She thought about Claude, and a pang of guilt hit her. Then she thought about Awan and Winn, and their promise to help take down Dayton.

"Keep your friends close," she said to herself, taking another sip of her Big Gulp. "But keep your enemies closer."

GLOSSARY/ BIBLIOGRAPHY

Blood Oath, Blood River is a work of fiction, set in a real place and culture. Local Mormon vernacular is used in the story to keep the characters authentic. People not familiar with the local and cultural terms might find some of them unusual and confusing. While the novel itself defines most of the important and relevant terms within the context of the story, this glossary is offered for those who would like to have the terms better defined. The type of definitions offered below (along with references to outside sources and more information) would have been too disruptive to include in the narrative.

Use of Wikipedia information is released by CC-BY-SA (http:// creativecommons.org/licenses/by-sa/3.0/), and attributions to various Wikipedia contributors can be found using the pages provided in each glossary item. Rather than listing here the URL's you'd have to type manually, visit the Wikipedia home page (http://www.wikipedia.com) and use their search feature; type in the name of the page I've provided, and you'll reach the page I've referenced. While I used Wikipedia to make sure I got the basics of each topic correct, I have attempted to relay each topic in harmony with the focus and tone of the novel. Note that links (or Wikipedia page names) can sometimes change; if you find a broken link, feel free to drop me a note at www.michaelrichan.com.

ADIT – An entrance to or passageway through a tunnel that is horizontal or nearly horizontal.

APOSTATE – someone who leaves a particular group or religion because their beliefs have changed.

BAPTISMS FOR THE DEAD – A proxy ordinance performed by the LDS Church in temples. Based on the belief that baptism is a necessary ordinance to enter heaven, and that the deceased person can choose to accept or reject the baptism performed by the living person in their name. Children twelve and older are allowed to perform these baptisms, often in organized youth group outings. Each person typically performs ten to forty baptisms by immersion during their visit. See *Wikipedia, "Baptism for the Dead"* page.

BEARING YOUR TESTIMONY – One Sunday church service per month in each LDS ward is designated as a "fast and testimony meeting." Instead of scheduled speakers as part of the sacrament service, which is the norm, a block of time is allocated for members to stand and speak, similar to a Quaker service, and address the rest of the ward. When they speak, the expectation is that they will "bear their testimony," which means to tell the other members what they believe. Typical elements of a testimony bearing are phrases such as "I know the church is true," "I believe Joseph Smith was a prophet of God," "I believe [insert name of current church president] is a prophet of God," etc. Sometimes the bearing of the testimony drifts into storytelling and travelogues, and there are usually one or two people in each ward who will use the time to spout crazy theories or supernatural stories, which is frowned upon. While there is no time limit for each speaker, five minutes is considered the maximum, so that others will have time to speak. See *Wikipedia, "Worship Services for The Church of Jesus Christ of Latter-Day Saints,"* page, *"Fast and Testimony Meeting"* section.

BISHOP – The leader of a local congregation of LDS church members, who holds responsibility for all of the temporal and spiritual aspects of the ward, much like a pastor or priest in other religions. They serve without pay and are selected from the ranks of the ward to serve for a period of three to five years. In the LDS hierarchy, they report to a Stake President. See *Wikipedia, "Bishop (Latter-Day Saints)"* page.

BLESSING CIRCLE – Newborn infants are presented at ward fast and testimony meetings to undergo a non-saving ceremony called "the naming and blessing of children." Provided the father is a holder of the priesthood, he conducts the blessing, and invites as many priesthood holders as he chooses to participate, which usually includes relatives, close family friends, and any visiting church dignitaries. They form a circle around the infant, each reaching in to support the child as it is held in its father's arms, while the father performs the ceremony by formally giving the child a name and pronouncing an extemporaneous blessing. Similar to the baptism of infants in other faiths, it is an important social event, usually drawing relatives from other wards. See *Wikipedia, "Naming and Blessing of Children"* page.

BLOOD ATONEMENT – The theological concept, popularized by Brigham Young in the 19th century, that there are sins so grievous, they cannot be forgiven through the atonement of Jesus Christ. To atone for these sins, a person must die in a manner that sheds their blood (such as firing squad or by a knife wound.) See *Wikipedia, "Blood Atonement"* page.

BLUE STAR PROPHECY – A Hopi legend describing the destruction of the world via a cataclysmic event, ushered in by a series of nine signs. The appearance of the blue star Kachina is the ninth and final sign, signifying the coming of a "Day of Purification" and a new world. Some consider eight of the nine signs to have already occurred, and that the ninth sign is imminent. See *Wikipedia, "Blue Star Kachina"* page.

CELESTIAL KINGDOM – The LDS believe that after death, the spirits of all people will wait in a "spirit world" until the second coming of Jesus Christ. At that time, all people will be resurrected. Thereafter, a judgment will occur, and people will be sorted into one of four places to reside for eternity: the worst is the LDS version of hell, called "Outer Darkness." The other three are considered "kingdoms of glory," of which the Celestial Kingdom is the highest, and best. The Celestial Kingdom itself is divided into three parts, the highest of which is reserved for people who have been sealed (which is why the LDS perform proxy sealings for the dead). In this highest section of the Celestial Kingdom, resurrected beings will live as gods. See *Wikipedia "Degrees of Glory"* page.

COUNSELOR (IN A STAKE PRESIDENCY) – When a man is selected to become a stake president, he is allowed to pick two men from within the geographical boundaries of the stake to serve as his counselors. The counselors are also given the title "president." The three men, together, are known as the "stake presidency." See *Wikipedia "Stake (Latter-Day Saints)"* page.

D.I. (DESERET INDUSTRIES) – A chain of retail thrift stores operated by the LDS Church. Locals often abbreviate the name, calling it "the D.I." It operates similarly to Goodwill Industries. The name Deseret is taken from the Book of Mormon, and is the name given to the provisional state that was essentially a theocracy created by the LDS when they emigrated to the American west. See *Wikipedia, "Deseret Industries"* page and *Wikipedia, "State of Deseret"* page.

DANITES – A vigilante group of LDS church members in the 19th century dedicated "to put to right physically that which is not right, and to cleanse the Church of every great evil" (- Joseph Smith). Their name was taken from the Book of Daniel in the Old Testament. The group operated in secret, supposedly executing the will of church leaders. There were rumors that the group persisted after the LDS Church moved to Utah, and that it existed into the 20th century. See *Wikipedia, "Danite"* page.

ENDOWMENT – A religious ceremony created by Joseph Smith and organized/instituted by Brigham Young. The LDS version of the ceremony is performed in temples. People who wish to be sealed must first perform this ceremony. The ceremony is considered to prepare people to become kings and queens in the afterlife, by taking part in a scripted reenactment of the Adam and Eve story. During the ceremony, the person makes several oaths, many based on Masonic oaths, including a promise to keep the oaths secret. The ceremony has been changed several times over the years, primarily to remove objectionable and violent elements. Prior to 1990, the oaths included penalties that involved ways in which life could be taken if the oaths were violated. Prior to 1927, the oaths included an Oath of Vengeance: "You and each of you do covenant and promise that you will pray and never cease to pray to Almighty God to avenge the blood of the prophets upon this nation, and that you will teach the same to your children and to your children's children unto the third and fourth generation." The "prophets" were Joseph Smith and his brother,

Hyrum, killed by a mob in Illinois. "This nation" was the United States. In addition to removing the Oath of Vengeance in 1927, the LDS Church also softened the language of the penalties from specific ways in which the penalties might be executed ("my throat ... be cut from ear to ear, and my tongue torn out by its roots...our breasts ... be torn open, our hearts and vitals torn out and given to the birds of the air and the beasts of the field...your body ... be cut asunder and all your bowels gush out") to a gentler "suffer my life to be taken." See *Wikipedia, "Endowment (Latter Day Saints)"* page, *Wikipedia, "Endowment (Mormonism)"* page, and *Wikipedia, "Oath of Vengeance"* page.

EXCOMMUNICATION – A disciplinary act of a church against a member. In the LDS church, an excommunication is conducted if church leaders determine that a serious sin was committed. The LDS teach that the excommunication eliminates the chance for that person to reach the Celestial Kingdom and nullifies all ordinances such as baptism, endowments, and sealings. If the person repents and rejoins the church, their ordinances can be restored. See *Wikipedia, "Excommunication"* page, *"The Church of Jesus Christ of Latter-Day Saints"* section.

EXIMERE – (*Spoiler alert: skip this paragraph if you have not read Eximere, the fourth book in The River series.*) Eximere is the name of an underground house in the novel of the same name. The house was created by a character that was gifted, but renounced his gift and worked to undermine the gift in others by draining their abilities, killing them, and stealing any memoirs and objects they may have possessed, keeping them locked away in the secret underground mansion. Steven and Roy Hall, along with Eliza Winters, discover Eximere under the haunted estate of Harold Unser on the Olympic peninsula of Washington State, and establish a way to take possession of the place, working to restore the stolen memoirs and objects to their rightful owners or heirs. Restoring memoirs has been an easier task than restoring objects, since the memoirs can be read and an owner more easily determined. The objects at Eximere, on the other hand, do not have obvious owners and most have unexplained abilities and powers that Steven, Roy, and Eliza have not discovered. See *"Eximere"* by Michael Richan.

EXTERMINATION ORDER – Missouri Executive Order 44, issued by the governor of Missouri, Lilburn Boggs, in 1838. Its most dramatic wording included: "...the Mormons must be treated as enemies, and must be exterminated or driven from the State if necessary for the public peace..." It was used as justification for forced expulsion of Mormons from their properties in Missouri. Some of the more notorious expulsions were done in the middle of cold winter nights, forcing Mormon families to abandon all of their possessions and run into nearby fields with nothing more than the clothes on their back, watching from a distance as angry mobs burned their homes and farms. It wasn't rescinded until 1976, when then-governor Kit Bond acknowledged the unconstitutional nature of the order. See *Wikipedia, "Missouri Executive Order 44"* page.

FUNDAMENTALISTS (MORMON) – In order for Utah to become a state, the LDS Church was forced to give up the practice of polygamy that it had condoned in the 19th century; US laws forbade polygamy. The LDS church formally renounced polygamy in 1890, after sixty years of teaching that it was only by polygamy that a person could reach the highest level of the celestial kingdom in the next life. Many members of the LDS church in 1890 weren't prepared to part with this teaching, and broke off from the church, becoming smaller groups known as fundamentalists. They continue to believe that polygamy is a divinely sanctioned practice, and they hold to several other teachings from the Brigham Young era, such as blood atonement, the "Adam-God theory," and that black males cannot receive the priesthood. Perhaps the most famous fundamentalist in modern times is Warren Jeffs, leader of the Fundamentalist Church of Jesus Christ of Latter-Day Saints, the largest of the break-off sects. See *Wikipedia, "Mormon Fundamentalism"* page, *Wikipedia, "Mormonism and Polygamy"* page, *Wikipedia, "Fundamentalist Church of Jesus Christ of Latter-Day Saints"* page, and the *"Jeffs, Warren"* glossary entry.

FUNERAL POTATOES – A delicious but unhealthy traditional casserole served as a side dish at Mormon after-funeral communal meals in Utah and Idaho. Often prepared by the sisters of a ward for those who are grieving or ill. See *Wikipedia, "Funeral Potatoes"* page.

GADIANTON ROBBERS – A secret organization of people, described in the Book of Mormon. They formed large criminal organizations, and identified each other by secret signs. They were responsible for assassinations in the Book of Mormon story. As a group, they appear in three different iterations over the span of the book. Modern folklore speculates that the organization still exists to this day. See *Wikipedia, "Gadianton Robbers"* page.

GARDNER, RONNIE LEE - Received the death penalty for murder in 1985, and was executed by firing squad by the state of Utah in 2010. The execution of Gardner at Utah State Prison became the focus of media attention in June 2010, because it was the first to be carried out by firing squad in the United States in fourteen years. Gardner stated that he sought this method of execution because of his Mormon background. See *Wikipedia, "Ronnie Lee Gardner"* page.

GENEALOGY – The study of families and the tracing of family trees. Members of the LDS Church are primarily interested in genealogy for the purpose of acquiring names for proxy ordinances in temples. See *Wikipedia, "Family History Library"* page.

GENERAL AUTHORITY – The highest levels of leadership in the LDS Church, including, in descending order, the president of the church and his counsellors, a quorum of twelve apostles, and a group known as the quorum of the seventy. Collectively, these men are colloquially referred to within the church as "the brethren." In the hierarchy, stake presidents report to members of the quorum of the seventy. Unlike the positions of stake president and bishop, general authorities are paid by the church. The president of the church is considered a prophet by default of his position, and members of the church are expected to support and sustain all general authorities. See *Wikipedia, "General Authority"* page.

INVESTIGATOR – LDS term for a person who isn't a member of the church but might be interested in becoming a member. Mormon missionaries call potential converts who are studying the church "investigators."

JACK MORMON – A lapsed or inactive member of the LDS church. See *Wikipedia, "Jack Mormon" page.*

JEFFS, WARREN – Leader of the Fundamentalist Church of Jesus Christ of Latter Day Saints. Convicted in St. George, UT in 2007 of two counts of rape as an accomplice. His conviction was overturned by the Utah Supreme Court due to improper jury instructions. He was extradited to Texas, where the church had a temple that had been raided by authorities. He was convicted in Texas of sexual assault and aggravated sexual assault of children. He was sentenced to life in prison plus 20 years.

KACHINA – A personification of a spirit or of something in the real world. Common in western Native American cultures, particular the Hopi. Each pueblo community has its own pantheon of Kachinas, which can represent anything including astronomical features, such as the sun and stars. Kachinas are not worshiped, but are venerated. See *Wikipedia "Kachina"* page, and the *"Blue Star Prophecy"* glossary entry.

LAFFERTY BOYS – Ron and Dan Lafferty, members of a fundamentalist Mormon sect known as the "School of Prophets." In 1984, acting on a revelation Ron claimed he received from god, they brutally murdered the wife and daughter of their brother, Allen. Brenda Lafferty and her infant daughter, Erica, were killed in their home, their throats slashed. Police found Ron's written "revelation" and Dan they were both convicted. Dan was sentenced to life without parole, and Ron is on death row in Utah. Their story was told in the bestselling *Under the Banner of Heaven*. See *Wikipedia, "Under the Banner of Heaven"* page, and *Under the Banner of Heaven,* by John Krakauer.

LDS – Abbreviation for Latter Day Saint, a name given to followers of any of the various religious sects which sprang from Joseph Smith. Latter Day Saints are commonly called "Mormons" because of their belief that Smith's work, the *Book of Mormon*, is divine scripture. The largest and most common of the sects is the Church of Jesus Christ of Latter-Day Saints, headquartered in Salt Lake City, UT, with an estimated worldwide membership of 15 million as of 2013. Communities in areas of Utah outside of Salt Lake City are heavily dominated by Mormons and Mormon culture, particularly southern Utah and Nevada, northern Arizona, western Colorado, and southern Idaho. See *Wikipedia, "List of Sects in the Latter Day Saint Movement"* page.

LEE, JOHN D.– An early prominent Mormon, executed in 1877 by firing squad for his role in the Mountain Meadows Massacre (1857). He was an alleged Danite. He was excommunicated, and tried twice for the massacre. Lee maintained that he'd become a scapegoat, drawing attention away from the church leaders who had authorized the action. Lee was the only person held accountable for the massacre. His final words were: "I do not believe everything that is now being taught and practiced by Brigham Young. I do not care who hears it. It is my last word... I have been sacrificed in a cowardly, dastardly manner." In 1961 his membership in the LDS Church was reinstated. See *Wikipedia, "John D. Lee"* page.

MORONI ("right out of Moroni") – A character in the Book of Mormon who authored the final section of the book. The most famous and oft-repeated part of Moroni's writings is a passage that is routinely used by Mormon missionaries to challenge a potential convert to accept the book as true. It's referred to as "Moroni's Promise," and it reads: "And when ye shall receive these things, I would exhort you that ye would ask God, the Eternal Father, in the name of Christ, if these things are not true; and if ye shall ask with a sincere heart, with real intent, having faith in Christ, he will manifest the truth of it unto you, by the power of the Holy Ghost." The idea is that, if something is true, God will cause some sort of sign to tell you that it is true. Moroni, incidentally, is the gold statue seen on most LDS temples. See *Wikipedia, "Moroni (Book of Mormon prophet)"* page.

MOUNTAIN MEADOWS MASSACRE – A series of attacks on an emigrant wagon train from Arkansas, passing through Utah on its way to California. Stopped at Mountain Meadows, north of St. George, UT, the wagon train was attacked for five days by a band of Mormons dressed as Native Americans, along with some Paiute Indians that the Mormons had solicited to participate. 120 men, women and children were murdered and hastily buried in the meadow. Fearful that members of the wagon train had discovered their disguises, the attackers ensured that anyone over the age of seven was killed. Seventeen children, under age seven, were placed with local Mormon families. Historians have decided the attack was a result of several elements, including strident Mormon teachings (such as the Oath of Vengeance), a strong mistrust of outsiders, a fear of impending war with the United States and invasion of the Utah territory by US soldiers, retribution for the death of Parley Pratt, killed by Arkansans that year, and taunting from the wagon train itself, claiming, as it passed through Mormon settlements, that they had in their possession the gun that killed Joseph Smith. The attack was organized by church leaders in Cedar City. Only John D. Lee was tried for the murders, although many others were involved. Historians disagree whether Brigham Young had knowledge of the event or sanctioned it. Today, the site of the massacre is marked by a monument. See *Wikipedia, "Mountain Meadows Massacre"* page.

OKAZAKI – A reference to Chieko N. Okazaki (1926-2011) who was one of the most-read LDS authors, specializing in books for LDS women. She confronted tough subjects honestly and with an unusual candor and insight. Her first book,

Lighten Up! is a collection of her speeches. See *Wikipedia, "Chieko N. Okazaki"* page.

PRIESTHOOD MEETING – All males in the LDS Church over twelve years of age hold the priesthood. A priesthood meeting is one of a weekly series of meetings that LDS men attend, usually held on Sundays. At the beginning of the meeting, all men meet together. After an initial prayer, hymn, and announcements, the men break into classes according to their priesthood office (if they are over eighteen) or divide by age groups (if they are under eighteen). See *Wikipedia, "Worship Services of The Church of Jesus Christ of Latter-Day Saints"* page, *"Priesthood Meetings"* section.

PRIMARY – A weekly meeting for children in the LDS church, held on Sundays. It is divided into two age groups. See *Wikipedia, "Worship Services of The Church of Jesus Christ of Latter-Day Saints"* page, *"Primary"* section.

SACRAMENT MEETING – A weekly Sunday meeting for members of the LDS church, open to visitors. The service is similar to most protestant churches where communion is offered. The meeting is characterized by prayers (invocations and benedictions) hymn singing, ward announcements, talks given by selected speakers, and the passing of the sacrament, which is consecrated bread and water, passed among the participants. See *Wikipedia, "Sacrament Meeting"* page.

SEALINGS – A sealing is an ordinance performed by Mormons. The LDS perform the ceremony in temples. Most sealings are marriages, "sealing" the marriage partners for both time and eternity, a bond that is considered to transcend death. Children born to the couple are considered "born under the covenant" and are automatically sealed to their parents. The LDS teach that a temple sealing is a necessary ordinance to achieve the highest level of the celestial kingdom. Proxy sealings are ordinances conducted on the behalf of a couple who is dead, with the belief that the deceased persons may choose to accept or reject the ordinance. See *Wikipedia, "Sealing (Mormonism)"* page.

SHILAH – Navajo for "brother."

SMITH, JR., JOSEPH – Founder of Mormonism and first president of the church. He was born in Vermont in 1805. By age 24, he had published the Book of Mormon. He led the church as it moved from upstate New York, where it was founded, to Ohio, Missouri, and finally Illinois. He originated almost all of the church's doctrinal teachings, including the Endowment ceremony, which he tasked Brigham Young with constructing for presentation in the Nauvoo, IL temple. He was murdered by a mob in Carthage, IL at the age of 38. He had attracted thousands of followers from around the world, most of whom chose to follow Brigham Young after his death. Many smaller groups continued on their own in Illinois, Michigan, and Pennsylvania. See *Wikipedia, "Joseph Smith"* page.

STAKE – A geographical collection of LDS wards (congregations). Usually five to ten wards form a stake. There is usually one meetinghouse in the stake that is larger than the others, and contains the offices for the stake officers (such as the stake president and high council.) This larger meetinghouse is called the "stake center." See *Wikipedia, "Stake (Latter Day Saints)"* page.

STAKE PRESIDENT – A position in the LDS church hierarchy. Local members are part of a ward, overseen by a Bishop. Five to ten geographically contiguous wards form an administrative unit called a stake. General Authorities appoint a state president, to whom all local Bishops within the stake boundaries report. The stake president chooses two men from within the stake to serve as his counsellors. The three men, together, are referred to as the "stake presidency." See *Wikipedia, "Stake (Latter Day Saints)"* page, *"Stake Officers"* section.

TAYLOR, JOHN – Third president of the LDS Church, following Brigham Young. Once a man is appointed the leader of the church, they serve until they die. Taylor was president from 1880 to 1887. He was a strong supporter of polygamy. See *Wikipedia "John Taylor (Mormon)"* page.

TEMPLE MARRIAGE (SEALING) – A sealing is an ordinance performed by Mormons. The LDS perform the ceremony in temples. Most sealings are marriages, "sealing" the marriage partners for both time and eternity, a bond that is considered to transcend death. Children born to the couple are considered "born under the covenant" and are automatically sealed to their parents. The LDS teach that a temple sealing is a necessary ordinance to achieve the highest level of the celestial kingdom. Proxy sealings are ordinances conducted on the behalf of a couple who is dead, with the belief that the deceased persons may choose to accept or reject the ordinance. See *Wikipedia, "Sealing (Mormonism)"* page.

UNSER, JAMES – (Spoiler alert: skip this paragraph if you have not read *Eximere*, the fourth book in The River series.) James Unser is a character is the book *Eximere*. Steven and Roy Hall, along with Eliza Winters, discover that Unser was gifted, but despised his gift and sought to eliminate it in others. He would capture and kill other gifteds, and keep their memoirs and objects, denying their heirs their inheritance. He built an underground area called "Eximere" as a home base for his activities. Steven, Roy, and Eliza, having discovered Eximere, are working to return memoirs and object to their rightful owners. See *"Eximere"* by Michael Richan.

VISITING TEACHERS – Most LDS women are asked to visit other women in the ward on a monthly basis, along with an assigned female companion, to check on the welfare of those they have been assigned. The visit usually includes the delivery of a spiritual message selected for that month by Salt Lake. Since most of those receiving visits are also Visiting Teachers to others, they're in the awkward position of listening to the presentation of a spiritual message they've likely delivered to other women already.

WARD – A local congregation of LDS members, usually from 25 to 500 members in size. A bishop, selected from among the congregation, oversees the temporal and spiritual needs of the ward, and serves without pay. The bishop reports to a stake president.

WINZE – A vertical passageway in an underground mine used to connect levels (as opposed to a shaft, which is connected to the surface.)

YOUNG, BRIGHAM – Second leader of the LDS Church, from 1847 to 1877. Under his leadership, members of the LDS Church emigrated from the United States to the west, settling in areas that are now the states of Utah, Nevada, Arizona, Idaho, Wyoming, Colorado, New Mexico, Oregon, and California. Prior to Young's exodus, the LDS church had struggled to survive in New York, Ohio, Missouri, and Illinois, constantly running into problems with neighbors, but in the western deserts of North America, they were able to gain a foothold and grow. Young wielded considerable power; in addition to being the president of the Church, he was also the first governor of the Utah territory. He essentially presided over a theocracy, and church doctrines and practices under his leadership reflected that. See *Wikipedia, "Brigham Young"* page, and *Forgotten Kingdom: The Mormon Theocracy in the American West, 1847-1896,* by David Bigler.

Michael Richan lives in Seattle, Washington.

. . .

Did you enjoy this book?

The author would love to know your opinion of the book.

Please leave your review at Amazon.com and Goodreads.com.
The author reads every review posted there.
Your feedback is appreciated!

. . .

Blood Oath, Blood River is the first book in
The Downwinders series, part of The River Mythos.
Other titles include those of *The River* series:

The Bank of the River, A Haunting in Oregon,
Ghosts of Our Fathers, Eximere,
The Suicide Forest, and *Devil's Throat.*

Deem and Winn first appear in *Devil's Throat.*

. . .

Visit

www.michaelrichan.com

for more information about all the books in *The River* series, and
where you can sign up to receive a notification
when a new title is released.

Made in the USA
San Bernardino, CA
29 June 2014